PRAISE FOR CHARLIE

THE HANGING CITY

"Lyrical and striking, *The Hanging City* is an enchanting story of romance within a harsh world and an even more unforgiving society. Navigating class conflict, rigid social rules, and bitter hierarchies, *The Hanging City* explores the many types of love that people can find between one another, and is as unsparing in its depiction of the consequences of love as it is thrilling, rewarding, and heart-felt."

—Robert Jackson Bennett, author of *Foundryside* and *City of Stairs*

"Holmberg's latest is rife with forbidden romance, monsters, and unique world building. Not only will readers enjoy delving deep into the canyons the trolls call their home, but Lark's journey will also leave a mark deep on their hearts."

—Tricia Levenseller, *New York Times* bestselling author of *Blade of Secrets*

THE WHIMBREL HOUSE SERIES

"Filled with delightful period details and artfully shaded characters, this whimsical, thoughtful look at magic and its price is the perfect read for a cold fall night."

—*Publishers Weekly*

"Readers will be drawn in."

—*Booklist*

"This is Charlie at her best—intriguing mystery, creative magic systems, with plenty of romance to keep me turning the pages."

—Jeff Wheeler, *Wall Street Journal* bestselling author

"The quirky characters, period detail, and personal journeys . . . are well wrought."

—*Library Journal*

STAR MOTHER

"In this stunning example of amazing worldbuilding, Holmberg (*Spellbreaker*) features incredible creatures, a love story, and twists no one could see coming. This beautiful novel will be enjoyed by fantasy and romance readers alike."

—*Library Journal*

THE SPELLBREAKER SERIES

"Those who enjoy gentle romance, cozy mysteries, or Victorian fantasy will love this first half of a duology. The cliff-hanger ending will keep readers breathless waiting for the second half."

—*Library Journal* (starred review)

"Powerful magic, indulgent Victoriana, and a slow-burn romance make this genre-bending romp utterly delightful."

—*Kirkus Reviews*

THE NUMINA SERIES

"[An] enthralling fantasy . . . The story is gripping from the start, with a surprising plot and a lush, beautifully realized setting. Holmberg knows just how to please fantasy fans."

—*Publishers Weekly*

THE PAPER MAGICIAN SERIES

"Charlie is a vibrant writer with an excellent voice and great world building. I thoroughly enjoyed *The Paper Magician*."
    —Brandon Sanderson, author of *Mistborn* and *The Way of Kings*

"Harry Potter fans will likely enjoy this story for its glimpses of another structured magical world, and fans of Erin Morgenstern's *The Night Circus* will enjoy the whimsical romance element . . . So if you're looking for a story with some unique magic, romantic gestures, and the inherent darkness that accompanies power all steeped in a yet to be fully explored magical world, then this could be your next read."
    —Amanda Lowery, *Thinking Out Loud*

THE WILL AND THE WILDS

"Holmberg ably builds her latest fantasy world, and her brisk narrative and the romance at its heart will please fans of her previous magical tales."
    —*Booklist*

THE FIFTH DOLL

Winner of the 2017 Whitney Award for Speculative Fiction

"*The Fifth Doll* is told in a charming, folklore-ish voice that's reminiscent of a good old-fashioned tale spun in front of the fireplace on a cold winter night. I particularly enjoyed the contrast of the small-town village atmosphere—full of simple townspeople with simple dreams and worries—set against the complex and eerie backdrop of the village that's not what it seems. The fact that there are motivations and forces shaping the lives of the villagers on a daily basis that they're completely unaware of adds layers and textures to the story and makes it a very interesting read."

—*San Francisco Book Review*

BOY

of

CHAOTIC
MAKING

BOY

of

CHAOTIC

MAKING

Whimbrel House Book 3

CHARLIE N. HOLMBERG

Published by 47North, Seattle

www.apub.com

Amazon, the Amazon logo, and 47North are trademarks of Amazon.com, Inc., or its affiliates.

ISBN-13: 9781662508738 (paperback)
ISBN-13: 9781662508721 (digital)

Cover design by Faceout Studio, Amanda Hudson
Cover illustration by Christina Chung

Printed in the United States of America

*To Dan Wells,
who is proof that sometimes it's
okay to meet your heroes.*

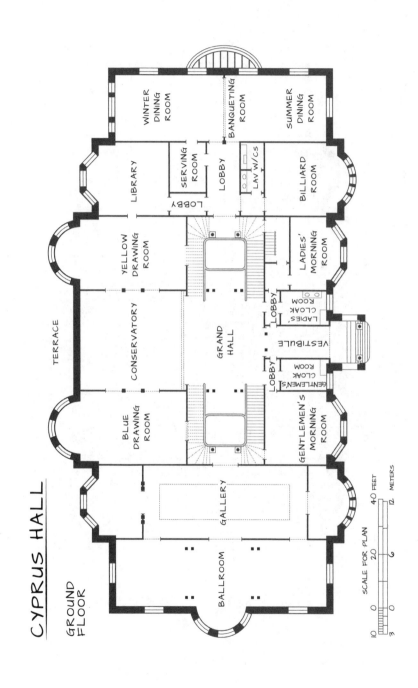

CYPRUS HALL

GROUND
FLOOR

TERRACE

WINTER DINING ROOM

BANQUETING ROOM

SUMMER DINING ROOM

SERVING ROOM

LOBBY

LAV W/CS

LIBRARY

LOBBY

BILLIARD ROOM

YELLOW DRAWING ROOM

LADIES' MORNING ROOM

CONSERVATORY

LOBBY

LADIES' CLOAK ROOM

GRAND HALL

VESTIBULE

BLUE DRAWING ROOM

LOBBY

GENTLEMEN'S CLOAK ROOM

GENTLEMEN'S MORNING ROOM

GALLERY

BALLROOM

SCALE FOR PLAN

40 FEET

20

10   0

METERS

12

6

3   0

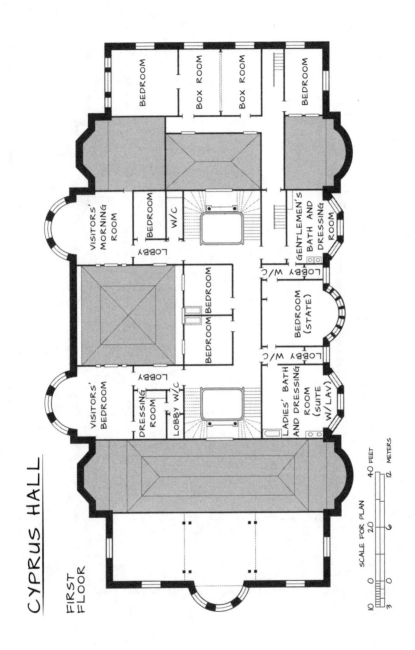

CYPRUS HALL

FIRST FLOOR

BEDROOM

BOX ROOM

BOX ROOM

BEDROOM

VISITORS' MORNING ROOM

BEDROOM

W/C

LOBBY

GENTLEMEN'S BATH AND DRESSING ROOM

LOBBY

W/C

BEDROOM BEDROOM

BEDROOM (STATE)

LOBBY

W/C

VISITORS' BEDROOM

LOBBY

DRESSING ROOM

W/C

LADIES' BATH AND DRESSING ROOM (SUITE)

W/C

W/C

W/LAV

SCALE FOR PLAN

10   0   20   40 FEET

3   0   6   12 METERS

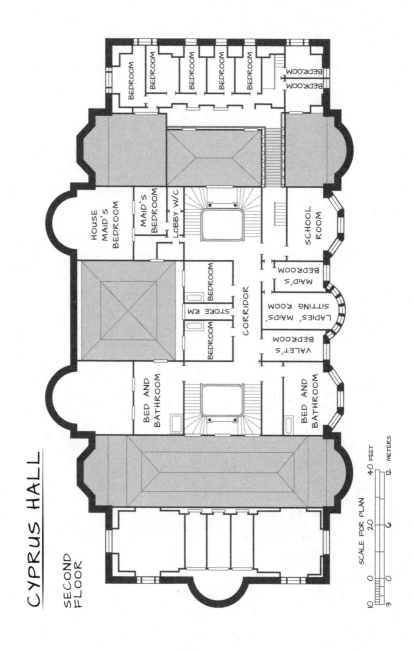

CYPRUS HALL

SECOND
FLOOR

BEDROOM
BEDROOM
BEDROOM
BEDROOM
BEDROOM
BEDROOM
BEDROOM

HOUSE
MAID'S
BEDROOM

MAID'S
BEDROOM

LOBBY W/C

SCHOOL
ROOM

BEDROOM

STORE RM

CORRIDOR

MAID'S
BEDROOM

LADIES' MAIDS'
SITTING ROOM

VALET'S
BEDROOM

BED AND
BATHROOM

BED AND
BATHROOM

SCALE FOR PLAN

10   0   20   40 FEET
3   0   6   12 METERS

DOCTRINES OF MAGIC

Augury • Soothsaying, fortune-telling, divination, luck
1. Repercussion: forgetfulness
2. Associated mineral: amethyst

Psychometry • Mind reading, hallucination, empathy, intuition
3. Repercussion: dulling of senses
4. Associated mineral: azurite

Conjury • Creation, summoning of natural components
5. Repercussion: loss of equal worth to summoned object
6. Associated mineral: pyrite

Necromancy • Death/life magic, life force, disease/healing
7. Repercussion: nausea
8. Associated mineral: turquoise

Wardship • Shielding, protection, spell-turning
9. Repercussion: weakening of physical body
10. Associated mineral: tourmaline

Element • Manipulation of fire, water, earth, or air
11. Repercussion: fire, chill; water, dryness; earth, vertigo; air, shortness of breath
12. Associated mineral: clear quartz

Alteration • Shape-shifting, changing, metamorphosis
    13. Repercussion: temporary physical mutation
    14. Associated mineral: opal

Communion • Translation, communication with plants/animals
    15. Repercussion: muteness, tinnitus
    16. Associated mineral: selenite

Hysteria • Manipulation of emotions, pain
    17. Repercussion: physical pain, apathy
    18. Associated mineral: carnelian

Kinetic • Movement, force
    19. Repercussion: stiffness, lack of mobility
    20. Associated mineral: bloodstone

Chaocracy • Manipulation of chaos/order, destruction, restoration
    21. Repercussion: confusion
    22. Associated mineral: obsidian

Chapter 1

February 16, 1847, Near Waynesville, Ohio

A normal person would probably be completely aghast, and perhaps faint, at the sight of the man who'd tried to murder her, suspended in a tank of . . . Hulda didn't want to know. But in truth, she'd expected much, much worse, so in a strange way, seeing Silas Hogwood's only *partially* decayed corpse in a cylindrical glass coffin was almost a relief.

The dolls he'd kept around in life, shriveled monstrosities that looked like starved cacti or fungal legumes, had been far more repugnant. Though those, at least, hadn't had discernible features. Silas Hogwood . . . he almost looked like himself.

Hulda drew in a deep breath, inhaling until it passed her navel and hit her hips, then let it out all in one gust. "This will see all of us in jail."

Us, referring to all four persons present. As far as Hulda was aware, they were four of only five people who knew about the hidden, unnamed laboratory Myra Haigh had siphoned funds to for years.

Speak of the devil.

"I know I've left it to you"—Myra stepped up beside her, an index finger crooked just under her bottom lip—"but it would be a great waste to destroy it. Mr. Hogwood aside, a lot of research has been done here. *Is* being done. I beg you to take all of that into consideration before you make a decision."

Hulda bit the inside of her cheek. At least the facility, while macabre, *was* well run. She shouldn't have expected anything less where Myra was concerned. The woman had caused her a great deal of trouble over the last six months, but she was nothing if not competent. And aggravatingly difficult to get a hold of.

Hulda glanced over her shoulder at the two employees, both in long coats, working at tables full of glass vials and other sundry objects. Or pretending to work. Likely eavesdropping, and Hulda couldn't blame them. Myra had sworn they were trustworthy. Hulda believed her.

Glancing back at the . . . tube . . . she asked, "What is he in?"

"Formaldehyde." Myra leaned closer to the glass. "Salt. Water. Magic. If you want the exact potion, I can call over Lisbeth."

Lisbeth, one of the workers behind her. Hulda had forgone introductions, though every iota of politeness and finishing school censured her for it. She'd only just assumed her new duties as the director of the Boston Institute for the Keeping of Enchanted Rooms a few months prior, and she didn't want to be any more tangled up in this mess than she already was.

Magic had been slowly but steadily leaving the world for centuries. The idea of synthesizing it *was* fascinating. World changing. But to do it like this? It made nausea brew.

"How did you get him in here without informing outsiders?" she asked.

Shrugging one shoulder, Myra said, "I have my ways." She hesitated. "I suppose you'll want to know—"

"I really don't."

Interrupting. Another faux pas her manners teacher would deplore. Merritt Fernsby was rubbing off on her a little too much. Drawing another steeling breath, Hulda added, "The best situation any of us can hope for is to make this operation as *legal* as humanly possible. Paperwork can be fudged. I'll speak to a lobbyist and—"

"It's too risky," Myra broke in, her voice low enough that the other two in the room would not hear her. "There's too much at—"

Hulda wheeled on the older woman. "I will not take the fallout for your choices, Myra." Her voice rang harsher than intended. Myra reeled back, sealing her lips. Pushing forward, Hulda added, "The cadaver law first." Just being in *possession* of a corpse, even that of a mass murderer, broke United States law. Only hospitals and medical researchers could skirt it. As far as she knew, this was the first *body* brought into the lab, but she didn't ask. The more ignorant she was, the better. "If we can portray this work as *research* into the field of medical knowledge, it will go much easier on us. I'll be as anonymous as possible. Magic is a dying art, yet it's something everybody wants. Why else would institutes like the Genealogical Society for the Advancement of Magic be federally funded?" She glanced at Mr. Hogwood's floating corpse, then turned her back to it. "I'll place my petitions carefully. Unless this becomes sanctioned, not a single stroke of a pen will breathe of this place." Myra looked like she wanted to speak, but Hulda pushed on. "It will take some time, yes, but I will do this right. *We* will do this right, and then we'll have a new, documented start. If we cannot achieve that, then this place shuts down."

Myra's mouth twisted. Hulda sensed a great many words building up in her throat, most of them ungenerous. But Myra swallowed them. She'd given up her power when she'd abdicated her position as director of BIKER. The very fact that Hulda was even considering aiding this grisly effort . . . well, Myra could only be grateful for it.

"I understand," she managed.

Hulda nodded. "I will make it clear, again"—she glanced at the two employees, who paused to meet her eye—"that this institute is no longer associated with BIKER. I did not create it, and I cannot support it. As far as any of you are concerned, I've washed my hands of this place. But"—she turned to Myra—"Miss Haigh is likewise no longer affiliated with BIKER. If she wishes to keep it running, that's her prerogative.

But absolutely no funding will come from BIKER unless the proper ratifications are secured. Until they are, you will be on your own."

After receiving silent nods of approval, Hulda started for the exit. Myra quickly fell into step beside her, heels clacking against the hard floor.

"Do you really think you'll get government accommodation for this?" Myra sounded incredulous.

"I intend to look into options. Perhaps, if handled gently, we could even get a grant."

Myra snorted. "I highly doubt it."

"Doubt all you want"—Hulda stopped and met her gaze—"but do not doubt *me*." She straightened her glasses. "Besides, I'm marrying a man who is very good with words. I'm sure he'll be able to draft up a wonderful proposal."

Myra frowned, clearly displeased that Hulda had brought Merritt into her confidence. Fine. Hulda was impenitent. Myra's actions had nearly gotten Hulda *and* Merritt murdered by the man in that tank, and then incarcerated for crimes they didn't commit. She really didn't have a leg to stand on.

Hulda tipped her head slightly. "I envy you your gift. I wish I knew what you were thinking."

Perhaps involuntarily, Myra's eyes shifted slightly to the right. Hulda followed them to a door she'd assumed was a closet.

Her chest tightened. "Do I want to know?"

Myra didn't answer.

Sighing and adjusting the black bag on her shoulder, Hulda marched toward the door. She was nearly there when Myra said, "You've washed your hands of the place, remember?"

Hulda wrenched the door open. The space within was unlit, and not much larger than a closet. After fumbling in her bag, she pulled out an enchanted light and bid it to ignite.

She nearly dropped it.

Two of those horrid, shriveled bodies were in here, hung from a shelf like curing meat. Those awful, gnarled things used to be people. Silas Hogwood had mutated them with spells, preserving them from death so he could keep the magic stolen from them. That ability was the reason Myra had taken his body postmortem in the first place, sure that the secret to replicating magic lay somewhere in his anatomy.

"For the love of heaven." Hulda slammed the door shut and reeled around. "Put them *out of their misery*."

Myra pressed her lips together. Thankfully, she nodded, skipping the fight Hulda had been more than ready to have with her.

She ended the spell on the light in her hands and said, "I'll see myself out." She swept down the hallway and to the exit, leaving at a pace far quicker than she'd used upon arriving. She wished there were a kinetic tram line this far west. She couldn't return to her hotel fast enough.

She found herself in desperate want of a bath.

～⑨

Merritt paced the length of the hall in the triple-decker house that had been turned into a small inn. The Bluebird, it was called, and admittedly the weathering on its blue-painted exterior walls did resemble feathers. It was right next to the railroad station, and he'd stayed there last night, though barely slept a wink. Not because house plants and rodents were trying to speak to him—no, he had that, blessedly, under control.

It was just that . . . he hadn't seen his sisters in nearly fourteen years.

Worcester didn't seem like the most ideal place to reunite, what with all the factories and construction and the noise from the canal, but it was a decent city somewhat in the middle of all their locations— Merritt was posted out in the Narragansett Bay, Scarlet had moved to Albany, and Beatrice was in Concord. Granted, he and Scarlet had access to a kinetic tram, which made it a little fairer for them, but—

He touched the faded scarf around his neck, uncaring that it didn't exactly add to his clothing. And he was wearing his nicest clothing—church-worthy clothing, with a new lavender vest. Beth, his maid and friend, had thought it looked well on him, but it didn't exactly blend with his multicolored scarf . . . the only token he'd been able to take with him from his oldest sister, Scarlet, when the man who'd raised him had kicked him out with little more than the clothes on his back. Only much later had he learned that Peter Fernsby was not his true father. Merritt hadn't been able to save anything of Beatrice's.

His mother, against Peter's wishes, had sent his sisters' addresses to him, and he'd written to them. They were both married, with households of their own, so there was no one around to tear up letters before they reached their destination. Not like before. And his sisters, both, had *answered*. Immediately. He'd even gotten a telegram from Scarlet.

He was to be reunited with his family any minute now. *Any minute now.*

He pulled out his pocket watch with clammy hands and checked the minute hand for the dozenth time. His hostess had asked him on several occasions if she could get him anything, then finally let him be to wear down the varnish in her reception hall with his relentless pacing. Forcing the watch back into his pocket, Merritt squared his shoulders and ran a hand back through his hair. Should he have cut it? Maybe he should have cut it. Or at least tied it back with a ribbon or something. Merritt had never cared about his hair. Why did he suddenly care so much about his hair?

He turned about for a mirror. Didn't see one. There was one in his room, but he wasn't going to trudge upstairs for the sake of vanity. What if he didn't like what he saw? What, precisely, was he going to do about it?

The front door opened. Merritt's heart lodged in his throat—but a wide man of about forty stepped through, two suitcases in hand. His trouser leg got caught on a splinter in the doorframe.

"Here, let me," Merritt offered, and grabbed one of the suitcases so the man could free himself. He might have wondered if this was one of his brothers-in-law, but both of his sisters had determined to come solo. First, to make this a more intimate and less stressful affair. Second, because they both had children, some of whom were in school, and it was easier to find help at home if their husbands could take over after work.

"Thank you." The man tipped his hat to Merritt, then accepted his suitcase back.

"Hostess is upstairs," he offered.

The man nodded and started up that way. Merritt moved to close the door—

And locked eyes with Beatrice Fernsby—Blakewell, now—coming up the path.

His organs evaporated. His spirit shot out of his body and dissipated into fog. She looked different—there was more weight on her, rounding out her features. More lines to her face. Her dress was well made, as was her coat. Good. It meant her family made a comfortable living. Her eyes were the same—blue just like his.

"Oh!" she cried, and dropped her suitcase right there on the winter-curled lawn. She ran toward the porch.

Merritt blinked, and suddenly he was in his body again, tripping over the doorjamb as he stepped outside. Blinked again, to clear tears from his vision.

"Merritt!" Beatrice shrieked, and bowled into him, nearly sending them both to the ground. Her arms went straight around his waist, and his fell over her shoulders. Had she always been this short?

"Bea," he whispered, and a tear traced the side of his nose and fell onto her hat. "Goodness, Bea, you're all grown up!"

She pulled back enough to swat him with a reticule hanging from her wrist, then embraced him again, burying her face into his chest. "I was practically grown when you left!" she objected, then started bawling into his shirt.

He blinked rapidly to control his own tears. Squeezed her tight and pressed his face into her hair, just under the rim of her hat. "I'm so sorry," he whispered, throat constricting. "I tried to reach out to you—"

"Oh, stop." She pulled back and fished into her reticule for her handkerchief, then carefully dabbed her eyes. "Stop it right now. We all tried." She sniffed. A tear fell free from her dark eyelashes. Quieter, she repeated, "We all tried."

Swallowing against a lump in his throat, Merritt gestured to the door. "There's a fire inside, and some chairs. I think I scared off the other guests."

Beatrice laughed—or maybe sobbed—and nodded. Merritt jogged out to fetch her suitcase. Urged her to take the chair closest to the fire. She lowered into it and then pulled off her gloves and warmed her hands.

"It's . . ." He sat beside her, still stunned and at a loss for words, his pulse racing laps from his head to his feet and back. "It's so good to see you."

She smiled, lips pinched together, eyes watery. Reached out to his face—he leaned forward in his seat so she could touch his jaw. She flicked back his hair. "This is nonsense." She laughed.

"I know."

She pulled back and looked him over. "All grown up."

Merritt grinned. "I was grown before I left."

"Hardly!" Dabbing her eyes some more, she added, "You were barely a man. Mother, well, she caught us up on everything." She needn't explain what; Merritt had let the ordeal with Ebba, his old fiancée, slip, and he imagined his father had been asked to account for his actions. After all, he'd known Merritt was a bastard long before Merritt did, and he'd orchestrated the whole mess. "Regardless, Merritt . . . you're my brother. I love you. Always have, always will."

His pulse tripped on a lap. Merritt found himself turning away, digging into his pockets for his own handkerchief. A minute passed as he found it, used it, and tried to work down that sharp ball lodged in his throat. "Thank you," he whispered.

She beamed. "I read your book. *A Pauper in the Making*. You absolutely drew on our trip to Connecticut for the train scene!"

He chuckled. "I did, I did."

"And the next one?"

Clearing his throat, Merritt folded up the handkerchief. "It releases in May. May 18. Did . . . Did you like it? *Pauper?*"

"I wouldn't have mentioned it if I didn't!" Beatrice slapped his knee, and the simple gesture shot him back twenty years to their shared home in Cattlecorn. So many of her mannerisms were the same—even the way she dabbed at her eyes. "I never thought writing interested you. Did you write much before?"

"Started in my early twenties."

"Well, you have a knack for it. A little scary for me. The book, not the knack." She winked. "But I read it all anyway."

His cheeks hurt from smiling. "But tell me more about your children. Bethany and Maggie. And your husband. Was . . . Was it George?"

"Yes." She grabbed the sides of her chair and scooted a little closer. "George. Our eighth wedding anniversary is coming up." She sighed and relaxed into her seat. "Bethany is almost seven. Maggie is four. There was another, but, well, it didn't work out."

Strength fled his shoulders. "Bea, I'm so sorry—"

She shrugged. "It happens, Merritt. Happened with our own mother, if you remember."

He nodded. "I . . . do. I hadn't thought about that for a while." A stillborn, delivered two months early. Had the baby survived, Merritt would have had a younger brother, right between him and Beatrice in age.

"But the two I have keep me plenty busy!" She slapped his leg again. "But I heard a rumor—"

"Merritt?"

Both of them turned in their chairs to see a newcomer, dressed in a long wool coat, her dark hair twisted up and pinned, a small purse in her hands. Her cheeks were flushed, either from the cold or exertion, maybe both. She was tall and lean, with high boots and a red scarf.

Merritt rose from his chair, pulse picking up where it'd left off. "Scarlet."

He crossed the room to her in a sort of trance. Beatrice was his younger sister by roughly four years; Scarlet was his older by two. His first playmate, his first defender. He still remembered her voice through the wall as Peter Fernsby tossed his things onto the lawn, yelling at him to stop it, stop it, *Please, Father, stop!*

When he neared, she lifted a delicate hand and touched the scarf around his neck. She let out a fluttering breath. "You kept it all these years."

Merritt couldn't answer. If he tried, his voice would be little more than the screeching of an old door hinge.

So he opened his arms instead, and Scarlet fell into them, leaving her tears just above Beatrice's. After a moment, he felt another pair of arms—Beatrice, coming to join them, his sisters' embraces warmer than the fire at his back.

This. Merritt had waited *so long* for this. There was so much to talk about, and so little time before they had to return home. How would he cover it all?

When they finally pulled apart, having exchanged their sorrys and well-wishes and regrets, they returned to the seats by the hearth. Scarlet hung up her coat and situated herself comfortably between Beatrice and himself, then said, "I hear you have something for us."

He paused. "Something?"

"Yes!" Beatrice exclaimed, dabbing yet again. "Yes, I heard a rumor about a woman."

"Oh!" Merritt reached into the inside pocket of his jacket and pulled out the folded papers, neatly addressed and sealed with wax. The paper had seen better days, but such was the toll of travel. He handed one to each of them.

Wedding invitations. The date was set to April 12, two months away.

Scarlet broke the wax reverently and unfolded the note as if it were woven from spider silk. Beatrice ripped into hers, nearly tearing it in two.

"You have to tell us all about her," Scarlet said, halfway to a whisper. "Hulda Larkin. Such a melodic name. I want to hear the story from the start."

Elbows on his knees, Merritt knit his fingers together. "I want to hear *your* stories. I want to know about my nieces and nephews."

"One thing at a time." Scarlet smiled, soft and genuine. "Tell me about Hulda, and then tell me about the house, and where you've been all these years. Tell me so I can stop dreaming about it, worrying about it, wondering about it."

Warmth enveloped Merritt's chest. "All right. First, the story of the house and the story of Hulda are one and the same . . ."

Chapter 2

After too many days of travel and another long day of catching up on work, Hulda met Merritt at Karlsson's, a soup-and-sandwich shop near the docks in Boston that had become a regular rendezvous point for the two of them when she could get away from BIKER and he had time to travel up from Blaugdone Island. This past month had seemed especially busy—BIKER was running much more regularly now, with only occasional checkups from its parent company, LIKER, or the London Institute for the Keeping of Enchanted Rooms. Merritt was writing a great deal and had taken a much-needed visit to reunite with his sisters. Hulda was elated to see him again, and relieved to see him so happy. They took a table in the corner, away from the drafty windows, and he recounted everything. She, on the other hand, had not disclosed her findings at the Ohio facility, though Merritt knew she'd gone. She couldn't risk it, not yet. Certainly not at a public restaurant, and she dared not tell him of it through their linked communion stones. Which were technically BIKER property, and technically should not be in Merritt's ownership anymore.

Technically.

"But," Merritt said, putting a hand in front of his mouth to mask the last remnants of food there. He'd been talking so long, answering all of Hulda's questions, that he'd barely eaten a bite. "I wanted to show you this. Picked it up on my way here."

He lifted his satchel onto his lap and pulled from it a folded newspaper. Opened it up, turned to the second page, and folded it down again. Hulda quickly wiped her fingers on her napkin before accepting it.

"Is this it?" She brought the paper to her face, pushing up her glasses with her free hand. It took her only a moment to find it.

Souls Over Blood

Local scholar theorizes magical heritage is linked to more than blood.

"How wonderful that it published!" she said, glancing over the article. She'd read early drafts of it already—it detailed, without *too* much detail, findings that suggested magical inheritance was connected to the soul first and blood second—hence the ability powerful spirits had to inhabit houses, which was becoming a far-less-frequent occurrence as magic continued to dwindle. The fact that Owein—once a boy, then a house, now a canine—still had full access to his magic seemed proof enough, though Merritt had purposely not named him or given many details on the matter. He valued privacy too highly, and there were those who might go to great lengths to study him. Myra came to mind.

"Scholar?" she teased.

Merritt shrugged. "Gifford edited it, so it counts. I'm not the first person to have made the connection, but they published the article anyway."

Mr. James Gifford from the Genealogical Society *was* quoted twice in the passage. While Merritt usually put his name to articles he sold, he'd requested it be left off this one. Again, for privacy. Both for himself and for Owein.

"How is he?" Hulda asked, softer, folding the newspaper again. "Owein, I mean. Nightmares?"

"Not for a bit now. At least, not since I got back, and if it happened while I was away, Beth didn't mention anything." He swirled his spoon around his chowder, took a bite, considered. "He seems all right."

Hulda nodded. "That's good." Owein hadn't been sleeping well. It wasn't every night, only on occasion. Perhaps that was normal, for a child. Then again, Owein was, if they were to be precise, 223 years old. He seemed reluctant to talk about it. Granted, he could easily communicate only with Merritt, but he'd learned his letters well and could speak with a letterboard when he needed to.

She folded the paper back up, but a smaller article on the same page caught her attention. She skimmed it. *Renowned Aristocrat and Wizard Passes Away.* It was half news, half obituary, naming a marquess who had died at Cyprus Hall in London. She'd paused because she recognized the name—Patrick Bryson Pratt, the Marquess of Halesworth. He was a direct relation to the Crown. She'd met him once, indirectly—he'd been a member of the King's—now the Queen's—League of Magicians, and Silas Hogwood had hosted him at a few dinner parties at Gorse End. That had been long ago, of course, before Hogwood's insidious affairs were uncovered. The marquess had been kind—a pity that he'd passed away.

She folded the paper, and her thoughts broke when she noticed the steam over Merritt's soup bowl looking rather . . . cubical in shape. She blinked. "You've gotten rather good at that."

The cube dispersed, letting the steam dissipate. "I've been practicing." He did so again, over Hulda's tea. The cube was smaller, and would have been unseen if not for the little wisps of steam licking its side. It didn't quite form all the way before silently shattering.

Hulda almost asked if Merritt had been in contact with his half brothers—he had three from his biological father, and one had wardship abilities. But surely Merritt would have mentioned as much, and

Hulda didn't want to needlessly remind him that he had family who didn't know he was a part of them. Thus far, Merritt had kept his biological father's secret. Perhaps he felt he owed the man, after Nelson Sutcliffe had so gallantly come their way to pay bail after their wrongful imprisonment. Perhaps Merritt didn't want to risk wounding the innocent people who would be hurt. Or perhaps it was simply too much for him to take in. He'd only just reunited with his mother and sisters, and getting him to take the first step there had been . . . difficult.

So Hulda didn't ask. She moved to hand the paper back to him, then paused. "Do you mind if I keep this?"

Merritt chewed and swallowed a bite of bread. "Go ahead." He waggled his eyebrows. "Going to brag about me to Sadie?"

Hulda rolled her eyes. "It might be useful for some letters I need to write." If she could prove there was a *need* for further study in the realm of magic to President Polk or Congress, it might open up some avenues for Myra's . . . projects. She could cut out this article and anything else she found and mail them as evidence. Magic regulations in the States were lax, but they still existed. Hulda was the head of BIKER, however, and had a better chance of getting through to key legislators than most.

"*Those* letters?" Merritt asked. He knew the general direction she meant to take, but not much more. Safer for the both of them to keep it that way, for now.

"Those letters," she confirmed, and slipped the paper into her bag.

"Letters, houses, résumés, assignments." He sighed. Stretched a leg out so his foot touched hers. "If only the pastor would let you marry BIKER."

Hulda snorted. "Perhaps I should ask him." They had a Baptist pastor in Portsmouth who had agreed to come out for their spring wedding. They were to get married on Blaugdone Island, of course, just as the blooms were bursting on the trees—the ones Merritt hadn't torn up in the discovery of his chaocracy spells.

It was a queer thing, contemplating—really *thinking*—about the wedding. That it was actually happening. Her insides danced, mingling elation with . . . uncertainty. Not about Merritt, no, but about *marriage*.

Hulda had wanted to be a wife and mother since she was a little girl. She'd fantasized about romance and a babe in her arms throughout her adolescent years and into adulthood. She'd focused harder on her studies when she struggled to turn a beau's eye, then dove into a very fulfilling career when it became apparent she was destined to live out her life as an old maid. Apparent for a time, at least.

Now, finally, at nearly thirty-five years old, she was tying the knot. *Finally* living out her dream. But she was so terribly used to being a single, independent woman that the idea of being someone's *wife* stirred anxiety. How much would her life change, once she was married? Once she had children? *If* children were even in her future . . . The older she got, the less likely she'd get pregnant. She wanted children, of course, but she also wanted BIKER. One change she certainly wasn't reveling in was the commute. Once she married and relocated to Whimbrel House, she'd acquire a two-hour, one-way commute to work. The best option for avoiding the inconvenience would be to move the office itself. Blaugdone Island was out of the question—BIKER had enough staff and clientele that moving so far out of the way would be discommoding, but perhaps she could find office space in Portsmouth. She'd need to run it all through LIKER, since it had proven wise in the past not to have a public face for the institute. All in all, it was a lot of communication and paperwork Hulda wasn't looking forward to.

Perhaps she could invest in a faster boat.

Even now, the line of dedication between her career and her fiancé stretched to a delicate thinness. How could she possibly keep it from snapping altogether?

Merritt sipped his tea, and in doing so broke the tangled line of thought. There were certainly *pleasant* things to look forward to in marriage, as Hulda recalled a premonition that had assaulted her from

Merritt's tea leaves months earlier. It had involved a bed and other risqué things—

"What are you thinking about?" Merritt asked.

She cleared her throat. "Nothing."

"Nothing doesn't make you pink."

Hulda took to folding her napkin, trying not to give attention to the blush beneath her skin, because minding it only made it worse. "No matter. I have every intention of standing across from you beneath the arbor."

And she did. Worry aside, it still astounded her that she was getting married. It was . . . surreal. Even now, she woke up in the morning wondering if Merritt were merely a figment of her imagination or she'd conjured his fondness for her in a dream. Why Merritt, why now, and not . . . then? If only her augury were strong enough to let her understand how God had laid out the cards.

Hulda didn't like showing affection in public. Admittedly, she struggled with expressing just how much she loved this man even in the privacy of his home. She'd buried her emotions and yearning for so long they seemed to prefer the metaphorical trunk in which she stuffed them. But not even the deepest box could contain all she felt in her heart. So, in a weak effort to show it, she reached across the table and laid her hand over his.

Merritt smiled coyly at her and asked her to talk about her day as he finished his meal; Hulda had already devoured hers. He made another wardship cube before his soup cooled off, and when they rose to leave, he knocked his knee on the table and hissed through his teeth.

He hadn't hit it very hard, but the weakening of the body was a side effect of wardship. All magic had side effects, often something seemingly opposite to whatever the spell had been cast to accomplish.

Hulda touched his elbow. "Are you all right?"

He rubbed the spot. "Serves me right."

They walked back to BIKER together, her hand in the crook of Merritt's elbow—a place where she'd found much comfort. The air had a crispness to it, but the sun was bright overhead, teasing the onset of spring. They moved aside for a coach, then crossed the street and took a shortcut between two shops—a shortcut Hulda took only when she was in a great hurry or when she was accompanied, as it wasn't the most unmolested alleyway in the city. They reached the hotel, then circled around its back to BIKER's entrance, near a large tree bare of its leaves. Still, as they neared, Hulda felt a sudden thrill of daring. Glancing about, she ensured there were no onlookers, and just before Merritt reached for the door, she grasped his collar and kissed him.

She hadn't realized how cold her face was until his warm lips pressed into hers. He caught his balance quickly, palm finding her neck as he deepened the kiss—only for a moment, before Hulda pulled back. They *were* still in public, after all. But she hadn't kissed Merritt for eight days, and, well, she'd wanted to.

"How uncharacteristic," he murmured, looking at her with half-hooded eyes. *Love eyes,* she thought, and that earlier thrill swirled around her heart.

She shrugged, feigning nonchalance. "I'm in charge here, remember?" She stepped back and fixed her hair, though her fingers found nothing out of place. "Who is going to tattle on me?"

Goodness, she felt like a sixteen-year-old. She couldn't decide if that was a positive or negative.

"Well," Merritt began, a lopsided grin pulling at his lips, "Sadie is right behind you."

Mortification stripped all the thrilling feelings as she spun around, an apology on her tongue—

To the closed door.

Merritt laughed. "I'm sorry. It's just . . . you make it so easy."

She turned back to him and smacked his shoulder. "You nearly gave me a stroke, Merritt Fernsby!"

He shrugged. "I have something to make it up to you." He reached inside his coat. "Close your eyes."

She glared at him with utmost suspicion.

A mischievous slant tilted his features. "I don't *have* to give it to you . . ."

Giving in to the enticement of curiosity, Hulda closed her eyes and held out her hand, expecting a small parcel of lemon drops to fall onto her palm. Instead, Merritt reached for her other hand—her left—and slid something onto her ring finger.

She opened her eyes, heart jumping into her throat. On her finger was a silver band with an inlaid pearl, catching the orange and rose light of the sunset. Simple yet elegant. Perfectly suited to her . . . and it matched her spectacles.

"Oh, Merritt," she whispered, touching the pearl.

"Admittedly the real reason I needed to come into town." He gently grasped her fingers in his own, tilting her hand so the light shifted and glimmered across the pearl's surface. "Feels more official now, doesn't it?"

Emotion constricting her throat, Hulda managed a nod. She was never taking it off.

"Wish I knew where my grandmother's went," he went on, releasing her hand. "I don't even remember what it looked like, but in a way, Anita Nichols is who brought us together." She had bequeathed Whimbrel House to Merritt after her death, and BIKER had sent Hulda to tame it for him. The rest had fallen into place, not so neatly, after that. "But from what I remember of her . . . I bet it was gaudy. Big. Not suitable for hands like these." He grasped both her hands this time and brought them to his lips, kissing the middle knuckle of each.

Heaven help her, she was going to cry. She squeezed his hands and took a deep breath, steeling herself. "It's perfect." Still holding his hands, she turned her grip so she could admire the ring. "Wherever did you get it?"

"Little jeweler in Portsmouth. Also sells ceramics, actually. We talked over what might be suitable and settled on this."

He'd had it *made* for her. Good gracious, despite everything, she could not wait the seven weeks to be married to him.

And yet BIKER loomed behind her, full of files and work they were still behind on from Myra's resignation and LIKER's audit, plus LIKER's reassignment of a few buildings' care to Boston. The reason the wedding had been delayed until spring was to give Hulda enough time to get things in order and delegate whatever needed to be delegated. Perhaps she *was* married to her work, as Merritt had joked earlier.

Repressing a sigh, Hulda stood on her toes and kissed Merritt's cheek. "I'll see you soon," she promised.

He kissed her forehead. "Remember to breathe, love."

She nodded, unable to school a very girlish smile. "Travel safely, Merritt."

Chapter 3

Despite the coolness of the day, Baptiste was working on his cow fence when Merritt returned home shortly before dinner. He had all the posts set into the ground just behind the house and was now nailing cross slats into place.

"You know," Merritt said, one hand on his satchel and the other in his trouser pocket as he approached, "cows can't swim. Don't think they'll get very far without a fence."

"Funny man." Baptiste drove a nail in with a single pounding of the hammer—impressive. Then again, much about the French cook was impressive. He was the largest man of Merritt's acquaintance and made absolutely mind-melting pastries. This past Christmas had been one of the best in Merritt's life, in part because he hadn't spent it alone, and in part because Baptiste Babineaux was an absolute god in the kitchen.

Christmas made him think of Scarlet and Beatrice again. Just reminiscing about their meeting warmed him against the late-winter chill. Would he see either of them next Christmas? Would they come out to the island and sip hot cider beside the fireplace while Owein chased around his nieces and nephews? Would Merritt *meet* his nieces and nephews, or . . . had too much time passed? His sisters had moved on to families of their own without including him in their lives. Without the *ability* to include him, yes, but it had happened just the same. Would they all be creatures too set in habit to rearrange for his sake?

He touched the old scarf he still wore, not liking the dreary direction in which his thoughts were heading, so he refocused on Baptiste, grabbed the box of nails, and moved it closer. "I'm just saying she's not going to run off." Merritt had promised Baptiste a milk cow if his next book did well, and Baptiste apparently had a great deal of faith that it would. Granted, with Hulda's income added to the mix once they were married, a cow wouldn't be too steep of a purchase, either way.

"I keep her close." He grabbed another nail, this time taking two swings of the hammer to knock it in. "I take good care of her. I not walk ten miles for milk if she wander." He paused. *"Wanders."*

He then said something in French under his breath that Merritt didn't catch. Granted, had he heard it clearly, he still wouldn't have known what it meant.

"Don't stay out too long," Merritt chided, and turned for the house.

"Dinner in one hour" was the only response.

Inside, Merritt hung up his coat and satchel on a hook near the portrait of an unknown woman. Even Owein didn't know who she was. The painting was faded, and when Owein's spirit had occupied the walls, it used to occasionally melt or walk about the house, as the boy saw fit. Now she just hung, the only life within her the paint strokes that the original artist had given her. It felt wrong to remove the portrait. And so Merritt tipped an imaginary hat to her before heading upstairs.

"Paper came for you," said Beth as she bustled by, a duster in her apron pocket and a broom in hand. "Left it on your desk."

"News or work?"

"Work."

"Thank you," he called, though she didn't slow for conversation, merely continued on to the library. Yesterday she'd decided to undertake reorganizing the volumes there by author's name. Merritt did not envy her. Mayhap the library had once been organized as such, but Owein, as a house, had possessed a nasty habit of throwing books, so titles were merely shoved wherever there was a space for them.

Sure enough, a great ream of paper sat at the corner of his desk in his office, as well as a stack of notebooks. The place was spotless, his breakfast dishes cleared away, the trash bin emptied, the glass window looking out into the bay free of marks. Owein was curled up in the corner on the oval-shaped bed Hulda had given him for Christmas. His fur had developed white patches over the last few months, albeit not ones usually associated with age; they seemed to sprout at random, all over his body, instead of around his eyes and snout as might happen with a geriatric canine. He showed no other signs of age; his dog body remained spry and young.

Owein glanced up when Merritt entered, then rested his head on his paws.

"Long day?" Merritt asked, crossing to the desk and pulling his latest notebook, nearly filled, from its top drawer. He was working on his third book, *Two More in the Study*. This one was a mystery about two feuding families locked in a magicked house for an entire weekend. Every six hours, someone was murdered. Everyone believed it to be the house at first . . . but indeed, it was one of the family members!

Merritt hadn't figured out which one yet. But he'd get there.

He had an hour until dinner, and a little light left, so he sat down and read his last page, catching himself up on where he'd left off. He'd written, very lightly, a few notes for himself on the next page. He erased them and started anew:

Yet surely Annie had not been in the kitchen that morning—Louis himself had heard her retching upstairs before breakfast, as the smell of eggs had greatly upset her pregnant constitution. He couldn't believe Benjamin capable of harming a soul, not when he'd cried over so much as a squished spider in childhood. Who, then, could have left the poison? And had he, or she, brought it with him, or had it been in the cupboards all along?

An idea struck him then. If he could—

His pencil, already down to half its length, snapped in his hand.

"Bother," he muttered, and opened his second drawer for a new one, as well as a sharpener. He began the slow process of peeling back wood from graphite, trying to keep his ideas in his head.

He slowed halfway to a decent point and glanced at the broken pencil, his mind drifting back to the article published today. Or, more specifically, to Gifford. He hadn't taken a magic lesson from the fellow in a few months, but he remembered them well. Had even reread the dry essays the man had provided for his enrichment.

Merritt possessed quite the odd concoction of magic spells, made all the more surprising by his discovery of them so far into adulthood. He could make wardship walls and talk with plants and animals, but he had some chaocracy as well, passed down from Owein's side of the family through his biological father. It was weak, but he'd done quite a bit of destruction with it once, unintentionally, of course, so it was certainly part of him.

Chaocracy. The magic of disorder, which caused disorder of the mind in retribution for its use. But there was another side to chaocracy—if something was already in a state of disorder, then the magic could be used to restore order. "Restore order" was a spell he and his great-whatever-uncle Owein shared.

So Merritt set down the new pencil and the sharpener, and picked up the broken ends of his pencil. Held them together and focused.

His magic, they believed, was tied to his instincts and emotion. Chaocracy, supposedly, to his temper. But did that mean he had to be blindingly angry to make it work?

He stared intently at the crack in the pencil. Tried to will it to mend the same way he willed wardship spells to form or mice to quiet. *Mend. Fuse. Fix.*

And for a moment, the crack began to repair itself.

Then stopped.

Sighing, his thoughts somewhat scattered, Merritt pulled the pencil apart, dropped it on the desk, and leaned back in his chair. "Not worth it," he muttered.

The pencil pieces then drew together like magnets and stitched into one whole. Merritt did not believe for a second that it was his doing.

You'll get there, Owein said, pawing over to the desk. Only Merritt could hear his words, thanks to his communion spells.

"Perhaps not. I've your spell, but it's been diluted by two centuries of plebian breeding." He continued sharpening the new pencil. By the time he was finished, he'd need a candle. "Normally I'd be put out that a child can do anything better than I can, but, well, I suppose you're not, really."

Which had become a very curious thing to Merritt. Owein had died at the age of twelve but lived for over two hundred years in this house. Often alone, sometimes with tenants. Yet he still acted every bit a child. "I suppose when you're not limited by society or body," he mumbled, "you can be whatever you want."

The dog tilted his head.

Merritt waved the words away. "Don't mind me." After setting the pencil aside, he petted the top of Owein's head, then scratched behind his ears. "What did you do today?"

Chased birds. He pulled back and scratched his neck with his back paw. *Helped Beth with the laundry.*

Merritt grimaced. "Do I have terrier spittle and tooth marks all over my clean shirts?"

Owein managed to make his canine countenance look affronted. *Only one hole, and I fixed it.*

Merritt snorted, then cleared his throat. Communion liked to take his voice away, but in truth, that was the mildest wizarding symptom he had to deal with. He could always whisper—ish—or write if he needed to. Long stretches of work were often done in quiet, besides.

He and Owein chatted a bit more before Merritt returned to his book and scribbled down another two pages. He was interrupted by a soft, barely perceptible knock at the door. Beth waited until he looked up, then said, "Dinner. Do you want it up here?"

Stretching his arms over his head, Merritt answered, "No, I'll come down." Owein trotted ahead of him, and they went down the hall, down the stairs, and into the dining room, where the table had already been set. Merritt still felt spoiled sometimes, having these things done for him, but he was grateful. It gave him more time to write, and to travel back and forth between the island and Boston. It was easier for him to get away than for Hulda—hopefully the distance wouldn't be too exhausting for her once she moved in again, this time officially, and this time in *his* room, no walls between them. April 12 couldn't come soon enough.

He was just about to sit down when Owein perked up and bolted to the front door, sticking his nose to the bottom corner of the jamb, sniffing. Merritt exchanged a glance with Beth as Baptiste walked out carrying a pot of soup.

"I'll get it," Merritt said, and hurried to the door. Was Hulda stopping by? Perhaps her plans had changed—

He opened the door, and Owein bolted out onto the porch, barking once at a man trudging up the path, his journey made easier by the wintery flattening of the island's flora. The twilight sky left much to the imagination, but the stranger wore a light-colored suit. He kept one hand on his hat to keep it from blowing away and the other on a cane, though his gait was even.

"Can I help you?" Merritt asked.

The man glanced up when he reached the stairs for the porch. "Indeed, Mr. Fernsby," he said in a heavy English accent. "I'm here to deliver a message."

Merritt froze. Not a stranger—Merritt recognized both the voice and the face, once the light of the house fell upon him.

"Mr. Adey," he said, stiff. Adey was the detective who'd come sniffing around last November, inquiring after Hulda's ties with Silas Hogwood.

The man held out a letter. "I need not come in this time. I'm merely the messenger."

Owein sniffed the man's shoes. Adey seemed not to notice.

Merritt hesitantly took the missive. "There are other ways to send letters." He glanced at the paper, but there was no return address.

"Sensitive query, this one." Adey looked past him to Beth, nodding a greeting. "I'll be back in a couple of days for your response."

The letter felt heavy in Merritt's hands. A cold breeze swept by. *Close,* murmured a bird, possibly nesting in the eaves. *Close, closer—*

Merritt tuned it out. Not bothering to hide the skepticism from his voice, he said, "Would it not be easier to come in and—"

"I believe," the British man said with a faint smile, "that you'll want to mull it over. I'll be back." He tipped his hat first to Merritt and then to Owein, which raised gooseflesh up Merritt's back. He thought about the article, but there was nothing in it that would point to Whimbrel House or Owein Mansel. He'd made sure of it. Even Gifford was still in the dark. Then again, Dwight Adey had proven himself privy to personal information in the past.

Adey turned to go. Using a communion spell, Merritt said, *Owein, inside.*

The mutt stepped indoors. Merritt closed the door to a crack, then said, "Baptiste?"

The chef cracked his knuckles. "I will watch." He pushed past them and stepped outside, ensuring Adey got on his boat, just as he had the first time he'd come by.

Beth lingered at the window, watching him go. Merritt stepped into the dining room for better light, Owein on his heels. *What is it?*

"I don't know." Merritt broke the seal and opened up the single-page letter, then caught his breath. "It . . . There's no way."

What? Owein asked.

Merritt's gaze shifted to the signature at the bottom, then back to the top of the letter. *I am interested in your dog,* it said.

And it was signed by none other than Alexandrina Victoria.

The queen of England.

Chapter 4

For a moment, Merritt didn't breathe. In that same moment, his cheeks cooled as blood drained from them, and his heart kept hard, even time.

He read the letter from the top.

Attention: Merritt Fernsby, or

To Whom It May Concern,

In short, I am interested in your dog.

I am personally addressing you as a situation in which you were involved has greatly impressed me. The incident I speak of was the sudden deterioration of the Suffolk County Gaol in the state of Massachusetts. Specifically, the report of a certain witness who detailed the involvement of a male, medium-sized, mixed-breed terrier.

As I'm sure you know, I come from a long line of magic users and consider it a personal responsibility to continue that line, and to protect a resource so many have forgotten is nonrenewable. My involvement in magic includes, of course, a vast education on its workings. This education informs me that dogs cannot be in the possession of spells. And yet, it seems yours is.

My necromancer assures me there is only one possible explanation, and upon examination of files from the London Institute for the Keeping of Enchanted Rooms, supplied recently by its Boston counterpart, I feel certain I understand completely and do not find it necessary to explain in a letter what we both already know.

I wish to introduce you and your dog to my cousins the Leiningens. I believe we can offer you and Owein Mansel an irresistible opportunity that will secure a most excellent future for the both of you. Your compliance, of course, is greatly appreciated, and all expenses for the trip, boarding, and otherwise will be covered.

With the utmost sincerity,

Victoria

Queen of the United Kingdom of Great Britain and Ireland

Merritt's free hand clamored for a chair and managed to pull one out before strength left his legs.

"Mr. Fernsby?" Beth padded over. Owein's nose pressed into his trousers.

Merritt said nothing, merely handed the letter over and stared into a dimension portaled somewhere between the table and the far wall.

Adey had not been wrong about the mulling.

"Oh my." Beth's hand pressed to her collar. Then, a moment later, another "Oh my."

What? What? Owein pestered. The words were loud. That was, Merritt couldn't technically *hear* them. They simply pressed into his mind, and his mind vocalized them in a way he could understand. A spare part of his brain wondered what Owein's true voice would have sounded like, if he'd still had it.

Blinking back to the present, Merritt rubbed his eyes. "Surely it's not real."

"I believe it is." She turned the letter over just as Baptiste came in. "That seal."

The chef approached. The letter rustled as it exchanged hands. After a moment, Baptiste asked, "What this mean?" and pointed to a word. Beth did her best to explain—an explanation that served as subtle harmony to Merritt's whirling thoughts.

The actual queen of England knew about Owein. She wanted Owein. Why? The letter was not threatening in the slightest—there was no reason Merritt shouldn't consider the offer she'd put forward. But then again, he didn't *have* to. The monarch of England had no jurisdiction here. He could ignore both it and Adey, next time the royal puppet came knocking. But . . .

Opportunity.

"*Qu'est-ce que c'est!*" Baptiste said as Owein leapt up and tore the letter—most of it—from his hands. Merritt shook himself and stood as Owein trotted to the stairs, spat the letter out, and began reading it. He had become a decent reader these last few months, though Merritt imagined he might get stuck on some of the same words as Baptiste.

After a minute, Owein turned toward him, dark eyes shining. *What does this mean?*

"It means the queen of England is interested in you. For the sake of her cousins . . . for whatever reason. I can't fathom that part." He inhaled slowly, exhaled slowly, and ran a hand back through his hair. "I . . . I need to talk to Hulda." He patted his pockets, but his communion stone wasn't there.

"I'll fetch it," Beth offered, and, picking up her skirts, quickly ascended to the top floor.

What are they going to do? Owein asked.

Merritt shook his head. "I don't know."

Folding his arms, Baptiste said, "If it were no legal, I think . . . she would not write such polite letter."

Merritt nodded. "Seems that way. But believe me, my imagination can conjure up all sorts of mires." He sunk back into his chair. "You know, none of this nonsense happened before I met you all. Before I got this house." He gestured widely. "Power-sucking necromancers, emotionally scheming lawyers, and now the most powerful wizard in the Western world?" He threw up his hands. "Well, why the hell not?"

౿

Merritt was no stranger to late nights, and he'd known tonight would be one of them, with so much on his mind. But he'd taken two cups of warm chamomile tea heavy with cream and managed to drift off—just before the house started shaking.

Again.

His eyelids slow to part, Merritt pushed himself off his mattress and stumbled toward the door, managing to wake fully halfway down the hallway as another quake hit. He followed a huffing sound, laced with a whine, to the office, where Owein lay on his side on his bed, his legs jerking.

"Owein." He crouched and rubbed the dog's ribs and lightly patted his snout. "Owein, wake up. Owein."

Alertness assaulted the dog suddenly, causing him to jerk up and collide the top of his head with Merritt's chin. Merritt fell onto his backside.

The shaking subsided.

Ears sagging, Owein plopped back onto his bed. *Sorry.*

Another nightmare.

"It's not your fault." Merritt ran a hand down the dog's sleek body. "What was it this time?"

Owein shook his head. After a few beats, however, he said, *Just darkness. Just black. All around me.*

Merritt's heart felt like a dish sponge wrung too tightly, left torn and dry. "I'm so sorry." He wasn't surprised, though. When he'd first come to Whimbrel House, Owein had been a broody, almost violent spirit. Surely spending decades on end without another human around and then, when they came, being unable to communicate . . . that would do something to the best of men. The loneliness Merritt had struggled with for much of his life failed to compare.

"Come on." He tapped Owein's butt, urging him off the bed, then picked up the large cushion and carried it into his room. Owein followed behind, droopy and slow, like he'd been scolded. Merritt set the cushion down near his bed, hesitated, then patted his mattress. "Come on."

Owein hesitated a moment—Beth did not like him on the furniture—before hopping up on the side of the bed still made—the half Hulda would be occupying soon enough. He set his maw on the pillow and sighed.

Stifling a yawn, Merritt slipped in beside him and stroked his fur with one hand until the terrier's breathing calmed. Slowly, together, they both fell fast asleep.

~☙~

"I imagine every paper in Massachusetts made note of it, and the states beyond," Hulda said, gazing over the torn note one more time. It floored her that she was holding a letter penned by *the* Queen Victoria. Would Merritt let her keep it? But that was a foolish thing to ask. Or was it?

Regardless, she ensured for the third time she hadn't missed anything, including any hidden meanings, of which the English were fond. She absently drummed the fingers of her left hand on her desk—she had only just become accustomed to being on this side of it. It was a large desk, cherrywood, directly across from the stairs in BIKER headquarters. One wall was lined with bookshelves, the other relatively sparse, save for a potted fern she had moved in here. Apparently it bemoaned of thirst to Merritt every time he stepped foot on the floor, so Hulda had taken it upon herself to keep it close and ensure it remained well watered.

Merritt sat across from her, chair pulled up close enough that he could prop both elbows on the opposite side of the desk. He'd given a little extra attention to his hair today—the waves in the light-brown locks were nearly uniform and shiny, save for a crimp that whispered he had tied it back at one point, then probably given up on it halfway to Boston and pulled the tie out. "I should have cashed in on that." He stretched his neck to one side, then the other. "I could have written a far more detailed article on the jailbreak than anyone else."

Hulda snorted. "The Crown likely has people everywhere. And they would easily be able to access the files on Whimbrel House." Files that contained everything *except* the moving of Owein's spirit from house to dog. As far as any of those papers were concerned, the house on Blaugdone Island was still enchanted. "She's being straightforward. And I agree with Beth; I believe this letter to be authentic." She certainly believed Dwight Adey to be authentic, and he was apparently the man who'd delivered it. "At the very least," she offered, finally setting the paper down, "you should hear her and the Leiningens out."

"Do you know anything of that family?"

"Not offhand. But the name is familiar." Hulda had lived in England for several years. The light caught on her pearl engagement ring, and for the twentieth time that day, she found herself both mesmerized by the band and surprised it was there. She tilted her hand a little to the right, then the left, watching sunlight from the window behind her dance across it.

Merritt lifted a fist and rested the side of his jaw against it. "I don't suppose you might accompany me?"

The offer warmed her. "I would love to. But BIKER—"

"But BIKER," he repeated, as though that was explanation enough. And it was. He punctuated it with a sigh.

A flicker of anxiety threaded around the base of her throat. *Just a sigh now, but what about later?* Merritt honored her commitment to her job, but what if a year or two down the line, he tired of it? What if he became the next Dickens and her BIKER paychecks became moot? What would she do?

"If," Hulda tried, glancing once at the clock on the wall, "this *opportunity* requires an elongated stay, I'm sure I could arrange a visit with LIKER. They're also stationed in London." Might as well keep her fingers in two pies for as long as she could manage it.

A soft smile tugged on Merritt's lips. She found herself matching it. "Thank you," he said. He took the letter, folded it slowly, and slid it into an interior vest pocket. It was a brocade vest, threaded with violet, carmine, and gold. For as plain as all his other clothes were, Merritt seemed to fancy extravagant vests. Hulda hardly minded—they made her smile. Now, if only she could get him to wear a proper hat—

"I think I might get some documentation notarized." He leaned back in his chair. "In Providence."

She blinked. "What documentation?" Their marriage license was already taken care of.

"I don't know." He fidgeted. "It's just . . . they know about Owein. All of this revolves around him. I honestly don't know what to expect, so I want to make sure we have any and every protection we need. I think . . . I think I'm going to adopt him."

Hulda's lips parted. After a beat, she said, "I-I'm not sure the law will allow you to legally adopt a canine."

35

"I'll see what I can finagle. In my experience, you can get away with just about anything if you pay the right amount."

She frowned. "Perhaps. Though I do not believe you are flush with cash."

Sweeping back his hair, Merritt said, "Just don't tell Baptiste I'll be dipping into his cow fund."

∽

Adey returned two days later, midsunset. Merritt had a letter ready for him—it was brief, accepting the offer and nothing else. Playing it safe until they had more information. Owein was anxious about traveling so far, and Merritt was anxious about traveling on so little. But they were going together, and that seemed enough to steady them both.

However, after Merritt opened the front door and handed the queen's man the unsealed note, he didn't take it. "May I ask, Mr. Fernsby, if the letter is in the affirmative?"

Merritt hesitated, arm still outstretched with the paper. "I've no qualms about you reading it."

The British man smiled. "If you would tell me."

Merritt sighed through his nose, wondering at the detective's game. "We are, tentatively, accepting Her Majesty's offer."

He nodded, grin still in place. "That is most excellent. In that case, I will wait for you to pack your bags."

Finally withdrawing his arm, Merritt asked, "Pardon?"

"Her Majesty instructed me to bring you straightaway upon your consent," he explained. "I've a ship awaiting us in Newport, ready to leave on the morrow."

Merritt stared at the man, incredulous. But he seemed all jovial seriousness.

He heard the clicking of Owein's nails on the floor before words communed with his mind. *We're going now?*

Apparently. His brain picked apart every word, every shift in Adey's stance, every possibility of subterfuge. He found none. His legal adoption of Owein provided some comfort, but to be safe, he would pack one of his pistols.

"I suppose I'll have you wait in the living room." His limbs moved woodenly as he stepped back to allow Adey enough space to step in, which he did. Beth, who had been lingering in the dining room, swept in to take the man's hat and jacket.

Adey nodded in acknowledgment. "Thank you." Then, turning toward Merritt, he added, "The swifter we are, the easier the trip will be."

"If you'd wanted swiftness, you should have called earlier." Merritt shut the door. Waited for Beth to escort Adey to the living room. Then, feeling quite odd, he walked up the stairs, Owein on his heels.

He packed enough for three days, because that's what would fit in his suitcase. Hesitating, he took the scarf Scarlet had made him and set it on his dresser for safekeeping. With luck, he'd have more memories to make with her in the future, and maybe this poor bunch of yarn could finally get some rest. He then spoke to Hulda through their communion stones to alert her—once he started across the Atlantic, the spell binding the stones together wouldn't work anymore. That finished, he came downstairs to say goodbye to his small staff. Owein took a long time with Beth. While Merritt waited, he quietly pulled Baptiste aside, out of earshot, and said, "Keep Beth safe."

Baptiste nodded.

After a beat, Merritt asked, "Are you ever going to tell me the story?"

The chef raised a dark eyebrow. "What story?"

"You know." He spun a hand in the air. "Why you had to leave France." Why he was a convict.

Baptiste's eyes narrowed while his lips pulled into an almost feline grin. "I do not know if you can handle truth. When I think you can, I will tell."

That gave Merritt pause. What sort of grotesque thing could the man have done? Surely not murder . . . he'd be in prison for murder. Would Merritt have to fire him if it was murder? That was something he'd have to consider.

Owein's goodbyes complete, they followed the queen's man into the twilight and sailed into Portsmouth by the gleam of lighthouses.

And in the morning, as Adey had promised, they embarked on the two-day trip across the waters on a kinetic ship to England.

Chapter 5

Owein had never been to England.

He'd thought Portsmouth was enormous. Thought it was—what was that word Hulda used? *Bristling* with people and smells and things. The buildings were large, the streets long, the city vast.

But as he followed Mr. Adey and Merritt from the docks, he realized the world was *much* larger than he'd ever realized.

London engulfed him entirely, like it was a great beast of stone and wood and mortar with an open maw. Instead of the bug song of Blaugdone Island, the air buzzed with the loud clamor of shod horse hooves ringing on cobblestones, wheels creaking on their axels, and heels clacking beneath thousands of shoes. People, people, *people.* Every nook and cranny had people, people of all shapes and sizes and colors and smells. The heavy scents of fish and sea slowly gave way to the musk of cigar smoke and yeast and . . . what was *that*? Owein couldn't identify it. His dog's tail wagged of its own accord as he followed the scent, losing it once to the pungent odor of freshly dropped horse manure—

Wait. Where was Merritt?

Panic flooded his chest. He barked. *Merritt!*

He felt a hand on his collar; Owein had just gotten a couple of steps ahead, that's all. Relief, cool as snowfall, settled over him at the realization.

"Stay close," Merritt advised. "Don't know how I'll find you if you get lost."

A burr of anxiety caught in his throat at that. *Don't lose me.*

Merritt nodded, like that was obvious, but it was desperately important. Owein didn't want to be alone again. Didn't want to lose himself in a city where no one could understand him.

A tendril of darkness, reminiscent of a forgotten nightmare, licked the back of his thoughts. He shook his whole body, causing his ears to slap loudly against the sides of his head. He took in their surroundings. They were near the crossroads of two streets. A few food vendors—had the new smell come from one of them?—a clock shop, an imposing building he didn't recognize. There was no sign, so he couldn't read for the answer—

"This way," Mr. Adey said. "Just there."

Owein huffed as his eyes landed on the biggest carriage he'd ever seen. Its colors were a little muted, like all colors were when he looked through his dog eyes. Sometimes he forgot what shades of green and red looked like; in this body, the grays ate them up. Even so, he was sure this carriage was black. Dark black, with goldish ornamentation on its corners and the center of its wheels. The roof was high enough that Merritt might be able to stand in it, though Baptiste wouldn't. But Baptiste wasn't here. Nor was Beth.

Owein moved closer to Merritt, pressing against his leg, nearly tripping when Merritt stopped suddenly for a man on horse to pass by. Then they were up a step on that carriage—a man in nice clothes held open a door—and he was inside, assaulted by the scent of leather and wood and bodies and . . . lemon? It was similar to the candy Hulda liked, but not so sweet. Older and . . . oily.

Owein marched straight for the opposite window and lifted his front legs onto the sill, sticking his head under the curtain to look out the window.

"Owein—" Merritt's hand touched his back.

"Perfectly fine." Mr. Adey chuckled. "He is a guest of honor, as are you. It's no trouble to get the marks off the glass."

The carriage jerked as the man loaded luggage onto it. Then again, harder, when it took off down the street. The city passed swiftly, though not nearly as swiftly as it did from inside a kinetic tram, which Owein had taken for the first time that week. The carriage moved slowly enough that Owein could take in the sights, sparing the details. Women in hats and men carrying barrels and driving wagons, riding horses. Another was shoveling dung off the road—there were two children Owein's age chasing each other—

Not your age, his mind whispered, but Owein ignored it, taken in by a bakery with a word so long and convoluted it had to be French. Someone passed out papers, and there was a kinetic tram station far larger than the one in Boston—

"My goodness," Merritt whispered behind him. "That's the largest tram station I've ever seen."

Merritt had never been to England before, either.

"Indeed, and there are many of them. This is an old country, Mr. Fernsby. We have the benefit of millennia of magic users who strove to make it better. We've lost some of the old family lines, of course. Time weathers all things. If you want to look out the other window at the Thames, you'll see one of our ships, the *Pearl*, out there. Her Majesty has the finest navy in the world, and our kineticists spare no—"

Their voices faded into the background as the carriage rounded a corner. Owein tried to keep all he saw in his mind, to make a map of it, but half went out his skull as soon as it went in. There was so much to *see*. A giant clock chimed the hour; they passed an immense stone courtyard with an enchanted water feature, from which spurts of water danced through the air before falling. Though the window didn't open, Owein smelled roasting meat just before passing a small restaurant with loaded spits in the window. A hat shop, a fortune teller, a block of apartments that made Whimbrel House look like an anthill—

He watched, amazed, mesmerized, forgetting for a time the uncertainty of his arrival and the question of where he was going. But Merritt was here, so he was safe, and he let his tail wag and tongue hang out as houses and factories and canals whizzed by, taking away any and all sense of importance Owein had ever felt about himself.

In truth, he didn't entirely mind it.

Hulda carefully dipped her pen into its little jar of ink and copied down the next line from the second draft of her letter to President James Knox Polk onto the third. She wanted everything worded precisely and professionally, with a neat and educated hand. This would be her first inquiry into seeking the permissions and possible grants for a facility to research magic under the BIKER name, a facility that *did not yet exist*, as far as anyone was concerned. She was the director of a prominent American institution of magic; even so, she expected her letter to be waylaid to a committee of Congress that oversaw United States wizarding laws before it ever graced the president's desk. Still, she had to try, and when Hulda Larkin tried, she put forth effort.

Her second attempt would include the backing of other prestigious wizards, or those within the community, such as Mr. Elijah Clarke from the Genealogical Society for the Advancement of Magic. She'd start drafting a list of possible allies next week.

If Hulda couldn't get the necessary approvals by the end of it, that would be that. She'd raze the Ohio facility that housed Silas Hogwood's corpse if need be. But if she could make this *work*, then everyone would be happier for it. The idea of synthesizing magic was incredibly appealing. But she wouldn't get ahead of herself.

Her hand started to cramp as she wrote the last methodical lines of the letter; she had a tendency to hold the pen too tightly when she was trying to be especially tidy in her penmanship. But she finished, signed her name, and set the last page aside to dry. After wiping the pen and returning it to her drawer, Hulda massaged her right hand at the base of her thumb. In doing so, she couldn't help but notice, again, the ring encircling the fourth finger on her left hand.

It really *was* suited to her, she thought as she tilted her hand back and forth, letting it catch the light filtering through the window behind her. Elegant without being ostentatious. The pearl shined a bright, silvery white, a fine complement to its sterling setting. Almost as if it were—

The sparkle of light snuffed out as her augury took hold, wiping out the office around her. The vision was dark, almost too dark to see, but she heard Merritt cough. Knew it was him, not just from the sound, but because it was his ring that had triggered the vision. He was in a hallway she didn't recognize. It was so murky—but no, that was smoke. He was surrounded by smoke!

Danger. The word pressed into her mind. Reeling, she found herself back in her office, all the sights and smells of the vision gone as quickly as they had come.

She gaped for a moment, forgetting herself, as she tended to do with her magic. Then she shook her head and shot to her feet, nearly tipping over the ink vial on her desk. She pushed her chair back and marched to the door, yanking it open with enough force to startle Miss Steverus, whose desk sat just outside.

"Are you all—" the secretary began.

"I need you to book me a ticket on the next kinetic ship to England." She spun around for her office, paused, and then turned back for Sadie, trying to orient herself and coassemble a plan. She couldn't simply drop everything to run to England! She'd need to pack, yes. And alert LIKER she was coming. At the same time, panic choked her, as the vision had surely concerned Merritt's trip. While she could do nothing to change the future, she could, at the very least, warn him of the danger.

If only she knew more.

"Miss Larkin?"

"Straightaway," Hulda said.

Miss Steverus nodded, grabbed a few things off her desk, as well as her coat, and hurried down the stairs to the exit.

Hulda turned inward. Her colleague Mrs. Thornton was presently stationed in New Hampshire; she could oversee BIKER while Hulda was away, which hopefully wouldn't be for long. The other woman was in possession of a BIKER communion stone—Hulda need only find its pair in the filing room and direct her to report to headquarters. As for Mr. Walker at LIKER, she would need to send a telegram. They didn't have connected selenite large enough to cover the distance of the Atlantic, which likewise meant her communion stone with Merritt wouldn't function again until she arrived in Europe.

Danger. The word rankled her as she hurried down the hallway to the filing room. She didn't often get impressions of words with her visions—in fact, the last time she could remember it happening was with Merritt, when the story involving Ebba and his father had unraveled. She didn't like it. And she wished desperately she could conjure forth that vision a second time. Curse the weakness of her singular spell!

She made it to the room and quickly found the stone she needed. BIKER had its own telegraph, so that would save her time as well. Then she'd head downstairs to pack her things. Miss Steverus would be back shortly with her ticket; if there were any ships departing today, Hulda had to be ready to run.

"It will be fine," she reminded herself, jogging to the telegram. "You've seen visions further out than that one. He will be fine."

Still, she had to try, and when Hulda Larkin tried, she put forth *effort*.

Chapter 6

Merritt felt like a little boy as their private, very expensive-looking carriage pulled up to a mansion that surely wasn't made of marble but certainly looked it. He'd thought the exuberant home looked, well, exuberant from the road, but as the horses trotted up its long drive, past manicured bushes and enchanted water features that looked like upside-down wedding cakes, it became utterly astonishing. Merritt found himself equal parts amazed and, due to his modest sensibilities, disgusted at the blue gabled roofs with bronze cresting, perfectly symmetrical chimneys, and rows of neat rectangular windows highlighting panels of pressed brick. There were pale stringcourses in high relief between each of the house's stories, of which there appeared to be four. The base of the glamorous monstrosity was textured with a mix of brick and stone in shades of white, gray, and blue to match the rest of the house. There were doors. Many doors. Which made sense—a man could easily get lost in a house like this, so numerous exits were smart. The whole thing was roughly the size of Blaugdone Island, and it sat on a lush green lawn roughly the size of Rhode Island. A hyperbole to be sure, but it seemed an apt one.

And he'd thought Whimbrel House excessive upon his first visit.

"Welcome to Cyprus Hall," Adey said, with a pleased look about him, though he'd borne a pleased look ever since Merritt and Owein had agree upon this eccentric adventure. The carriage pulled around, revealing a long line of people waiting outside massive double doors—most were in matching black-and-white uniforms, four women and two men. At their center stood three middle-aged people, two men and a woman, all looking onward with bright eyes and brighter smiles. Two of them, likely a couple, stood in front of the other man. He wore dark clothes and had a receding hairline and light-brown hair speckled with gray. Of the couple, the woman had dark hair, nearly black, meticulously curled and pinned. She was tall with a healthy amount of stoutness. The man was taller still, with a long nose and thinning gray hair neatly oiled and combed. His jacket was nearly the same color as the roof, and Merritt wondered if he'd done that on purpose.

I don't know. Maybe, Owein replied, surprising Merritt, who hadn't realized he'd sent the thought on their communion line. There was magic all about in this place—those water features didn't move by machine, and there appeared to be enchanted lights, currently unlit, along the path and exterior of the house. Other spells likely lurked about as well. It was incredibly interesting. How much would these folk let him poke around?

The carriage stopped, and one of the men in uniform—footman—approached as the driver dismounted. The footman opened the door. As Merritt hesitated to rise, Adey stepped out first, then off to the side to allow Merritt through, followed by Owein.

Goodness. The house was *immense.* Merritt took a moment to gawk at it before his eyes lowered to the approaching middle-aged couple.

The man extended a hand. "Merritt Fernsby?" He had a notable German accent and an equally notable graying mustache.

"As my mother named me." He accepted the hand and received an overly firm shake.

"Wonderful, wonderful! I am Friedrich, and this is my wife, Helen. We are very happy to welcome you to our home."

Clearing his throat, Adey added, "This is Prince Friedrich Karl Heinrich Ludwig, third prince of Leiningen, and his wife is Lady Helen de Clare, daughter of the Marquess of Halesworth."

Merritt took in the information like he was sipping honey. Hulda would have understood it a little better, surely. He wished, not for the first time, that she'd been able to attend. "Meaning that you are both very important," he tried.

To his relief, Friedrich—Prince Leiningen?—laughed. "Or so we would have others assume."

"Please," said Lady Helen—Merritt was fairly certain that would be the correct way to address her—"allow me to introduce you to our dear friend William Blightree." She gestured behind her, and the man in dark colors stepped forward, nodding his head in greeting. "He is a royal necromancer, here to help us with discussions."

The term *necromancer* immediately put Merritt on edge. He'd met only one in his life, but Silas Hogwood had been more than enough for a lifetime. Still, Merritt found himself erring on the side of politeness and extending his hand, which Blightree graciously took in both of his own.

"It is very nice to meet you. Both of you." His gaze drifted to Owein, who seemed more interested in the prince's shoes than in the introductions.

Prince Friedrich placed a hand on Blightree's shoulder and, perhaps sensing Merritt's hesitation, said, "He is a good man. The best of wizards. He saved my life when I was only seven years old."

Merritt nodded. "I am glad to hear it. I . . . don't suppose you're the necromancer Her Majesty spoke of in her letter?"

Blightree smiled. "The very one. I am aware of the situation at hand." He reached for Owein, who retreated behind Merritt.

He smells like licorice, Owein said.

48

Merritt chuckled. "I don't suppose you've been in contact with any anise today?"

Blightree leaned back. "I . . . have, actually." He pulled back his hands and sniffed his fingertips. "Does it bother you?"

"Owein merely commented on it."

All three of them paused. Blightree passed a glance to Adey. "You said he was a wardist!"

Holding up his hands in mock surrender, Adey said, "The intelligence is not perfect."

"Communion?" Lady Helen asked with a grin. "Do tell me you're a communionist. Or are you a psychometrist? Would that work with a human soul?"

Merritt was unused to speaking so openly about his still-new abilities, and yet their enthusiasm was enticing. "They can, but I am no psychometrist. Communion and wardship, yes. A very little helping of chaocracy—"

Lady Helen gasped.

"—which I inherited, indirectly, from him." He jutted a thumb toward Owein.

"Really!" Her hand flew to her breast. "What an excellent mixture! And"—she glanced at his left hand—"you're not married!"

His skin warmed. "*Yet*, my lady. With any luck, my fiancée will be joining us. Though I'm unsure how long we're staying . . ." He glanced at Adey, who merely shrugged.

"Oh, oh yes, I've been too forward." She batted at the air like the action alone could clear it. "We'll discuss it all in good time. And there is so much to discuss! I'm sure dear William is eager to move forward"—she tipped her head to Blightree—"but manners are manners. Please, come in, the both of you. And, Owein, dear, if there's anything you need, please don't hesitate to let us know. It will be so good to have a translator here! And . . . relative?"

"He's my uncle," Merritt filled in, "a couple of times removed."

Prince Friedrich clapped his hands together. "Fascinating!"

I need the grass, Owein pressed. He needed to relieve himself.

Pinching the bridge of his nose, Merritt replied, *Now?*

Owein answered with a whine.

"I will personally give you a tour of the hall"—Lady Helen gestured to the house—"and show you to your rooms. Are you hungry? I can have a tray brought—"

"I am terribly sorry to interrupt." Hopefully being American would let Merritt get away with that. Lowering his voice, he continued, "But my dear uncle is in need of a lavatory."

"Ah! Yes, right this . . ." Lady Helen paused. "That is . . . well, it's not quite built for dogs."

"Any bush will do," Merritt assured her.

Lady Helen deserved credit—she moved with the changing current well, her countenance barely flickering as it hurried to catch up. It wasn't easy to mesh a canine in with polite society. "I have a most excellent bush. Right this way. Or, Friedrich, perhaps you should lead the way? Since Owein is . . ." She merely circled her hand around.

Merritt bit down on a smile. It wasn't like a terrier had any real sense of modesty; he didn't wear clothes. Everything to be seen was, well, easily seen.

Still, Prince Friedrich obliged with a nod. "This way. And afterward, we do have a very fine lavatory for the rest of you. Have you ever used an enchanted commode? It will change your life."

∽

The tour of the house was, indeed, impressive. Actually, *impressive* didn't seem to be the right word for it. It didn't seem to encompass what he was seeing. But he didn't have his well-worn thesaurus with him, so he couldn't, for the time being, find a better term.

Hulda would know, he thought absently as they passed through the hall that had christened the tour. The walls were hung with dozens of portraits of varying sizes, some that could fit in a pocket and others that were taller than Merritt, who was neither notably tall nor notably short.

A great deal of horses and mantels were featured.

With the same pleasant enthusiasm she'd exuded on the house tour, Lady Helen led them into a sitting room off the dining room. The scents of dinner hung in the air, reminding Merritt that he was hungry. The size and expense of the house made him quite eager to see how the food fare compared.

"Please, take a seat." Lady Helen gestured to an array of settees and armchairs. When Owein hung back, Merritt crossed the room to the far side, choosing a scarlet settee with elegantly carved armrests and legs— something Hulda would certainly remark upon, were she here. It was comfortable, and he settled in. Owein settled on the floor beside him.

"Oh no, that won't do." Lady Helen took a plush pillow off the settee and set it before Owein. "I know, well, this is a little awkward. We've never hosted a pup like yourself in this capacity. But please, make yourself comfortable."

Owein's dark eyes glanced at Merritt. He nodded, and Owein resituated himself on the cushion.

All right? he tried. Shorter messages tended to have fewer side effects.

Owein didn't answer; Merritt masked a frown. He'd tried speaking with him on two other occasions since they'd begun the house tour, and he hadn't responded either time.

Once their small party settled, William Blightree approached. "If you don't mind"—he had the decency to address Owein directly—"I'd like to examine you."

A slight whimper slipped from Owein's throat, but he stood.

Blightree stepped back immediately.

Reaching a hand over, Merritt stroked Owein's back. "Forgive him, we had a . . . negative experience with a past necromancer."

Blightree's forehead creased with the raising of his eyebrows. "Hm? Who?"

Merritt simply shook his head. Best not to drop *that* name anytime soon.

You're safe, Merritt assured Owein, who, after a few seconds, settled down again.

After approaching with caution, Blightree knelt on the carpet and gently took Owein's canine head in his hands. If he did anything, Merritt couldn't detect it. In truth, he just looked like an aging man enamored with a mutt.

"It's true," the necromancer said after a moment, pulling his hands back. "He's no Druid. This is indeed a human soul trapped within a dog."

"Goodness." Prince Friedrich leaned forward from his own armchair. "I suppose I didn't quite believe it!"

Merritt met Blightree's eyes. "I'm sorry. Druid?"

Blightree's knees cracked as he rose to his feet. He settled himself on the settee, taking the seat closest to Merritt, before answering. "Druid, yes. They're a dwindling group of people, mostly hailing from Ireland. Shape-shifters and wood-speakers. I haven't heard of any covens in the United States, but one never knows."

Alteration and communion spells, Merritt figured. All those dry essays on magic Gifford had tasked him to read were proving surprisingly helpful.

Blightree continued, "You yourself would be eligible to join their ranks, should you ever have the urge to shun polite society." He smiled, not unkindly.

Merritt leaned back in his seat.

"Forgive me." He gestured to Owein. "My family line has a psychometry spell that allows us to read spells in others. That's how I confirmed Mr. Mansel's present state . . . and the details of yourself, when I shook your hand. I should have asked first."

"Well." He shrugged. "It's not really a secret."

"Americans are very open people," Lady Helen explained to her husband.

Again, Merritt's thoughts shifted to Hulda. "Not all Americans."

Lady Helen turned. "Pardon?"

"Nothing. Just a passing thought." He absently stroked Owein. "But . . . now that this is out of the way, why did your cousin write us directly? Why bring us here? She mentioned an opportunity—"

Just then a man in a well-tailored uniform stepped into the room. He clasped his hands before him, waiting for Merritt to finish, but Merritt's words wafted away from him. After a brief pause, the newcomer announced, "Dinner is ready, my lord."

"Excellent." Prince Friedrich clapped his hands, rose, and then offered a hand to Lady Helen. "If you'll excuse our casual manner tonight, Mr. Fernsby, I think a comfortable dining experience will make talk easier."

Merritt rose as well. "I know little about the formalities you're omitting, so we're all probably better off this way."

The prince grinned. "Perfect. Shall we?" He looped his wife's arm through his and led the way to the adjoining room. Blightree motioned for Merritt to go ahead of him, and Owein followed closely behind.

The dining room table was long enough to comfortably seat twenty, but only the close end of it had been set, including four different silver bowls on the floor surrounding a cushion for Owein. The dog went straight for it, his stomach apparently overriding whatever nerves had kept him quiet.

There was a vegetable and chicken soup already in the bowls at the complex place settings, as well as silver trays of what looked like fried sole, veal with a sort of spinach gravy, an encrusted leg of mutton, and a lemon-scented pudding farther out. It was Merritt's understanding

that food at dinner parties like this were typically served in courses, so the setup was either intended to deformalize the event or for the sake of privacy. Merritt glanced around the room and noticed a lack of servants. And as he'd learned from his tour, there were *always* servants.

Regardless, the spread looked absolutely delicious. What would Baptiste think of the setup?

They settled in, forgoing grace, and finished their soup course before Lady Helen addressed him in a very businesslike tone. "How much do you know about British wizardry, Mr. Fernsby?"

Merritt lowered his fork. "I admit to not being well studied in it, though I'm more familiar now than I used to be. My fiancée and I spoke at length on it, after the queen's letter."

"Is that so? Is she a scholar?"

"Not formally." Merritt allowed himself a bite of mutton. Chewed and swallowed before adding, "She's the director for the Boston Institute for the Keeping of Enchanted Rooms."

"Oh!" Lady Helen's fingers flew to her breast. "Really? The director?"

"A woman director?" Prince Friedrich asked, apparently unaware of the institute's previous master.

"Hulda Larkin, if I'm not mistaken." Blightree spoke more evenly.

Merritt nodded. "You are well informed."

"Isn't that something." Lady Helen set down her silverware. "That's something, isn't it, Friedrich?"

Her husband chuckled. "Any plans you had brewing for him are certainly pointless now."

Lady Helen swatted his arm. "Really, Friedrich. Let's have some propriety at the table."

"The interest," Blightree politely, softly interjected, "is with Mr. Mansel, of course."

Lady Helen composed herself. "Yes, thank you, William." Her gaze refocused on Merritt. "The British wizarding pedigree is the strongest in the world, you see. It's been taken very seriously since England could even be called such. It is one of the greatest duties of the peerage to uphold it, to nurture it. To continue the line. Thus Her Majesty's direct missive to you."

Merritt nodded, stomach suddenly tight. Where was this going?

"We heard about the prison break," Prince Friedrich explained. "Animals can't inherently possess magic. You said as much in your article."

Merritt stiffened. "That article hasn't been published a week yet." And Owein was never named in it.

"We have our ways." That same, gentle smile touched Blightree's mouth.

"It is clear," Lady Helen continued, "that Owein's—I can call you Owein, can't I?" She glanced at him.

Owein nodded.

She smiled. "Owein's magic is strong and enticing. How old is his spirit?"

Merritt clasped his hands together. "He was born in 1624. Roughly two hundred and twenty-three."

Lady Helen nodded, smiling enough to show her dimples. "As I thought. No wonder it's so strong! A miraculous way to skip natural dilution."

"What my dear wife is dancing around," the prince said, "is that we wish to add Owein's abilities to the family line."

Merritt stiffened like someone had taken an iron fence post and shoved it right up his backside. "P-Pardon?"

"He is common, yes," Lady Helen explained, "but where magic is concerned, such things can be overlooked."

What do they mean? Owein asked.

Merritt could barely process the communion. His pulse had doubled in speed. "You want to . . . but he's a *dog*. It isn't possible."

"That is where I come in," Blightree interjected. "My family line is also well cultivated; I have strength in a number of spells, including the one I believe was used on your uncle."

Merritt shook his head, not understanding.

"What we're offering"—Blightree glanced at the Leiningens to ensure it was appropriate for him to continue—"is a human body for Owein."

Chapter 7

Merritt's ears were ringing. Or was that some sort of bizarre enchantment in the room? He only vaguely picked up Owein's attention swiveling from his bowl to the company.

"I could move his spirit to a new vessel," the necromancer explained, moving his hands in undefined loops as he spoke. "In exchange, he would sign a marriage contract with Prince Friedrich's youngest daughter, Lady Cora."

Owein came over, rose onto his back legs, and placed his paws on the edge of the table. *What?*

At the same time, Merritt stuttered, "P-Pardon?"

"It's possible," Blightree explained slowly, turning fully in his chair to face Merritt and illustrating with his hands. "With a viable human vessel, that is. I can't resurrect Owein Mansel's body—only, perhaps, the very first necromancer would have such power. Even a body a day past wouldn't work. A living body, yes, but there are ethics to be considered. But the right specimen at the right time, I have the spells necessary, both to keep it viable and to move Owein's spirit when the time comes."

Merritt tried to sort through the information but felt like he was hammering puzzle pieces that didn't fit together. "I . . . How? Who?"

"I don't know. But with your agreement, and Owein's"—he nodded to the dog—"we would begin searching."

Owein's dark eyes lifted to Merritt. *A body? A human body? For me?* He barked.

Merritt shook his head. "But . . . if this *is* possible . . . why would his spirit be worth more than that of the deceased?" He glanced to Owein. "I don't mean to devalue you, but"—his gaze switched back to Blightree—"isn't this a little close to playing God? Moving around spirits to keep those with magic in their family line?" He gestured to the Leiningens but didn't look at them. "Necromancers are healers, aren't they? Why wouldn't you just heal the sick or the injured instead of waiting for them to pass so you can use the body for a more suitable spirit?"

Owein's ears drooped. *But, Merritt—*

I don't mean anything by it, Merritt insisted telepathically. *Would it feel fine with your conscience to take the life of another kid just so you can have ten fingers and a larynx?*

Owein lowered his head and shook it almost imperceptibly.

Lady Helen interjected, "Of course all of that would be taken into consideration, right, William?"

Blightree nodded. "I've discussed it with Her Majesty directly, and we would sign a contract with Owein, ensuring everything was acceptable for all parties."

"Including"—Merritt cleared his throat, shaking off communion effects—"the deceased and his family?"

"Of course." Blightree spoke with measured grace. "However, such a thing wouldn't be possible at this time, as we wouldn't know who the deceased and his family would be."

"And the party who signs it would be me," Merritt pressed. "I'm legally Owein's guardian."

There seemed no end to Blightree's patience. Still, he said, "Legal guardianship of a canine is not—"

"It is, and I brought the paperwork to prove it." Merritt's tone had taken on a slight edge. He tried to dull it; if Blightree could remain calm, so could he. "And we both know he's more than just a canine." Shaking his head, he glanced at Owein. "I'm sorry. I don't mean to speak for you as though you're not here."

Owein huffed. *I haven't been able to speak for myself for centuries.*

Merritt's stomach sunk. *I'm so sorry. I'm . . . I'm doing my best.*

"What is he saying?" Prince Friedrich asked.

Merritt ignored him and focused on the necromancer. "How would we know you didn't just select some random, innocent adolescent off the street?"

"We're not barbarians." Blightree's voice was a little softer. "I promise you that. It could be years until a suitable host is found. It will be handled with the utmost care."

The hope in Owein's eyes nearly broke Merritt. And the offer . . . Victoria was right. It *was* irresistible. For Owein to live as a human again—after losing his own body so young and being trapped in that house—why not take the opportunity, if it were to present itself in a moral manner? And dogs . . . they didn't live long. Owein would be gone before Merritt's fortieth birthday, and he'd last until then only with interventions. Once his dog life was done, he'd either move on or live inside Whimbrel House again, with all the magic of his spirit at his fingertips and all the sensations of the body and words of the mind lost.

I want to sign it! Owein pressed.

Merritt let out a long breath. "We're willing to at least look at a . . . contract."

Owein's tail thumped against the side of his chair.

After taking a deep breath, Merritt asked, "How would it work?"

"We would have to work quickly, to ensure function of the mind. That would deteriorate before the rest of the body, which is what makes finding a suitable host difficult," Blightree explained. "But just as this boy's soul was moved from the grave to a house, and then to this dog, it would be moved again. Resituate itself. Owein would understand the method better than any of us." He met Owein's eyes. Then, with a small smile, he added, "Might be easier if you didn't care for the sex."

Owein's ears lifted.

Blightree chuckled. "I'm joking, of course. We would need you to remain male to ensure the family line. But age . . . I can't guarantee age. The host might be a ten-year-old boy or a fifty-year-old man. Only time will tell."

"Yes," Lady Helen interjected. "My dear Cora. Oh." She looked over the table, then to the wall, before patting her skirts and retrieving a bell from the thick gathers of fabric. She rang it loudly; a moment later, a footman discreetly entered the room. Lady Helen murmured something to him; he nodded and exited the room. "My Cora dined in her room; she's aware of the situation, of course. We didn't want to spring too much on you at once."

Too much was an understatement, Merritt thought. This all seemed quite *too much* to him. But he nodded. There wasn't really a simple way to make such an offer, was there?

"She's thirteen," Lady Helen continued. "Fourteen this summer."

Merritt tried not to cringe at the idea of a thirteen-year-old girl being married off to a fifty-year-old man.

"Quiet child, but very kind, very smart. Well educated, of course," Lady Helen went on.

Merritt chose not to mention that Owein had only recently learned how to read.

"She'll be here in a moment," Prince Friedrich added.

"We've four children altogether," Lady Helen explained. "Cora is our youngest—the contract would include marriage to her, in exchange for what we've discussed."

Merritt whistled. It probably wasn't polite, but it seemed warranted given the situation. Marriage contract. New body. *Are you understanding all of this?*

Owein sat. *I marry their daughter, and they make me human again. More or less. You don't need to make any decisions yet—*

Lady Helen continued, "Palmerston and Colin are our oldest, both with estates of their own. Then there's Briar, who married last year and will be joining us tomorrow. If . . . If it wouldn't be too direct . . . what, precisely, does Owein have in his repertoire?"

It took a moment for Merritt to realize she was asking after his spells. It seemed crass considering what they were asking of him . . . but he supposed it was no more so than the work done by the Genealogical Society. And well, *If we don't tell them, the offer might be rescinded.*

I'm not embarrassed by my magic, Owein retorted.

Merritt shrugged. "Owein"—his voice came out raspy; he pushed through it—"has spells of alteration and chaocracy. We have rough approximations from a scholar back home."

Lady Helen beamed and clasped her hands together. Prince Friedrich said, "That is good—we have an alteration spell in my lineage, and all our children have inherited it. Mere recoloring, but still. Our dear Queen Victoria must have caught on to that. She's very bright. Do you, perchance, know his percentages?"

Merritt was not used to such discussions, but at this point, there was no use holding back. He'd focus on what could help Owein. "Supposedly around twenty-four overall."

Lady Helen put a hand on her husband's forearm. "That's very good. Better than we had hoped. Cora, she'd got quite the mix. Alteration, yes, which will make for an excellent combination with dear Owein, and ether manipulation, in the discipline of elemental magic. Hysteria, conjury, augury, and wardship, just one spell each—"

The footman from before stepped into the dining room. "Lady Cora Karoline of Leiningen," he announced, and stepped aside.

The girl who walked in took after her mother—she was short and well dressed, with a pale complexion and dark-brown hair carefully curled and pinned. She had the slightest bit of childhood left in her cheeks, but the rest of her had started the ascent into womanhood. She held herself well, straight-backed and with her hands clasped before her, shoulders squared, chin lifted. The stance, in all honesty, reminded Merritt of Hulda.

That's her? Owein asked, peeking around Merritt's chair.

Merritt nodded. It was easier than working around the tightness communion had left in his throat. Blightree stood, reminding him that he should do the same, and her parents rose as well, all in respectful greeting. Cora curtsied, then crossed to the seat beside her mother. Another footman pulled out the chair for her.

Farm boy married to a princess, Merritt said.

Owein didn't reply. His eyes watched Cora.

"Cora," Prince Friedrich said, "this is Merritt Fernsby and Owein Mansel, come all the way from Rhode Island to meet you."

Cora nodded. "How do you do? Thank you for your time and effort. I hope the trip was gentle."

"Uh, yes," Merritt rasped. He cleared his throat again, but it did little to help. "Forgive me, I've been using communion."

With a family so indoctrinated with magic, he needn't explain further. All of them just nodded with understanding.

"As I was saying," Lady Helen continued, "we do have alteration in the family line; Cora specifically inherited the ability to alter color, which will mesh very well with Owein's magic. She also has air movement, infliction of pain—don't worry, it's moderate and never used—conjury of stone, luck, and spell-turning. There are actually both alteration and chaocracy further up the family line. Who knows—perhaps they will come about again!"

"Of course," Cora's father interjected, "there would be no union until she was eighteen. And until Owein was eighteen, depending on the age of the host."

Merritt studied Cora's face as her parents spoke, but her expression remained unaffected. She maintained a demure quietness. Merritt couldn't blame her. What would he think of all of this, were he in her position? In Owein's?

The latter was easier for him to piece out.

"The contract could be drafted tomorrow, with revisions as necessary," Blightree said.

"Perhaps," Merritt pushed in, raising a hand as though he could halt the procession of wild ideas, "we give it a fortnight. Give Owein, and your family, time to mull over the idea. Ensure the two . . . suit."

"Yes, it's all a bit to digest, isn't it?" Lady Helen sounded apologetic. "And after such a long trip, too. But of course, we should see how they suit! This is a large step; all parties need to take it into the deepest consideration. I seem to have exhausted my manners!" She rose from the table. "A fortnight can easily be spared. For now, rest. Let me personally see you to your rooms."

"The housekeeper can do that, love," Prince Friedrich said.

She shook her head. "I insist. Unless . . . Cora, do you have any questions?"

Cora smiled kindly. "It's all been explained thoroughly, thank you. It's nice to meet you, Owein." She nodded to him.

Owein, head barely able to see over the table, nodded back.

"Excellent. This way." Lady Helen gestured. Merritt pushed back his chair and followed, Owein slow to copy him. His eyes remained on Cora until he'd passed into the hallway.

What do you think? Merritt asked as they continued to follow Lady Helen.

I want to sign the contract.

Merritt pressed his lips together. *The contract would involve you getting* married, *Owein.*

The dog leveled his stare as much as he could. *I'll marry a toad if it means getting my body back. Or a body back.*

Merritt rubbed warmth into his hands. *Nothing is legalized yet. Marriage is a big—*

I don't want to die.

That sentiment had Merritt tripping over his own heels. "What?" he asked aloud, voice a whisper.

But Owein didn't respond, physically or through their magicked connection. Merritt reached down for him, stroked the top of his head, but no more words came.

At the top of the main set of stairs, Lady Helen paused. "You know what, I have something better in mind for you." She turned toward Owein and took on a soft, maternal expression. "If you will be part of the family, and I hope you will, you should sleep closer to us. The rooms I had prepared . . . they're far away. And likely drafty. Let me set you up somewhere nicer."

Merritt whispered, "It's no problem—" then coughed.

She gave him a wry look. "I do wonder what you two are discussing." Then, with a wink, she said, "It's no trouble at all. This way."

She led them down a marble hallway lined with Indian rugs, bronze busts, and a few Grecian vases—a part of the house that had not been included on the earlier tour—and Merritt had a feeling they would be staying here far longer than either of them had initially planned.

Chapter 8

The preparations were made in quick order, with Mrs. Thornton alerted and on her way to Boston, a windsource pigeon sent to Beth at Whimbrel House, Hulda's bags packed, and the kinetic ferry ticket purchased. Unfortunately, due to the limited number of ferries, Hulda could not depart across the Atlantic until tomorrow.

Which was how she ended up staying the night with her sister.

"It *is* an awfully *long* time to wait for matrimony is all I'm saying!" Danielle spoke with a mouth half full of food, which would have been an atrocity if any guests besides Hulda had come to dine in her home in Cambridge. Danielle, wearing a cream gown with far too much lace for Hulda's liking, paused, chewed, and swallowed. Then, wielding a fork like a sword, added, "Though I suppose a winter wedding wouldn't be very nice, especially on an island. But really, wouldn't you prefer a church?"

"We're having a Christian wedding," Hulda pressed. "No need to move the entire household across the bay to wed in a church." Or at the church Hulda attended in Boston, which was a fine building with beautiful windows. It would just be a pain, in the long run. And the streets would be crowded.

Danielle shrugged. "When John asked me for my hand, I couldn't wait! Each day was painful."

John, her husband, simply smiled from the head of the table and cut into his portion of chicken.

"Boys," Danielle addressed her children now, "don't ever make your belles wait on you. If you're going to marry them, marry them!"

"Gross," Benjamin retorted, also around a half mouthful of food.

Hulda rolled her eyes. "I told you, he's not making me wait—"

"No, you are the cruel one in this matter!" Danielle stabbed the air with her fork. "Really, Hulda, men have needs—"

"Danielle," John said softly, no food in his mouth. "Perhaps not in front of the children."

Danielle sighed and slumped in her chair, not even having the wherewithal to blush. "Very well." She set down the fork. "I'm finished. Hulda, meet me in the parlor when you're done."

Pushing away from the table, Danielle sauntered out. Her maid slipped in, graceful as a swan, to remove her dishes.

"Good luck," John offered.

"Thank you." Hulda speared a potato. "I fear I'll need it."

Hulda did not rush her meal but finished in an orderly fashion. She was antsy to reach Merritt, yet the matter was entirely out of her hands until she arrived in London. Things she couldn't control often frustrated her, but what was she to do for it? Augurists, even those weak as herself, were a rare breed. Her grandmother had taught her everything she knew, but her grandmother had been neither a master nor a scholar. Still, perhaps while overseas, Hulda might be able to find a tutor of some sort, or a very well-written book on the subject, thus ensuring she learned more in future readings.

In the meantime, Hulda forced equanimity into her thoughts and actions. Forced herself to be meticulous, and to stay occupied. She offered to assist the small staff with cleanup, but was turned away, so she found herself trudging to the parlor, where far too many candles had been lit. Danielle sat on a powder-blue sofa within, working on a cross-stitch of a sunflower. She held it up as Hulda took the seat beside her.

"I'm going to hang it in James's room," she said, naming her youngest son. "What do you think?"

Hulda nodded. "It looks well." Danielle had a knack for tiny, uniform stitches. Hulda had always considered her fingers too long to achieve such a thing, though her sewing was generally considered neat.

Setting the cross-stitch aside, Danielle said, "I'm sorry if I was brash at the table. I was just having some fun. I so seldom get the opportunity to tease my beloved sister."

Hulda waved the apology away. "I'm very accustomed to your antics. No offense was taken."

"Still, an apology is due." Reaching forward, Danielle grasped Hulda's left hand in both of her own, admiring the ring there. "He's got good taste." She grinned. "He's a fine-looking fellow. Just needs a haircut."

Hulda snorted. "I don't think it will ever happen. In truth, I believe it grew long out of sheer laziness, but at this point he keeps it to vex people, most of all me."

Danielle shrugged. "Perhaps it will come back in fashion. But perhaps not. One cannot set a trend if he spends all his time alone on an island." She paused. "Are you all right, living there? Away from the city and all the people?"

"I lived there before."

"But permanently! Won't you get bored?"

Hulda plucked at a loose thread on her cuff. "Hardly. With the commute into Boston, I'll barely have time to—"

"Commute?" Danielle interrupted. "You mean you'll keep the position with BIKER?"

"Of course I will."

"Is he poor?" She grasped Hulda's hand. "He didn't look poor."

"Oh, for goodness' sake." Hulda pulled free and adjusted a pillow behind her back. "He is not poor, though if he were, it wouldn't matter. I *want* to work, Danielle. BIKER has been my life and will continue to be my life until the day I die."

"Do you plan on dying very soon?"

Hulda moved to pinch her sister, but Danielle dodged with a chuckle and situated herself on the far end of the sofa, which was still within pinching distance, should Hulda choose to lean forward. Still, the comment prickled. She knew what her sibling was thinking; Danielle had been married over a decade, and the idea of Hulda continuing to work surprised her. Was Hulda completely ignorant of the callings of a wife? Was she kidding herself to think she could keep both roles?

Smiling brightly, Danielle said, "He is not the only one who enjoys vexing you. I do think it's my favorite pastime!"

"I'll be sure to visit more often," Hulda retorted. "I would hate to leave you bored. John does not seem like he would be pleasing to vex."

"Indeed he is not." She sighed dramatically. "But speaking of John. Or, rather, men in general—"

A flush began to work its way up Hulda's neck. "Spare me."

"I shall not!" Danielle bounced back to the center of the sofa so that her knees pressed into Hulda's. "I cannot let a dear sister go into matrimony without every piece of advice and warning I have to offer."

The flush crept higher. Hulda ignored it. She was tempted to blow out some of the candles to better mask it . . . and to cool down the room. "I am well aware of what a marriage consists of, Danielle."

"But the marriage *bed*—"

"Oh, for heaven's sake." Hulda folded her arms. Leaned toward a side table and blew out two candles.

"Hulda!"

"I read a book on it," she admitted, softer. "Though I was well aware beforehand."

Danielle paused. "Did Mother tell you—"

"She had less hope in me than I did." Hulda absently fixed her hair. "It's nothing you need worry about."

When Danielle didn't respond right away, Hulda glanced over to find her leaning close, eyes squinting to scrutinize her. Several seconds passed before Danielle's face turned gleeful as a clown's. "You've seen it, haven't you!"

Hulda leaned back, desperate for personal space. "Seen *what?*"

"Seen *it!*" Danielle laughed. "Oh, but the way your face is blooming, I know it's true! If only the augury blood had chosen me. I would use it for so many things!"

The room was most certainly too warm now. "I have not."

"Yes, you have. Else you wouldn't know what I meant."

"I know what you mean because it's simple deduction of the c-conversation—" Hulda stammered, trying to find her words. She hated being taken off guard! "And besides, the augury is only snippets. I hardly see enough to determine—"

"So you admit it, then." Danielle pulled her legs onto the sofa, kneeling, and faced Hulda full on.

Perhaps some of the heat beneath Hulda's skin was simple temper. "I admit to nothing, and if you do not drop the subject, I will retire early."

Her sister's face fell. "You are no fun at all." She pouted. "I've so few women friends willing to discuss private matters."

"Perhaps because they are *private.*"

Now Danielle rolled her eyes. Their mother had always hated the habit, and Hulda wondered, briefly, if Danielle had gotten the foible from her. "Give it a year or two and we'll have late nights talking all about *private things*, just you wait. You'll be dying to have me as a confidant."

Merritt will be my confidant, she thought of retorting, but determined it might be too harsh. Her younger sister was, well, a younger sister, and an eccentric one at that. But Hulda loved her and had no desire to hurt her feelings.

"We shall see," she settled on instead. "In truth, I have had a vision, but I couldn't make much of it. As is usually the case with the trickle of magic I have." She allowed herself to slouch. "But Merritt seemed to be in a dangerous situation. Or at least an uncomfortable one. And I can't yet reach him, and it's putting me out of sorts."

"Ah." Danielle's hand found Hulda's knee. "Well, I'm . . . sure it's nothing too terrible." She hesitated. "Would you read for me while you're here? You have such a calming voice, and you never mispronounce anything."

Hulda's lips ticked upward. She knew Danielle meant only to distract her. In truth, Danielle hated the way she read. Not enough *inflection*. But Hulda was not one to turn away a diversion. Not tonight.

"Why don't you select a book, then?"

Danielle grinned and leapt to her feet. "I know just the one! Bought it last week because the cover was so lovely. You'll be the first to crack the spine. I know you'll like that."

She did. Fresh spines and the smell of clean pages. And so Hulda took the book, opened it, and began to read. She read well into the night, even after her sister had fallen asleep on the sofa.

Chapter 9

The darkness had claws.

A room with no walls, no floor, no ceiling. Just shadows cast without light. Water and soot sloshing and staining, and low, black claws on crooked pitch fingers, too many to be a real hand, reaching and bending like spider legs. Reaching, reaching—

Owein startled awake. Found himself shivering despite the blankets on the enormous bed in his room. It was still dark, but it wasn't mind-dark, because pale-blue moonlight whispered through the window. Lady Helen had drawn the curtains. He'd opened them back up.

A whimper escaped his throat as he nosed deeper into the covers, hunkering there until the shivering stopped. Then he poked his head out and looked around. Searched for anything crumbled or broken. Maybe he'd woken up before his spells kicked in this time. He didn't feel any of their effects. His mind was keen (Hulda had taught him that word) and his body normal. So he scratched behind his ear with a back paw, laid his head down, and waited.

Sleep didn't come.

He waited a quarter hour, or so was his guess, before sliding from the heavy blankets and dropping to the enormous rug upon which his enormous bed sat. Everything was enormous, like the people who'd made this house had forgotten how to build things small. He walked to the door and rose on his hind legs, pushing down the handle with his paws. It gave, and he slipped out into a hallway with no traces of window-screened moonlight.

He paused, seeing a dozen inky claws in the back of his mind. Swallowed a whimper and trotted with his side brushing the stone wall. His dog eyes could make out the doorframes and sconces just fine in the dark, but there was comfort in touching something solid. When he reached Merritt's door, he stood on his hind legs and pawed at the knob. This time, however, he couldn't get it to turn. Maybe it was locked. So he melted himself a hole. Slipped inside silently, save for the faint clacking of his nails on the stone.

Merritt's room looked just like his, but in reverse. It even had the same trimming, which in the candlelight had looked cream and gray, although Merritt had told him the gray was actually burgundy—Owein had a hard time seeing burgundy, though he remembered what it looked like. In the dark, especially with the curtains closed, everything looked black and gray.

Another chaocracy spell forced the curtains open a little roughly, but some calming moonlight streamed in. Merritt stirred in the bed. He woke up fully when Owein jumped onto the high mattress.

"Owein?" he asked blearily, then a calloused palm stroked Owein's shoulder. After letting loose a yawn, Merritt mumbled, "Nightmare again?"

Huffing, Owein folded all four legs beneath him and set his dog chin on Merritt's stomach.

The petting continued. Owein liked being petted. Or maybe it was the dog part of him that liked it. Silas Hogwood hadn't bothered clearing out the terrier's body before shoving Owein inside of it, but Owein's soul overwhelmed the simplicity of the animal's soul. Still, sometimes the dog made its preferences known, and its instincts had a mind of their own. "You're fine to stay here."

So Owein did. Settled in for about two minutes, long enough for Merritt's breath to start an even pattern. Then he asked, *What will it mean to be married?*

Merritt startled. Yawned. "You're very aware of what marriage is."

For other people. Not for me.

With a soft groan Merritt sat up, slightly displacing Owein. He stretched his arms overhead. "Is that what's keeping you up?"

Owein shook his head. He knew Merritt could see it, because he'd opened the curtains.

Merritt frowned. Considered. "It means when you're old enough . . . old enough in body, I suppose . . . you'll come back here to England and marry Lady Cora. *If* you agree, of course."

I will, he said. *I want a body.*

"I don't blame you. It would be a good thing, mostly—you'll never want for money. All those needs will be taken care of. But you won't be able to choose your own wife. If you fall in love with another . . ." Merritt shrugged.

I'm not in love with anyone.

A light chuckle escaped him. "Not yet, I suppose. And maybe not ever. It would work out better that way. But you'd be bound to her." He ran a hand back through his messy hair and glanced at the newly revealed window. "You would take care of her when she's sick. Listen to her when she's sad. Comfort her when she needs it."

I think the servants do that.

"*You* will do that," Merritt pressed, a raspy edge leaking into his voice from communion. "You first. As if there were no money and no servants and no family to speak of." He paused for a moment. Kneaded his hands together. Maybe he was thinking about Hulda. They talked about marriage and weddings a lot now. "You'll attend her gatherings and her dinners, and because it's the royal family, you'll have a certain level of"—he swirled his hand in the air—"*prestige* to uphold. I don't know if they'd require a lot of public appearances from you. And you'd become a father, and take on all the responsibilities of that."

Owein mulled it over for a moment. He'd never really imagined himself as a father. Then again he'd never imagined himself as a dog, either.

Before a new question could form in his mind, the room began to quake. Not roughly, but gently, like a cat purring unevenly. The tremors were disjointed, uneven.

"Owein?"

Owein rose to his paws. *Not me,* he said.

A crack and a rumble followed, almost like a storm, and then everything was still.

Owein met Merritt's gaze. Merritt flung the blankets off himself, hurried to the foot of the bed, and grabbed his trousers, nearly falling over as he struggled to pull them on while rushing for the door. One perk of being a dog was not needing clothing, so Owein made it there first.

The hallway smelled faintly of dust. Merritt spun, trying to orient himself. Owein raced ahead, following the heady scent of dust. Not wanting Merritt to lose his voice, he barked to communicate his location, and Merritt followed him down the hallway and around the corner, where the smell became nearly overwhelming. There was a short, wide set of stairs, and then dust clouded everything.

Merritt waved his hands, trying to clear the air. He coughed and pulled his shirt over his nose. Owein didn't have the luxury. He sneezed twice and blinked, eyes watering.

"My goodness!" It was Lady Helen's voice, and suddenly air swept through the hallway, pressing against Owein's backside, clearing the dust. "What happened?"

A lady's maid in a night-robe hurried behind her, protecting a candle from the gusts.

"These rooms," Merritt said, then coughed, "they seem to have collapsed."

"Good gracious!" Lady Helen met them, then cast her hands out, sending another gust down the corridor. She sounded a little out of breath—the side effect for elemental air spells—when she said, "Belinda, bring the light closer!"

The lady's maid hurried forward, holding the candle high. The hallway was mostly clear, though up ahead some stone had broken off the left wall and spilled into the hallway. Since Belinda was the only one with a light, she led the group. They'd just reached the pile when more footsteps sounded behind them—one set belonged to a man Owein didn't recognize, one to a haggard Prince Friedrich, and the last to a baffled Lady Cora.

Owein's heart squeezed a little at the sight of her. Then he sneezed more dust from his nostrils.

"Goodness!" Cora's hands pressed into either cheek.

"Whatever happened?" Prince Friedrich asked as he and the other man met up with Belinda. Both were carrying candles, which cast more light on the destruction. Merritt tried to open the door nearest the rock pile. It didn't budge. He slammed his shoulder into it.

Owein barked, using an alteration spell to shrink the door, so when Merritt hit it a second time, it burst open. He stumbled back, gasping, waving his hand as more dust assaulted him.

Lady Helen hurried forward.

"Careful!" the male servant warned.

Several gusts of wind left Lady Helen panting. "It's absolutely horrid." She took Belinda's candle and peered into the room without stepping into it. "Oh, Friedrich, half the ceiling has fallen!"

"How?" The prince moved forward, only for the male servant to stop him.

"I must ask you, Ladies Helen and Cora, to retreat," he pleaded. "It's not safe."

More footsteps sounded down the hallway; probably more servants coming. Padding forward, Owein peered into the room. It was dark, hard to see, but he could make out clusters of mortared stone scattering the floor. Some larger chunks had fallen onto the bed, snapping its frame.

"Is anyone in there?" Cora cried.

Lady Helen, finally retreating, shook her head. "No. No, dear. No one. But . . ." In the flickering candlelight, she looked pale as milk.

"But what?" Merritt asked.

Helen's wide-eyed gaze fell to Owein before shifting to Merritt. "But . . . this was meant to be your room." Her voice quivered with each syllable. "Mr. Fernsby, I'd initially intended *you* to be *here*."

Chapter 10

Despite lack of sleep, Merritt found himself very awake at the breakfast table the following morning. The breakfasting room was, in size, at least, one of the more modest areas of the house, meant to serve just the family, sans guests, or so Lady Helen had told him. The furnishings, however, were still quite grand. The ceiling, trim, table, and chairs were all painted a brilliant white that seemed to reflect the east sky billowing in from the enormous window at Merritt's back. The walls were papered a deep navy blue with white fleur-de-lis in neat, vertical rows. There were two entrances to the room, one to the north and one to the south, and the servants seemed to use only the former. Lady Helen apologized for the meager meal, which wasn't meager in the slightest—Merritt had a boiled egg in a little egg cup with a genuine silver spoon the length of his pinky, a plate full of eggs, sausage, ham, cheese, and braised tomatoes. There was also bread, butter, and preserves and a tray of little tarts that hadn't made its way to his end of the table yet, not that he could possibly spare room in his belly for it. The most excellent part of being a guest in a lavish home was the equally lavish food.

He focused on the food so as not to dwell on the fact that he would not be here to enjoy it if Lady Helen hadn't determined to move his room closer to the family suites.

A chill coursed from elbows to shoulders at the thought. He'd taken a peek at the damage after the constable left this morning. Had he slept in that space, he would most definitely be dead.

God knew he was getting tired of people trying to kill him. But who could hold any animosity toward him here, of all places? It was a coincidence. It had to be. His sanity *needed* it to be.

"The incident last night does seem to be the working of magic," Blightree said in a solemn tone, which made breakfast gurgle in Merritt's gut. The necromancer appeared to have gotten less sleep than Merritt, judging by the heavy bags under his eyes. "It couldn't have been natural causes, isolated as it was. The constable agrees with me."

"A sound judgment," Prince Friedrich said. He hadn't touched his plate, while Lady Helen's appetite seemed well. Lady Cora picked at hers sleepily. Owein sat in the corner—Lady Helen had tried to get him a feasible chair for sitting at the table, but it had proven more awkward than it was worth. Cora herself had set him up in his present position—a good sign. Owein had already finished and was sniffing around, only occasionally passing a thought to Merritt.

"Even if any of ours had the ability to break stone"—Lady Helen looked at Merritt specifically—"so much magic would have caused enormous side effects. We would have discovered the culprit straightaway."

An assurance that his host wasn't trying to murder him. And it did assure him, a little—he'd seen all of the family members shortly after the incident, and none had appeared to be experiencing the kickbacks associated with magic. Only Lady Helen had seemed discomfited, and that was from overuse of her spell of air movement to clear the hall. He wondered if anyone suspected himself or Owein, who *did* have spells that could cause such destruction, but again, their lack of magical symptoms marked them as innocent. That, and lack of motivation. Blightree had come late to the event, but he was a necromancer. None of his spells could have wreaked such havoc. But all that had already been discussed and recorded with the constable.

Merritt knit his fingers together and placed them beneath his chin, feigning surface-level calmness. "And none of the servants are gifted?"

Lady Helen shook her head.

"There's Elizabeth," Cora offered.

Lady Helen met her daughter with a patient smile. "Yes, but she is only a hysterian, darling, and barely one of note." She met Merritt's gaze. "Elizabeth works in the kitchen. She has a slip of joy in her from her grandfather."

"Perhaps she made the house chuckle itself into breaking," Merritt offered.

Lady Helen shook her head. "I don't think . . . Oh, but of course you jest." Another patient smile.

Perhaps now was not the best time for jesting. But Merritt found he could best stomach the uncertainty—especially as it seemed to involve him directly—with a little mirth. He'd learned to cope with a lot of things with laughter, for better or for worse.

"Let us hope," Prince Friedrich said, finally cracking into his egg, "that the police turn up something in their search and we can let it be done and over with."

"Mr. Fernsby," Blightree added, "I assure you that very few persons know you're here, and for what purpose. I believe your involvement to be happenstance."

"I prefer to think so," Merritt agreed. And yet, logic dictated it must have *something* to do with him. It was no isolated earthquake or failure of construction; both Blightree and the constable had confirmed the damage appeared to be of magical make. Merritt prided himself on his imagination, but he could not begin to fathom a story that made sense of the situation.

Owein lifted his head. *Someone is coming.*

A moment later, the south door opened to a footman who bowed and announced, "Baron Ernst Freiherr von Gayl and Lady Briar Feodora of Leiningen."

Cora leapt from her seat as a tall blond man with a shockingly wide mustache stepped through, followed by a demurer woman who appeared to be around twenty, with brown hair similar to Hulda's, pinned up modestly, though her dress was certainly of expensive make.

"Briar!" Cora cried, instantly crossing the room to her. She embraced Lady Briar around the middle, and was embraced in return. If Merritt remembered last night's conversation correctly, this was Friedrich and Helen's eldest daughter.

"I'm so sorry, Mama," Briar said midembrace. "We meant to arrive earlier, but there was a problem with a horse."

"Tossed a shoe?" Prince Friedrich asked.

The . . . baron with the enormous name . . . Ernst was the beginning of it, Merritt thought, took an empty seat. "No, just a fit." He had a heavy German accent that put Prince Friedrich's less pronounced one to shame. "Driver said it was newly broken and unused to the travel. We stayed at the Red Rabbit last night. The place has really gone downhill."

"Red Rabbit?" Lady Helen frowned. "That's only a few miles from here. You should have stayed the night."

"It was more trouble than it was worth," Briar said as she and Cora pulled apart. She gave her sister a genuine smile. "But I noticed damage on the west hall—was there a storm?"

Briar made no effort to sit at the table; meanwhile, Ernst was helping himself to every tray. Merritt watched them quietly.

Lady Helen threw down her napkin. "I'll let William catch you up on all of it, because I'm tired of it all!" After steadying herself with a breath, she said, "Baron, Briar, this is Mr. Fernsby and Mr. Mansel, whom I wrote you about."

Briar started, seeming to see Merritt for the first time. "My apologies." She offered a mild curtsy. "I hope you are enjoying your stay. And . . ." She searched the room, two fine lines forming between her brows.

Owein walked up beside Merritt so he could be seen.

"Oh. Oh, right." Briar's face notably fell. She plastered on a smile, but it affected only her mouth, leaving the rest of her expression tight. "How . . . peculiar. I hope you, too, are finding everything well."

We were almost crushed, Owein responded.

Merritt set a hand on the dog's shoulder. "He is, thank you."

Owein shot him a scorning look that was surprisingly human.

The sound of distant barking outside caught Merritt's attention. Owein's, too, by the way his ears rose.

"Don't mind that," Lady Helen said as Cora tiredly resumed her seat. She waved Briar over, but Briar replied with a subtle shake of her head, which made Merritt curious. "That's just our kennel master readying the hounds."

"I thought a fox hunt might be a splendid way to start the morning." Prince Friedrich helped himself to a bite of ham. "Good thing to get our minds off it all, eh, Mr. Fernsby?"

Owein's voice chimed in, *Don't leave.*

Merritt kept his eyes forward. "I've never hunted a fox before." *And maybe I'll be harder to randomly murder if I'm on horseback.*

Those thoughts would not get him anywhere.

Baron von Gayl wiped his mouth and said, "But surely you ride, yes?"

Merritt managed a smile. "I know how to stay atop the saddle, at least."

"You should join them," Briar said to Baron von Gayl, still looming near the door. "You do love a good hunt."

"Surely you both want to rest," said Lady Helen.

"We're quite rested," Briar pressed. "Aren't we, Ernst?"

Seems she's not fond of her husband, Merritt said to Owein.

Owein tipped his head.

"Yes, yes, I think I shall." The German nodded.

Don't leave me behind, Owein repeated. A slight whine followed.

Merritt hesitated, unsure what decorum required of him. "Uh . . ."

Lady Helen perked up. "Is he speaking?"

To Briar, Cora explained, "Mr. Fernsby is a communionist. He can tell us what Owein—I mean, Mr. Mansel—says."

Owein glanced at her. *She can call me Owein.*

Clearing his throat, Merritt relayed the message. Cora seemed pleased.

"He'd also like to attend the hunt," Merritt added.

Lady Helen paused. "Well . . . I suppose that would work. He's about the size of the hounds. He could keep up."

Briar grimaced. None of the family seemed to notice. Merritt couldn't entirely blame her for feeling distaste . . . The situation was bizarre, at best.

Owein let out a soft woof of delight.

"Then it is settled." Lady Helen clapped her hands. "Afterward we'll have luncheon, and Cora will give you a tour of the grounds, if the weather permits. She's become much more involved with them. Then we shall have afternoon tea—I have a violinist coming in to play for us, and Cora has been working on a wonderful song on the pianoforte. Briar is also an excellent player. Oh! You both should do that duet of yours, if you remember it. Then I thought we could all take part in a game of cards, and I've a soothsayer coming in to look at the match— just for fun, of course! I wish dear Victoria could join us, but of course she's terribly busy running things, but she would be at the union itself, most certainly—"

Chapter 11

The adults seemed quite put out by the fox hunt by the end, since they hadn't actually caught any foxes. Owein got a whiff of one's scent at one point, he was pretty sure, but he and the hounds had been unable to find it or its den. But the run had been the best run of his life. Fallen trees and moist earth, new scents and clamoring bodies . . . that was, he enjoyed the clamor of the dogs, *not* the horses. He'd nearly been stepped on multiple times.

The hounds weren't possessed by a person, like he was, but those lingering terrier instincts inside Owein understood them, in the simplest of terms. Their wants and reasons weren't complex like people's were, and after all this jumble about politics and marriage, Owein rather liked simplicity. Perhaps it was a bad thing, to prefer the company of hounds to people. But after they returned to the house and he took a nap in the kennel, he quickly got bored with the dogs and their eagerness for a friendly hand and a treat. He left to spend time with Merritt, half suspecting his nephew was the actual reason they hadn't caught the fox.

"I just feel bad," Merritt had remarked after lunch, under his breath, "hunting something we're not going to eat."

Charlie N. Holmberg

Merritt seemed distracted. The bad kind of distracted. But didn't he know Owein would protect him, should anything bad arise?

Nothing bad did arise; the rest of the day was just as packed as Cora's mother had promised. Cora did play the pianoforte well; Owein enjoyed listening to her, though he did so from the back of the room, finding the instrument too loud for his ears. He couldn't tell Cora he liked her song, so he had Merritt tell her for him, and she scratched his ear and smiled, so maybe this marriage thing wouldn't be so bad after all.

Merritt let Owein sleep in his room again, and when he woke, he couldn't remember whether his dreams had been dark or light. They'd only just exited to the hallway when a muffled sound caught Owein's attention. He paused, lifting his ears to listen. Merritt noticed a beat later. "What?"

I hear Hulda. He pushed his way back into the room—Merritt hadn't latched the door—and followed the sound to Merritt's suitcase. He huffed.

"Hulda?" Merritt knelt by him and quickly opened the case, digging through it until he found his communion stone. Pulling it free, he heard Hulda say, quite distinctly, "—send a telegram, but I ought to be near enough—"

"Hulda?" Merritt asked the pale stone.

"Merritt!" she replied. "Merritt, I'm in England now, on my way. Are you and Owein all right? I had a vision of a smoky hallway in the dark—"

Owein barked.

"You're here?" He smiled. "Yes, we're fine. And yes, there was a rather dusty hallway two nights ago." *Better,* he communicated to Owein, *not to tell her the details until she gets here, or she might panic.* "I'll tell you all about it when you get here. We're at Cyprus Hall. Do you know it?" *Might not be a bad idea to have another ally here. We'll keep her safe.*

84

Owein huffed his agreement.

"I do," the stone chimed, "and I'll be there shortly."

ᘒ

"This is where it happened?"

Hulda would never have guessed anything was amiss from the appearance of the hallway; the corridor was swept and polished and looked every bit as it should. But when Merritt opened the door—which stuck to its frame—her lips parted in surprise. The entire ceiling had collapsed. Sunlight glinted through slits where curtains didn't quite touch. The bed frame had buckled. The shattered glass from the windows and other debris—it had been *dust* clouding that hallway in her vision, not smoke—had been cleaned up. It was the tidiest disaster Hulda had ever beheld.

To her great relief, no one had gotten hurt. But news of the room's original assignment put her on edge, as did that sense of *danger* from her vision.

When a vision had concluded, and moved itself from future to past, did its warnings still pertain to futurity? There had been danger, yes—Hulda could see as much—but it had passed. Still, Hulda found herself wishing for something *extra*. If only she had a class or even a pamphlet to help her hone her minute skill. The thought brought another one—a reminiscence of Myra's attempts to synthesize magic and the possible merits therein, but she pushed it from her mind. Priorities. There were always priorities.

After setting her black bag down, Hulda removed her dowsing rods and gingerly stepped into the room, surveying the ceiling first, then the floor.

"Should be safe," Merritt offered, stepping in behind her.

It looked secure enough, at least. Still, Hulda trod lightly, circling the room with her dowsing rods in hand, then crossing its center, circumventing the bed. She lifted her hands toward the ceiling as well.

"Nothing here that I can find." She tucked the rods under her arm and slowly turned, surveying the damage. Merritt had drawn the curtains; every window was cracked, but only one pane had shattered. "And you just found it like this?"

"Heard the rumbling from my room. Thought it was Owein at first."

Stepping to the nearest window, Hulda peered out over the manicured grounds. Owein was on a walk with Lady Cora, chaperoned by both Lady Helen and Lady Briar. He'd seemed hesitant to leave Merritt's side, but if the boy was willing to "marry a toad" for a human body, he could also go on a walk with his potential intended. Fortunately, Owein *did* seem to be adjusting to Cyprus Hall well enough.

"And you can't think of anyone"—she chose her word carefully—"who might wish you ill?"

A dry laugh escaped Merritt as he stuck a hand on the back of his head. "No one. I've never *been* here before, Hulda. I don't know anyone. And I'm certain my books aren't *that* offensive, if any copies made it overseas."

Hulda didn't smile.

He lowered his hand. "Truthfully, though. I'm supposedly here on the queen's errand, and the Leiningens have been nothing but hospitable. Lady Helen's apologized to me . . ." He counted on his fingers. ". . . maybe a dozen and a half times already."

Pressing her lips together, Hulda lowered the dowsing rods and carefully studied the room with her own eyes. It *didn't* make sense for Merritt to be a target, but she was far too monomaniacal to rule it out. How could it be happenstance? Perhaps the Leiningens had enemies, and said enemies didn't know where they slept. Perhaps it was errant magic . . . somehow. If the house had suddenly gained sentience, her rods would have picked up on it. And the matter of the collapsing room was not the only issue at hand . . .

"I can't fathom how they'll do it." She kept her voice low; Merritt had left the door ajar. "How could they possibly find a body for Owein? Other than what happened with Silas Hogwood, I haven't heard of soul-switching happening in centuries . . . If Mr. Blightree is powerful enough to make the switch, would he not be powerful enough to save whatever boy or young man he selected?"

"My thoughts precisely." Merritt seemed eager for the subject change, drawing closer and folding his arms. The gesture emphasized his shoulders, and Hulda took a brief moment to appreciate them.

"The contract?" she tried.

"We've some time to ponder on it," he offered. "But I wanted to get your thoughts. I know it's been drafted. Honestly, they probably had it written up before we arrived."

Tapping her fingers against the dowsing rods, Hulda said, "I suppose if the ethical boundaries are clearly stated . . . but how does one clearly state it? Perhaps we should hire a lawyer."

"I don't know how much lawyers understand ethics."

She rolled her eyes at the joke.

"Regardless," Merritt continued, "the family wants to keep this close to the chest. I don't know how well the general public would take to a princess being betrothed to a *dog*. Briar certainly doesn't seem to care for it."

"Do take care to use their titles where they can hear you," she pressed, "and the correct ones at that. Prince Friedrich's title is from his German estate, but Lady Cora's comes from her mother." While his casual demeanor could be refreshing, Hulda didn't want to risk any faux pas.

Merritt merely shrugged a shoulder.

She added, "And he's not a dog . . . not really."

"Not judging Owein by the body he's in is like not judging a book by its cover." He scanned the room. "Not possible." He waited a beat. "Anything else in that bag of yours that might prove handy?"

"I don't think so. Not after the fact. If I'd been there . . ." But there was no point in tracing the possibilities of the situation. "Perhaps I'll find something of use at LIKER headquarters. You're sure this was supposed to be your room?"

"Yes, but Lady Helen moved both Owein and me closer to the family after meeting us." He chewed on the inside of his cheek. "I would honestly consider it happenstance if I'd never met you. You keep me looking over my shoulder."

Because Silas Hogwood and Alastair Baillie had taught them to be suspicious of happenstance.

"Perhaps it's haunted," he continued.

"Unlikely. Though—" Her train of thought caught as a trickle of memory lit. She focused on it, whisking back to a table and a bowl of soup in Boston.

Merritt touched her arm. "Hulda? Premonition?"

She blinked. "What? Oh, no. I was just remembering something." She snapped her fingers. "There was an obituary in that newspaper that published your article on Owein. An announcement. It was . . ." She closed her eyes a moment, thinking. "Yes, it was about the death of the Marquess of Halesworth. Member of the Queen's League of Magicians."

Merritt's brows drew together. "And this is relevant because . . . ?"

A shiver coursed up her arms as she pictured that newspaper in her hands. "Because, if I'm not mistaken, I believe he died *here*, at Cyprus Hall."

§

Lady Helen, Lady Cora, and Owein were just returning from their walk when Hulda and Merritt found them near the kitchen. Heavy cloud cover promised rain, but so far the weather had stayed dry.

"Oh yes." Lady Helen's face fell when Hulda inquired about the marquess. "My poor, dear father. His health had been in decline for some time." She took a moment to breathe deeply and still her emotions, and Hulda almost regretted asking. "It wasn't a surprise, that he passed, but yes, he was staying with us when it happened." Turning to Cora, she said, "Why don't you show Owein the library, my dear? Perhaps share a book with him."

Merritt tilted his head—something he did when Owein was speaking to him. He said nothing, however, only shifted his eyes to and from Owein, as though offering silent encouragement.

Lady Helen waited until the two had departed before saying, "Why do you ask?"

"I'm curious about the incident with your guest room," she explained, then hid a wince when Lady Helen blanched. "I'm sure it's no misconduct of yours," she hurried to add. "Indeed, Merritt told me your gift was advantageous in clearing the air after it happened."

"Well, thank you." She rubbed her hands together, perhaps banishing the chill from her walk. "And you are, of course, more than welcome to stay. I know LIKER is accommodating, but we've rooms to spare, and the others shouldn't collapse. Oh dear." She touched a hand to her face.

"That is very generous of you. I would love to accept, if it doesn't put you out." Hulda had been hoping the offer would come along; she'd rather be near Merritt and Owein than across town at LIKER headquarters. Especially with yet another magicked house mystery to solve. She happened to be a specialist in that area.

Her acceptance seemed to warm Lady Helen, who lowered her hand and smiled. "It's always lovely to have guests. But about my father?"

"Did he," Merritt asked, "pass away in that same room?"

Lady Helen's eyelashes fluttered as she blinked, gaze shifting from Merritt to Hulda. "Hm? Let me think . . . No, I believe he was staying elsewhere, near Briar's old room."

"We ask," Hulda explained, "because I wonder if his spirit might not be inhabiting Cyprus Hall."

"Oh. *Oh.*" Lady Helen pressed a palm to her chest. "Oh dear, I see. That can happen, can't it?" She looked upward, as though her deceased father might manifest himself in the moldings.

"Have there been any other manifestations of magic not intentionally caused by you or members of the family?" Hulda asked, mayhap with a little too much animation. If the hunch proved sound, it would both elucidate their problem and allow for it to be quickly resolved.

Lady Helen took a moment to consider. "No . . . none that I can think of at all, though I will ask the staff. But my father . . . he wasn't a destructive fellow."

"Nothing less than a gentleman, or so I thought when I had the pleasure of meeting him," Hulda agreed. "But death can be, understandably, a shocking experience."

Lady Helen nodded. "Of course. But it's been . . . oh, almost two weeks now." She blinked rapidly, then smiled. "I've seen and heard nothing that might indicate a . . . a *haunting*. But if you think there might be a chance, is there something you or LIKER could do? Don't misunderstand me, I loved the marquess, but I also love my house being in order and . . . standing."

Merritt chuckled.

"Once I confirm a haunting, the London Institute for the Keeping of Enchanted Rooms would be more than happy to offer assistance in keeping Cyprus Hall tamed and protected. Enchanted homes are becoming quite singular; I would take care of the registry, special staff, and auxiliaries personally."

Lady Helen folded her hands together. "I appreciate the offer, Miss Larkin, but there is plenty enough magic in this house as there is."

Hulda tipped her head in acquiescence. The world could do with more magicked abodes, but she had to respect the wishes of the family. And of course, if the spirit was indeed in residence, he *was* causing exorbitant destruction, which was a non sequitur, given her past experiences. "I'll perform an exorcism to be thorough," Hulda offered. She'd love to dive in deeper, but Cyprus Hall was a large abode, and not one she'd been hired to oversee. She'd be overstepping her bounds. "I'll collect what I need today."

"Let me send for our driver, if you need to head out."

Hulda smiled. "Thank you. That would make it easier." She glanced at Merritt, wishing she could commune with him mind to mind the way Owein did.

Fortunately, Merritt caught her intention. "Afterward, *Lady Helen*"—he bit down on a smile, and Hulda knew the emphasis had been for her benefit—"I know you and your husband have been eager about the contract."

She lit up. "Yes! The contract."

"If I could review it. Just to assure everything is in order."

"Of course, of course. And Miss Larkin, I'll have a very sturdy and nonhaunted room ready for you by supper. I can situate you near Mr. Fernsby. Oh"—she touched her bottom lip—"that is, unless a farther room would be more appropriate?"

Hulda's ears warmed. "I'm happy to go with your recommendation."

"Wonderful. Freddy!" she called past them, and Hulda turned to see a footman passing by. "Would you alert Mr. Hensfork to bring the curricle around for Miss Larkin? She has some business in town."

The footman nodded and departed.

A curricle was a two-person carriage, so it wouldn't do to ask Merritt to come along with her. Best he stay with Owein. With the puzzle of her vision so nearly solved, she felt comfortable leaving for a short time. She nodded her thanks. "I'll be sure to return in time for supper."

⌒☉

91

After Hulda departed, Merritt put on his coat and stepped outside for some fresh air and fresh thinking. The idea of dealing with another ghost, oddly enough, lent him some confidence, but the thought of the marriage contract still made him uneasy. Then again, if a usable body wasn't found—a very likely outcome given the demanded ethics clauses—the issue would be null. Of course, Merritt had no idea how the extended royal family worked behind the curtains. They could simply kidnap someone, annex his spirit, and present a body and an entirely innocent backstory, and Merritt would be none the wiser.

That idea sat uncomfortably in his gut as he passed by a winter-trodden flower garden. Spring was on its way and would certainly brighten up the gray grounds, but Merritt didn't intend to stay long enough to witness it.

An icy drop of rain hit his cheek. Merritt glanced skyward, waiting for another to fall. If it did, it struck him where he couldn't feel it. He quickened his pace. He'd like to get at least a lap in before returning indoors. The Leiningens were hospitable folk, but Merritt wouldn't say he was *comfortable* here. Especially if there was a ghost lurking in the walls. But in truth, he got his best thinking done when he could walk out in nature. Figuring out what to eat for dinner, unwinding plot holes in stories, deducing how to best confess his feelings for his housekeeper . . . all had been accomplished on purposeful strolls.

While he'd intended to sort out this mess with Owein on this particular jaunt, he passed a leafless rosebush, which made him think of *Rose*, his mother, and the tight redness on the face of his father, Peter Fernsby, when Merritt had finally returned home. It had so starkly contrasted his mother's teary joy.

He'd sent his mother a wedding invitation. To the house, in case she was able to receive it before Peter got his hands on it, and a backup had gone off to Ruth Portendorfer, her neighbor and the mother of Merritt's best friend. His ribs squeezed. Would his mother be able to come to the ceremony? He had to accept that she might not. So long as Peter

Fernsby had his way, Merritt would have no place in that family. He wondered, briefly, if the separation was meant to punish him or *her*. His father had known from an early age that Merritt wasn't biologically his. A better man might not have penalized him for the sins of his mother. Then again, Merritt would gladly bear the penalties on her behalf.

She'd insisted Peter was good to her. His sisters, too, had promised Rose Fernsby lived well. He'd have to take solace in that, even if he didn't see his mother again until her husband's funeral.

As he followed the walking path between bare trees, he noticed another body moving toward him. It took only a beat for him to recognize her as Lady Briar, Cora's older sister. She had an umbrella in hand, though it wasn't unfurled, and strode alone. She must have been lost in thought, for she didn't notice him until they were only a few paces apart, and only then with a start.

"Mr. Fernsby! I didn't see you."

Merritt dug cold hands into his coat pockets. "I don't blame you; the pavers are vastly interesting."

She glanced down at the stones underfoot. "Ah yes." She smiled. "Very interesting."

Merritt really should start wearing a hat; this would have been a prime opportunity to tip one. "I hope I didn't disturb you."

"Not at all." She glanced back the way she'd come. "Are you against company for your stroll?"

That surprised him. She'd seemed of a mind to be alone. "Not at all. To be honest, I'd love a conversation that doesn't involve magic or weddings in some form or another."

She nodded. "I absolutely understand." She turned and fell into step beside Merritt, retracing the way she'd come. "The woman in taupe, wearing glasses—was that Miss Larkin? I didn't have an opportunity for an introduction."

"Yes. She took your curricle out to LIKER headquarters for some supplies for an exorcism."

Briar missed a step. "An exorcism?"

"Just in case your grandfather is haunting the walls."

She studied his face as they walked. "Goodness, you're serious."

"I am serious at all times."

She studied him a little longer. "I think you're fibbing about *that*, Mr. Fernsby. I've heard about your sense of humor, and I don't for a minute believe you find the pavers interesting."

"Oh? What are they saying about me behind closed doors?"

She waved a hand. "Nothing worth gossip, I assure you. Cora merely told me everything that happened before our arrival."

"And Cora—Lady Cora—how is she handling things?"

Briar's steps slowed. She waited a beat before speaking. "Thank you for asking. She's involved in this more closely than anyone, and no one seems to ask how she's faring. But." She sighed. "All things considered, she's doing well. She's optimistic. It's expected, in our family, to have things like this arranged. Just never . . . I mean, no offense, Mr. Fernsby—"

"Never to a suitor with four legs?" he offered.

She looked relieved. "Precisely that." She flushed. "My goodness, here you've specifically requested we not speak of magic and weddings, and I'm prattling on about them anyway."

He enjoyed her candor. "It's all that's on our minds. What else is to be expected?"

She nodded, and they followed the path toward the front of the house, silent for several seconds. Briar broke the beat of their footsteps by asking, "Miss Larkin. You're engaged to her, correct?"

"I am."

She grinned. "Tell me how you met."

Hands growing warm, Merritt moved them from his pockets and clasped them behind his back. "That is a story that deserves an entire novel. But in short, I inherited a house that *was* haunted. By Owein, actually."

"I . . . that is, I'd heard that he'd only recently become a dog."

He nodded. "Anyway, Hulda was sent by BIKER to oversee the transition and make everything comfortable. I suppose we took a liking to one another." That was the *very* condensed version of it.

"How charming." Her grin faded slowly, a little with each step. "We, my siblings and I, that is, weren't permitted to search among common folk for a spouse." She laughed. "Not that we had the freedom to choose from among the elite, either."

Her tone was light, but there was a slight edge to it. One Merritt might not have picked up on had he not breakfasted with her twice. Had he not seen how cool she was to the Baron von Gayl, her husband. It didn't take a scholar to know that marriage had been arranged, just as Cora and Owein's would be.

"I'm sorry," Merritt offered.

"It is what it is. It's been only a few months. Who knows? Perhaps we'll learn to care for one another." The statement was devoid of hope. "We're very . . . different," she went on. "But he does have an excellent magical pedigree."

A kineticist, if Merritt remembered correctly. His pace slowed a bit.

Would someone with strong kinetic powers be able to collapse the ceiling of a house?

Gooseflesh rose over his skin. Merritt returned his hands to his pockets. Realizing he should speak or else draw attention to the revelation, he said, "Hulda is an augurist."

"Is she?" Briar latched on to the change in subject. "I am, too. Not exclusively, but I've a streak of luck. Proves useful, at times."

Merritt looked her way and waited for her to meet his gaze. "Perhaps you need only give it time for it to be useful again."

Pinching her lips together, Briar looked away. "Thank you. I should remember that."

"Hulda is a soothsayer—sees flashes of the future. Frustrates her, though. She's not as rich in the ability as your family seems to be."

She perked up. "I know a great teacher I could put her in touch with, if she's interested. Magic is all in the blood, yes, but understanding how to wield it can multiply its effectiveness. Such has been the case in my learning, at least."

"Mine as well. I'll let her know, thank you." He had a feeling Hulda would appreciate the opportunity to study.

Briar clapped her hands. "I'll write to him as soon as we return to the house."

LIKER's headquarters were seated on the Thames, just across Westminster Bridge, almost parallel to Big Ben. While it was no Palace of Westminster, it was far more eye-catching than the Bright Bay Hotel in Boston. Gothic in design, the narrow four-story building had dark-ribbed vaults and pointed arches around its doorways. It resembled a cathedral but without any spires or stained glass to beautify it. From the outside it looked a thing of the past, and from the inside it appeared entirely modern. The tiles underfoot as she entered were blue and yellow, where they weren't covered in scrolling Indian rugs, and there was an alarming number of large potted plants, nearly enough to qualify the place as a jungle. The hallways and reception area were tastefully beige with the occasional flourish of fleur-de-lis, while individual offices and rooms sported a variety of patterned wallpapers. The place had twice the space and far more people than its Boston counterpart.

It was good to see a familiar face as Hulda approached an overlarge, polished oak reception desk. "Miss Richards, it's a pleasure to see you."

Miss Richards, whose attention had been split between an open novel and a cup of tea, startled, spilling a few drops of the latter onto her skirt. She didn't seem to notice as she stood. "Miss Larkin! You certainly travel fast. Are you wanting to speak with Mr. Walker?"

"That would be lovely, if he's available. I realize I'm arriving outside his normal schedule." Her own schedule had been decimated by the time change.

The secretary checked the clock. "I think you're fine to go up. It's been a slow week." She set down her teacup before resituating herself in her chair. "Anything else I can help with?"

"Yes, actually. I need materials for an exorcism."

"Exorcism?" She thumbed through several open files before her.

"I'll be sure to make a full report." She pushed her glasses up her nose; no matter how tightly the arms were adjusted or how large her nose grew, the lenses never would stay in place.

"I'll get right on it; I cataloged the stones just last month, so I know we're flush." She turned the novel upside down on the desk to mark her place. The secretary jaunted off toward one of the materials closets.

Hulda knew her way around, so she set off down the corridor behind the desk, heels clacking on tiles, and took a spiraling staircase up to the second floor. A muffled noise from her ever-present black bag caused her to pause and fish out her communion stone, which glimmered with a smooth, unbroken sheen as she pulled it into the light.

"Come again?" she asked.

"Lady Briar says she knows an augury professor in London." Merritt's voice was a little garbled, but Hulda understood him, and her pulse picked up as he spoke. "I thought you might be interested—"

"Very much so." She cleared her throat, lowering her volume. "Yes, please get his—her?—information, and I'll send a contact card immediately."

"Already have it." She could hear his smile. "I'll leave you to it."

The stone quieted. Hulda clasped it in her hand. A professor! Would he—or she—be willing to meet with Hulda? Surely it was a possibility, or Lady Briar would not have suggested it. Perhaps God had heard her quiet prayers and was sending her a much-needed boon.

Bolstered by this revelation, Hulda continued on her way. Mr. Walker's office was just down another hallway. She couldn't help but tense as she passed the one for LIKER's lawyer, though a new face lingered over the desk, buried in work and unaware of her presence. Mr. Baillie, of course, no longer worked at LIKER. Or anywhere, unless they were giving him unpaid tasks to complete in prison.

Mr. Walker's door was open, but she knocked anyway. The man was halfway through a crumpet.

"Mm!" He swallowed, waving her forward with a free hand. "Miss Larkin, wonderful to see you. Come in, come in. How are things in the States?"

"As to be expected. I've nothing new to report." That was a partial lie. She had a great *deal* worth reporting, and it included a dead wizard suspended in goo in a glass tube in Ohio. But the laboratory was neither an enchanted room nor under LIKER's jurisdiction, and by all means, she didn't know a thing about it. Still, out of habit, she found herself quickly focusing on a portrait of the queen on the far wall. She was used to working with a superior who had the ability to read minds. Though even without psychometry, it had always been difficult hiding a secret from Myra Haigh.

Unfortunately, that had not been a two-way street, but she mentally digressed.

"I've a rather interesting conundrum I'd like to discuss with you." She sat on a chair on the opposite side of Mr. Walker's desk and situated her bag on her lap. "Without giving any specific names, for the sake of propriety."

As she disclosed the facts pertinent to the situation with Owein and the offer of a body, Mr. Walker's eyes doubled in size. His half-eaten crumpet lay forgotten near his elbow.

"That is . . . quite a surprise." He rubbed his chin. Stubble was already growing in from his morning's shave. "For many reasons. Most necromancy spells only work on humans."

"He *is* human. Or at least, he was. His mind and his soul are human," Hulda offered. "But you understand the predicament."

Nodding, Walker knit his fingers together. "I can't think of any specific laws that would apply, but then again, the royal family sort of *is* the law, aren't they?"

"Has it been done before?"

"Not to my knowledge, but I highly doubt any documentation would be at my disposal. And . . . this dog of yours is a very special and extreme case."

"That he is." Hulda let out a long breath. "Obviously we would be against murder. Stripping the soul from an able body would be nothing less than that. Nor from an unable body that might be healed from a master necromancer's services. So what else is there?"

"Volunteers, I suppose."

Hulda blanched. "You think someone would just *volunteer* their life for the Crown?"

Mr. Walker shrugged. "There are many poor lads out there who might be willing, if it meant financial comfort for their families."

Hulda found herself twisting the handle of her bag. "But accepting the sacrifice of a boy who has volunteered out of desperation is hardly ethical."

"I agree. I'm merely thinking aloud," he offered. "Perhaps one might volunteer because he is unhappy."

A shiver coursed through her shoulders and into her neck. "I cannot fathom a single situation where obtaining any body, volunteered or not, would feel right and honorable." She sighed. "I *do* want it for him. He died very young. He hasn't had human form in centuries. But . . ."

"But," Mr. Walker said in absolute agreement. "There are occasions when a babe is born without a mind, or an accident befalls a man and strips away his ability to think or function beyond anything a doctor, necromancer, hysterian, or psychometrist can hope to mend. Perhaps in the days of old, when magic was stronger, but today, even with advancements in science, there is little to be done for it. Perhaps the unnamed nobles in this situation are looking for something like that."

Hulda mulled this over. "I could see something of the sort working. But to find one in the next few years, before Lady—before the girl this concerns comes of age, and to find one suited to her. If they put the boy in question into the body of an infant, well, his adulthood will come too late. And to find a lost mind among the elderly . . . all sorts of things could go wrong." How utterly unfortunate it would be for Owein to gain a human body, only to approach death shortly thereafter. Then again, as a dog, his years were already limited.

Would this be his destiny, then? To constantly pop between bodies and buildings, never truly having one of his own, the only escape being death? Death was not something to fear—they would all have to meet their maker someday. But Owein . . . what did he think about the situation? Was he afraid to pass on?

He's just a boy. The thought saddened her. And yet, regarded in a different light, Owein had lived longer than any of them.

She stood. "Thank you, Mr. Walker. You've given me something to think about. I hope you don't mind; I'm concerned there may be a recently deceased wizard in the walls of . . . an undisclosed manor nearby." To name Cyprus Hall would banish any sense of privacy Hulda had been trying to give the Leiningen family. "I'll write a report."

Two lines formed at the center of his brow, then relaxed. "Yes, go ahead. I've already learned the hard way to trust you, Miss Larkin. I look forward to reading your findings after my trip to Constantinople."

She paused. "The manor in Çengelköy again?"

"The very one."

She replied with a tip of her head, then saw herself out.

Miss Richards had the stones and spells waiting for her.

Hulda returned to Cyprus Hall as the family was meeting for dinner; she had just enough time to change into something a little more formal and then meet the others in the sitting room connected to the dining hall. Lady Cora was playing the pianoforte when she arrived, her sister, Briar, turning the pages; Owein seemed to be asleep in the far corner of the room. Lady Helen de Clare, Prince Friedrich, Merritt, and two men she didn't recognize sat on two sofas, enthralled in some sort of conversation. Merritt lit up at the sight of her, and his expression sent pleasant nerves drifting down her torso like snowflakes. He crossed the room to her, took her hand, and brought her over. "Miss Hulda Larkin of the Boston Institute for the Keeping of Enchanted Rooms. I believe you've acquainted yourself with everyone but the Baron von Gayl, Ernst, uh . . ." A lopsided smile tilted his mouth. "I'm so sorry. Your names are so formal and . . . long."

Back in September, Hulda might have been embarrassed by the confession. Now she merely appreciated that Merritt was honest.

As did the baron, for he slapped his thighs and laughed. "Ernst Freiherr von Gayl." He stood and offered a shallow bow. "It's excellent to meet you, fräulein. Mr. Fernsby has spoken of you at length."

"Hopefully only positive things," she said with a smile and a curtsy. "It's very nice to make your acquaintance."

"Don't worry," Merritt assured her, "this one is much simpler. This is William Blightree, of the Queen's League of Magicians."

Mr. Blightree was the oldest of the group, and he nodded his head respectfully. "I'm here to help oversee the contract and any questions that might arise with the arrangement. Mr. Fernsby has put all of us off, insisting he get your opinion." He said it in a kind, almost teasing way. "He thinks very highly of you."

Hulda felt herself flush. "Thank you. You must be the queen's necromancer?"

Lady Helen put a hand on Mr. Blightree's shoulder. "Yes, he is very esteemed at court. You won't find a more skilled magician than he in all of Europe, I assure you that!" She grinned fondly at him. "Mr. Blightree is a longtime family friend as well. He's put off his own personal business to stay with us."

Merritt said, "I hope nothing too unsettling."

Mr. Blightree opened his mouth to respond, but Lady Helen beat him to it. "More settling than unsettling! He's finally come into a long-overdue inheritance. The whole mess was tied up in the courts for *years*." She turned toward him. "And we're so excited to visit the place when things calm down. I've always wanted a tour of Gorse End."

Hulda's smile froze on her face.

Gorse End. She *knew* Gorse End. Knew it far too well. She'd dug through Hogwood's family tree to find no direct relatives, and the Crown had yet to seize the estate. But if William Blightree was its heir . . . heaven help her.

This man was Silas Hogwood's *family*.

Chapter 12

Hulda had never lost her appetite more quickly.

Her manners kicked in even as her mind reeled; she nodded to the servants, sipped her soup in utter silence, smiled, and addressed her hosts graciously, always keeping one ear apprised of the conversation. She knew whom to turn to when and the best dinner topics for easy conversation, as well as tricks for turning attention away from her and to the hosting family. She'd been seated between Merritt and Baron von Gayl and, in a piece of luck, nearly as far from William Blightree as she could be. The only person farther from her was Lady Cora, who sat at the end of the table, nearest to Owein, who took his dinner on the floor. Still, despite Hulda's automatic manners, she could not stop her gaze from shooting down the table between nearly every forced bite of food.

His name might not have *been* Hogwood, but he was a Hogwood, and Hulda could not talk herself down from that very high limb.

Sudden warmth on her knee startled her; she glanced down to see Merritt's hand there, then lifted her eyes to meet his. Leaning in closer, he said, "You're tense as a spring hare."

Forcing a deep breath to relax her chest, she said, "Nothing I can say here."

"Gorse End?"

Hulda gave him a look that she hoped read, *Please do not speak*, and forced her attention onto her uneaten meal. A pity—it looked and smelled wonderful, but she could do little more than pick at it. Were they at Whimbrel House, she might have snuck a few morsels under the table for Owein, but alas, such was not proper, and he had his own elegant dinner to consume.

As the servants delivered the dessert dishes, Lady Helen said, "Miss Larkin, I believe you wanted to peruse the contract as well. I know your role in Owein's story and his ability to come here was significant."

Hulda set down her napkin, trying not to glance at the man beside Lady Helen. "Yes, thank you. My apologies, Lady Helen. I'm afraid I'm not feeling well."

Merritt's gaze settled on her.

Fortunately, Lady Helen clasped her hands together in utter sympathy. "But of course! You've been traveling all day, poor thing. How could I not consider it?"

"You've been more than considerate," Hulda assured her. "And might I add that the dinner was lovely and your home very accommodating."

"Coming from a housekeeper, that is high praise," Prince Friedrich said.

Lady Helen beamed. "Thank you." She waved to the corner, and a pretty maid hurried over. "Anabelle, would you kindly show Miss Larkin to her room?"

"You're sure it's no trouble?" Hulda asked, neck growing stiff from the continued effort not to look at Mr. Blightree.

"None at all! None at all. Anabelle will take you." Lady Helen gestured, Anabelle curtsied, and Hulda gratefully followed the younger woman out of the winter dining room, into the lobby, and then the grand hall, from which they took steps upward, away from the hall with the damaged room and down to where she believed Merritt and Owein were staying, very near the family quarters. She thanked Anabelle, accepted an offer of tea, and slipped into the space.

༄

Cora's mother referred to the pastry on Owein's platter as a Genoese fancy, and it looked excellent . . . but Owein worried that, should he scoff it down, he'd be retching shortly after. Too much food. His dog stomach could handle a lot—in fact, it was alarming what the canine side of him sometimes found appetizing—but something about all that sugar and pastry cream told him he was about to overdo it. Dogs weren't meant to eat like people.

Yet another thing to look forward to, in a new body. The first thing he'd do was get the biggest Genoese fancy he could find and devour it. With a human tongue, it would taste amazing, he was sure of it.

A clamor of silverware on porcelain pierced his ear, punctuated by a gasp. Owein turned his attention back to the dinner table. Cora's sister, Briar, was standing, her shoulders tense, her hands pressed to the table's edge.

"I cannot possibly go along with this farce any longer." Her voice was hard as a thrown book.

"Good gracious, Briar!" Lady Helen reached over as though to grasp her sleeve, but since her husband sat between the two, she couldn't quite reach. "Sit down! What is the meaning of this?"

"I *mean* to point out how absolutely absurd and unfeeling this entire affair has become!" Her voice pitched high on the last few words. "It is one thing to insist we abstain from any sort of amour when court-ing because we're merely horses for breeding—"

"Briar!" Lady Helen snapped.

Cora merely placed a hand over her mouth.

"—but to insist my sister, *your daughter*—betroth herself to a *dog*? How much further could we possibly take this?"

Owein. Merritt's voice popped into his head, though Merritt hadn't turned toward him. *Perhaps you should step out.*

Owein didn't.

Still seated, Prince Friedrich said, "You've made your stance on the situation very clear. You embarrass yourself with this outburst."

Briar's husband, the baron, took on a queer shade of gray. Was he flushing?

"And yet it seems no one in this room has heard me." Briar spun toward Cora. "Surely you realize the insensibility of all this!"

Cora, soft-spoken even in quiet moments, didn't answer. Her eyes watered. Owein took a step forward, wanting to comfort her, but Merritt heard him—he put out a hand, warning him to stay.

Stay, like a good dog.

Owein didn't want to be a dog anymore.

"Mr. Fernsby." Briar wheeled on Merritt. "You are a sensible man."

Lady Helen left her seat and came around Prince Friedrich's chair, snatching Briar as though to physically make her sit down.

Briar was undaunted. "A sensible man with American ideals of *freedom*." She spat that last word at her mother, successfully stilling her attempts to quell her outburst. "You must see how hurtful this is to my sister."

"Briar," Cora protested meekly, but no one seemed to hear.

"I . . ." Merritt's gaze shifted from Briar to Cora to her parents. "I'm not sure—"

"You needn't answer her," Prince Friedrich said with a calm coldness, slicing into his Genoese fancy. "She is acting the part of a child."

Briar whirled on him. "How dare you cite immaturity for my reasonings when *you* married for love."

Her father had nothing to say to that.

Owein barked, gaining the attention of every person in the dining room, even the servants trying to disappear into its corners. *I'm not a dog!* he shouted. *I didn't choose this body! Can't you understand? I haven't been a real person for over two hundred years. If it makes this family happy, why is it such a terrible thing? I'm a human first! Why can't you see that?*

But of course, they couldn't hear him. They weren't communionists or psychometrists. Only Merritt's expression dipped with the weight of sympathy. To everyone else, he was just a worked-up mutt.

Seething, Briar turned her attention back to her mother. "I will address Victoria herself if I must."

With that, she stormed from the table.

⟲

Hulda inspected her bedchamber with the eye of a woman who'd specialized in them the past fifteen years. It was a very commendable room, with copper fixtures and a large west-facing window, heavy brocade draperies pulled aside. Her two bags were already set on a trunk at the foot of what was perhaps the plushest bed she'd ever seen in her life, complete with four tall posts and a dozen ornately embroidered pillows. A soft fire crackled in the hearth, making the room smell a little earthy and, oddly enough, a little rosy. Hulda crossed to it and gently set two quarter logs atop it. Then she closed the curtains to block the chill from the window; it was already dark outside, so leaving them open was no benefit to her.

Next, she paced. Her reasonable side sewed half-spun excuses for why it was perfectly natural for Mr. Blightree to be presiding over these proceedings. Few necromancers alive could successfully execute an entire body transition, so it made sense that a family connection existed between the two who could. All was well, the reasonable voice insisted, but her experienced side reminded her that reason hadn't protected her from Mr. Hogwood and Mr. Baillie. The first had nearly killed her, and well, she supposed the second nearly had, too.

Well. She'd sort this out swiftly, then.

Anabelle returned with a tea tray, which she set on a little breakfasting table near the bed. Hulda took a few sips, but her stomach was still too tight to hold much, so she left it to cool and crossed to the small mirror on a side table above a pitcher and washbasin. Cleaned her glasses. "I still have an exorcism to perform," she murmured, rubbing at the scalp under her pins. She sighed, considering propriety. Surely she could just put her hair up in a simple knot. She really could not tolerate the pinching in addition with the fraying of her nerves, so she carefully removed the pins, feeling minutely better once they were free. She'd just begun to run a comb through the locks when a soft knock sounded at her door. She nearly feigned sleeping to avoid answering, but the rhythm was familiar, so she crossed to the door and carefully opened it.

Sure enough, Merritt stood outside. His presence was a relief.

"Might I come in?" he asked.

Propriety said *no*, but she certainly wasn't going to relay her revelation out in the hallway, and goodness, she was old enough not to get into trouble, and foreign enough that no one here would care to gossip about it. So she opened the door wide enough for him to slip through, then shut it.

She tugged the comb through another chunk of hair. "Are you aware—"

"You're beautiful."

The compliment caught her off guard. She nearly dropped the comb as she gaped at his blue-eyed gaze drifting over her unbound hair. He'd seen it down before, once or twice, surely. When he reached for it, she held very still. It wasn't the most elegant . . . that is, she'd *just* unpinned it. There were unnatural kinks throughout, and she hadn't tamed all the knots—

He ran his fingers through it, causing a shiver to course over her scalp.

Biting back a habitual dismissal, she managed, "Th-Thank you."

He smiled as he twisted the end of a lock around his fingers. "You know, the Leiningens are far more trusting of us than they should be."

She set the comb on a table. "What makes you say that?"

He tilted his head toward the wall the bed was pressed against. In the flickering candlelight, Hulda hadn't discerned the narrow door there.

"That, my dear"—a roguish grin overtook his face—"leads to my room."

Clearing her throat, Hulda squared her shoulders. "I hate to disappoint you, but I've had easy access to your bedroom for a great deal of our acquaintance. That door is nothing alarming."

"Hmm. If only Owein were still in the walls."

Now she did warm—surely Merritt referred to that time, before they ever courted, when a mischievous boy spirit in the walls had thought it would be humorous to split their bedrooms during the night and fuse their beds together. Owein had been playing matchmaker before either of them knew what they wanted.

Merritt reached forward and clasped her hand. "I don't suppose you're ill—"

"No." She pulled him away from the door, closer to the hearth.

"Which means you're either uneasy about the mention of Gorse End or you foresaw the incredibly awkward dinner discussion that followed your departure."

She turned. "Awkward? What happened?"

"Briar giving everyone an earful on how very against the match she is." He slid his hands into his pockets. "Owein and Cora, I mean. As far as I know, *we* still have her approval."

Hulda rolled her eyes. "Heaven forbid. Owein is not too hurt, is he?"

Merritt shook his head. "He seems fine. Was willing to stay behind with Cora, anyway, when I wanted to come up. He's been staying in my company most of the time. Hopefully this means he's adjusting well."

"Hopefully." She wrung her hands.

Merritt crossed to her. "So. Gorse End."

Pulling her hands apart, she answered, "Did you know William Blightree is related to Silas Hogwood?"

He paused. "Not until tonight, but I suppose it makes sense."

Hulda paced to the window and back. "We're sharing a house with a Hogwood."

Merritt chuckled, completely disarming her. "Hulda, Blightree is one of the most amiable fellows I've ever met. In this case, bloodlines don't mean anything."

"But his alliance might be to Silas Hogwood—"

"Who is dead." He enunciated each syllable, then softly grasped her upper arms. "And Blightree is employed by the Crown. Perhaps that's why he's the appointed heir. After the mess with Silas, I'm sure they're on high alert."

"*Someone* tried to kill you," she pointed out, jabbing a finger at him. "Why could it not be a relative—"

"Yes, I suppose he's the most obvious suspect of all." He squeezed her arms. She did not like how calmly he was taking this. "Believe me, Hulda. It's never the most obvious person. That would make for a very boring story."

She frowned. "Baillie was connected to Hogwood."

"We're all connected in one way or another." He shrugged. "You do make a good point. I just . . . He's like a jolly grandpa. Might as well be ol' Saint Nick. Baillie was a scrub and a lobcock from the beginning."

She frowned. "No need to be crude."

He paused a moment. "I suppose that was. Sorry."

Hulda bit her lip. Considered. "It's just . . . in the past, I have told myself similar rationalizations, and then ended up in a prison cell or facedown in the dirt." She thought, momentarily, of the collapsed room, but Blightree wouldn't—*shouldn't*—have the spells to do something of the sort.

Even so, she desperately wanted to look at his pedigree.

"If I were writing this book," he said, gesturing to the room around them, "I think I would set up Blightree as a sort of diversion, to draw the reader's eye away from the true culprit, if we've even met him yet. Or her."

"This isn't a storybook," Hulda protested.

He squeezed her arms. "I will help you look into it. Tomorrow. It's late, and you still have a ghost to discipline." He lifted one hand and ran it through her hair again. It was a simple brown, not dark or light, but it took on a bit of an auburn glow in the firelight.

"I think that door is quite alarming," he continued, his voice husky in a way that set the nerves in Hulda's arms and torso alight. "You might not use it, but I find it very tempting."

He gingerly pinched the arms of her glasses, slid them off her face, and set them beside that washbasin. Her pulse sped beneath his touch. Would it always speed like this, or would she someday get used to such words, such caresses, such attention?

She supposed that didn't matter at the moment. When Merritt turned back, she readily met him, touching her lips to his and sighing softly at the warm contact and blissful spark it ignited, one that started in her mouth and sizzled all the way down to her hips.

Merritt tilted his head and claimed her, sliding both hands into her hair, pulling her closer. She grasped fistfuls of his vest, feeling his own quick heartbeat beneath her knuckles. The smell of his petitgrain had become so familiar it felt like coming home, and despite her worries over balancing her future life with him and her allegiance to BIKER, the thought of coming home to him always was nothing short of blissful.

Where have you been all my life? she wondered as she tugged at his lower lip. But had duty not forced them between the same walls, would she ever have considered him? Or he her?

He was certainly *considering* her now, the way his palms slowly draped down her neck, her shoulders, her back—and suddenly grabbed her elbows and yanked her away.

She choked on a breath, the room tilting for a moment blurrily, as he'd removed her glasses. Protest launched up her throat—

"Owein, I didn't hear you." He cleared his throat, and the blur of him shifted until Hulda felt him press her wire spectacles into her hands. "You're welcome to knock."

Fire burned beneath Hulda's skin as she practically smashed her glasses onto her face and whirled toward the door—the one that connected her room to Merritt's—just as Owein sealed up a melted hole with magic. She hadn't heard a thing—he must have spoken to Merritt while they were . . . occupied.

Oh good heavens. She pulled her loose hair back. There wasn't a lock in existence that could keep that boy from barging in where he wasn't wanted!

While she bristled, however, Merritt's stance softened. "Of course you can stay in my room tonight."

All the humiliation and aggravation fled her instantly. "Are you sleeping poorly still?"

A soft, almost imperceptible whine escaped him.

"He says he just feels it coming tonight," Merritt murmured, then, quieter, "He slept well last night, but . . ."

"Of course." She smiled. Smoothed her hair again. "Nothing could keep a door from being tantalizing more than the presence of an apperceptive canine."

Merritt smirked. "I love it when you speak dictionary to me." He kissed her chastely on the lips before burying a hand in his pocket and heading toward the door. Looking down at the dog, he said, "I can't wait for you to have thumbs again, old man."

Owein's tail wagged as Merritt opened the door. Merritt passed her an apologetic yet impish look before slipping into his own quarters. She really ought to lock that door.

A thorough examination of the ethics of the door would have to wait, however. She had a spirit to exorcise.

Chapter 13

The problem with exorcising a noble manor was the excessive amount of salt it required.

The staff and Merritt helped Hulda spread it by lamplight, thankfully, so the perimeter around the mansion went down quickly. The entire family stood outside as well, bearing the March chill, though Hulda had already assured them it was unnecessary. The spells targeted wizards' ghosts floating about within the walls, not the ones still entrapped in living, breathing bodies.

That made her think of Owein.

She set eleven stones—one representing each of the eleven doctrines of magic—inside the house, along with small red bags containing alteration and wardship spells that would allow for the expunging of any spiritually inclined resident wizard. With the salt in place, she stepped into the large receiving hall and read her spell.

Nothing happened. It was quite similar to Whimbrel House.

She inspected the stones, spells, and the full name of the suspect again, then took a quick jaunt around the property to ensure the salt circle was thick and unbroken, which it was. Out of breath, she returned to the hall and recited her spell once more. No change. She tried to ignore the sinking feeling in her gut, but it insisted on sinking nevertheless.

The family had gathered round when she exited this time. As she tucked her spell papers into her black bag, she put on her most professional façade and said, "Prince Friedrich, Lady Helen, I'm sorry to say I haven't any answers for you. The collapse of that bedchamber was not the working of a ghost. At least, most certainly not the doing of the deceased Marquess of Halesworth."

Lady Helen's hand flew to her collar. "But if not that, then what?"

"Might I suggest," Hulda tried, "speaking to a contractor about the build of the house itself?" That would provide an answer and, in some senses, a comforting one. Though staying in an abode that might degenerate at any moment was not an appealing prospect.

Prince Friedrich sputtered. "This house has stood for generations without a problem!"

Lady Helen touched his arm. "We have a crew arriving tomorrow to begin the repairs. I'll have them inspect the area."

Hulda nodded. "I would advise that, yes."

Lady Briar, who stood several feet apart from her husband, gave him an uneasy look. The others did not appear unaffected, either—Lady Cora stepped closer to her mother, Owein not far from her, and Merritt just behind him.

Merritt tipped his head suddenly, listening to a voice no one else could hear. "M'lady," he offered a moment later, garnering Cora's attention, "Owein is wondering if you might still like to adjourn to the drawing room, and if so, whether my presence wouldn't be a bother. He'd like to speak with you."

The delicate adolescent's gaze hopped between Merritt and Owein before resting on her mother.

"Tomorrow would be best," Lady Helen advised. "If not for the light, then because I have some things to think about, and Cora will of course need a chaperone."

Merritt nodded. "Of course."

Chapter 14

Merritt awoke to the sensation of falling.

He gasped, his mind taking a beat to identify where he was—not Whimbrel House, but Cyprus Hall. Shadows engulfed the ceiling overhead; the curtains were drawn against the depth of night. And he was sinking.

Merritt bolted upright and a little to the left as the too-soft mattress bowed beneath his weight. His comforter, shifting into a thick liquid, stuck to his hand like bread dough.

"Owein!" he barked, scrambling back with what little purchase he had. He smacked into a still-solid headboard and rolled onto the floor from there, a few drips of blanket coming with him. "Owein, *wake up!*"

His shoes danced across the carpet—which shifted from burgundy to navy to white—as though they had invisible legs. He crawled away from the bed, spying Owein at its foot. Where the trunk had gone, Merritt hadn't a clue. But the dark terrier huffed and whimpered, his legs quivering like they were trying to run but the joints kept catching on something.

"Owein!" he shouted louder. "Wake—"

A box the length of his forearm flew at him, pelting him in the shoulder hard enough to knock him over. Merritt shook himself and leapt to his feet.

The trunk. It was the trunk, now a fraction of its original size.

Before he could call Owein's name again, a cup came soaring toward his hip; he dodged, and the ceramic shattered against the wall behind him. Next came the basin and pitcher; the first flew wide, but the second sailed straight for his head.

It broke into three uneven pieces against an erected wardship spell. Another time, Merritt might have prided himself on his quick handling of the magic.

Owein whined. Anything that wasn't nailed down or over two hundred pounds flew into the air—portraits, combs, clothing, dust clods, a chair, and so on. They flew back and forth, faster with each pass. In moments they'd reach a deadly speed.

Merritt threw up a wardship spell to block a hatbox, palms held out, then another connected to it to deflect the chair. He *pushed* the magic away from himself, feeling the strain in his bones. His shoulder, where the shrunken trunk had hit, began to ache as he added a third section to his invisible wall.

"Hulda!" he bellowed. "I need help!"

A key grazed his crown. A fourth section of wall began corralling the orbiting objects closer to Owein. None struck him, but the shards of teacup whipped with alarming speed, and his shoes were flashing mulberry. The carpet beneath Owein began to bubble and pop, but still the terrier slept on, jerking and wheezing. One of his ears had gone bulbous, and his back legs were too long—his body changing in response to his unconscious use of alteration spells.

"Good heavens!" Hulda called, likely from their shared doorway. The only thing Merritt could see through the flying mess was a blip of candlelight.

Merritt's knees creaked as he put a lid on the bespelled box. He felt the items pelting the wardship magic as if he were personally embracing it. The flying stuff soared faster, until he could barely make out individual items, and then—

The box blew with a great *boom*! Clothing and ceramics and furniture exploded in all directions. Something broke the window. Merritt fell onto his backside and put his hands over his head; fortunately only a few socks and his notebook collided with him.

The stillness after the burst was deafening. Everything settled. The only sound was Merritt's own heartbeat and a rustle as a breeze from the hole in the window sucked at the curtain.

Merritt? Owein hobbled in the mess, his legs not quite returned to normal. He whined again, spinning around. *Where are we? What happened?*

The chaocracy-induced confusion would wear off soon enough. After crawling over, Merritt put a hand on Owein's neck. "We're safe." He let out a long, shaky breath. "We're safe."

Chapter 15

"It was Owein."

Merritt sat in the parlor with Prince Friedrich early the next morning, before breakfast had been served. The encounter last night had stirred a few in the house, but Merritt had managed to put off an explanation until daylight. Hulda had her first meeting in East London today with the tutor Lady Briar recommended; at the moment, however, she was poring over Owein and Cora's marriage contract. Unfortunately, Owein's magically charged nightmare hadn't gone undetected, and thus Merritt found himself assuring his host that it wasn't the dead marquess acting out after an attempted exorcism.

Merritt ran a hand down his face. "He's been struggling with sleep lately." He wanted to explain the situation without invading Owein's privacy. This sort of thing had happened at Whimbrel House, too, but not so . . . severely. Merritt wondered if the new place—and the new stressors it brought with it—was affecting the poor boy's nightmares. "Bad dreams. I suppose it's a wizardly form of sleepwalking. I'm terribly sorry for any damages. I'm of course willing to compensate you."

Hopefully the Leiningens would accept the funds in installments.

"Don't worry about that. It's a few dishes, really." Prince Friedrich nodded, punctuating the statement.

And a few pieces of furniture, but Merritt didn't feel the need to remind him. In truth, the episode had been . . . alarming. Not just for the injury it had caused him—which, thanks to wardship's weakening of the body, Merritt was still nursing—but the intensity, particularly at the end. Like all the chaotic energy Owein put out had been amplified inside the box Merritt had created, setting it off like a bomb.

Friedrich continued, "Honestly, I understand. My dear sister used to have bouts of anxiety that had similar outcomes. She grew out of it."

Merritt nodded. "That gives me hope."

Prince Friedrich stroked his mustache. "But the first room, in the other wing?"

Merritt leaned back. "Not Owein. He was with me. He can't project his spells so far, regardless."

"Blast." The prince snapped his fingers. "That would have been a simple answer to it, no?"

"If you want to worry about the house collapsing around you as you slumber each night of our visit, I suppose so."

To his relief, Friedrich grinned. "Well, all of this has certainly brought some excitement to Cyprus Hall."

Merritt countered, "I have a hard time believing you lack for excitement."

His smile faded. "I must apologize, again, for my daughter's unseemly outburst."

"It's quite all right," Merritt assured him. "I understand where she's coming from. It's hard to—"

The door to the parlor opened, and Lady Helen stepped in, blue skirts swishing around her. She wore a high-necked dress with layers of lace draping off the collar, something Hulda would likely find excessive, though it suited the woman well. She took a seat on the sofa beside her husband. "Will Owein be able to keep his appointment with my dear Cora today?"

It took Merritt a beat to recall the promised drawing room visit. "Yes, that should be fine. Though, I must ask—our arrival and stay here was somewhat . . . obscure in details—"

"Oh, but you must stay as long as you like!" Lady Helen batted at the air as though intending to slap his knee, but her arm wasn't nearly long enough to do so. "You're practically family now."

"Or will be, when that contract is signed," Prince Friedrich added in a stern tone, obviously still upset about last night's dinner.

Lady Helen snapped her fingers. "Oh, yes, I'm to meet with Miss Larkin this morning about that."

Merritt smiled. "Of course, and thank you for your hospitality. It probably would be good for Owein and Cora to spend a little more time together."

Lady Helen leaned across her husband conspiratorially. "Do you think he likes her?"

Merritt tried not to fish-mouth. "I mean, he doesn't dislike her, certainly." He would not relate Owein's claim that he'd be equally ready to marry a toad. "All of this is very new to him." Worried he'd been offensive, he added, "But your daughter seems very well mannered and kind." Soft-spoken and shy, but good-hearted.

"Mother." A new voice entered the room—Briar stepped in from the hallway, and Merritt wondered how long she'd been lingering there. There was no sign of anger in her bearing. She wore a simple pink gown, a stark contrast to her mother's, and crossed the room quickly, perching at the far end of her parents' sofa. "I've something I'd like to speak to you about."

Feeling the tension instantly rise, Merritt stood. "I'll excuse myself." He nodded to the three of them, earning an appreciative smile from Briar, and slipped into the hallway. He honestly did not think Briar a hotheaded or unkind person; by all means, it was good to be protective of one's sister. But her actions affected Owein, and therefore him, so

Merritt allowed himself to linger long enough to catch the beginning of their conversation.

"I know what you'll say, but hear me out. The Earl of Derby has a nephew who shows great promise in the earth element. He's only a couple of years younger than Cora. The spells wouldn't add, but perhaps they would make a better match—"

"Briar! Enough of this," Lady Helen snapped, and it was the first time Merritt had heard anything truly unpleasant pass her lips. "You weary me! Be more open-minded. Go to Victoria if you must! But the queen herself approves of this match—"

Feeling an intruder, Merritt quietly continued down the hallway, out of earshot of the conversation. He couldn't blame Briar for trying— it was, truly, an absurd situation.

At the same time, he feared Owein losing his one chance to be human again. Perhaps it was time he started taking these arrangements more seriously.

 ͡

Hulda's glasses perched low on her nose as she studied the six-page contract. She was a quick reader, but here she mulled over each and every word. She'd passed through the contract once already, and now scrutinized it even more closely. It gave her a headache, even with Blightree's clean handwriting, but she persisted.

When she finally turned over the last page for the second time, Lady Helen quietly asked, "What do you think?"

"The provisions for the ethics of finding a body are sufficient." She pushed her glasses higher on her nose and turned in her seat to better address her hostess. "I appreciate the effort put forth there."

Lady Helen smiled.

"I do not see, however," she continued, "anything clearly stating Owein Mansel's rights."

Lady Helen blinked. "His rights?"

"As to his person."

The woman hesitated a moment. "Miss Larkin, why would he not be treated as any person would be treated?"

Hulda took a moment to collect her thoughts. "Mr. Mansel will be marrying into a noble family. *Your* noble family. In doing so, he will become a nobleman. But the specifics of that change of title are not clarified within the document."

A patient smile curved Lady Helen's mouth. "He will, of course, be given a courtesy title and treated as any other member of the family."

"I'm sure you would do no less." Hulda pressed her index finger into the center of the contract. "However, this is a legally binding document. Mr. Mansel needs these protections and promises in writing—what title he will be receiving, how his marriage to Lady Cora affects her inheritance, what dowry he'll receive, whether he'll be given a seat in the House of Lords, and of course the granting of British citizenship. Without these things delineated in the contract, I will have to advise both Mr. Mansel and Mr. Fernsby to forgo signing."

Lady Helen frowned.

"Please understand I am only looking out for the well-being of my family." Her future family, but she didn't feel the need to specify.

The patient smile returned. "But of course. I am embarrassed to think neither myself, my husband, nor Mr. Blightree considered it!" She moved forward and collected the papers. "I will see it redrafted at once." She turned from the table but stopped halfway to the door. "I truly do think it will be a good match."

Hulda nodded. "I think so, too."

And with that, Lady Helen departed. Hulda gathered her things and followed right after. It was time to meet with the man who might have the answers to controlling her foresight.

Gethin Griffiths, augurist and professor at Durham University, did not live quite as far from Cyprus Hall as Hulda had anticipated, which meant she arrived rather early for her appointment. His office was located in a house that had been converted into office space not far from the Admiralty House; three stories of white brick with simple trim, dark oak door left ajar. Hulda pushed it open and peered within, immediately greeted by a stairway. Though she had the instructions memorized, she checked the note written in Lady Briar's hand: *Second floor on the right.*

In Britain, that meant the third floor.

Picking up her skirts, Hulda climbed two flights, her trusty black bag a weight on her right shoulder. Fortunately, *Griffiths* was written on the door, assuring her she had the right place. After smoothing her skirt and adjusting her glasses, she knocked firmly.

A bass "Come" responded.

She pushed the door open. The office within was cluttered, stacks of books, journals, and papers on nearly every available surface. Three sets of ink vials and four assorted pens occupied a modest desk. Three simple chairs lined the wall directly to her right, though two of them also sported teetering stacks of paper, as did some of the floor, which was carpeted scarlet. Scents of wood polish and ink hung heavily in the air, and the morning sun hit the window in just such a way that made everything look slightly yellow. Not in a putrid way, but in an old-book sort of way.

Professor Griffiths himself looked to be in his early fifties, with a well-trimmed beard speckled gray. He still had a full head of hair, also speckled gray, though it had gone nearly white over his temples. He wore dark, round spectacles and a broad-shouldered tweed jacket, giving him the refined look of an academic.

It took a beat for him to finish his sentence and glance up. He blinked a few times.

"I apologize for being early, Professor Griffiths," Hulda said, remaining in the doorway. "My name is Hulda Larkin. I'm here on recommendation of Lady Briar Feodora of Leiningen."

She *had* sent a telegram.

"Right, yes." He stood abruptly, removed his glasses, and looked her up and down. She envied the ability—the second one, that was. He only needed his glasses for reading. Hulda, unfortunately, was cursed to keep hers perched upon her nose regardless of activity.

"You're American," he added.

"I hail from Boston, yes."

"Excellent." He stepped around the desk. "You've come all the way here for training?"

"I . . . am here on business."

"Of course." Professor Griffiths gestured to a door on the far side of the room that led into another, smaller office, somewhat less cluttered but not without its stacks of books and newspapers. A table that could seat six sat within, as well as four chairs matching those from the first room. Hulda followed him inside.

"Please, sit." He indicated the closest chair, and Hulda obliged. He didn't take his eyes off her as he took his seat, though he managed to slip his glasses into a front pocket. "A recommendation from Lady Briar is quite the recommendation."

She nodded. "Indeed. I happen to be staying at Cyprus Hall, as is she. The meeting was fortunate."

"Ah! Very good. The Leiningens are good folk. How are Prince Friedrich and Lady Helen?"

"They appear to be in good health."

He nodded. "And if I may be so bold, how are you acquainted with them?"

Knowing she was unable to relate the details of the situation, she merely offered up a separate but distantly related fact. "I'm the director of the Boston Institute for the Keeping of Enchanted Rooms. I've come across the pond to speak with my London counterparts, and Lady Helen was gracious enough to offer me a room."

"You don't say!" Professor Griffiths beamed, and Hulda couldn't help but be charmed by the reaction. "What an accomplishment, and from one so young."

She barely held back a snort. "I have not been called young in some time."

"My dear, when you get to be my age, *everyone* is young. Now." He pulled out his glasses, slipped them on, and grabbed a piece of paper from a random stack. A pencil appeared from within another pocket. "You're an augurist. I know it's in bad taste, but might I ask your concentration? It will help me understand what we're working with."

"I am. And only eight percent, I'm afraid."

"Eight is rather good, for today." He jotted it down. "I myself am twelve, and only because of a few carefully selected marriages once upon a time."

That gave Hulda pause. "Might I make further inquiries?"

He stabbed the paper with punctuation before glancing up. "Ah yes, it's rude to bring up things of interest without explaining them, isn't it? Especially to a woman in your line of work." He grinned. Removed his glasses. "My bloodline is purely English, save for a bit of Swedish influence in the 1600s. My uncle was a baron. At this point, there's no special title reserved for my father, nor for me, but we do descend from a noble line. You know how the English are with their nobility."

"Indeed." It was the very reason Owein had been summoned, to keep magic in the blood of Queen Victoria's kin.

"What spells have you manifested?" he asked.

It felt strange to so openly talk about her limited gifts, but Hulda forced herself to relax. She'd get nowhere otherwise. "Divination only."

"Truly!" He wrote without looking down. "That is also my situation."

"Diviner?" Hulda leaned forward, interested.

"Only." He cut the air with his pen in emphasis. "We will be a most excellent fit, Miss . . ." His eyes shifted to the pearl ring on her finger. "Mrs. Larkin."

"Miss, for now," she corrected. "Unless you'd like me to begin keeping house for you."

He chuckled. "I obviously need it." He patted the nearest stack of papers like it was a dog. "Ever since Evelyn's passing, it's been a bit of a wreck."

Alarm straightened Hulda's spine. "Oh dear, I'm so sorry. Was she your . . . wife?"

He nodded. Put the glasses back on and scribbled away. "Thank you, but I'm quite all right. It was some time ago." He underlined something, but from her angle, she couldn't quite read the tight, messy handwriting. "I haven't had a student of magic for over a year. This will be a breath of fresh air. Is it reasonable to conjecture you can't control the ability?"

"Yes! It merely comes and goes as it pleases." In truth, one of the outcomes she hoped for in this tutoring was not merely better control of her magic, but *control*, period. Something to make her feel purposeful and in command of herself. Something to ease her occasional bouts of uncertainty about her impending marriage.

"We might not be able to fix that entirely." Professor Griffiths now looked over his glasses instead of removing them once more. "But we can hopefully hone your skills well enough to take out the guesswork. Now, I've a set of dice here . . ."

Chapter 16

Merritt took a seat in one of the Leiningens' two drawing rooms—the yellow one beside the conservatory. Brown-tinted ivy hung outside the window, and as the enchanted lights came on, Merritt heard it murmur, *Suuuuunnnnn.*

Soon enough, he thought, without relaying the message. He needed to save those delightful communion side effects for Owein. *Though if you could whisper of any murder plots, I'm all ears.*

The ivy didn't respond.

A servant finished stoking the fire, curtsied prettily, and excused herself without a word. Cora sat in an armchair near the ivy's window, close to the fire. She smoothed her pale-blue skirt, crossed her ankles, and rested her hands on her lap. A dark, carefully curled piece of hair bounced as she nodded her thanks to Merritt. Owein sat on the floor about two paces from Cora, just in front of the fire. Anabelle sat closest to the door and pulled out some knitting.

"I'll try my best to be invisible," Merritt offered.

Cora's blue-eyed gaze shifted to Owein. "What would you like to talk about?"

Merritt expected Owein to look to him for help, but he simply answered, *Does it ever snow here?*

Merritt relayed the message.

"Yes, though we had more storms when I was a child." Cora folded and unfolded her hands. "I saw a few flakes this winter, but they never stuck."

It snows where I'm from, but not as much as inland, so I'm told.

"I'd like to go somewhere very snowy," she said with a tip of her head. "Just for a few days. Where it reaches up past my knees and there are hills for sledding. Not too long. I don't really like the cold. But I do think it would be rather novel."

Or skiing.

"I think I'd be too afraid of skiing." Cora glanced out another window, as though she could see snowy hills through its panes. "And I don't believe it would suit with a skirt."

You could wear trousers.

Cora blinked. "My mother would be beside herself."

I won't tell her.

A faint smile touched Cora's lips. "Maybe it would be nice, to get away from her reach." She hesitated, glancing up toward Anabelle, but the maid was far more interested in her knitting than the half-formed secret. "But whether we'd go somewhere like Austria, or deeper into the US? Austria would be closer."

What's Austria like?

A distinct tickle made Merritt cough as he translated the words. Anabelle rose instantly and tugged on the bell pull. Over a slight ringing in his left ear, Merritt said, "Pardon me." His voice croaked. "Just a moment."

Cora offered him a look of sympathy. "It must be frustrating, to lose the ability so quickly."

"Were it just Owein and I," Merritt rasped, "it wouldn't matter. He wouldn't need to hear my voice." Realizing how that sounded, he added, "Not that this is a bother at all. It is what it is."

At the door, Anabelle murmured, "Some tea for Mr. Fernsby, if you would."

"I've a few effects that make me quite cross," Cora offered, seeming unsure whether to address Owein or Merritt. "Conjury is harsh; it takes something of equal value to whatever you conjure. I can only conjure stone, and there's plenty of that around here, so it's not particularly useful. But if I were, say, to conjure a rock the size of my fist, it might, oh . . . take that quarter log over there in retribution, or perhaps the pins out of my hair."

"Really?" Merritt's voice was barely more than a whisper.

"Of course, there's a way to do it," she went on. "I could get a handful of sand and then trade that sand for a stone of what the universe considers 'equal.' It's not always by weight or worth. Or perhaps it would be, if I had a little more of the blood in me."

Merritt nodded; this was the most he'd ever heard Cora speak.

"But the air is the worst." Cora folded her arms, then checked herself and let her hands fall daintily into her lap.

The air? Owein asked.

The ringing amplified.

"Lack of breath," Merritt whispered, "if I recall correctly."

The door opened, and a new maid brought in a small tea service. As she set it down on the nearest table, Cora said, "More than that—"

"Lady Cora is asthmatic," Anabelle interrupted, dismissing the maid with a nod and taking on the tea service herself. She didn't ask Merritt what he cared for, but the little bit of cream and sugar she added to his cup were fine enough for him. He nodded his thanks as he took the warm cup and sipped. "To use her magic, more than a puff, would threaten her life."

Owein shifted onto all fours. *Really? You shouldn't use it ever.*

Merritt held up a finger to Owein, begging for a moment to recover before sending more words his way. The tea was hot; he sipped it gingerly.

Owein watched him impatiently. Unfortunately, the muteness would take a good moment to wear off.

In the interim, Owein padded to the unoccupied couch against the wall perpendicular to the ivy window. Slipped behind it and pulled out a letterboard not dissimilar from the one Hulda had crafted him in the States. Had Hulda helped him find one? But she hadn't had the time . . . Perhaps the family had put it together, wanting Owein to be able to communicate if Merritt wasn't around to translate.

He didn't miss the faint flush on Cora's cheeks as Owein dragged out the chart and smoothed it out as best he could. Was she embarrassed by the ordeal?

Owein began tapping out letters with his paw. *H-A-S-I-T-E-V—*

"I think I need to retire," Cora said suddenly, softly. "I'm so sorry. I think the smell of the tea is making my stomach ill."

Owein paused midword.

She stood and offered a quick curtsy to the both of them. "Anabelle, if you would inform my mother I'll be resting upstairs."

The maid nodded, then stepped aside and held the door for Cora's uncomfortable exit.

Merrrrrriiiiiitt.

Merritt was vaguely aware of a strange tugging sensation on his arms as his dreams—which he was already forgetting—blended and bled from his thoughts. Words formed in his head that weren't his.

Merritt! I'm bored. Let's go play!

Opening bleary eyes, Merritt took in the bedroom illuminated by bright sunshine pouring around the edges of the heavy curtains. He stared at it for a couple of seconds before rubbing his eyes and propping himself up on one elbow. "What time is it?"

Owein jumped off the bed, ran across the room, and jumped back on again, shaking the mattress. *Clock says ten forty-five.*

Groaning, Merritt rolled over and stretched. He'd stayed up late last night with Hulda in that same yellow drawing room, talking through other possible magic sources for the collapsed room, though the lack of further incidents had her strongly favoring worn beams in the house itself, which was probably why Merritt had been able to sleep so soundly. They'd meandered on to the topic of the wedding, of course, and Merritt's family. Though he owed his biological father, Nelson Sutcliffe, a great deal, he hadn't invited him, nor any of his half brothers, to the wedding. He wouldn't make it awkward for his mother, should she find a way to attend. And his half brothers still didn't know he was their blood relation. Merritt understood Nelson's desire to keep his family happy and intact, of course, but it felt like one more man penalized Merritt for something he'd taken no part in.

For now, Merritt would honor Sutcliffe's wishes. Just not Peter Fernsby's.

He desperately hoped to see his mother and sisters at the wedding. Desperately wanted it to be the doorway from a life with no family to a future with two—the Fernsbys and the one he'd begin with Hulda.

Owein grabbed his sleeve and tugged; Merritt wore only a long nightshirt, now that there was no immature ghost within the walls threatening to merge his bed with his housekeeper's and leave him in an awkward entanglement with no pants on. *I've been waiting forever for you to wake up. Let's play!*

"You'll put a hole in it," Merritt grumbled, unsure if the rasp in his voice was from sleep or communion. Stifling a yawn, he sat up, tangled hair falling into his face.

Owein's tail beat against the mattress, and a soft whine emanated from his furry throat.

Merritt glanced at the bright sunlight around the curtains. Was it rude to sleep in so late? No one had come to wake him, so hopefully he was all right on that point. He stretched again.

Owein whined.

"Question," Merritt said. "You've lived a great deal longer than me, albeit in a multitude of bodies." He swept hair back from his face. "You're centuries old."

Owein dipped his head. His tail beat against the blankets impatiently.

"So why do you still act like a child?"

The tail stopped.

Sighing, Merritt reached out and stroked between Owein's ears. "I don't mean it negatively. I just wonder. I understand you died at twelve, but your consciousness has never stopped. Yet you still seem very much a boy."

Owein shifted on the bed. Glanced around the room.

Rubbing a crick in his neck, Merritt offered, "You don't have to answer. Just a thought I—"

It's easier, Owein said, quietly, in his not-voice. *It's easier to deal with it, when I'm just a kid.*

Carefully choosing his words, Merritt asked, "What's easier?"

Owein's dark, canine eyes met his. *Dealing with the . . . hurt.*

The mattress seemed to suck down on him. Getting up on his knees, Merritt put a hand on either of Owein's shoulders. "Owein, I'm so sorry."

Owein didn't respond. But if Merritt had learned anything over the last year, it was the importance of getting things off one's chest, not bottling them up and letting them simmer until the glass shattered.

"Nightmares?" he tried.

Owein took several seconds to think. *I was alone for a really long time.*

Merritt nodded. Waited. Waited a little longer.

Owein settled down, laying his chin between his legs. *I was always alone. Sometimes someone would come by, every twenty or thirty years, but they could never hear me. It's different, inside the house. Different without eyes and ears and . . . skin. I saw and heard and felt things in a strange way.*

Distantly. And it was always dark, even when the sun was up. Even after Silas put me in this body, the darkness followed. And it hurts.

Merritt ran his palm down the length of Owein's spine. Once, twice, three times. His heart felt heavy, like it needed to slumber.

I don't know how to grow up, he finally finished.

Merritt considered this for a long moment, wanting to say the right thing, if there even was a "right thing" to be said. *I think,* he began in communion, not trusting his voice to hold up, *it's like a child—a young child—thinking there are monsters under his bed. And he hides under the blanket, and the monsters disappear.*

Owein's gaze lifted to his.

Children are very forgiving, he went on. *You hurt them, and moments later it's forgotten. Children always look forward to the future because they don't yet value the past. There's certainly something alluring about the idea. But you do have a past, Owein. And yes, it is a dark one. I'd like to think I have an expansive imagination, but I can* only *imagine how hard such a past must have been.*

Even though Merritt had spent a good many years alone before moving to Blaugdone Island, he'd never been completely solitary. He'd made friends. Expressed himself. *Moved.* Being trapped on Blaugdone Island in a house must have felt little different than imprisonment. In truth, it said a lot of Owein's character that he wasn't more psychologically damaged.

But you are too smart and too old to believe a blanket will muffle the bad. You have to face it. And it's going to hurt. Honestly, it never stops hurting. Even with all the balms one could hope for, the hurt carves your soul and leaves a scar. But, Owein . . . you're not *alone anymore. That twelve-year-old boy who got sick and fled into the walls of Whimbrel House will always be a part of you, but you and I are together now. Always will be.*

Another soft whine. Owein lifted his head. *Hulda, too? And Beth? Baptiste?*

Merritt smiled. *Hulda, certainly. I'm not letting her go anywhere. I can't make promises for the others, but I'll eat my shoe if Beth ever leaves you behind.*

Owein leapt to his feet and licked Merritt's face.

"Ugh," Merritt rasped at the same time Owein complained, *Scratchy.*

Wiping off the slobber, Merritt felt his stubble. Shaving was such a pain. If Hulda allowed it, he'd become a hermit on Blaugdone Island and grow out a beard to his chest. Anything past the nipple line would be excessive.

After shaving, dressing, brushing his teeth, and combing his hair, Merritt headed into the hallway, Owein on his heels.

"I wonder what we'll do if the food's already put away." His voice had mostly returned to normal. "Is it uncultured to go straight to the kitchen?"

Owein huffed, considerate enough not to tax Merritt's communion further—until they reached the bottom of the stairs near the reception hall, where Owein exclaimed, *I have to pass water.*

Merritt gestured toward the front doors. Fortunately, the terrier didn't request Merritt's presence this time, and simply went on his own, using magic to melt one of the double doors and slip into the cool March . . . afternoon? Was it noon yet?

Fortunately, upon entering the breakfast room, Merritt was pleased to see he wasn't the only late riser. There was food atop the table, and Baron von Gayl and Lady Briar sat across from one another, both of them eating. Briar had nearly finished her meal; the baron appeared to be working on recent seconds.

Briar looked up as Merritt entered, her icy blue eyes sharper than they'd been when last he'd spoken to her. "Mr. Fernsby."

Merritt nodded, thinking his name a greeting, but as he reached for a chair, Lady Briar continued.

"How is it that you can continue to live under this roof with the knowledge of how hurtful your presence is to both me and my sister?"

The baron lowered his utensils. "Again, Briar?" His voice wasn't harsh, but pleading.

Briar ignored him, never taking her glare from Merritt.

Merritt grasped the chairback with both hands. As kindly as he could manage, he replied, "You have made your feelings abundantly clear. Unfortunately, your sister has not yet expressed a similar sentiment." Not where he could hear, anyway, but that was beside the point. In truth, this was Owein's decision, not his.

Briar's lips pressed into a thin line. Setting her utensils atop her plate, she threw her napkin onto the table and escorted herself out, leaving the dishes for the staff to clean up.

Merritt let out a long breath and pulled out the chair.

"I'm very sorry," the baron offered, German accent polishing his syllables. "She's very passionate about this."

"My condolences as well." Merritt sat and reached forward for a cherry pastry. "It must be hard hearing it, considering your . . . circumstances."

The baron—Ernst—shrugged. "It is what it is. I knew from a very young age that I would marry to create a magic lineage, not for love. I never expected anything different." He looked at the door Briar had left through. "I think the same for her, but she had . . . hope. I've tried to win her over. Really and truly. But not yet." He sighed.

"Have you tried battling a necromancer in a dank basement?" Merritt asked.

A bite of egg stopped halfway to Ernst's mouth. "Pardon?"

Merritt cleared his throat. "I asked if you've tried reading. Her favorite books, perhaps."

"Ah." He chewed the egg, swallowed. "She does love reading. It feels too . . . slow for me. But I could try." He shrugged. "By the way, Mr. Fernsby. What is your occupation?"

"I'm an author, actually."

Ernst laughed. "But in truth."

Merritt mimicked the same shrug.

Ernst blushed. "My. I'm sorry. I thought you were joking."

"Your question did have excellent comedic timing." Merritt smiled. "But I do think the books might help."

Ernst took a full minute to consider this, long enough for Merritt to grab a sausage—two, that was—and an egg for himself. He'd just cracked the shell when a scurrying of clipped-clawed paws sounded outside the door.

He looked up. "That must be O—"

He paused as a young hound scrabbled through the door. Not Owein. The dog came right up to Merritt's side and snuffed around, then jumped up so its paws were on his thigh.

"Maksim, no!" shouted an adolescent boy in the doorway, scrabbling much as the dog had. "I'm so sorry," he said to Merritt. Then, noticing Ernst, he went red in the face. He bowed at the waist. "My apologies, sir. He's just in training and got away from me. Took 'im to the kitchen for a treat. Which he will *not* be getting now."

The hound sniffed at Merritt's plate, completely undaunted by the threat.

"Not a problem." Merritt pushed the enthusiastic animal down. "Pups are like that."

"How old is he?" Ernst asked.

The boy grabbed Maksim's collar and hauled him toward the servants' door. "Nearly a year, sir." His eyes shot between Ernst and Merritt. "Don't tell Mr. Coldwell. Will you?"

Merritt imagined Mr. Coldwell was the kennel master.

"It will be our secret." Ernst grinned. "Now hurry out before Lady Helen sees you. She is far less forgiving than I am."

The boy nodded and dragged Maksim toward the door, but the pup must have gotten a whiff of sausage, for it pulled free and jumped at the table, turning its head sideways to grab at Briar's forgotten morsel—

A loud *crack* sounded through the room, giving everyone but the dog pause. Merritt stood, knocking back his chair. Dust fell from the ceiling.

The crystal chandelier quivered.

"What is—" Ernst began.

And the ceiling fell down.

Chapter 17

A quiver and crack like thunder reverberated through the library where Hulda and Lady Helen were talking. Hulda's heart seized. Her skin pebbled beneath her dress. Her eyes met Lady Helen's round ones.

In an instant, they were both rushing for the door, cutting through the lobby to the breakfast room. Dust clung to the air like fog.

Hulda coughed. "Is anyone in there?"

Wind shot from Lady Helen's palms, blowing back the cloud as they approached the door.

"Hulda!"

Hulda's bones turned to ice. "Merritt!" she screamed, and rushed in. Lady Helen barked for her to wait, but Hulda was already inside, stepping over broken pieces of wood and stone. She collided right into Merritt, who looked like he'd just come in from a snowstorm. Rubble sprinkled his head and shoulders, but he was upright. He looked all right.

She grasped his arms. "Are you hurt?"

He turned away as Lady Helen's gusts blew in, whipping through the air, blowing away most of the debris covering him.

"You've got to come quick!" cried a servant boy within the room, climbing over a large chunk of the ceiling with oddly smooth edges. "The baron and Maksim! Hurry!"

⁓

Cora sobbed into her sister's lap at the far end of the visitors' morning room, where everyone had gone while Mr. Blightree saw to the baron's injuries. Owein had heard the rumble and come in as the servants began crowding around the breakfast room.

Just like the bedroom . . . though the damage wasn't as bad. This time there had been injuries, however.

The chunk of ceiling that had fallen from the corner, right past the servants' entrance, had crushed the baron's arm. Skimmed the shoulder of a boy who worked in the kennels. Shattered the back leg of the dog he'd been trying to lure outside.

It was the damage to the dog that had upset Cora the most. "She loves those dogs" was all a very choked-up Lady Helen could manage. The leg would have to come off; Blightree couldn't use necromantic healing magic on an animal. Might have been better to put the animal down, some people were saying, but Cora promised through streaming tears she'd nurse the hound back to health, and her parents had relented, for now.

Owein wasn't sure what to do with himself. He wanted to stay by Cora, see if he could comfort her . . . especially if she loved dogs so much. But her sister didn't like *him*, so he hesitated to approach. Lady Helen and Prince Friedrich spoke in quiet tones near the door; she occasionally dabbed at her eyes with a handkerchief, and he occasionally reminded her the baron would be just fine. Merritt had gone with Blightree, despite insisting he was unharmed.

Hulda came in just then. The hem of her skirt was white with dust, and Owein could smell the debris even before he trotted over. She nodded at him, then turned to the Leiningens with a gray cloth in her hand . . . or maybe it was red. Owein couldn't be sure.

"I found this in the rubble," she murmured, handing it to Cora's father.

Prince Friedrich turned it over. "A spell?"

Oh, Owein recognized it now. Hulda had hung little bags of spells around him when he'd still been a house. To keep him from breaking things. This looked like one of those bags.

"It's unlabeled, but I believe from the color and residue that it's an alteration metamorphosis spell, specifically of shape change."

Owein's ears perked. *I have that spell.* Not that anyone could hear him. And not that it mattered; *he* wasn't the one who made the ceiling cave in. Or the floor, from the viewpoint of the bedroom situated above the breakfast room.

The bedroom . . . oh. No one in the breakfast room had noticed anything amiss, so someone must have used a spell in the bedroom to make the ceiling come down!

Owein pawed at Hulda's dress. *Maybe I can smell who did it.*

"It's a packageable spell, often used in construction and demolition for debris management." Hulda's voice had a cool edge to it. "It would explain why the piece that fell had such rounded edges. Someone used it on a specific piece of the floor, changed the edges so they no longer fit with the whole, and, well . . ." She clasped her hands together.

"Very purposefully done." Prince Friedrich's tone sounded low. "Who can purchase spells like this?"

"Anyone with a license," Hulda answered. "Or with the right connections. I could inform LIKER, but this strikes me as subterfuge rather than any enchantments within the house. Cyprus Hall isn't haunted; if it were, by a spirit other than the marquess, we'd see much more activity than this. This damage was caused by a purchased spell." She gestured to the cloth in the prince's hands. "I am fairly certain this spell is not what collapsed that bedroom, however. Too much widespread damage. Surely it was something else entirely."

Prince Friedrich stood. "Either way, I'll send word to the police."

The door opened again, nearly hitting Hulda's backside. Merritt stepped in; his hair was damp as though he'd washed it, but he was in the same clothes from this morning. The smell of dust and mortar made Owein sneeze.

Merritt, tell her I'll smell for it, Owein pressed.

Merritt held up a hand to him. "Baron von Gayl is doing just fine. He'll be tired from the healing spells, as is Mr. Blightree, but he's hale."

Briar stood, and Cora, her eyes swollen, stood with her. "I'm glad to hear it," the former said.

Excusing himself, Prince Friedrich left. Probably to contact the police.

"Smell for what?" Merritt asked.

Owein pawed at the carpet. *Smell for the person who did the spell. In the bedroom.*

Merritt paused. "That's not a bad idea." He relayed the message to the others.

Lady Helen perked up. "Yes, yes! Right this instant. I want to know who is hurting my family!"

Or who is hurting mine, Owein thought, only realizing he'd projected the words when Merritt's gaze met his. Because *Merritt* was the connection between the two incidents. He'd been in the breakfast room when the ceiling fell, and the room that had collapsed had been originally assigned to him.

Lady Helen opened the door. Owein forced himself to hold back so as not to trip her—running out into the hallway was something a child would do. But as soon as the way cleared, he hurried after her, not entirely sure how to get to the room in question. He followed her up the stairs, through one hall, then another. The bedroom was dusty but undamaged other than the hole in the floor, utterly unlike the first bedroom. The windows were still intact.

Owein sniffed around, sneezed. Sniffed and sneezed. Sniffed again, even when the dust hurt his nose. But all he could smell was dust and Lady Helen.

He didn't need to have words to express that his efforts had failed. He saw it in the slump of Lady Helen's shoulders as she stood safely by the door.

"It was worth a try," she offered, and dabbed her eyes once more with the handkerchief.

⁓

One of the perks of living in London and being an aristocrat was the timeliness of police. The inspector himself came to answer Prince Friedrich's summons. Hulda introduced herself early and made herself available, expressing to the men what she herself had gleaned—that the house was very unlikely haunted and that the second incident was the result of a purchased alteration spell. She supposed it was fortunate that the repair crew had not yet begun work on the damaged guest bedroom, as the devastation was available for the police's further perusal.

While the officers interviewed the family and servants, Hulda retreated to the guest drawing room. She pulled a crochet project out of her bag but found herself unable to focus on it.

Why hadn't she foreseen this happening? Or anything else, oh, *useful* to the situation?

One of the reasons she'd been employed at BIKER was due to her magic, diluted as it was. And it did come in handy from time to time. Indeed, it was that same diluted power that had first alerted her to Silas Hogwood's crimes. Still, it was impossible to rely on her gift. What was the point of being an augurist if the majority of future glimpses she saw were pointless? Wouldn't it be just dandy if she could foresee the culprit now and save them all some trouble?

Hulda set her yarn aside and stared at the weak fire in the finely decorated hearth. The damage to the guest bedroom was different from that of the breakfast room. Given the broken windows in the guest room, it was possible the damage had been done from a spell originating on the exterior of the house. Not so with the breakfasting room. Someone had deliberately unleashed magic in the room just above it. The Leiningens had no guests outside of Hulda, Merritt, Owein, and, she thought with a shudder, William Blightree.

So logic suggested that one of them might be behind the attacks—attacks that could very well be aimed at Merritt.

A sick, heavy feeling crawled through her chest like an obese slug. She shook herself. *All is well. He was unharmed.*

Returning to her bag, Hulda pulled out a receipt book. She'd taken notes in the margins of it. It wasn't the most enticing receipt book she'd read, so she wasn't particularly disconcerted at the idea of marking it up. She wrote down a few more details she'd gathered while following the police about, then turned back a page—to where she'd listed the spells of every known magic user in Cyprus Hall. Granted, one of them might possess an unknown talent. Merritt had been an unknown until recently, after all. She must also take into account that the spell had been purchased, not made, and anyone with a license or influence could have acquired it. Indeed, it needn't be a magic user at all.

One of the servants? Hulda wrote in tiny letters in the corner near a drab cinnamon bread recipe. Everyone was being interviewed; perhaps she could pull some strings and see the police reports herself.

She considered her notes on the guest bedroom, her mind recalling the devastation there. Who had spells that could have caused such damage?

Owein and Merritt, both. But neither had the motive, and truthfully, Merritt's chaocracy was finnicky, much like Hulda's own augury. Besides, such an act would require a surge of magic so great it would have left the user addled long enough for a witness to notice. Neither Owein nor Merritt had felt such symptoms.

William Blightree was a necromancer, though he must have some kinetic ability if he claimed he could transfer Owein's spirit. But did he have enough strength to destroy an entire bedchamber? Hulda would need to come back to that.

Baron von Gayl had been bred like a show poodle to excel at kineticism. He certainly would have the spells necessary to do a great amount of targeted damage to a room. But he also wouldn't have broken his own arm—nor could he have been in two places at once to do so.

Were there two culprits at hand, then?

Hulda shook her head and turned back a page. Baron von Gayl and Lady Briar hadn't arrived at Cyprus Hall until the day *after* the demolition of the guest bedroom. It couldn't have been them.

Unless it was.

It was an errant thought, but one Hulda lingered on. They'd arrived the next morning. Might they have concealed the true time of their arrival to enact their scheme? Lady Briar was certainly against any marriage contract between her sister and Owein. According to Merritt's account, she'd pledged to do *anything* to prevent the nuptials. Lady Briar would also be familiar with the rooms her mother customarily used for guests. And unlike Lady Cora, she hadn't seemed apoplectic about the injuring of the dog.

That last bit was speculation, but Hulda had come to find her speculation was often, more or less, correct.

Since Lady Briar didn't seem keen on her husband, his presence in the breakfast room might not have impeded action. But what could she have against Merritt? He was Owein's caretaker, yes . . . Would Merritt also be signing the contract, since he had guardianship of Owein? But how could Lady Briar have been aware of that fact before coming to Cyprus Hall?

Hulda's thoughts drifted to Mr. Adey. The royal family *did* have their ways.

She jotted down a few of her ideas. Still, the elder sister didn't have much to gain by eliminating Merritt, unless she was entirely off her head. Other than, perhaps, providing an advantageous body for Owein.

Hulda's pencil stilled. The marriage contract hinged on that, didn't it? And what better body than one whose blood was infused with magic? It would certainly help with the enchanted lineage. Then again, Lady Briar seemed to object to arranged marriages altogether. If anyone *were* considering killing Merritt for his magic-limned corpse, it would be Briar's parents.

That heavy, sluglike feeling returned, only this time in her stomach. Hulda pressed a fist into it, sure she was going to be sick.

Perhaps this is too much speculation. She closed the book. Besides, Lady Briar had made it clear she had no interest in helping the contract along, and the only spell she retained that could create that sort of destruction in the guest bedroom was her wind spell. To use it so forcefully would mean risking her own life, since elemental spells of air took one's breath away in compensation. She'd suffocate, as would her sister, who was an asthmatic.

There was Lady Helen, whose air spell would be more potent than either of her daughters'. But why would she destroy her own house? She was quite disconcerted by all of it, and Hulda didn't believe her to be an excellent actress, merely a distressed noblewoman.

After shoving everything back into her bag, Hulda rose and strode for the door. She'd share all of this with Merritt and get his thoughts on it. Perhaps even lend it to the police. She was no detective, but surely she was digging in the right hole.

She'd just exited the room and started for the stairs when her path crossed with the last person she wanted to encounter: William Blightree.

She nodded and continued on her way.

"Miss Larkin."

Her manners halted her step before her self-preservation could form remonstrance. Cursing inwardly, she turned around. "Yes, Mr. Blightree? I'm terribly sorry, I'm in a bit of a hurry—"

"Yes, of course. I'll walk with you." He gestured ahead of them.

Hiding a cringe, Hulda continued on her way, hoping to outpace him.

She did not.

"I've been meaning to speak with you," Mr. Blightree said, his smooth, cordial voice causing the sensation of ants beneath her bodice.

"Oh?" She didn't look at him.

"It's just . . . and please, correct me if I'm wrong, but I seem to have upset you."

Hulda paused and turned to him, caught off guard. He wasn't a large man—indeed, in these shoes, Hulda was a finger's breadth taller. He had a benevolent face and balding head, but she could see the Hogwood in his eyes and the curve of his mouth.

"Not at all." Hulda put on her stiffest mask, trying not to sound flustered. "Indeed, we've barely had a chance to acquaint ourselves since my arrival."

He nodded. "This is true. Then perhaps I imagine it . . . but, Miss Larkin, even now, you seem discontent."

A flush threatened to crawl up her neck. Hulda forced her spine to relax. *Well, better now than never.* "I admit I'm aware of your relation to Silas Hogwood." There. She'd said it.

"Ah yes." He rubbed his chin, seeming not at all surprised at the statement. "That one does come up a fair bit. First cousins, we were."

Sensing opportunity, Hulda pressed, "Might I ask how you were related?"

"His mother was my aunt," the necromancer answered honestly.

Hulda considered this. She was well aware of Mr. Hogwood's pedigree; his mother had been a solid necromancer. Everything else he had came from his father's side.

"And," she pressed, "if you're the one to be performing this potential body switch, you are also a kineticist?"

He looked impressed, of all things. "Indeed, I have a fractional ability with movement, as well as in psychometry, for detecting magic. My real skills lie in necromancy."

Fractional ability. So the man was, essentially, a pure necromancer. And necromancers couldn't break bedrooms . . . assuming he was being truthful on that front.

"He is," Mr. Blightree went on, "a dark spot in the family history. Necromancy is considered by many to be a dark art, but it also does a lot of good . . . such as healing the poor baron's arm."

Hulda dipped her head in hesitant agreement.

"I hope to give it a better name. And the family a better name, though fortunately I don't bear the title of *Hogwood*." A weak smile touched his lips. "I, uh, assume you know the story of my cousin."

"Indeed, Mr. Blightree. I was involved in it."

She waited to see his reaction—surprise. Interesting.

"I didn't realize." He rubbed his hands together. A few age spots mottled them. "I . . . I was called in after they found his . . . cache, if you don't mind my bringing it up again. It was rather . . . unsettling, what he did."

Hulda let out a long breath through her nose in hope of better disguising it. She had a suspicion that Merritt was right—Mr. Blightree was simply a kind old man, here to enact his queen's will. She'd keep an eye on him, however. She'd learned not to be too trusting with those she didn't truly know.

"Then, while I have you"—Hulda resumed their walk toward the stairs—"I want to know what might go wrong, when and if you move Owein's soul. How is the search coming? I am well aware the royal family is powerful, but we will not accept a body *taken*."

He nodded. "Neither will I. When your life is as dedicated to the workings of life and death as mine has been, you learn not to trifle with it. In truth, I think the likelihood of Cora marrying another suitor is high. If we haven't found a means of making Owein presentable by, oh, the time she's twenty-five, I think another pairing will be arranged."

Hulda clasped her hands together. "Owein will not live that long in his present body. Unless you intend to stave off its aging."

But Mr. Blightree shook his head. "Alas, my abilities only work on mankind. I can do nothing for animals, however much I wish it were otherwise." They reached the stairs, and he took a firm hold on the railing. "Had a horse once. Loved that beast. He was fast and noble and everything good. Couldn't do a thing for him when he broke his leg."

Her posture softened. "I'm sorry."

"Twenty years ago now." He took the stairs slowly; Hulda matched his pace. "But I will do my best, for the queen and for your family."

"Thank you." And she meant it.

They reached the base of the stairs; Hulda heard the police chatting in the reception hall up ahead. As she neared, she spied Merritt and Owein loitering near the entrance. The former noticed her and hurried toward her. Mr. Blightree gave her a congenial nod and went off to join the family.

"Well," Merritt offered, combing a hand back through his hair. "There's not much new to report."

A few strands of hair came loose on his fingers; he shook them off his hand. As they drifted toward the floor, however, a pattern formed between the delicate threads, throwing Hulda into a vision.

In it, she saw Merritt standing in the depths of a forest. Hanging off his neck, pressed together chest to chest, was a woman she didn't recognize, naked as the day she was born.

Chapter 18

March 5, 1847, London, England

The hairs passed out of sight, color blending with the surroundings, and the vision ended. And Hulda . . . Hulda had stopped breathing. She stared at a spot just past Merritt's shoulder. Her back and shoulders were so erect, so tight, they began to ache.

"Hulda?" Merritt waved a hand in front of her face. "What's wrong?"

Slowly, like her eyes were pestles grinding in their mortars, she met his gaze. His face began to blur as though painted on a wet canvas. Then she blinked, and a tear rolled down her cheek.

Too good to be true, a quiet thought creaked.

Merritt blanched. "Hulda, what?"

She still wasn't breathing. She didn't know how to answer. She *couldn't* answer. This . . . why did she have to see *this?* Why couldn't the magic just let her be happy a little longer?

Merritt reached for her. His fingertips grazed her sleeve just before she turned from him and stalked back through the hall toward the stairs that led up to the rooms. Long, desperate strides that finally demanded she inhale or pass out. Her shoes clacked loudly on the floor, or perhaps that was just the sound of a slow-breaking heart.

"Hulda!" Merritt ran after her and grabbed her elbow. She tugged it free. Grabbed her skirt and rushed up the stairs.

But damn that man, he was faster than she was. Hulda had made it only halfway up the flight before Merritt swung in front of her, blocking her retreat. She tried to step around him, but to no avail. Her skin heated with embarrassment as another tear escaped. One would think she'd be tough as iron by now. Heaven knew she wanted to be tough as iron, but that awful image of him and *her* had tattooed itself on her eyelids.

He grasped her shoulders, locking her in place. "Damn it, Hulda, what's wrong? What did you see?"

"The future," she spat, hating the way her throat constricted the words. "Because that's how it works, Merritt. I see the future *as it is*, not how it *might* be. *Always*." She wrenched free, but gained only a stair before he snatched her wrist.

"Did someone die?" His voice took on an edge. "Did I do something? What did I do? For heaven's sake, Hulda, at least tell me the crime before you punish me for it!"

Gingerly trying to dab her eyes with her free hand, Hulda attempted to respond, but a sore, hard lump had formed in her throat and forbade it.

A voice downstairs—one of the servants—neared.

Releasing a sigh but certainly not his grip, Merritt said, "Let's go somewhere private." When he led her upstairs, she followed, each step zapping her strength, turning her into little more than a rag doll.

Hulda's room was closest, so they went in there. Merritt shut the door with more force than was necessary. She fled to the far window when he did, grabbing a handkerchief off her dressing table and desperately trying to dry her eyes, but the tears wouldn't stop. She pulled off her glasses and set them on the windowsill.

"Talk." His words were much gentler now as he crossed the room to her. "*Please*, Hulda."

It took her a good minute of deep breaths and biting the inside of her cheek to manage anything coherent. "I saw you."

"I figured as much."

"In the forest."

Merritt's brow ticked. "All right . . ."

"With a woman."

He waited.

Hulda drew in breath until her chest threatened to pop. "With a *naked* woman draped over you like she was a sinner and you were the *Madonna of Bruges*!"

He reeled back at that, his features slackening. "Pardon? What? Who?"

"I don't know!" she snapped, hiding her face with the handkerchief. "I've never s-seen her before."

"Hulda, I would *never*." He touched her shoulder. She wanted to lean into the weight of his hand and rip away at the same time. The latter won out. "I mean," he went on, "in a *forest*? I think I'd be a little more circumspect than—"

She glared at him over the cloth.

"Right. Not a great time for jokes." He ran a hand back through his hair again. "Okay . . . how old was I? What was I wearing? *I* was clothed . . . wasn't I?"

Hulda sniffed. New tears pressed out. She waited a moment to speak. "Y-Yes, but I don't recall in what."

Merritt stepped forward and clasped his hands around her upper arms, forcing her to look at him. "Hulda. I love you. I love *you*. I would never be unfaithful to you. I've waited my whole life for you!"

The sweetness of the declaration fought against the utter sourness overtaking her.

"Surely you trust me by now. You know me."

She did. Admittedly, it had never once crossed her mind that Merritt would leave her for another. But she'd seen what she'd seen.

For the moment, her shattered mind couldn't come up with another reason for it.

He smoothed loose hair from her face. "I mean . . ." He hesitated. "The future is the future for your visions, yes. But surely you've seen something of *us* as well?"

The heat in her skin changed temperature and flooded her face. She hadn't seen their wedding yet, but she *had* seen intimacy. Graphic intimacy. On more than one occasion.

A lopsided and mischievous grin formed on Merritt's mouth. "Well, that's good, at least. If the future is set, you must forgive me for this eventually."

She swatted him with the handkerchief. "Really, Merritt." But he had a point. Anything she did now contributed to the future she'd seen. She knew she married Merritt. Or at least, slept with him. But she certainly would never do that outside the bounds of marriage. So she would marry him. In some way or another, she would conciliate what she'd seen in the vision and say her vows.

But what if this happened *after*? Did Merritt grow tired of her? Would she not be . . . adequate?

His hands caressed her face, bringing her attention back to him. He was close enough not to be too blurry without her glasses.

"I've made mistakes before," he murmured. "I will not repeat them. And I will *never* make the mistake of leaving you. I will marry you right now if you want to find a pastor. I will also wait as long as you need. I will take a vow of celibacy and simply worship you until I draw my last breath." He kissed the tip of her nose.

A shuddering exhale escaped her. She believed him. She did. Or at least, she dearly wanted to. Throat closing up again, she managed a nod.

"Though apparently I won't need to." That grin returned.

She swatted at him again. "You really are impossible, Merritt Fernsby."

He kissed her chastely. "I'll do anything you want to prove it to you, Hulda Larkin."

Anything she wanted. The problem was, Hulda didn't know *how* to feel better. She didn't know how to prove or disprove anything, not with the way her abilities worked. If only she could revive the vision and force it to play out a little longer, or start a little earlier, she might have the answers she needed.

It seemed what she *needed* was another meeting with Professor Griffiths. If she could control the magic, perhaps it would stop controlling her.

Merritt embraced her. Letting go of all of it, she buried her head in his neck and sunk into the embrace. She loved him. She couldn't bear losing him. *Please,* she prayed. *Please let me keep him.*

They stayed like that for a long while.

"This might not be the best time," Merritt tried, grasping her shoulder, "but time isn't on our side today."

She waited.

He sighed. "I'm not sure it's a good idea for us to stay here any longer . . . after what happened in the breakfast room."

Her organs shrunk. "That . . . is probably wise. But Owein . . ."

"I want to give him time to acclimate." He spoke softly, as though any volume might shatter her. And it very well might. "To the culture of this place, and to Cora. But we still don't understand what's going on with these . . . very purposeful destructions of rooms I occupy. It might do to just sign the contract and leave."

She nodded. "I believe it's been redrafted to my specifications."

He rubbed her upper arm. "Let's ask for it, then. Let's sign it and then go home."

She bit her lip. "All right."

Perhaps she wasn't meant to get a handle on her augury. And thinking on the vision, perhaps she wasn't meant to have a happy ending, either.

Still, looking into Merritt's sincere eyes, she believed everything he'd said to her.

That would have to be enough.

⁓

Owein waited with Merritt and Hulda in one of the drawing rooms—a funny name for the space, really, since he'd yet to see anyone draw in it. He himself hadn't had the opportunity to draw in a very long time. Had he been good at it, in his life before? He couldn't remember.

Lady Helen sat in a blue chair nearby, her spine stiffer than Hulda's, her hands working and reworking in her lap. She smelled like lilacs. Lilacs and worry, which were scents that didn't mix well. Perhaps she wore the lilac to mask the worry. And perhaps it worked . . . on human noses.

After a long silence—they'd been discussing the virtues of a game called cricket—Lady Helen said, "Are you sure you won't stay? I will post a guard on the grounds and move your room right next to mine, even. Owein and Cora hardly know one another still, and you *did* suggest a fortnight in the beginning, Mr. Fernsby."

Merritt smiled. Not his normal smile, but his *I'm trying to look friendly but I'm tired* smile. "I did, and I would love to, but the situation . . . it's not a comfortable one. To put it lightly."

He clasped one of Hulda's hands in both of his own. Hulda seemed . . . distracted. Owein found that interesting, since she usually seemed very attentive whenever one of the Englishmen was around. And Lady Helen was right there.

Owein would ask about it, later. He didn't think Merritt would tell him much if he asked now. But what was really important was that the contract would be signed, and Owein would get a body . . . hopefully . . . and then they would be going home. There was so much more left to explore here, and part of Owein yearned to do just that, but he missed Whimbrel House, too. He missed Beth, especially.

He didn't recognize heavy footsteps outside the door and was surprised when Prince Friedrich entered. Owein knew Prince Friedrich's steps. He never walked that quickly. It was the tempo that had thrown off Owein. Behind him, Mr. Blightree approached as well.

Lady Helen stood, her scent of worry pungent.

"It's gone." Prince Friedrich shook his head, flabbergasted. "We can't find it anywhere. The contract is gone."

Chapter 19

"Gone?" Merritt repeated, rising from his seat as well. "You mean it's missing?"

"I had it in the study," Blightree explained, clasping and unclasping his hands. "I'd recently redrafted it. I need Her Majesty's approval, of course, but I understand your reasons for departing." He stepped forward to be better seen. "It's not there."

Hulda said, "You misplaced it?"

Blightree shook his head. "I am getting on in years, but I assure you, I left it in Prince Friedrich's study, which he's graciously lent to me during my stay."

Friedrich nodded. "I recall. It was folded in thirds on the left-hand side of my desk."

Lady Helen shook her head. "But . . . a contract doesn't merely get up and walk away!" She cast an apologetic look toward Merritt, Hulda, and Owein. "We must have simply . . ."

She paused. Set her jaw. Grabbing a fistful of skirt, she marched toward the door; Blightree stepped out of her way. After wrenching it open, she must have found a footman or a maid waiting nearby, for she said, "Fetch Lady Briar at once."

They think Briar took it? Owein asked.

"I guess," Merritt murmured, catching Hulda's attention as he did so. "She's a likely suspect."

Hulda stood and gently placed her hand on the inside of his elbow. "Well," she tried, pulling on her business tone, "contracts are not carved into gold. We can simply draft a new one."

"Aye, we can draft a new one," Blightree said, "though not *simply*. We'll need to review everything to ensure I haven't forgotten anything, especially with the new amendments."

Hulda frowned. "Which we haven't had a chance to review."

Blightree nodded. "My apologies, Miss Larkin. Mr. Fernsby, Mr. Mansel. I did not think it necessary to place it in the safe." He sighed. "It was only a draft."

"You mentioned it needed to be reviewed by Queen Victoria," Merritt tried, rubbing the bridge of his nose as a headache began to sprout in his forehead. "If we were to sign it and she did *not* approve it, we would need to review and sign an entirely new draft, correct?"

"Correct," the necromancer replied.

They can mail it to us, Owein suggested.

Merritt cleared his throat. "Owein makes a valid point. Perhaps the contract could be mailed to us."

Blightree and Friedrich exchanged a glance.

Merritt released a long breath. "What is it now?"

"English Soil Law," Hulda said.

Prince Friedrich gestured with a turn of his wrist. "It's my understanding . . . magic laws in the United States are not very strict."

We don't have required breeding programs for it like you do here, Merritt thought to himself, but nodded.

Lady Helen returned to her chair, obviously flustered. Prince Friedrich continued, "They are much stricter here. Any charter or decree of magical origin pertaining to British land or British citizens must be signed on British soil. It's a protection, really. With the empire expanding as it was, laws in India weren't matching laws in the islands, or there was that whole mess with Ireland . . ."

"Such a bother," Lady Helen murmured.

Merritt glanced at Hulda. "Perhaps . . . there's always LIKER."

She considered.

Lady Helen interjected, "I swear to my Lord in heaven, Mr. Fernsby, there is no plot against you. Not in my house!" Her voice rose enough to startle Owein. "I want this to work. Truly I do. I want Cora to have the fortnight promised to her. I will hire and post guards around this house and all its grounds, day and night. I do not mind the expense. We will get to the bottom of this, and to this bloody contract."

Prince Friedrich paled. Less at the promise and more at the language, Merritt suspected.

"I could," Hulda began, withdrawing her hand from his arm, "go to LIKER on the morrow and obtain some more wards and stones. Wardship stones that can detect magic, and perhaps even counter it." She looked at Merritt. "If anyone did attempt a spell, the stones would catch it."

"Like with Baillie," Merritt supplied.

She nodded. "Like with Baillie. The house is large . . . but if I can get my hand on some counterspell wards, those could be placed around your person."

Merritt considered this. "Isn't it detrimental to wear a ward?"

"*Around* your person, not on it." Knitting her fingers together, she added, "It might be a pain, but with the guards, I'm sure we can get the new contract drafted and ready in record time. Yes?"

Blightree said, "Of course."

The door opened, revealing a young footman. "Pardon my intrusion."

Lady Helen motioned him inside. "Well?"

The servant swallowed. "She's not here, my lady."

Lady Helen surged to her feet. Her hands balled into tight fists. "What do you mean, *she's not here?*"

Bowing his head, the footman answered, "The baron explained she'd left for the borough of Westminster."

Lady Helen rolled her eyes and barely held in a growl. "This child of mine!" She pointed accusingly at Prince Friedrich. "She's gone and done just that, I tell you! I hope Victoria refuses to see her!"

"My dear"—the man came forward with his hands raised, as though Lady Helen were a rabid wolf—"let's consider this rationally—"

What's happening? Owein asked.

Merritt slumped down into his chair. *I think we found the contract thief. And I think we'll be staying here another night, at least.*

Lady Helen was true to her word—guards roamed the estate the very next morning, and Merritt and his retinue slept the night without any disaster. Slept, thanks to the tincture Hulda had ordered up from the kitchens. *Bless that woman,* he thought as he walked, Owein taking two steps for his every one.

Saturday rolled in as all English days in March seemed to—overcast and crisp. The Leiningen grounds were looking quite green, thanks to magic from a grounds crew, though in the wooded area beyond what the family had manicured, a few daring leaf buds were starting to peek out of winter branches. Mayhap it was better for Merritt to stay indoors, where the guard was thicker and magical wards would soon be placed, but he had the desperate need to stretch his legs. He would also be hard to target if no one knew where to find him, and Owein was the best guard he could possibly ask for at this point, truthfully. Still, Merritt rubbed his fingers together in his trouser pockets, not because they were cold, but because he was ready to cast a wardship wall at any moment. He'd need only a second to do so. The collapse in the breakfast room had taken him so off guard he hadn't had a chance, but he wouldn't make that mistake twice.

In addition to the hired guard, the repairmen for the damaged rooms in Cyprus Hall had arrived and taken over the house, and Hulda . . . who *seemed* to be faring better today . . . had gotten an appointment with that augurist in town, so Merritt had decided to take Owein out, away from the noise and the expectations. Lord knew they had a lot to chat about, and Merritt had a lot to think about.

He wasn't entirely sure how to process this vision of Hulda's. Could she have misread it somehow? But Hulda wasn't a woman prone to flights of fancy. It had physically hurt him to see her cry, to see the look of betrayal in her eyes, even though he hadn't yet *done* anything. And he wouldn't. He'd made a mistake with Ebba, but even then, he'd been loyal to the woman he'd pledged himself to. Ready to own up to everything and be there for her and their nonexistent child.

He sighed. Climbed over a log while Owein squeezed under it. The only future Merritt wanted was with Hulda. He'd convince her of that, however long it took. Hopefully this Griffiths fellow would help her home in on the vision, though Merritt would prefer it if she didn't relate too many details.

Hell, the way things had unraveled for him, maybe Merritt had a secret twin brother. He honestly wouldn't be surprised at this point, though the revelation would be a little melodramatic for his taste.

After the missing contract debacle, Hulda had privately shared her sleuthing into who could possibly be breaking Cyprus Hall and why. Merritt had taken notes—stress aside, this would make for an excellent book. And it eased his anxiety, thinking it a work of fiction instead of his life. He really did hope no one was trying to kill him. Again.

He listened to the fall of his footsteps punctuated by Owein's for several seconds, a rhythm just a little too off to be even.

But enough of his problems.

"Do you want to talk about it?" Merritt asked when the trees thickened. Owein would know what he meant. He'd had another nightmare last night, though he'd woken himself up from this one before he could do any unconscious magical damage.

Owein didn't respond immediately. Merritt took in their surroundings, trying to picture the forest in the lush greens of summer. There was a deer nearby, listening to him as he listened to it. He sensed it more than heard it. No more guards this far out, but when he looked over his shoulder, he saw one patrolling in the distance. Fingers and magic ready, Merritt trudged forward. A trail wound through the trees, so he didn't worry about getting lost.

I was alone a lot, Owein said. *I would get so bored. I kept waiting for someone to take the house, to move in, and no one did.*

"The witches?" Merritt asked softly.

They didn't stay. Whimbrel House had been a safe house for women accused of ill deeds during the Salem witch trials—the only reason BIKER had known of the house's existence in the first place.

They stepped around a mud puddle and ducked beneath a fallen branch caught on the boughs of another tree.

I watched them die. My parents, I mean.

Merritt's stride slowed. "I'm so sorry, Owein."

My dad went first, then my mom. I remember it, and I remember them, but at the same time, I don't. But I think they were in my dream last night. Not their faces, not really. But they were there, and they were far away, and they were calling for me.

Heavy stuff. Merritt mulled it over.

Do you believe in heaven, Merritt?

"I do." His voice took on its usual communion-induced rasp. "What's the point of all of it if there isn't something beyond? Seems life would be pretty dismal if it were strictly sealed cover to cover."

Owein took a moment to consider that, which gave Merritt's voice a chance to recover. *I wonder if they're there, waiting for me. My family.*

"Maybe." Merritt quickened his step and let his hand drop from his coat pocket so his first knuckles grazed Owein's head. "And you have family waiting for you here."

I miss Beth.

"You'll see her soon enough. I—"

Wait.

Owein slowed, stopped. Merritt followed his lead. His nose pointed ahead and to the south, ears perked, tail erect. Tensing, Merritt readied a spell. How large could he make a wall? His practice was usually on a smaller scale—

A gray hawk flew through the trees ahead, landing on a branch, regarding them.

Merritt let out a breath. "Just a bird. Don't scare me like that."

A woman's voice behind him said, "We don't mean to be frightening."

Both Merritt and Owein jumped. Merritt whirled and threw up an invisible wall. Two people approached, one a woman about Hulda's age, another a man in his midforties. The first wore a gown that didn't look warm enough for the weather, reminiscent of something one might find on a Greek statue. Her long, dark-blonde hair was loose down her back. She had large, deerlike eyes and full lips, which smiled at him. The man was tall, dressed as a dedicated hunter might be, in colors of the forest. The material of his clothes seemed foraged from everything and anything, patchworked to fit over broad shoulders and long legs. His hair was dark, and he wore a beard that fell about to his Adam's apple.

Merritt backed away. "Who are—"

Merritt! Owein barked. *He can hear me!*

Merritt's voice caught in his throat. *What?*

Owein danced in place. *The man, he can hear me! His name is Sean.*

Merritt met the dark eyes of the stranger. ". . . Sean?" he tried.

"I would confirm that you are Merritt Fernsby," said the man in a distinctive Irish lilt, "and this is Owein Mansel. I don't know any other creature that has a mind like that."

All right, Merritt admitted it. He *could* still be surprised.

As though sensing his thoughts, the woman said, "The royal family is not the only one with eyes and ears." Her gaze lifted up toward the hawk in the tree. She stepped off the path, her footfalls oddly light, and walked around the wall, fingertips grazing it as she went. "We're not armed," she assured him. Her dialect matched the man's. "When we heard of you, we wanted to meet you."

Merritt turned, unsure of whether it was more important to watch the woman or man. "And since you're familiar with us, perhaps you'd like to formally introduce yourselves." He willed himself to relax. If nothing else, he could throw up another wardship spell and Owein could, oh, throw some trees or the like and give them time to run back to Cyprus Hall.

"My name is Morgance," the woman said. "We're Druids."

That gave him pause. "Druids?"

She nodded. "We live off the land, outside of the queen's rule. We let her believe we're small in number and weak so we're not bothered." She stopped walking and smiled. Tipped her head. "If you want a better look, then come have it."

The hawk sailed off the branch farther up the trail and took perch on Morgance's arm.

Merritt dismissed his unseen spell. Tried to commune with the bird, but it didn't answer. "And that . . . is also a Druid?"

She nodded. "Fallon's abilities allow her to see what many of us cannot."

Owein turned his head, catching something behind them.

"And how many of you are there? Here?" Merritt asked warily.

"Only one more," Sean answered this time. "Hurry up, boy!"

Once the demand came, Merritt heard what Owein must have—a trudging through the brush. Seconds later, a boy of about ten appeared, wearing clothing similar to Sean's. Something about the arrival of the child immediately put Merritt at ease.

"This is Kegan, my son," Sean said. "He'll be able to hear you, too."

Owein's tail wagged. He was silent a long moment, presumably speaking mind to mind with the new arrival. It was awkward. Was this how Hulda, Beth, and Baptiste felt whenever Merritt and Owein had private conversations? He'd need to do something about that.

"Druids," Morgance went on, "are those with Druidic magic. We have many in our numbers without gifts, of course, but that is how we started."

"Druidic magic?" Merritt asked.

"Communion, elemental, and alteration spells." She gently stroked the hawk's—Fallon's—neck. "Or anything else that lends to Mother Earth."

Sean added, "We've a necromancer who specializes in equines back home."

Merritt processed this quickly. "And home is . . ."

"Wherever we choose, but our kind hail from Ireland," Morgance answered, which made Merritt think about *that whole mess with Ireland* that Prince Friedrich had mentioned. She took the hawk off her arm, letting it perch on two fingers, then held her arm out so it could flap to a close branch. "We heard of you and wanted to see for ourselves. But Owein is not a shape-shifter, is he?"

"No. He's human, or his soul is. A necromancer put him in that body."

She nodded. Knelt so she could look Owein in the eyes. "It's a beautiful body," she offered.

A moment later, Sean stiffened. "A human one? Really?"

Merritt supposed Owein had just offered up information about the marriage contract. *That's private, Owein.*

To you, maybe, the boy countered. Then, suddenly, *Can I play?*

"What?" Merritt asked aloud.

"Please?" The boy, Kegan, clasped dirty hands in front of his chin. "We've been traveling *forever* and I'm *bored* and can we please play?"

The hawk screeched from the branch.

Merritt rubbed the heels of his hands into his eyes. "This is bizarre." *I don't know if it's a good idea.*

Please, Merritt?

Merritt suddenly remembered what they'd been talking about before the newcomers' arrival. Death and darkness and loneliness. In truth, Owein needed more friends. Friends who weren't adults trying to care for him, teach him, and corral him. Even before Owein had died and joined his spirit with Whimbrel House, he'd been cloistered on that island.

He eyed the Druids. "I don't suppose you're part of a secret murder plot, are you?"

Sean's brows drew together. Morgance asked, "Pardon?"

Merritt sighed. To Owein, he said, "Go on. Not too far."

Owein barked and took off into the trees, followed by Kegan and Fallon.

Once the children were gone, Merritt asked, "So what interest do the Druids have in blokes like us?"

"We are always interested in our own kind," Morgance said, dropping to the dirt and smoothing her skirt around her legs.

"Owein isn't your kind. He has alteration spells, yes, but not the sort I imagine that hawk possesses."

"Yes, I can see that, but I spoke of *you.* You speak to them. Animals."

"Only animals?" Sean asked.

Merritt chewed on the inside of his lip, wondering how much to share.

"You have nothing to fear from us. We might not like the rule of Britain," Morgance murmured, "but neither are they our enemies.

We simply ask for peace and freedom—not much different from the pilgrims who settled your own country. We mean no ill to the Crown or the Leiningens."

"Do they know you're here?" Merritt asked.

"Land cannot be owned," Sean countered. "At least, it shouldn't be."

Merritt searched his face, seeing no malice there. Letting his shoulders relax, he said, "I can also hear them." He tipped his head toward the tree Fallon had been perched in. "They're not saying much. Still waking up."

Morgance smiled. "How wonderful. You would fit in with us well. Teach us what you know."

He snorted. "I don't know much. Only discovered the abilities some months ago."

"Oh?" Her brows rose. "Perhaps we could teach you, instead."

"Let the children play," Sean said, crossing the trail to sit on a half-rotted log. "And we'll talk. If we only accomplish one thing today, it will be to earn your trust."

"You're one of us, Merritt Fernsby, even if you don't live the way," Morgance offered. "A man who can hear the thoughts of the creatures around him can never truly step out of their world."

Chapter 20

March 6, 1847, London, England

"It bothers me," Hulda clarified, again sitting at the cluttered table in the back room of Mr. Griffiths's office. "It was a critical occurrence. Someone was injured, nearly killed! Why did I not foresee it?"

"Even if you had"—Professor Griffiths adjusted his glasses—"you would not have been able to do anything about it. Attempting to change the future is all part of the future."

"But I could have been prepared," she countered, stabbing the table with her index finger. "The repair crews could have been ordered, a doctor would be on call!"

He smiled at her. "Such is the bane of an augurist, Miss Larkin. Would have, should have, could have. They will plague your life. Sometimes, the gift of future-seeing is *not* seeing."

Hulda sunk back in her chair, then remembered herself and straightened her spine. "I understand the philosophy. I do. But I feel so *useless*. I'd rather not be an augurist at all than such a pathetic one."

"*Not* pathetic," he said firmly, and Hulda immediately felt chastened. "Magic is a gift, however small. But that's why you're here. Let's see what we can do with what you have. Make the most of it. Anything else of interest?"

That vision of Merritt and the nude woman rose in her thoughts; she quickly began counting in Latin to banish it. "When I do see things, they're often quite random," she offered instead. *One problem at a time.* She didn't want to flush—or worse, cry—in front of this esteemed man. "Such as, oh, a plate breaking in three days' time. Or I once had a vision of myself being flustered from losing a pen. It happened that afternoon."

Professor Griffiths nodded, and it was a relief to have another person instantly understand the vexation of the thing without further explanation. "Soothsaying is often tied to your own thoughts. When you read a pattern determined by another individual, it is that individual's future you see more often than not. But, well . . ." He rubbed his chin. "Say you are entering a pie into a county fair. It's heavy on your mind. It's important to you to win the blue ribbon, so to speak. And so, when you peer into the tea leaves of a neighbor, you might see her experience at the fair, such as, oh, petting the head of a lamb. As opposed to a vision of the chimney in her home collapsing. The chimney is arguably the more life-affecting incident, but your own concerns direct the augury elsewhere."

Hulda scribbled down notes in a clean ledger she'd purchased specifically for these lessons. "That does seem consequent." Merritt was always on her mind, as was their wedding. Never a fear of his fidelity, however . . . not until now.

He wouldn't have relations with another woman. He won't!

"Are you all right?"

Hulda blinked. "Yes. I was just pondering something."

He nodded. "How far into the future do your visions usually stretch?"

"A few weeks or so. On occasion, months. Never more than a year," she answered. Thus why she'd never seen Merritt when she was in her twenties and despairing of her spinsterhood. Or seen herself as director of BIKER.

"Let's try some exercises." The professor pulled himself closer to the table. "I want you to close your eyes."

Hulda felt silly doing so, but she wanted to learn, and so she clasped her hands in her lap and obeyed.

"I want you to think of what you'll do when this exercise is over. Your best guess is fine. And then what you'll do after that; leave this office, most likely. And then, whatever comes after that, regardless of how inconsequential. We're going to flow with the entirety of the day. Now we're approaching lunch. What will be served? What will you eat, and how much?"

Hulda pictured all of it as keenly as she could. By the time she mentally went to bed, she felt as though she could lie her head down right there and fall asleep. But then Professor Griffiths had her think it all through again backward, from bedtime to this exercise. Then forward again, only this time imagining very unlikely things. Hulda imagined her skirt ripping on her way out, then heavy snowfall, an Italian luncheon with children all under the age of three, Owein being moved into the body of a hippopotamus, Merritt shaving his head, her learning to play the harp in a matter of minutes, and then falling asleep on a bench out in the garden.

Then, as before, she imagined it backward, all the way back to the office.

By the time she opened her eyes, the late-morning light seemed too bright. Professor Griffiths watched her with a pleased expression.

"Most certainly my best student. Now, let's try focusing on a specific incident you *know* will be in your future."

The first thing that came to mind was her wedding.

Professor Griffiths set out an array of sticks, some as short as her pinky, others as long as a cubit. They were flat, with one side dark and the other light. He handed them to Hulda, and at his direction, she scattered them across the table.

"Let your vision go out of focus," he said softly. "Let your thoughts revolve around that future event."

She thought of Blaugdone Island. Of Merritt. Wondered what he might wear. She had her dress ready; it was a rich blue with lace trim, the kind of frippery she normally didn't prefer, but it was a wedding after all. She'd yet to show it to anyone or don it. She tried to imagine the flowers, the guests, the pastor. For a moment, she felt a prickle in her mind, almost like a sneeze—as though her augury were about to kick in but refused at the last minute.

She tried again. No luck. *But the wedding happens! This means nothing.*

Right?

Leaning away from the sticks, Hulda rubbed her temples. "I'm afraid it's not working."

"That's quite all right." He gathered the sticks and offered them to her. "Let's try again."

She accepted the bundle, then paused. "Might I try something?"

He gestured to the table. "All yours."

Hulda reached into her black bag, pushed aside a little wrapped gift she'd brought from the States, and retrieved her receipt book—the one with all her notes on the goings-on at Cyprus Hall. She opened it to her most cluttered page and set it on the table before her.

"What's this?" Professor Griffiths inquired.

"Some personal sleuthing," she said, glad she'd written everyone's name either too tightly to be easily read or in code. *Briar*, for instance, was *Bush* here.

She took her time to look over her notes—if there was anything she'd learned in these lessons, it was not to rush—and tossed the sticks again. Most fell onto the open pages. A few scattered onto the table, and one dropped to the floor. She left it there.

Letting the sticks and notes blur to her eyes, she considered the breakfast room and the bedroom. How her dowsing rods picked up on nothing. The failed exorcism. The family, and Blightree. The stolen marriage contract—

The magic swelled, swallowing the receipt book and the sticks and replacing them with an onslaught of images.

A pen scraping the bottom of an ink vial.

A shod foot as it came down, as though running.

A bead, or perhaps a marble, rolling across the floor.

William Blightree, with tears in his eyes.

They happened in such quick succession she couldn't garner more details than that. The images rushed her in the space of half a breath, then vanished.

"You saw something." It wasn't a question.

Hulda paused, trying to cement the strange vision in her mind before looking up. "Yes, several things." She repeated all of them, if only to better remember.

Two deep lines appeared between Professor Griffiths's eyebrows. "Interesting. A cluster vision. Those are rare. Whatever this is"—he pointed to the receipt book—"it must be complex."

"Very," Hulda agreed. "If you'll give me a moment."

"Of course."

With her pencil, Hulda jotted down each vision on the following page of the book, recording any other details she could recall. The morning light in the room where she'd found the ink vial. The floor where the little sphere had fallen—there'd been some cream carpeting, but in the distance, hardwood. The shoe had a large gold buckle on it. It was brown . . . or perhaps maroon? With a slight heel. And Mr. Blightree. His head was bent, nodding just barely.

The image of him stuck with her the most. Why was he so melancholy, and what did it have to do with her notes, her sleuthing?

"I've time for another exercise," the professor offered.

Hulda closed the book. "Thank you, but . . ." She paused, her mind going blank.

"But," he encouraged her.

She shook her head. "But . . . I thought I had something. I can't for the life of me recall . . ." She reached into her bag for her planner.

"Such is the second bane of being an augurist." Professor Griffiths stood. "I can't tell you how often I've forgotten something on the stove or missed a class because I had a vision."

She followed suit. "It is nice to know I'm not alone."

"But of course. I think we have quite a few things in common, Miss Larkin. Should I still expect you tomorrow?"

She nodded. "If you're available, yes. I'll be in town."

Clasping his hands behind his back, he said, "I look forward to it. Allow me to walk you to a cab."

She did.

For a moment, upon his return, Merritt thought the hired guards were having a foray in the east yard of Cyprus Hall; they were all clustered together, speaking in low tones. Someone even had a hound on a leash. As he neared, however, he recognized Prince Friedrich among them and, even closer, noted about half the men were not contractors, but police.

"Lordy," he muttered, quickening his pace. The chill had seeped into his boots—he'd spoken to the Druids for about an hour—and his toes smarted with each step. What terrible thing had happened this time?

Owein panted but kept up with him. One of the policemen indicated Merritt, causing Prince Friedrich to turn around.

To Merritt's bewilderment, the man grinned.

"Glad to see you! I have half a dozen servants searching for you both." He nodded to Owein. "I've good news."

Merritt stopped, searching the faces around him. Some of the policemen had already headed back for the front drive. "Good news?"

He nodded. "We've found a suspect. Well, *they've* found a suspect." He gestured to the others. "He's already been loaded up and carried away."

"We have a few questions for you, Mr. Fernsby," said the constable.

Who? Owein's tail wagged.

"Who?" Merritt parroted.

The constable flipped through papers in a binder. "Do you know a man by the name of Benjamin Dosett?"

"I . . . can't say I do." He glanced to Owein, who merely shook his head. "Is he American?"

"No, British," the constable replied. They were meeting so often, Merritt really should learn the man's name. "This is his second arrest."

"Some of the hired men found him snooping around the west wood," Prince Friedrich supplied.

That gave Merritt pause. What if he and Owein had decided to walk west, instead of east, that morning?

"He's not a Druid, is he?" Merritt asked.

Both Prince Friedrich and the constable exchanged a glance. "No," the constable said after a beat. "He's a revolutionary. Mr. Fernsby, have you attended any Chartist meetings since arriving here?"

"I beg your pardon?"

"Merely asking questions."

"No," Merritt clarified, "I mean, what is a Chartist?"

Prince Friedrich answered, "They're part of a political movement that's gained popularity in recent years. Reformists, to put it delicately."

"I think I'd remember that," he said with a soft chuckle, which wasn't well received. "But no, I haven't. This Dosett fellow is one?"

"A radical one, yes." The constable flipped another page and asked a few more questions, but none of them were able to find any sort of connection between Merritt and this man. Still, the constable walked Merritt personally to the prison wagon that had been brought around and let him look through the bars. The single occupant, a man who appeared to be in his midtwenties, glared at Merritt before staring down at his feet.

"I'm sorry," Merritt apologized, "I don't know him."

After the wagon pulled away, the constable explained, "I believe you, Mr. Fernsby. There have been a handful of attacks made against noble estates in the name of *equality*"—he scoffed as he said it—"many by revolutionaries we've been able to track to a specific Chartist organization."

Merritt mulled over that for a second. "So you're saying it's not personal."

"I need to question this man to see if I can find any other accomplices he might have had, but no, I doubt it was personal. Unless you wrote a book that might have stirred discontent among readers such as Dosett?"

Merritt blinked. "You know I'm an author?"

The constable sighed. "From our initial interview, yes."

"Oh. Right." That had been after the bedroom crumbled. *Lots* of personal questions. Merritt really should learn the man's name. "But . . . no. I can't say my fiction is any more inspirational to revolution than the next book on the shelf." But that *would* make for good publicity.

The constable nodded. "I'll send an officer if any more questions arise. Good day." He tipped his hat and made his way back to Prince Friedrich.

So we're okay now? Owein asked.

Letting out a long breath, Merritt planted his hands on his hips. "I suppose so."

Chapter 21

I'm excited to see them again, Owein said as he and Merritt wound their way through Cyprus Hall, careful to avoid the crew of men hastily repairing the breakfast room. They passed another hired patrolman; would they be relieved of their duty, or would Lady Helen keep them on in case another "revolutionary" came by? Not that Merritt condoned the violence in any way, but he could certainly understand why a poor man—and Benjamin Dosett was poor, judging by the clothes he'd worn—would be frustrated by the privileges granted to a small elite class while others toiled endlessly for their bread. There were a lot of similarities between the States and England, but there were a lot of differences, too, and Merritt found himself noticing them in stark contrast.

As for the Druids, to whom Owein referred, Merritt believed they were genuine. His interest in them certainly was. However, that outing, plus the walk, plus his questioning had left him very cold, and Merritt wanted nothing more at that moment than a fire. Owein, of course, seemed completely unaffected by temperature and recent arrest alike.

Still, it was good to see him with friends, even if one was a hawk. But was tomorrow too soon to reunite with these folk? Granted, they didn't live here. There would be only so many opportunities before they departed for Ireland.

"We'll go," Merritt agreed, "if the Leiningens don't have need of us." He imagined there'd be some sort of church attendance and luncheon on the morrow, but Lady Helen hadn't disclosed any plans in particular.

The door to the blue drawing room was ajar, so Merritt slipped in, instantly relaxing when warm air hugged him. Then tensing when he spotted Briar on the sofa. She sat with Cora, a book in her lap.

"I didn't expect you," he blurted, then politely amended, "that is, I didn't mean to interrupt." He dipped his head. "I'll . . . go upstairs."

"You're quite all right," Briar said, gesturing to chairs by the fire. "Your nose is red; might as well warm up here. I'm hardly going to bite you. Have the police left?"

She asked so casually Merritt wondered if law enforcement came by regularly. "They have." Doing as directed, he removed his coat and slung it over the back of the armchair near the fire. Owein padded in as well. *Hi, Cora.*

"Owein also sends his greetings."

Cora smiled. "Did you both go on a walk?"

"Yes, a rather long one." Merritt rubbed his hands together. The fire was burning brightly, slowly driving back the chill. "But perhaps not as long a trip as you took," he suggested, looking at Briar, who frowned.

"It's much more pleasant in the spring," Cora offered, then rubbed her eyes. "My apologies, I don't mean to be rude, but I was about to retire. All this excitement has left me tired."

Briar put a hand on her shoulder. "Go on, then."

She stood, offered a brief curtsy to both Merritt and Owein, and departed the room. Merritt watched her go. Such a quiet girl, save for that last conversation they'd had. He wondered what had prompted her to open up. Was it dependent on her health, or how well she knew a person? She was certainly being patient with the entire affair. More so than her sister.

As though hearing his train of thought, Briar said, "She is still young and naïve. She doesn't wholly understand what our parents are signing her up for."

Merritt kneaded his hands together. "I don't think anyone really knows. Not to repeat myself, but there is more at stake here than what pertains to you and your sister."

The noblewoman frowned.

Merritt steeled himself. "Where is the contract, Briar?"

She scoffed. "Now I suppose you'll interrogate me, too, hm? I've gotten plenty enough of it for the day. Why do you think I've escaped here?" She looked away, perturbed, but her expression relaxed after a moment. "I have solicitors of my own, you know. Victoria is the queen, but she is not the law, not entirely. I will do what I must to protect my own. Surely you understand that."

Merritt considered her a moment. "And where is the contract *now*?"

She flipped a curl of hair over her shoulder. "Dear me, I believe I misplaced it." Her tone was dry and flat, and her eyes dared him to challenge her.

Goodness, Lady Helen must have been exhausted, dealing with this.

I think we should leave, he pushed to Owein, but just as he moved to stand, Briar blurted, "If I could get Owein a body without a betrothal contract, would you accept it?"

She looked at him, not Owein.

Owein lifted his head. *Yes.*

"Yes," Merritt repeated. "If it were morally come by."

She blinked. "Well . . . that is a relief."

"Is it?"

"That it's not about power or money," Briar affirmed. "Though if I'm completely honest, I've no idea how to go about it, especially when the *lineage* is at stake." Her tone took on a sour note. "My parents are quite decided. Which is why I will continue pressing the queen."

Merritt watched the fire dance for a moment. "I find it interesting that you waited for Cora to leave when discussing the matter," he said carefully, "but don't give a second thought to Owein's presence."

Her gaze shot to Owein. She sniffed.

"He's human. Just as human as I am. He simply doesn't look it." Merritt reached over and stroked between Owein's ears. "He was a boy who became a house, who was torn from his walls and shoved inside a dog. His own body was taken at the age of twelve." He sighed. "What he wants, what *we* want, is the opportunity for him to live the life he lost too young."

Briar's mouth twisted. She mulled over that for a few beats. "I do appreciate you being open to the discussion, unlike my parents. It is my understanding that Owein is quite old. Not merely a boy."

Owein laid his head on his paws, pulling from Merritt's grip. Merritt said, "It's complicated." Seeking another line of conversation, he asked, "What were you reading?"

"Nothing my mother would care for," she said, turning back a page. "It's American fiction called *A Pauper in the Making*. It's different. Rather interesting. Perhaps considered a little grotesque by polite society."

Merritt couldn't help grinning. "I don't think it's grotesque. Perhaps *enthralling*."

She glanced at him. "Have you read it?"

"I wrote it."

Her eyes widened. She turned to the cover and checked the author's name. "My goodness. Right there. Merritt J. Fernsby." A laugh choked out of her. "What are the odds?" She studied the cover a second longer before turning back to her place. "It *is* enthralling."

"No need to appease me," he offered.

"I think I've made it clear my goal is not to appease either of you," she said, though not in an unfriendly manner. "I don't think I could ever write a book, but I do enjoy reading." She paused, looking him over much as she had the book in her hands. "It's a pity you didn't come around sooner. You've probably enough magic to appease even my family, and then at least I'd have someone to discuss books with."

Merritt wasn't prone to flushing, but the fire did suddenly seem a few degrees warmer. He thought to make a comment about her being a little young for him, but it died on his tongue.

Fortunately, Briar, unruffled, added, "I do hope you and Miss Larkin will be happy."

Owein lifted his head, ears up.

An awkward chuckle escaped him as he rubbed the back of his neck. "Th-Thank you. I think—"

Lady Helen walked in just then, hip hitting the door and opening it wide. "I've come up with the most splendid idea!" She passed a peeved glance at Briar before sitting as far from her as the room would allow. "Now that this predicament has cleared up, we shall have a distraction. A tour of the Tower of London and a grand luncheon! Outside, if the weather cooperates, but of course we won't hold our breath for that, unless I can hire some wizards to make it pleasant for us. I think it will be a great opportunity for Owein to get to know us and the royal family a little better, and to get out of this dreary house. As early as Monday, I think. Wouldn't that be pleasant?"

Rising to his paws, Owein asked, *What's the Tower of London?*

Before Merritt could ask, Briar said, "I'm afraid I will not be in attendance. I'm scheduled for Buckingham."

Lady Helen's good mood instantly evaporated. "Really, Briar. Even if you're still set on that fool's errand, must you bring it up in front of our *guests*?" She shot an apologetic look to Owein, then to Merritt. "All the better you don't come! As I said, I want the outing to be *pleasant*."

Briar closed the book and stood. "If you'll excuse me."

Lady Helen waved a hand in dismissal. "I think it would be quite fun. And a great way to learn a thing or two before our dinner Tuesday night. Did I mention that? I'm having some cousins over, and"—she glanced behind her to ensure Briar had departed—"I've invited the queen herself, ha! Whether or not Her Majesty can attend is undecided; she's a very busy woman, but it was *she* who had the brilliant idea of arranging this match, however much my eldest daughter wants to deny it. As for the Tower of London, we've turned it into a royal agglomeration in recent years, after filling in that dreadful moat. Some of the Crown Jewels are kept there, as well as a display of our magical history I think you'll find most interesting. And the armaments are certainly impressive. Now, in regard to food, Mr. Mansel, do tell me if you have a preference between fowl. I mean to make up for every harrowing happenstance that has occurred under my roof and work my way into both of your good graces! My cook has a most excellent pheasant recipe, but it's come to my attention that canines cannot consume raisins—"

Once Lady Helen moved on to a general discussion of weddings and noble life, Merritt slipped from the drawing room—after making sure Owein was comfortable, of course. Owein had his letterboard, not that replying was particularly essential when Lady Helen got into one of her orations. He'd come back for his coat later. He was warm again, thank goodness, and had other things on his mind he needed to address.

Fate sensed he needed to address them as well, for the number-one item on his list walked through the front doors just as he entered the vestibule. Hulda nodded politely to the footman letting her in but didn't look up enough to notice Merritt. Seemed she had quite a bit on her mind as well.

He met her near the stairs. "How was it?"

She started, hand flying to her chest. "Oh, Merritt. Well enough, though my brain feels like it's been filtered through a very fine sieve."

"You were gone awhile." They started up the stairs.

"I stopped at LIKER." She patted her black bag. "And Professor Griffiths had me do a number of exercises, and when it comes to the mind, nothing can be rushed. Granted, augury isn't strictly of the mind, like psychometry, but it's what's used . . . oh, I don't need to detail it to you." She rubbed her forehead.

"Headache?" he asked.

"Only a small one. It will pass."

"I can get you some tea. Or ring for tea. You ring for tea here. Did you know that?"

She rewarded him with a small smile. "I am aware, yes. I used to be one of the people rung."

"They arrested the man who's been wreaking havoc on the house. Well, suspected of."

Merritt hadn't quite gotten the words out before Hulda whirled on him. "What? Who? When?"

Standing one stair below her, he summed up what had happened with the constable, who Benjamin Dosett was, and also that he had no recollection of the man.

Hulda considered this a moment. "I suppose that bedroom is closer to the drive. Easier to access, if he meant only to make a statement."

"If I were making a statement"—Merritt touched her elbow and guided her up the stairs—"I'd leave a note. Broken windows and such have a habit of being lost in translation."

Atop the stairs, they passed through the lobby toward the visitors' morning room, which was a little dark, given the time of day, but empty. Hulda pushed open the door and hung a dark-orange bag half the size of Merritt's palm on an unlit brazier—one of the promised wards. "If he's only a *suspect*," she said, "then I might as well stick to the original plan." The original plan being stones and wards throughout the house, to either stop or detect anyone trying to use magic. Lady Helen had banned her family from doing any spells without express permission.

A fire was going within the hearth, but not as robustly as the one in the blue drawing room. Merritt added only a quarter log to it as Hulda sat at the edge of a sofa, spine erect and hands daintily folded in her lap.

"Hulda, darling"—Merritt took a seat next to her and pulled one of her hands loose—"there is no one here to witness your weariness. Relax."

Letting out a long breath, Hulda let her perfect posture go and leaned back on the sofa. "There's just so much going on."

"And so much of it is finished, for now."

She sighed. "I am not one for naps, but I'm sorely tempted."

"If it will make you feel better, you should." He shrugged. "No one here has a real occupation. Napping seems to be a favorite pastime."

"They are not *without* occupation, it's merely different."

"Very different," Merritt agreed. "Lady Helen wants us all to go on a tour of the Tower of London Monday, and she's currently describing Owein's son-in-law duties to him."

Hulda snorted. "I do feel a little sorry for him."

"I think he likes it. People don't talk directly to him that often."

She sobered. "That is true."

"But"—he opened her hands and massaged her palm with his thumbs—"we did meet some interesting folk on our walk. Are you familiar with Druids?"

That had Hulda sitting up. "You met Druids?"

He took that as a yes. "Four of them, two children—well, I assume the hawk was a child—and two adults, a man and a woman. Kegan, Fallon, Morgance, and Sean. Friendly folk. Also, apparently we are the most entertaining thing in the Western Hemisphere, because they've *also* been tracking us. No offers of marriage, though."

He went on to describe the meeting in detail. "And they want to see us again tomorrow."

Hulda mulled over this. "Whatever for?"

Merritt shrugged. "They seem to see us as kin because of our 'Druidic abilities.' Honestly, it's not very different from the Genealogical Society and the desire to preserve and extend magical lines."

"Owein is not a Druid," Hulda pointed out. "And you are certainly not permitted to extend any magical lines with anyone outside this room."

He smiled. Wondered if that vision of hers was popping into her head again or not. He didn't ask. "I've no desire to. Outside of this room, that is."

The faintest dusting of pink crossed her nose. How long would it be, Merritt wondered, before Hulda grew used to his teasing, and such fetching blushes became extinct?

"You should come," he offered. "Tomorrow."

She sighed. "I would like to. It's been a long time since my last conversation with a Druid. But I'm not sure I can spare the time. I have to return to BIKER soon, and these lessons from Professor Griffiths are already proving useful; I want to get in as many as I can while I can. And if Cyprus Hall is safe again, I need to utilize the spare time. I suppose that's one benefit of this nonsense with the contract. More time." She scoffed. "But more so—" She reached into her skirt pocket and withdrew a telegram. "Stones and wards aren't the only thing I found at LIKER. Myra sent this."

He took and unfurled the paper. This new book is interesting. You should read it.

"Starting a book club?" he asked.

Rolling her eyes, Hulda retrieved the paper and shoved it into her pocket. "She won't say it right out." She glanced at the door, but they were still alone. Still, she continued at a quieter volume: "Myra's discovered something new and interesting at the facility. Something she wants to talk to me about. Nothing monumental, I'm sure—not this early on, and not with our—her—limited resources. But something consequential enough that it spurred her to contact me here. Perhaps the start of a road that leads to what she's been hunting."

Merritt nodded. Murmured, "I wonder what Blightree would think of this."

"We will not tell him," she whispered. "I don't want to discuss it outside the challenge of obtaining approval for a lab dedicated to the study of magic, which I'm presently querying." She eyed him, a look that said, *This is all I know, and all I want to know.* Smoothing her skirt, she added, "I considered querying the British government as well. If we were approved, we could move the facility here, though it would be difficult to maintain privacy while doing so, and honestly, there isn't a government in Europe more open to experimentation than that of the United States. But either way, it will be a slow process, and the hebetude of it all makes me nervous."

"Pardon?"

She met his eyes. It took her a beat to understand. "The languidness. The waiting. The longer we wait for answers—"

"The more anxious you feel, of course," he finished. "Perhaps you could move it farther west. Won't have to worry about the law, then."

"For a time, perhaps." She turned her hand around and clasped his fingers. "But sooner or later, secrets catch up with everyone." She looked away, not at anything in particular. Almost like she was future-seeing, but not quite.

She was thinking about that bizarre vision of him with another woman. He knew it, somehow.

With his free hand, he touched her chin, encouraging her to meet his gaze. "Hulda. You trust me, don't you?"

She searched his eyes a moment. "I do."

He nodded. It would have to be enough.

Hulda did retire to her room for a nap, although she did so only after placing some wards and stones. The guards were still about, as Lady Helen intended to keep four of them on in case another revolutionary came knocking.

Once in her room, Hulda rang for tea. And while she waited for it to arrive, she debated whether or not she could sleep on her hairpins. Napping was not conducive to good hair. Unfortunately, it *was* conducive for headache relief, so out the pins came and off the dress went.

She drank her tea in a plush chair by the window, feet pulled up, sipping slowly. *What is your secret, Merritt?* That was the thought that had come to her in the morning room. She'd chided herself for it. She hadn't lied, either—she *did* trust Merritt. But her augury was also never wrong.

She reminded herself, yet again, that Merritt had been entirely clothed in the vision. That fact was somewhat helpful.

Tea half finished, she glanced to her black bag, set at the foot of her bed. Putting down the teacup, she crossed to it and pulled out her receipt book with all her notes regarding the goings-on in Cyprus Hall.

Flipping toward the back of the book, she wrote new notes—everything she knew about the vision, and everything she'd thought since the vision. It took longer to jot it all down than she'd expected.

Then, making herself comfortable at the small table, she set the open book before her, took off her ring, and laid it on top—something of Merritt's, technically, that might help with the reading. Eyes closed, she practiced one of the exercises Professor Griffiths had led her through, focusing all her attention on Merritt. She replayed her first trip to Whimbrel House, recalling the disheveled manner in which he'd answered the door and pled for her to *get him out*. The bathroom nearly flattening them. The dejected look of him in that hole in the kitchen. The gradual way he'd started to light up whenever he saw her. Untying him in that dreadful basement in Marshfield *in her underwear*. Their first kiss. He'd been so gentle, so perfect.

The way he'd shoved Mr. Baillie up against the wall after the hysterian hurt her. Ice skating. Prison sitting . . . *that* had been a low, though it was also the first time they'd discussed marriage, and Hulda had nearly wept at the idea that he wanted her. Running off to the docks, hiding from the police, finding a new normal once Myra cleared everything up. Lunches in Boston and dinners at Whimbrel House. The way his hands felt on her waist—

Hulda opened her eyes and rolled her set of dice. Nothing. Reread her notes, rolled again—

Merritt filled her vision. He was shadowed, like someone stood over him, but his gaze was fixed downward on something else—something Hulda couldn't make out. And he was panicked. Breathing hard, sweating, tense.

Something rolled across the floor.

A shod foot came down.

Hulda's heart thudded in her chest, and the vision dissipated as quickly as it had come.

Picking up her engagement ring with trembling fingers, Hulda whispered, "What's going to happen, Merritt?"

But she didn't have the answers.

Chapter 22

Kegan screeched when Merritt and Owein entered the grove some two miles north of Cyprus Hall, startling a few roosting songbirds overhead. Owein bolted through the foliage, surprisingly agile, to meet up with them. Moments later, that gray hawk swooped down and perched on Kegan's shoulder. The boy didn't blink twice at the fact.

"I found fairy treasure," he announced, puffing out his chest. "Well, there's no treasure *in* it, but it's just the sort of tree a fairy would use to hide some. Want to see?"

Owein glanced up at Merritt.

"Off you go." He waved a hand. It wasn't quite as chilly today, though a steady sheet of cloud covered the sky. The Leiningens—minus Lady Briar and the baron—had headed to church, and Hulda had gone into town again, so it was as good a time as any to visit the Irish wizards. The guards had actually walked out with them a ways before heading back. Thus far, everything seemed fine.

Owein barked and ran off. A voice in his head said, *They're waiting ahead.*

Merritt startled, glancing at the hawk perched on Kegan's shoulder. Then into the trees, wondering if there were yet more Druids lurking about the woods. Well, he'd know when he'd know. Trudging ahead with far less grace than Kegan had, he did, indeed, find both Sean and Morgance beneath a thick oak tree, sharing some bread and cheese.

Morgance spotted him. "Are you hungry?"

"Perhaps a little." He found a sturdy root and sat, then accepted a piece of bread. "Thank you."

She nodded. "We don't buy and sell, back home. Everyone works and everyone gives. Everyone eats. No rank, no judgment."

"No judgment?" Merritt asked. "Whatever do you do for fun?"

Morgance paused.

Sean chuckled. "He's jesting, of course." He popped the end of a crust into his mouth. "Morgance is always looking to increase our number. We have strong men and women in our flock, but time dwindles all of us."

Morgance turned up her nose. "You make me sound like a salesman."

He tipped his head. "Forgive me."

After a few bites, Merritt asked, "Have you spied any revolutionaries in these parts recently?"

Morgance tipped her head, confused.

Merritt changed direction. "So, what did you have in mind today? Besides the sales talk and the play session." He jutted a thumb in the direction Owein had gone.

Morgance frowned at the *sales* term, but said nothing. "I wanted to teach you, actually."

Merritt lowered the bread. "Teach me? What?"

She drew her hand down the base of the oak tree's trunk. "You speak to plants. I want to show you just how great an ability that can be."

"It will be harder for you," Sean added, leaning back and folding his arms. "If I may make the assumption. The Druid lines are still relatively strong in their magic; yours will be diluted."

"And only recently discovered," Merritt reminded them. "I had many a poor night when the communion first presented itself."

Morgance and Sean exchanged a knowing glance. Perhaps insomnia was commonplace for communionists.

"The earth," Morgance went on, "is all connected. Every bit of it. Cities and railroads try to break it up, but beneath everything, there is earth. And where there is earth, there is life." She grasped Merritt's hand and placed it palm down on the root he sat upon. "The first communionist could feel her way through root systems clear to the other side of the world. Not only could she speak to flora and fauna, but she could command them, too."

"She?" Merritt asked. "I don't recall a woman among Christ's apostles."

Morgance clucked her tongue. "The Christian apostles as the incitement of magic is only a speculation, Merritt."

"Point taken. Then what is the Druid lore?"

"Druid lore is also only speculation," Sean said, earning a disapproving look from his companion. "Some say there are more than eleven doctrines of magic, but I've never seen anything to prove otherwise. Some insist there are but ten—a rounder number and more pleasant—and that augury and psychometry hail from the same progenitor. One belief is that the first communionist was not a man, but a hart."

Merritt straightened. This had the sound of an excellent story. "Really?"

Sean nodded. "His magic was full, untainted by the blood of others. He could transform into any other living thing on earth, including plants. Including humans."

"That branches into alteration," Merritt pointed out.

"In that story," Morgance cut in, "the hart is the progenitor of both. But he fell in love with a human woman and gave the ability of earthspeech to her, splitting the magic."

"Intriguing." And it was. Merritt found himself leaning closer. "And the elements? That's also Druid magic, is it not?"

Sean nodded. "The first elementist possessed ability with all four. Some say she completed four great tasks from the gods to earn each one, others say her mother gave birth to her at the center of the earth, with all four infused into her skin."

Merritt cocked an eyebrow. "I find that unlikely."

"Because the modern world limits your beliefs," Morgance said. "Were we able to stand with the progenitors, their abilities would astound us. The first soothsayer could not only see the future at will, but *change* it, even assign different fates to those around her. The first conjurer could create anything; he made ships to sail the oceans and balms to heal the sick. He even created beads for each of the first— beads that would absorb the ailments magic created so the progenitors could cast spells without consequence."

"That would be incredibly handy," Merritt said. "I wonder what he had to sacrifice to make them." The consequence of conjury was the loss of something of equal value.

"What I wouldn't give to know." Sean went on, "The first wardist made the seas. Hostilities between men grew so severe he erected a great wall that split the land into a dozen pieces, and into those chasms flowed rivers and rain."

"The first necromancer," Morgance said, "received her powers after the grave, and used them to bring herself back. She ferried lost souls back and forth, between the mortal realm and the realm beyond."

Merritt whistled. "Please tell me you have these stories written down."

"Of course." The question seemed to almost offend Morgance. "Our stories are protected, orally and in writing, writ on paper and in stone. There is much to learn among our kin. But first"—she touched his hand, the one still pressed to the oak root beneath him—"I want to show you. Speak to this tree. Cast out anything else. Focus only on it."

Merritt hesitated, but getting an encouraging nod from Sean, he did. He listened first. The oak was stirring, sensing the onslaught of spring. It moved water inside of it, readying leaves for sunshine. *Raaaaiiiinnnn,* it whispered. It had rained last night. *Driiiiiinnnnnk.*

"Close your eyes," Morgance whispered. "Sense the spirit of the tree, from its highest branches to its deepest roots." She placed her hand beside Merritt's and closed her eyes, following her own advice. Merritt followed suit. It took a moment—first, for him to take it seriously, and then for him to expand his thoughts the way she'd instructed. After several minutes, he got a sense of depth, of dark moisture. It was unlike anything he'd experienced before. Almost like . . . a voice without sound, but also without words.

"This tree's roots overlap with the next's." Morgance's whispers sounded far away. "Find where they touch. Where they harmonize."

Gradually, the sound of Merritt's breathing, of his heartbeat, melted away. He thought he'd found the place—no, two—Morgance had mentioned. Deep, dark, wet, cold. The pattern repeated over and over in his thoughts.

There was something else, a dogwood, perhaps—something with deep roots but not nearly as tall as the oaks, tangled in the underground web. Its voice blended into the trio. *Reeeaaach,* it drawled. *Reeeaaaach.*

Beings moved amidst the tangle. Merritt focused on the rhythm of their movement. Earthworms, again speaking in a manner he was unable to translate into human terms. They slid toward other roots, thick roots. A tree. Not an oak, something else. And beyond that, a fungus, singing a melody so haunting and strange he could barely understand—

His ears rang loud enough to hurt.

Gasping, Merritt ripped his hand from the tree and brought both up to cover his ears, but the ringing came from within. He winced, urging the side effect to die down.

Sean was gone. The sun was a little lower, warmer. Good heavens, how long had he been doing this? It had felt like only minutes . . .

With one cold hand he fished out his pocket watch. Gaped. *Two hours?*

How? he tried to ask, but even the ability to whisper had been stripped from him.

Morgance slowly opened her eyes and smiled. They sat like that for a full minute until her own voice returned. "It will go a little easier, with practice," she rasped.

Merritt didn't respond. He literally couldn't. So he did not point out that no amount of practice could multiply the slivers of communion in his blood, in his spirit. Nor could he explain the strange concoction of emotions swelling through him—the fear of utterly losing his voice, his hearing, the passage of time. The elation of having discovered an ability so novel and different. The uncertainty of what any of it meant or could mean, and if that was really a path he wanted to go down. It seemed like one a man could lose himself on, and Merritt had only just found so much *above* ground that brought him happiness.

Perhaps it was fortunate that he could not speak. He'd already chosen his path, and he did not think the Druid Morgance would agree with it.

Owein tumbled through the damp grass, then lay on his back, front legs curled, to stare up at the sky. It was just an off-white sheet, but if he stared long enough, there seemed to be subtle twinkles in it, like the entirety of heaven was covered in a thick coating of salt.

Kegan toppled next to him, laughing, and set his head on Owein's belly. Fallon flew above them, arced around, and flapped hard to land on the grass, where she pecked at Kegan's leg. Without comment, Kegan sat up and reached into a parcel slung over his shoulders, pulling out a homespun dress. He gathered it in his hands as though he were going to put it on, then set it next to the hawk instead. Fallon jumped into its collar and shimmied her wings into the armholes.

The bird began to grow, darken, and pop. Owein shot up to his legs—he knew that feeling. Alteration. Though he'd never used it to such an extent.

In a matter of seconds, the bird's head enlarged, wings coalesced and grew, legs thickened and stretched. Then there was a girl there, probably about Cora's age, a little odd angled, but that was the effect of the changing spell. She had dark skin, though not nearly so dark as Beth's, and long, wild black hair. Vivid green eyes. Green like the forest around them, green like melting winter and budding spring, though not quite so vibrant as the greens of summer.

After a moment, the angle in her neck popped back to place, and she looked wholly human.

You're a girl, Owein said.

Kegan laughed. "Well, she's not a hawk! Not always, just lots of the time. Otherwise she'd a—"

"Easier to travel that way," she interrupted, breaking into a grin. She spoke with the same Irish accent as Kegan.

You can hear me?

"She can't," Kegan answered. "But I can! Fallon's just a shape-shifter."

She gave him a withering stare. *Just* a shape-shifter. Before encountering the Druids, Owein had never met anyone who possessed enough alteration prowess to change their entire body. Those were different spells than he had, maybe even different percentages.

He nodded, yawned.

"Am I so boring to you?" Fallon laughed.

He shook his head. *Sorry. I just don't sleep as well as I should.* He usually made up for it with naps during the day, but Lady Helen had kept him a little too busy for much more than a snooze.

"He says he doesn't sleep well," Kegan translated.

"Why not?" She raised a black eyebrow.

Owein lowered his head, choosing not to respond.

But Kegan poked him in the ribs. "Why not?" *Why not why not why not?*

Owein nipped at him, which only made the boy giggle. *Because,* he said, and hoped to leave it at that. But two sets of eyes stared at him with the patient curiosity of children, and Owein inwardly sighed. *Because I have nightmares.*

"Because he has nightmares."

Fallon lay down in the grass on her stomach and propped her face on the heels of her hands, her head only a foot from Owein's. Her skin pebbled, but she seemed unaware of the March chill. Owein had fur to protect him. The Druids must just be used to the cold.

"What kind of nightmares?" She sounded fascinated.

A soft whine emitted from Owein's throat.

Kegan petted his back. "He doesn't have to say."

"Sure he does," Fallon challenged. "Nightmares are things that scare us. But if you stop being scared, you stop having nightmares."

"That doesn't make any sense." Kegan spoke for him.

"How does it not make sense?" She reached over and pinched him; Kegan slapped her hand away. "Remember how you were scared of those stupid green spiders?"

"Was not!"

"You'd jump whenever we saw them! Then Sean made you keep one in the corner of your room and make sure it got fed, and then you named it and called it your pet until it died."

Kegan looked away. "Sorcha was a good spider."

"See?" Fallon's eyes shot back to Owein. "So what are you scared of?"

Owein squirmed. *I'm not really afraid, I don't think. I was just . . . I'm really old. But for a lot of those years, I was alone in a dark house by myself. And the darkness is still there.*

Kegan related, growing a little hoarse as he finished.

"In the house?" Fallon asked. She must have had some skill in reading canine expressions, for she amended, "Ah, just in your dreams. In your head. I get that. I had to stay in the dark for a long time when I was little."

Owein's ears perked.

"I mean, I'm not secretly an old man." She grinned. "But one time some English soldiers were coming by and being bastards and stuff. This is when we were in Scotland."

"I hate Scotland," Kegan grumbled.

"No, you don't," she countered, and he didn't argue. Continuing on, she said, "They were being weird about who owns what, and my mum put me in this cabinet in the cellar of an old house of a friend we were visiting. Told me not to leave no matter what. She didn't want me to try and fly away on my own. I was still really little. So I stayed. For two days. Which maybe doesn't seem like a long time, but when you're in a box in a dark cellar without anything to eat, it's forever."

Were you okay? Owein asked. Kegan cleared his throat and translated.

"I mean, I'm okay now, aren't I?" She rubbed her arms as though suddenly aware of the temperature. She shrugged. "Mostly okay. But I get it." She paused. "I have an idea. I found this place a few days ago, before we found you. Let's go."

"Where?" Kegan asked.

"You'll see!" She jumped to her bare feet. "Faster to fly, but I won't leave you slowpokes behind. Hurry up, though." She took off sprinting through the grass.

Owein stood, hesitated. But Kegan followed immediately, so Owein loped behind. They picked their way through the forest for a good half hour—probably farther than Merritt would have wanted him to go—until they reached a cliff. Fallon led the way down to a place where the moss and grass peeled away to stone and earth. Across a gully, there was a small cave.

"Kegan, make us a bridge to there," Fallon pointed.

"That's far!" Kegan complained. "I'll get dizzy."

"I'll carry you."

The boy relented. He held out his hands and furrowed his brow, and Owein barked in excitement as rocks and dirt pulled up and remolded themselves against the cliff edge, making a narrow path to the cave. He'd never seen someone use earth magic before.

Just as it finished, Kegan teetered back onto his rump and held his head in his hands. He seemed to struggle to sit up straight.

Fallon, undaunted, merely put her hands under his arms and picked him up, then bent over and shimmied until Kegan made it onto her back. He had enough wherewithal to put his arms around Fallon's neck; she looped an arm around each of his legs, carrying him like a knapsack. "Let's go."

She led the way. The earthy trail held.

When they approached the cave mouth, Owein's fur stopped working. That was, now *he* felt the chill of the late-winter day. He peered inside, but couldn't see anything past three feet in.

"Let's go in."

Owein shook his head.

"Darkness isn't scary." Fallon bent her knees and shot up quickly, using the momentum to lift Kegan higher on her back. "Nothing is really scary. We just make it that way in our heads. That's what my mom said." She glanced into the cave. "She's dead now, but she wasn't scared when she died. She was brave. So I'm always going to be brave. And Owein? Life is a lot easier being brave than being scared."

Owein considered this while he stared into the shadows.

"If you're saying something, I can't hear it."

He hadn't said anything. He wasn't sure what to say.

"Hey." She waited for him to meet her gaze. "I mean, I'm not *always* brave. A lot of times I have to pretend. But pretending is kind of like practice. And the more you practice, the easier it gets. Just like those fancy girls and their push-button musical instruments."

You mean pianofortes? he asked, but she couldn't hear him, and Kegan, who was coming around, didn't translate.

"I'll stay close." She smiled, and there was something very assuring in her smile. She took the first step, then the second. The fourth took her out of the light, into the shadows where Owein's eyes couldn't penetrate.

He scratched at the ground a moment, uneasy. Then, pretending as best he could, he followed his friends into the darkness.

Chapter 23

Outside of an augury lesson, collecting one's hairs on a tabletop might seem eccentric, if not somewhat unsanitary. But Professor Griffiths's methods had proven nothing but beneficial, and so she followed this suggestion as well, snipping and scattering several hairs from the back of her head. The more she could learn of her future, the more she could protect her *now*. Finally, unfocusing her eyes, she waggled her fingers over the hairs as though she were about to perform a parlor trick.

To her utmost delight, a vision came. Of her exiting the building in the same dress she had on now. A vision just shortly in the future, but there it was!

"You're smiling." Professor Griffiths sounded amused.

Withdrawing her hands, Hulda picked up her glasses and propped them on her nose. She didn't have to focus on being unfocused when her eyes did so naturally. "It worked! I saw myself exiting this very building."

"Without any trouble, I hope."

"None at all." She'd had more visions since arriving in London than in the last month, maybe even two months, combined. "To think how much more concentrated this ability would be if I'd met you earlier!"

"It is certainly unfortunate." He held a pipe in his hand with the tip just in his mouth, though it wasn't lit. His eyes dropped down to Hulda's left hand. "When did you say you were getting married, Hulda?"

The question took her aback, as did the use of her first name. Was this the first time he'd used it? She couldn't recall. But the man had been nothing short of a blessing, especially with his willingness to meet with her on the Sabbath. "April 12," she answered.

"That's quite a ways out, still. Banns take only three weeks. Is it a complicated affair?"

"Not at all." She swept her hair up; it felt silly to have it just lying there in plain sight. "I've a lot of responsibility with BIKER. I only recently became its director; there's quite a bit to reorganize."

"Of course. I'm sure it's in most excellent hands." He reached over and collected a stack of cards upon a stack of newspapers in the crowded room beside his office. Shuffled them, then began laying them on the table face up; the cards were either black or white and had simple shapes upon their faces: circle, star, oval, square, and so on. "Remind me of his name?"

It wasn't unusual for them to share conversation during these visits, but outside of her first arrival, Professor Griffiths had never showed an interest in her upcoming nuptials. "Merritt Fernsby. He's a writer."

"A writer? That is precarious employment." He said it in a friendly tone, not looking up from the cards as he started a second row. "And he's American?"

"About as American as one can be."

He chuckled at that. "And you two went to school together, was it?"

"Hardly." She nearly snorted and inwardly congratulated herself when she didn't. "He inherited a magicked home last September and used BIKER's services to tame it."

"Only this past September?" He glanced up. "So you haven't known him long."

That gave Hulda pause. *Haven't known him long.* Many couples wed in a much shorter time frame. By all means, were it not for BIKER, they'd probably have held the ceremony before Christmas. But she also reflected on his remark about Merritt's being a writer. Yes, it wasn't a *steady* income, but Merritt lived comfortably. And Hulda's employment sealed any concern for—

For . . .

She completely lost her train of thought, and this time it wasn't a side effect of augury. Professor Griffiths was single—he was a widower. He always seemed happy to see her. He was even willing to come into the office to meet with her on a Sunday. And now he was interrogating her over her fiancé, hinting at subtle negatives . . .

Surely Gethin Griffiths wasn't . . . *interested* in her . . . was he?

Of course he isn't! What a bizarre place for her thoughts to go. *No one* was interested in Hulda, save for Merritt Fernsby. Merritt was a complete and utter anomaly in her life. Literally the only man who had ever, in all her nearly thirty-five years, returned her feelings. Merritt was kismet. The dangling carrot at the end of a *very* long rope. No one else had ever or would ever suit her.

To be fair . . . had she never met Merritt, Gethin Griffiths would certainly be the kind of man she'd aspire to know better. He was a little older, yes, but healthy and well kept, with a highly esteemed profession and keen mind. Not unlike Silas Hogwood's steward Stanley Lidgett, before Hulda realized the man was a humbugger.

Professor Griffiths laid down a third row of cards. What was it he had asked? Oh, September. "We've been through a great many ordeals together."

He simply nodded. "I do hope this Mr. Fernsby isn't causing you any undue stress."

Another pause. Why would he suggest something like that? Hulda certainly never had . . . though her upcoming vows *did* cause her some anxiety, and there was that awful vision she'd had of Merritt with another woman. She really did *try* not to dwell on it, but it was etched in her brain. She'd even dreamed about it the other—

The shapes on the cards highlighted a pattern of triangles, and Hulda's augury kicked in. Not for Professor Griffiths, who'd laid the cards, but for herself. And Merritt, being forefront on her mind, immediately swirled into it. And that was Whimbrel House, specifically the north wall of his bedroom, and he had Hulda pressed up against it with his hands under her skirts—

"Dear me." Her own voice sliced through the vision, killing it instantly, and her entire body grew hot as a whistling kettle. She fanned herself, touched cool fingers to her cheeks and neck, desperate to cool the instantaneous flush consuming her entire body. The thought of burning red as an apple in front of Professor Griffiths only increased the heat, and therefore her utter humiliation.

The professor stood. "My dear, are you quite all right?"

She cleared her throat. "I will be in just a m-moment. Some water, if you don't mind."

He thankfully swept from the room, giving Hulda an opportunity to fan herself to the extreme.

At least she was fairly certain she still had Merritt's ring on in that premonition. Oh, heaven help her. She needed to stop thinking about him *period* during these lessons. How embarrassing! Professor Griffiths was going to ask what she saw, because surely he knew she'd seen something.

Hulda stood, back erect, and focused on squirming one toe at a time, anything to put her mind elsewhere. She also started reading the headlines of the nearest errant newspaper. Much to her relief, she felt only warm by the time Professor Griffiths returned with a cup of tepid water. She accepted it gratefully and drank slowly.

"Whatever happened? Something I said?" he inquired, standing perhaps a little too close . . . *Don't think about that, or you'll redden up again.*

Lowering the cup, Hulda cleared her throat. "My apologies—"

"No need to apologize—"

"I merely saw a pattern in the cards. I'd been thinking of my sister and witnessed an event that she wouldn't care for me to have seen. Family drama." She purposefully rolled her eyes, hoping that would lend to the lie.

Thankfully, Professor Griffiths, being the gentleman he was, didn't pry. "Yes, of course. Would you like to end for today?"

Hulda checked the nearest clock. "Perhaps show me what you'd intended with these cards, and then I shall adjourn until tomorrow."

He nodded, a smile tempting his mouth, and sat down. "Now, the idea is randomization . . ."

⌒

And it was okay, Owein was saying as the sun began to sink in the English sky, disappearing beyond distant trees and the peak of a cathedral. *We went all the way to the back of the cave. I touched the stone with my nose.*

How fortunate there were no bears. Merritt chuckled. They approached Cyprus Hall and had been communing long enough that he had no voice left to him, and in his ears sounded a faint, constant ring. In truth, he'd used more communion today than any other day in his life. Mayhap he would never speak again.

It's just a color, Owein went on as Merritt entered a side door of the building. A bustling kitchen hand nodded to him before hurrying down the connecting corridor. *Darkness, I mean. It's just a part of the world. Part of life. It makes sense to me now. And my darkness . . . that's a piece of my story, like a chapter in one of your books. I'm not supposed to tear it out. It makes me stronger. It adds to what I'm facing now, and what I'll face in the future. It's part of me, just like my legs or my magic or my mind.*

Merritt paused as they came upon the gallery. One of the guards glanced at them and passed by. *That is very astute. I dare say a very mature philosophy. One that I should remember.*

Owein seemed to smile. *It's about time I grew up, I think.*

Merritt smiled. *Not too quickly, now.*

They walked a little farther, coming up on the blue drawing room. Owein said, *Hulda's here.*

Merritt listened past the steady ringing. *How can you tell?*

She has the clackiest shoes, he answered, and Merritt emitted a voiceless laugh. *Her strides always sound the same. She doesn't walk slowly to anything.*

Agreed.

They entered the grand hall. Sure enough, Hulda was there, crossing from the vestibule. She spied them immediately and clacked her way over. "Merritt, I would really like to speak with you. Privately, if it isn't too much of a bother, Owein."

Owein barked his compliance and headed to the blue drawing room.

Merritt held up a hand in an attempt to ask what was wrong.

"Perhaps we should . . ." Hulda turned about, looking for an appropriate place to converse. There were some chairs set out in the hall, near a pillar, and she gestured to them. "I suppose no one is really about on a Sunday." As though to test the claim, another guard passed in an adjoining hall. Still, she crossed toward the seating arrangement, and Merritt followed. It wasn't until they'd sat that she asked, "You're mute, aren't you?"

He shrugged his apology. With Owein gone, his larynx would begin readjusting.

She sighed. Glanced around once again—there was little Hulda disliked more than the risk of another eavesdropping on a private conversation. "I, well . . ." She flushed. "I have something I want to say, and

I find it highly incredulous, but I thought I should tell you regardless, especially before my next lesson tomorrow."

He cocked an eyebrow. This wasn't work related. Hulda never got flustered about that.

"I feel that . . . I *think* that . . ." She worried her hands. "Well, it's come to my attention . . . that is, the *possibility*, and it's only just that. An assumption—"

Merritt put his hands on both of hers, stilling them.

She drew in a deep breath. "I have an odd feeling that Professor Griffiths *might* be . . . perhaps . . . interested in me."

Merritt laughed.

She ripped her hands away. "I know it's preposterous, but hear me out—"

"Hulda." Her name was only a whisper between chuckles, but at least he could form the basic sounds. "I am not laughing because another man has noticed you. I'm laughing because you're so adorably uncomfortable about it."

She drew her brows together. "Well . . . then I suppose . . ." She sighed. "Men are not usually interested in me."

"You surround yourself with foolish men. Which I thank you for." Still a whisper.

Her posture softened. "Professor Griffiths and I get along very well. We're both academics, both augurists. I would like to think our time together has been pleasant. And today he suddenly began inquiring somewhat intensely about you, about our wedding date—"

"Inquiring how?" There was a slight squeak that time.

"How long we've known each other, which he suggested wasn't really very long at all. And he said writing isn't a reliable occupation."

"That's the truth," he murmured.

She gave him a pointed look that told him he tested her patience. "He seemed to hint that you may be a source of stress in my life, and that it was peculiar we were waiting so long to get married."

"I believe," he rasped, "both are accurate."

"Merritt Fernsby, take this seriously!"

He smiled, and when she moved to swat at him, he caught her hand and pulled her in, placing a delicate kiss on her mouth. Then, staring quite directly into her eyes, he croaked, "I do take it seriously, Hulda. And I believe you. Anyone worth their stones would see you're a catch. But I'm not *worried* about it."

She frowned. Searched his face. "Not at all?"

"Do you love me?"

Hulda never liked discussing vulnerable emotions, but they'd been together long enough that the question didn't catch her off guard. "Of course I do. That's a rubbish thing to ask."

"Then I'm not worried." He released her hand.

She considered that a moment. "In truth, I'm not sure what I wanted you to say. Dismiss it, accept it, fly off in a jealous rage . . ."

"I can try for the last once my voice returns, if you'd like." His words were already clearer and less wheezy, but he wouldn't sound quite himself for at least another quarter hour. In truth, part of him *did* want to meet this professor, to size him up. He was a man, after all. He had *protective instincts*, as Mr. Gifford at the Genealogical Society would say. But he and Hulda were perfectly shaped cogs in a slightly eccentric clock. His future was and always would be with her.

She bit down on a smile. "I suppose it's too late for a stroll."

"I've been strolling all day." To punctuate that, he stretched out his legs. "But I think you'd be interested to hear what the Druids told me about root systems. Perhaps I could interest you in a short walk to check our wards, and then in a library getaway until Lady Helen summons us for supper?"

Hulda smiled. "I would like that very much."

Chapter 24

With no more attacks upon the house and the grounds clear of revolutionaries, the tour of the Tower of London commenced immediately
after breakfast the next morning, the group having traveled via the
Leiningen family's exquisite coaches rather than the fast but more public
kinetic tram. Lady Helen started the tour herself as soon as they reached
the river Thames. The boxy fortress came into view as they crossed
Westminster Bridge.

Merritt whistled softly, pressing his temple to the window to get
a better look. Owein sat beside him, while Hulda and Ladies Helen
and Cora sat across from them. Prince Friedrich, Baron von Gayl, and
Mr. Blightree were riding in a separate carriage. As promised earlier,
Lady Briar had not come along on the tour, nor had she come down
for breakfast.

Merritt had to admit that London had a sort of ancient dazzle-
ment about it. Nothing in the States was as old or as regal as the things
they passed, and he had a funny feeling they never would be. America
was new and innovative, always looking to build quickly and expand,
while England was a place that dug its roots deeper and deeper, so that
nothing—a conqueror, a tsunami, an asteroid from space—could ever
wipe it out.

"—Norman military architecture," Lady Helen said with pride, as though she herself had commissioned the castle. "The other additions, there and there, were added in the thirteenth and fourteenth centuries."

She explained more about the fortress, hardly pausing long enough to take a breath, until the carriages pulled into an elaborate carriage house and servants in a livery Merritt didn't recognize came to escort them out. There was a bit of a chill in the breeze, so Merritt buttoned his coat up to his chin, then offered his elbow to Hulda. *Are you cold?* he asked Owein.

I'm all right.

Lady Helen didn't seem to feel the temperature as they approached the Tower of London—which was really several towers—whereas her daughter hunkered down in her cloak. There were quite a number of guards standing on and around the fortress, which the lady remarked upon only seconds after Merritt thought it. "We don't plan on any wars anytime soon." She chuckled. "But there are valuable things within, so the tower is protected. You'll note a few men in blue—they are from the Queen's League of Magicians. Owein, you would be eligible to join their ranks, once you secure a human form. They are very particular. Even my Cora can join when she's eighteen, though she hasn't shown a lick of interest in it. I can't blame her. It's not a very feminine occupation, though there are women in the ranks. Perhaps I would have joined had I not been married so young. Both Friedrich and the baron are members."

"Not active," Prince Friedrich said, hands clasped behind his back. He'd been in a quiet conversation with his son-in-law, but still caught his wife's words. Lady Cora said nothing on the matter, merely walked in the back, taking in the sights with her large blue eyes. Owein dropped back to walk beside her.

"The moat was filled in just last year," Lady Helen continued as they passed what Merritt assumed *used* to be the moat. There was a large number of armed men staring at them, which made him walk a little stiffly, but none stopped them; Lady Helen must have sent word ahead when she'd arranged all this. "There were issues with it, disease and other nonsense." She swept the idea away with a flick of her wrist.

Dipping his head toward Hulda, Merritt whispered, "I wish I could dismiss disease with a swipe of my hand."

She pinched his bicep. "Please behave yourself."

He grinned at her, taking in the grand walls as they passed through them. Lady Helen pointed out the construction of barracks in the inner ward, but insisted they weren't "important" and should be ignored, then launched into a long list of historical sieges upon the tower, occasionally corrected by her husband when she muddled the dates or, in one case, invented a siege that had never happened.

"There were no Spaniards," Prince Friedrich insisted.

Lady Helen dismissed him just as she had the moat diseases. "I shall look it up when we return home. Really, Friedrich." She scoffed, then dove into the imprisonment of Anne Boleyn.

"Perhaps," Merritt said quietly to Hulda, "I should write a novel about Henry VIII."

"Perhaps you should write something a little sunnier," she suggested.

He glanced over his shoulder, checking on Owein and Cora, who followed close behind. It was unfortunate Cora didn't have communion spells so the two could speak. But Cora caught his eye and smiled softly. "Is he saying something?"

Merritt looked at Owein.

Um, he started. *The history is . . . fascinating.*

Merritt relayed it, and Cora gave a polite nod.

Inside the tower was surprisingly cold, but then again, it was composed mainly of stone, and it was early March in London. Lady Helen now detailed how the tower had morphed from a royal residence to a house of munitions. They approached an armory, also guarded, but they were allowed to peek in and act appropriately impressed. Merritt nodded to one of the guards, who made no effort in word or expression to reply. Lady Helen launched into a one-sided discussion of the English Civil War as they took the steps up, but Merritt found himself studying the walls, imagining the lives of the people who'd lived there long ago, and how maybe it *would* be interesting to write a story that took place in a castle. *American Castle* had an interesting ring to it, as a title.

Hulda's pace slowed, and between their tour guide's breaths, she asked, "Lady Helen . . . have those shoes always been in your possession?"

Lady Helen paused and pulled her skirt back, revealing modest women's shoes, deep maroon in appearance, with a slight heel. "Indeed, I bought them just last year. Why do you ask? Would you like a pair?"

Hulda pinched the inside of Merritt's arm, which was how he recalled her telling him about a cluster vision she'd had during her sessions with Griffiths. One of them had involved a shoe of that color. *Interesting,* he thought.

"Oh yes," Hulda lied, "but forgive my intrusion. Please continue."

Lady Helen beamed and held up her hands to stop the rest of the procession. "Now, this is the really fascinating part. Up ahead are the Crown Jewels and the wizardry artifacts. I've been instructed to have us all walk single file and keep our hands behind our backs. But it really is such a treat that we get to walk this hall!"

The group did as instructed; Merritt let Hulda, Owein, and Lady Cora walk in front of him. He took up the back, and not surprisingly, an armed guard—this one in red, called a "yeoman"—tailed them. They passed an impressive array of jewelry that must be worth a *fortune*, then approached the coronation regalia, and the baron actually took over to explain how the different items were used in a royal coronation. The sovereign's scepter was especially impressive, as was Saint Edward's Crown, the frame of which was solid gold and adorned with semiprecious stones, "One for each doctrine of magic," Baron von Gayl explained, "and then some."

"Now, the wizardry artifacts." Lady Helen faced forward, but Merritt could hear her smile. *These* Merritt paid close attention to, because before meeting the Druids, he hadn't even known they existed. Hulda, too, seemed fascinated by the brief display, while Owein complained that he couldn't see.

The first was a delicate tube, almost like a short, wide straw. It appeared to be made of glass, but Lady Helen reported it was neither glass nor crystal; no one knew what material composed it. Believed to be from the first generations of water elementists, the tube could be used by anyone to draw water from the surrounding air, so that it was always on hand. "You would never be thirsty," she explained. "And the water would always be clean."

The next was a little wooden bead, nondescript, about the size of a shilling. This was one of a number of beads—the rest lost to history— that the first conjurer had supposedly made to strip away the side effects of magic. Queen Victoria was believed to be personally in possession of a second, but that had never been confirmed.

The next was the largest piece of amethyst Merritt had ever laid eyes on, nearly the height of his forearm, with strange runes etched into its sides. This relic was connected to augury, and—again, supposedly— allowed an augurist to pick and choose what she saw. Hulda's nose got very close to the glass on this one, enough to earn a stern coughing from the guard behind them.

"I don't suppose we're allowed to handle them?" she asked.

Lady Helen looked utterly crestfallen. "I'm afraid not. They're quite potent, so I've been told. The spells we possess now are mere whispers of what the originators had at their disposal! I had to pull strings just for the tour."

As they reached the last relic, Mr. Blightree took over as tour guide. "Lastly, this bottle is believed to have the power to hold souls. I've never been allowed to examine it myself, and there is reason for it. Any talisman with such power could be deadly in the wrong hands."

Merritt swallowed, imagining what might have happened had Silas been able to trap his soul and Owein's in that bottle instead of hauling their bodies to Marshfield. He would have made far quicker work of them.

He wondered if the Druids had anything like this, or if their stories had any truth to them. He doubted anyone would ever truly know the birth of magic, its hows and whys.

They came around a corner, where some historical armor—or pieces of it, anyway—were on display beneath magical lights. Lady Helen had to read a placard to detail any of it. They descended a narrow set of stone stairs, along which hung old portraits no longer wanted for display in the palace, namely paintings of long-forgotten dukes, duchesses, and the offhand cousin.

The air didn't feel quite so cold when they stepped outside again. Merritt stretched his hands over his head, while Owein stretched his front paws before him. The sun was peeking out from between long clouds.

"Might be decent enough for a game of cricket today," Baron von Gayl suggested. "What do you say?"

Prince Friedrich laughed. "With what team?"

"Surely you've some neighbors itching for exercise," the baron countered. Their single-file line remerged into a group. Hulda's arm looped through Merritt's, and Lady Helen summoned Cora to come closer and whispered something in her ear.

"A last-minute cricket tournament?"

"Just for fun. *Tournament* is too serious," the baron protested.

Hulda stopped walking, her grip tightening on Merritt's elbow. He glanced at her, catching just the end of that blank look she got when her augury ignited. The way her face paled had his heart squelching.

"What did you see?" he asked, hoping it wasn't another questionable glimpse of him. He'd spoken quietly, but the words had come right in a break of conversation, so the others heard and turned curious heads their way.

Hulda blinked. Looked at Merritt, then to Cora and Lady Helen. "I . . . I'm not sure I should share . . ."

Two delicate lines formed between Lady Helen's brows. "You had a vision? Please tell."

Hulda swallowed; Merritt placed his free hand on her shoulder for support. After a beat, she replied, "I saw Lady Cora. I saw something heavy falling on her, not unlike what happened in the breakfast room."

Cora gasped. Owein licked her hand, but she didn't seem to notice.

"Mercy!" Lady Helen exclaimed at the same time Prince Friedrich replied, "Surely not!"

Hulda only managed a nod. "I'm afraid I'm not mistaken. It was Cora—I couldn't tell where she was. It looked to be morning, perhaps. There wasn't a lot of light around. I heard a cracking and saw her look up right as something—I'm sorry, I couldn't decipher what—fell atop her."

Cora asked, "C-Crushed?"

Dipping her head, Hulda answered, "I don't know. It cut out too quickly. I'm not strong in soothsaying. I only see slivers of the future, really."

"Could you summon it again?" asked the baron. "Hold on to it a little longer?"

She stiffened. "I . . . I doubt it. I'm working with a professor to hone my ability, but—"

"We must get another augurist at once!" Lady Helen demanded. They were starting to earn the attention of the guards, likely wondering why they were carrying on in the bailey, but Lady Helen paid them no mind. "We must fetch Cousin Margaret. Surely she would be able to see it better!"

Prince Friedrich frowned. "Margie is on her honeymoon, dear. She's somewhere in the islands of Italy right now."

Tears began to well in Lady Helen's eyes.

Lady Cora gripped fistfuls of her skirt. Then, expression tight with determination, she said, "Your professor, Miss Larkin. Is he adept in soothsaying?"

Merritt felt Hulda relax a fraction. "He is. More so than I am."

Lady Helen sprang forward like a puppet stuffed with a new hand. "Then we will have him to the house as soon as possible."

The glimpses Hulda had seen could not be changed, but if she didn't see fit to point this out, neither would Merritt. Lady Helen was resolute and, at that moment, more terrifying than any general who'd earned the honor of having his armor displayed in the tower behind them. If nothing else, they might be able to see a closer look at *when* her vision would come to pass, so they could arrange to have someone like Blightree around for a quick healing. Though it might not be possible to change the future, one could certainly cushion it.

"We'll contact him straightaway," Merritt offered, and that seemed to quell the fire behind her countenance.

Needless to say, the ride home was a tense one, with few words spoken.

Chapter 25

Owein had entirely forgotten about the dinner party Tuesday night, which the now-much-sought-after Professor Griffiths would be attending. The house filled with complementary smells—pork and bread being the strongest. Owein really liked both, especially when butter was involved, but he had to fight the dog side of him to savor anything. It wanted to snork down dinners like food would stop existing on the morrow.

For now, he watched Lady Helen pace back and forth in the reception hall, occasionally directing a passing servant, though the staff seemed preoccupied with the dinner. He'd already heard her say, more to herself than to him or anyone else, "Of course the reading will need to wait until after dinner, as is polite" and "If he doesn't come, we shall have to issue a new invitation."

Owein thought the priorities of the matter quite stupid. There was a very real possibility that Lady Cora was going to be hurt in the future—shouldn't they have taken the tram to the professor's college and pled for help right there and then?

This isn't America, Merritt had remarked when Owein asked about it. What nonsense. Why would—what was the word?—*propriety* take precedence over the well-being of his friend?

Owein and Cora *were* friends, sort of. Not the same way he, Kegan, and Fallon were friends, no. He couldn't even speak to Cora, not directly, though when they did speak, she was polite. Kind. Not very open, but kind. She deserved to be protected, and to reiterate, Owein was not happy about the priorities.

He could hear Hulda's vocabulary leaking into his thoughts. *Good.* He'd need to sound smart if he ever got a properly functioning mouth. He'd spent a lot of time with Hulda today, helping her check the stones and wards around the house just in case, though none so far had indicated the use of magic (which Lady Helen had strictly forbidden, save for Owein, who'd been granted permission to do so when he needed to use the bathroom, though there was usually a servant about to open the door for him).

Growing impatient, Owein tried to relay his frustrations to Lady Helen, to tell her where her daughter's life was concerned, propriety could and should be set aside, but of course she couldn't understand him. His inability to communicate became more and more frustrating with each passing day. So, determined to fetch his translator, Owein trotted into the sitting room to find him.

The room was more occupied than usual; the Leiningens had invited cousins to this party. Owein paused a moment, trying to recall who was who. The older couple was . . . Earl. Earl and Earless—wait, no—*Countess* of . . . North . . . folk. Norfolk. That was it. Which meant the others, who were very plain-looking but sparkled with gemstones and other things Owein couldn't name, were the Viscount and Viscountess of Leiningen. Essentially, if he called an English person a Leiningen, he had a very good chance of being correct. He knew the earl also had alteration spells, which was where Lady Helen and Cora had gotten theirs, but they hadn't dove into the details of it. Lady Helen was too distracted, waiting for Professor Griffiths.

Titles were annoying.

Owein marched up to Merritt and asked, *Will you translate for me?* But Merritt was engaged in conversation with Baron von Gayl and Viscount Leiningen, something about deep-sea fishing, and didn't seem to hear him. *Merritt, Lady Helen is being—*

"Miss Larkin!" came a new voice, and Owein turned to see an older man, well dressed without being overly so, entering the room with a very relieved-looking Lady Helen trailing behind. "Good to see you."

Hulda came out of the crowd. "Professor, I'm so glad you could join us on short notice."

"Anything for you," he said, not seeming to notice Owein's approach. He smelled like pipe smoke, newspaper, and gingerbread. Not a bad combination.

"We'll start in just a moment," Lady Helen announced, smiling for the first time since the tour yesterday.

Owein hesitated, wondering if he should stay with her or seek Merritt's help again . . . or perhaps it was better he stay with Cora. They weren't engaged, not yet, but that seemed the chummy thing to do. And yet . . . Briar and the baron were married and hardly spent time together. What did propriety call for, and where could he get a book on it? Better yet, he could ask Hulda to simply explain it to him, but everyone was so *busy.*

Owein moved through the room, nearly getting stepped on once. He found Cora speaking to a girl a little older than her, a daughter or niece or something of the earl. In the back of the room, he caught Briar's voice as she spoke to the viscountess: "—failed to persuade her. I've yet to determine what my next course of action will be."

"I'm surprised you were able to get an audience with her at all," the viscountess replied.

"Only a brief one." She sighed. "She said she would *consider* if Cora reached twenty-five and a body had not yet been found. The ridiculousness of the situation—"

That was about him and Cora, Owein new. But he could hardly interrupt her and make his case, so he turned back around in time to catch Hulda introducing Merritt to the professor.

"Ah, Mr. Fernsby. I've heard so much about you," Professor Griffiths said, shaking Merritt's hand. His grip seemed tighter than necessary, but Merritt didn't appear to notice.

"I must say the same. Hulda speaks very highly of you. We both appreciate the time you've put into her instruction. It's certainly helped boost her confidence with augury."

"I'm glad to hear it." They still shook hands. This was a very long handshake. "You're quite a character, Mr. Fernsby."

They finally dropped hands. "Oh?"

"I've never seen a grown man with hair that long."

That was a lie. Although it was not common, to be sure, Owein had seen plenty of men on the street with hair like that. Most usually wore it in a ponytail, but still.

Hulda rubbed the bridge of her nose.

"Well, it wouldn't make sense to cut it until summer." Merritt's tone was easy.

"Pardon?" the professor asked.

"By means of the temperature."

You wear your hair long in the summer, too, though, Owein insisted, and got a very subtle *Not now* gesture from Merritt. Owein grumbled, which came out more like a growl.

Hulda interjected, "Merritt and I just discovered a poetry book by an author I'm not familiar with. Have you heard of Ronald Jonstone?"

Lady Helen called them in for dinner, forcing the cacophony of conversations to either break up or be carried inside. Owein was supposed to walk in with Cora, so he waited for her, earning his usual nod and smile when she approached. She didn't say anything else as they walked into the dining room and she took her chair, while he found his elegant doggy corner set up with the first course of soup. He approached and settled himself, bowing down to have a taste.

And then everything grew very quiet.

Owein glanced up. Everyone who'd been seated rose, and everyone who'd been standing turned statuesque. On four legs, Owein was shorter than everyone there and couldn't see over their heads and shoulders. He took a step past the soup bowl, curious, before Prince Friedrich broke the silence.

"Your Majesty, we're so glad you're able to attend."

And then everyone bowed.

A strange shiver coursed up Owein's legs. He padded softly around the table to get a better look.

"Forgive my tardiness, Cousin."

"But of course you must take the seat of the table! I did leave it clear just in case, didn't I, Friedrich?"

Owein grew close enough to spot her. A woman about Briar's age stood at the entrance to the dining room in the heaviest gown Owein had ever seen, with cream and white fabric and intricate trimmings; long, wide sleeves; a full and sweeping skirt; and a wide collar. She was a brunette, though not as dark as the Leiningen women, her hair pulled back simply from her pale face. Her blue eyes, however, were the exact same hue, and they surveyed the room. Two men flanked her, neither offering conversation nor introductions, but thanks to the distinctive blue uniform they wore, Owein guessed they were part of the Queen's League of Magicians, likely bodyguards.

As Queen Victoria approached her seat at the table, Owein backtracked to his corner, watching with a strange reverence. Not because she was a queen, not really. Owein had never had a queen before; he'd been born and raised in the United States, albeit before they were ever called that. He'd been a house in the middle of the bay when the revolution broke out, and seen none of it. But Victoria had a *presence*, for lack of a better term. A presence that made his thoughts slow and caused those shivers down his legs. Even among the well-bred English aristocracy, Owein wasn't used to standing in a room with a wizard more powerful than himself. And the English monarch resonated *power*.

The men attending her pulled out her chair, and she sat. They took two steps back at the same time, like it was practiced, and remained there. Lady Helen directed that the dinner should begin, and servants brought out the first course to everyone else. Gradually, like sand tinkling down from the top of an hourglass, conversation built up again, quietly at first, then with growing confidence.

It is good to meet you, Owein Mansel.

Owein froze and glanced at Merritt, who was midconversation with Baron von Gayl. So his attention slid around the room to the queen herself, who delicately ate her soup.

You can hear me? he asked.

But of course. Forgive me, I did not want to stall the meal when I'd already arrived late. And I do think it would be discomfiting to the others for us to be seen sitting in a corner staring at each other for an extended amount of time. How are you enjoying London?

Owein positioned himself in front of his cooling soup but didn't eat. *It's been fine. Cold. But the family has been good to me.*

I'm glad to hear it. I appreciate you and your . . . nephew, isn't it? Taking the time to consider my offer.

Trying to sound regal, Owein replied, *I intend to accept, Your Majesty. I would have already, if the revised document hadn't . . . gone missing.*

Victoria smiled and stirred her soup. *Oh yes, I heard about that. But never mind it now. I intend to review the addenda when time allows. I think you will make a splendid addition to this line. And I have complete trust in William Blightree when it comes to moving your soul. You needn't worry about it. I just ask that, after you've returned home, you be ready at a moment's notice to sail back. A body can only be kept fresh for so long. In fact, I have an offer for you to make it easier on everyone.*

Owein's ears perked.

I'm sure Lady Helen would be happy to house you, but this is my handiwork, and I will take responsibility as needed. I have a little cottage not far from here that you may take for your own while you await a suitable body. Your caretaker may live there as well, if he wishes.

Owein's breath fluttered in his throat. Stay, here? In England? But Hulda's work was in the States—neither she nor Merritt would stay here. And Beth was back on the island. Baptiste, too. He'd be closer to the Druids, though . . . but other than that, he'd be alone.

Think on it, she said, and directed her attention to Prince Friedrich on her right, who'd asked her a question.

Owein nodded, though she would not perceive it. Nor did he truly mean it, because he already knew his answer.

He would sign the contract. But once that was settled, he was going home.

୭

"We would be happy to host you," Queen Victoria said as the servants cleared away the dishes from the last course. "That is, on such short notice, Albert and I will not be able to conduct the tour ourselves—"

"Of course not!" Lady Helen interjected, reaching across the table toward Victoria. "We would never expect you to."

Victoria smiled patiently. "But you are welcome to Buckingham Palace. I always welcome family, present and future." She glanced over at Owein, offering a subtle wink before standing. "Thank you so much for your invitation, my dear. I'm afraid I cannot stay for any entertainment."

Lady Helen jolted to her feet and curtsied. "We were honored to dine in your presence again, Your Majesty. Please take care and travel safely."

Victoria smiled and said her goodbyes. Then, out loud to Owein, added, "Until we meet again, Mr. Mansel."

The queen's departure was a scene, with the Leiningen family and guests trotting behind, getting their last words and compliments in as Victoria picked her way to the door. It took long enough that Owein was glad for her late entrance. They'd still be on the second course, otherwise.

Gradually, everyone made it back to the sitting room. It was customary, Owein had learned, for the gentlemen to linger behind and drink port or some such after dinner without the ladies. Owein and Merritt always attended, though neither of them drank. (Owein did try, once, and ended up vomiting it up on the carpet. Thankfully, a little chaocracy spell took care of it before anyone noticed.) And Merritt simply didn't drink; a habit he'd made over the years, to "keep him out of trouble," he said.

Tonight, however, the port and manly meeting was passed over for the sake of Cora. Merritt and the baron pulled a bench over for Professor Griffiths to use as a table, and Prince Friedrich carried over a chair right across from it for Cora. Everyone else sat around them, as though the reading of Cora's potential demise was, indeed, planned entertainment. Owein lingered nearby. He could smell Cora's nerves; they were sour, like bread dough forgotten on the counter. She clasped her hands together and sat upright, proper and Hulda-like, though her fingers wriggled together, trying to escape the cocoon of her grip.

Professor Griffiths, beneath the light of extra candles, laid out several cards, along with dice numbered with lines instead of dots. He accepted a few strands of Cora's hair as well.

"Give me a moment." He focused on the table, eyes moving back and forth, back and forth, only occasionally breaking the pattern by glancing up at Cora's face, smooth and blank save for a distraught line between her brows. Several minutes passed in hushed silence, and then the professor inhaled sharply. His eyes stopped moving, taking on that blank look Hulda sometimes got. A few seconds later, it ended.

"I did not see a falling ceiling," he said carefully, a little too much space between each word. "Which does not discount Miss Larkin's reading. I believe what I saw was farther in the future; Lady Cora appeared a little older. She stood in a room with a balcony overlooking the Thames. There was a man with her, though I'm afraid he's not one I recognized. Her grandfather, perhaps, judging by the white hair."

Lady Helen and Prince Friedrich turned to each other. Mouthed something, then shook their heads. "Neither of Cora's grandfathers are alive, I'm afraid."

Owein wondered at this. The old man could be another servant—the family had a lot of those—but servants dressed a certain way, and the augurist hadn't specified, and Owein couldn't ask. Perhaps it was him; maybe, in the future, he *did* get a body, but it was that of an older man. Better an older man than nothing, he supposed. How old would he have to be for white hair?

Or maybe the vision was far enough in the future for the man to be Prince Friedrich.

Professor Griffiths nodded. "Nevertheless, she did not seem to be in harm's way. She did prick her finger on a broken clasp to a necklace," he added with a subtle smile. "That is the worst I see for her. If I am seeing beyond what Miss Larkin beheld, which I believe I am, then I can assure you that whatever happens in the near future, the lady will survive it well." He made eye contact with Cora then, and tension visibly left her shoulders. The room, as a whole, released a held breath. Even the house seemed to settle.

"Well then," Baron von Gayl asked in his heavy German accent, "how about that port?"

He was the house again.

It was night, or it was very dark, it was hard to tell. There were no candles to tinker with, no moonlight on his shingles, no mice scurrying beneath his foundation. No eyes, ears, mouth. Only that means of sensing things the way a spirit does, which is almost like a person's, but subdued and pulled back, as though in a dream.

Somewhere, in the back of his thoughts, Owein felt this was a dream. But in the depths of slumber, feeling something and knowing it were two different things.

The darkness was impregnable. It was heavy and thick, like castor oil. Like the *thump*s of the mallet as Baptiste brought it down on a cut of venison, flattening it for schnitzel. Like a heavy cough too wet in the lungs, trying to drown every breath of air. Owein *knew* that. He remembered. That was how he'd died. Hot and drowning, tucked in the bed he shared with his sister.

But it wasn't hot here. It was cold. Cold and dark and heavy, and the darkness shifted in, closer and closer, a box built with long iron nails. Closer and closer, tighter and tighter. It meant to crush him. It *was* crushing him.

The faintest trickle of light flared in his periphery. Desperate, Owein whirled toward it. It was too far to have shape or even color. But it was there. And Owein ran, ran, *ran* toward it. He ran for hours. Only after hours did he start to get closer, the light bigger.

He blinked, and he was at the cave in the forest. Glancing over his shoulder, he saw Kegan's makeshift bridge had crumbled; there was no way down but to jump, praying his hands caught a shrub, and that the shrub had roots deep enough to hold him.

Hands. He held them before his face. He had hands. They were pale and small. Were these *his* hands? He couldn't remember.

The cave coughed in front of him. Kegan and Fallon were gone. The bridge was gone. The sun was setting, threatening to take its gift of light with it.

Swallowing, Owein stepped into the shadows. He closed his eyes; seeing made no difference, anyway. He was used to not having eyes.

He walked into the darkness, heel to toe, keeping his path straight. Reached out his right hand and felt for the back of the cave. Any moment now he would touch it. He would—

Owein awoke, curled on the foot of Merritt's bed. Moonlight peeked through the drawn curtains. A few desperate embers glowed red in the fireplace. He lifted his head and saw that everything was as it should be; no furniture had sprung to life and danced around the room, no walls had altered, no additional glass broken.

He blinked. He waited. The night continued onward, still and unthreatening. Peaceful, even.

Dogs didn't cry. Not really. Not unless pollen, a fly, or the like flew into their eyes. But deep inside, a little boy remembered having hands, and he passed out of the cave and wept for sight of day.

Chapter 26

Merritt laughed at the way Owein bounded through the slow-sprouting foliage the moment he laid eyes on Kegan and the gray hawk, tongue hanging out like it was a warm summer day. It *did* seem a bit warmer today, somewhere in the fifties, though perhaps their long walk out into the forest had helped. Owein had woken that day eager to go out to see the Druids, though they had no official appointment to do so. He'd had a dream that felt like progress, so he'd explained that morning, but for whatever reason, he felt the hawk and the boy would grasp the meaning better than Merritt did.

Merritt did understand, in his own way. He knew the bliss of relief, coming out of darkness.

He found Sean first, tanning the hide of a boar. Merritt wondered if the animal had been hunted in these woods, and if it would have broken the strict poaching laws England had. He assumed the Druids didn't care either way. Sean nodded a greeting, as his hands were busy. "Good morning to you!"

"Morning," Merritt offered. "Glad you haven't moved too far." It had taken him and Owein a little longer than usual to find them. "How much longer will you stay?"

Not long, sounded a voice notably feminine. Merritt turned to see a doe step out from amidst the trees, limber legs carefully picking their way over the uneven ground. *I'm glad you came out to see us, Merritt. I'd thought to send Fallon to fetch you so we could speak.*

It took Merritt a moment to recognize the animal. "Morning, Morgance."

The deer seemed to smile.

"How is he faring?" Sean asked, looking the way the children had gone.

"Good. Better, certainly. We've another five days or so with the Leiningens." Based off the original fortnight that had been proposed. Hulda might return sooner, if work demanded it. She was still a bit restless over that telegram from Myra, but she wanted to squeeze out as much augury workshopping as she could while she was here.

So soon. It was more a statement than a question.

Sean leaned over and rinsed off his hands in a bucket, then dried them on his slacks as he stood. "We've been chatting about that. Here." He moved closer to Morgance, to a leather satchel propped up against a tree trunk. It was almost camouflaged there, something Merritt imagined was intentional. "We prefer pigeons," he explained as he dug around in it, "but I imagine you don't want to take care of a bird while you're here." He pulled out a stone and crossed to Merritt, handing it to him. It was long and cylindrical, selenite.

"A communion stone?" Merritt asked.

"I have a friend not far from here who can enchant them. If you cross the Atlantic, neither this nor a pigeon will be able to reach us here. But while you're here, and if you do extend your stay, that will be able to reach us."

"I don't know how long we'd extend, if we could." Merritt turned the selenite over in his hands. "These are expensive. Should I return it before we go?"

"Keep it."

Is Owein not staying on?

Merritt was unsure how much Morgance knew. She'd said the royal family weren't the only ones with eyes and ears. "No, he'll be returning with me and Hulda. For now."

"You don't *have* to return."

Merritt met the taller man's eyes. "Pardon?"

Somewhere beyond a copse of trees, Owein barked and Kegan shrieked with delight.

"You're welcome to come back to Ireland with us," Sean continued. "You've Druidic skill; you'd be accepted among our folk. Owein as well."

Merritt gaped for a moment. "I . . ."

Let go of the material world, Merritt, Morgance said, coming closer. *The British will always have their nobility, but our kind is dwindling. We don't want to lose the ways of our ancestors. Soon enough, there will be none of us left.*

"It's a good life," Sean offered. "Simple, and without some of the amenities you may be used to, but they're good folk. We could teach you to hone your abilities better. And Owein. We've none with his spellwork, but he and the others already get on so well."

"They do," Merritt agreed, then cleared his throat from the effects of communion. "They get on splendidly." Running a hand back through his hair, he sighed. "Honestly, if we'd met even a year ago, I think I would have said yes. The idea of leaving it all behind and starting fresh would have been appealing." He dropped his hand, feeling . . . not quite sad. Something like nostalgic. Wistful, perhaps. "I appreciate all you've done for the both of us, truly. But I've already started anew, in a way. I've a life and a family"—old and new—"back in the States. And Hulda."

Sean nodded. "I had a feeling that would be your answer, but we thought we'd offer—"

As he spoke, Morgance's form warped, sandy fur turning to pale skin, ears growing long and shifting into hair. Within two breaths, she was a human woman again, a very *naked* human woman, and she draped her arms around Merritt's neck before he could fully process what had happened. "Please, Merritt, surely you must reconsider."

Merritt's arms immediately swung out like he was surrendering to watchmen so as not to touch her. His body flashed cold and hot at once. He tried to step back, but Morgance rooted them both.

And suddenly he knew *exactly* what Hulda had seen last Friday.

"Uh. Um." Merritt shifted his eyes skyward. "This isn't really—"

"I wouldn't mind," she said softly, "taking you as a mate."

Merritt shut his eyes entirely and tried to think of anything else. "I don't think that would be a good idea. I *do* think clothing would be a *good* idea."

"Mor," Sean warned, but didn't try to pry her off. Apparently this was not unusual behavior for her.

"If you would please unhand me," Merritt pleaded.

"You needn't be so bashful," she said, but did loosen her grip. "There's no shame in it."

Merritt stepped back, keeping his eyes averted. "I know a woman in London who would disagree with you."

A few heartbeats passed. "Take the night to think on it."

"I'm afraid that won't be necessary." He made himself incredibly interested in a small patch of clover on the forest floor. "I do appreciate the, um, offer. I do. But I have every intention of returning to Rhode Island and marrying my housekeeper."

He heard a rustle of cloth and dared to look back; Sean had settled a cloak over Morgance's shoulders, covering most of her. He murmured something into her ear. Morgance frowned. "Very well," she said. "But our arches will always bloom for you. If you ever change your mind, come to the Lagan Valley. It wouldn't take us long to find you."

Merritt nodded, turned the selenite stone over in his hands, then left to find Owein.

๛

Hulda sat at the wooden table across from Professor Griffiths, her hands flat, palms down, on the surface. The professor had a silver spring-driven clock in front of him, ticking away the time with brass hands, sounding like a metronome in the otherwise silent room.

As she studied the pattern of the movement, Hulda's vision changed. She saw Professor Griffiths, wearing a different suit than what he wore now, collecting his things into a briefcase. He tossed a coat over his arm, adjusted his glasses, and stepped out the door.

The vision ended. Professor Griffiths reached forward and paused the cradle. "What did you see?"

Pulling back from the table, Hulda rubbed her eyes, the first prick of a concentration headache starting. She'd had quite a few of those since beginning these lessons. "I saw you, actually. Nothing important, merely you collecting yourself at the end of a day's work and departing."

"Were you focused on me?" The corners of his lips ticked upward.

She warmed. "You *are* situated behind the spring-driven clock."

He nodded. "But of course." He set the cradle aside, behind a stack of ledgers. "In truth, Miss Larkin, you've been an exemplary student. I don't have a lot more I can *teach* you, but I'm more than happy to help you through exercises as you see fit. They are often better carried out with assistance."

"Thank you." She smiled. "I appreciate your time. I do feel like I have a little more of a handle on it. Best not to tell anyone, lest I get more requests for fortune-telling."

He chuckled. "Of course, such is the bane of any augurist."

She reached for her bag.

"The exercises?"

Pulling the bag onto her lap, Hulda collected her things. "Of course I would appreciate the practice, but I intend to return to Boston next week." She gave him a grateful, earnest smile. "I am truly appreciative. Are you sure I can't compensate you?"

He waved a hand, dismissing the notion. "No." A beat. "That is, not with money."

She snapped her bag shut. "Pardon?"

"I have no desire for monetary compensation for our time," he clarified, knitting his fingers together and setting his hands atop the table. "I've enjoyed getting to know you. You've a keen mind, Hulda. It's hard to find that in a woman, at least in my circles. I'd like to get to know it better."

Her stomach tightened. "I apologize; I don't understand."

"Give me a chance to change your mind." His resolute expression seemed set in marble, and his eyes never left hers. "Allow me to take you to dinner tonight."

Heat rushed into her cheeks, but Hulda was too startled to care that she had reddened. "P-Professor Griffiths, are you . . . are you insinuating an intention to court me?" She felt foolish even asking! She was not a desiderative woman, one an esteemed educator would desire—

"Yes, I am."

Her jaw dropped. Her brain emptied. She gaped like a freshly caught fish with a hook still in its mouth.

"As I said," he continued, "give me a chance to change your mind. Mr. Fernsby is an amicable fellow, I'll give him that. But you've no legal promise to him. I merely wish you to consider—"

"No."

She hardly registered the word leaving her mouth; it was the abrupt ending of Professor Griffiths's plea that brought her thoughts back together. She swallowed, spine straightening out of habit. She clutched her bag—not tightly or with any dramaturgy, but because it was there. "That is," she amended, "I am incredibly flattered. Truly. And I would certainly have considered it in another time and place. You are an . . . admirable suitor." Was she, *Hulda Larkin*, really having this conversation? Never in her wildest dreams had she ever imagined having to reject such a man!

She forced her posture to relax a fraction. "But whatever you may think of him, I am deeply in love with Merritt Fernsby, and nothing will sway my decision to marry him."

Professor Griffiths smiled. It was a small smile, a sad one, but he was polite and nodded. "But of course" was all he said, nothing more. Not wishing to make the situation graceless, Hulda wished him well and rose from her seat, taking even, measured footsteps to the door and down the stairs. Her heart beat . . . not quickly, but firmly, as though her body were still digesting the furor of the offer.

She and Professor Griffiths did have several similarities. Once upon a time, she would have been utterly rapturous at his interest. But she realized as she opened the door to the cool afternoon, Hulda had no desire to court herself. She didn't want to be immutable, never changing or growing. She wanted to spend her life with a man who would challenge her, forcing her to stretch and evolve. Someone who made her think differently, who argued the other side, who made her laugh.

Her strides paused on the street, forcing a chimney sweep to step around her. That was it, wasn't it? That was what she *wanted*. And she had it in Merritt. And Merritt wanted her for the same reasons. He relished her independence. They'd been to prison together, but he would never imprison *her*. Being a married woman didn't have to change who she was.

She searched for those anxieties, the bouquet of worries she'd been keeping close to her chest these past months, and couldn't find them. Instead, she found resolve. She would marry Merritt Fernsby. She *trusted* Merritt Fernsby, with all that she had. There was not a better person in all the world she could give her heart to.

Grinning like a little girl, Hulda quickened her step, eager to return to Cyprus Hall, to *him*, and to their future together.

⁓

She found him in the guest drawing room, a picked-at tray of meat and cheese near him, his feet propped by the fire. He must have been out this morning. He leaned against the armrest of his chair, a book in one hand, the other casually knotted up in his hair. He looked up as she approached, and grinned.

"Well, your premonition came true."

Hulda froze a few paces from him. Her mind whirled . . . Which premonition? Cora? Or . . .

Merritt snapped the book closed and sat upright, setting it beside the tray, uncaring that he hadn't marked his place. "Did you know that when a Druid changes into an animal, she doesn't take her clothes with her?"

Hulda sank into the chair across from him as he recounted his outing with the Druids and their offer to accept him into their clan, and Morgance's very direct method of trying to persuade him. He didn't attempt to palliate the story at all, including all the details of the incident, which matched up perfectly with what Hulda had augured.

"And then we left." He laughed and rubbed the bridge of his nose. "I have the stone still. Don't think I'll use it. Might be a bit awkward. Honestly, I might have been more of a mess if you hadn't warned me. How was your morning?"

Hulda blinked. Then laughed. Harder than she needed to, but she couldn't help it. Old stress bubbled up and escaped her on the wings of mirth, and she laughed until her ribs ached. To think, while she was being propositioned by the professor, Merritt was being seduced by a Druid!

"Is the thought of me being so fetching to the Irish funny?" He grinned.

Hulda put a hand on her breast and forced deep breaths to calm down. "It's all lunacy, isn't it? These situations we find ourselves in."

He shrugged. "Keeps life interesting."

She met his eyes. "I love you, Merritt Fernsby."

He crooked an eyebrow at that. He knew as much, but Hulda didn't *say* it as often as she should. She was still overcoming her allergy to expressing herself.

"I love you, too," he said.

And without bothering to check that the door to the room was shut, Hulda crossed to him, dug her hands into his unkempt hair, and kissed him.

April 12 couldn't come too soon.

Chapter 27

E-X-I-T-E-D, Owein spelled with his paws on his letterboard.

Cora, perched tall and straight at the edge of the settee in the drawing room, ankles crossed and tucked under her, examined the board, blinking her large blue eyes. "Exited?" she asked. "You mean, excited? Am I excited for the palace tour?"

Owein nodded his head. He didn't have Merritt—or Kegan or Sean, for that matter—to translate for him, but he figured it might be better not to have a third person around all the time. Might give him and Cora a chance to know each other a little better. People liked to prattle to dogs, or that was his understanding. Merritt and Beth prattled to him all the time, even when he didn't respond or show interest. Owein didn't mind simply listening. A person—or a dog—could learn a lot simply from listening.

Problem was, despite his best efforts over the last quarter hour, he couldn't get Cora to prattle. She was reserved in her words as she was reserved in everything else, and Owein had only a few words, slowly and apparently incorrectly spelled, to offer in return.

So he sat up, straightening his spine the way she had, attempting a dignified look, and nodded.

"I suppose it's always exciting to go," she answered, examining her nails. "It's the queen's home, after all. An exquisite place. I've been before." She paused, listening for people outside the room. A minute passed. "We go about twice a year, for varying functions."

Her voice trailed off, like it was an effort to use it.

Owein spelled out a new word, *W-E-N*, but the door opened just then, and Lady Helen announced, "Carriages are ready, dears. Come along."

Cora stood immediately. "Is Briar coming? Might I ride with her?"

Lady Helen's face fell. "She insists on staying. I don't know why she bothers to visit if she won't participate in anything. Come along." She smiled brightly at Owein. "You'll both share a carriage with me."

Lady Helen split up Hulda and Merritt, so Merritt could ride and play translator on the way to the palace, though it was more between Lady Helen and Owein than Cora, who seemed occupied by the passing city outside the window.

"She seemed very pleased with you," Lady Helen affirmed for the dozenth time, referring to Queen Victoria and the dinner the night before. "I received a letter from her this morning thanking me—she's always been very gracious—and she mentioned as much."

"Glad to hear it," Merritt replied, and glanced at Owein, who didn't know what else to say on the matter. They hadn't talked very long. So he, too, decided to look out the window, watching the city pass with Cora, occasionally glancing her way. Their gazes never met.

The carriages pulled into a large carriage house outside the palace, four guards standing at quiet attention outside the four massive doors. Owein put his paws up on the window to get a better look at the vehicles within. They were large and small, four-wheeled and two. One of the carriages was completely gilt in gold, and it hurt Owein's brain to imagine how much such a thing must be worth, and how aggravating it would be to clean without magic, but he supposed the royal family had plenty of that to spare. The footman came around and opened the door; Cora stepped out first, then Lady Helen, followed by Owein and

Merritt. The other carriage was likewise emptying its occupants, which included Prince Friedrich, Baron von Gayl, and Hulda. Mr. Blightree had been called away before breakfast, for reasons Owein didn't know.

He went up to an enormous carriage that could have easily fit twelve people, its side black and polished, with the royal insignia painted boldly on the door. The spokes of its wheels were bright red, and the gold ornamentation on top depicted cherubs and a crown. A temptation itched him, urging him to use a spell to melt off the silly statuettes, or change the color of a single wheel to blue . . . but that was something a child would do, and Owein wasn't a child anymore. Still, the thought niggled at him.

Ridiculous, isn't it? Merritt asked as Lady Helen detailed the "splendors" of one of the adjacent vehicles to Hulda. The others had stepped outside. *How many carriages does a person need?*

I suppose a lot of people live in the palace.

Point taken. But I doubt they're all using these. Merritt ran a hand over one of four gilt lamps attached to the black carriage as he walked toward the others.

"Impressive, isn't it?" Lady Helen called. "That one was commissioned by King—"

Owein didn't catch the rest of the sentence as a hefty gale rushed through the carriage house. He bent his head low, waiting for it to pass, but the wind increased in speed, bouncing between the walls and swirling in on itself, catching dust as it went. Carriages creaked under the force. Owein's nails scraped on the floor as it pushed him sideways.

Hulda screamed, "Look out!" just before the wind force doubled, and the enormous carriage beside Owein toppled over.

A yip escaped Owein as he dropped to the ground. He had an instant, a moment, an *instinct*, and acted.

The toppling carriage erupted into black, red, and gold confetti all around him, swirling into the air. Only seconds after the gale had started, it stopped, leaving the chaocratized bits of carriage to flutter down as snow.

"Heavens!" Lady Helen rushed forward, her hair in complete disarray. She dropped to her knees before Owein. "Are you hurt?"

"Owein!" Merritt barked over her, running to his side. Owein tried to recall where he was and what had just happened. In the back of his mind, he understood that he would remember momentarily, as soon as the confusion from the spell wore off.

"What happened?" called out a distant man, perhaps one of the guards. Owein couldn't see past Lady Helen, Merritt, and now Hulda grouping around him.

Oh, right. The carriage.

"Search the premises!"

"Call for assistance!"

"That was no revolutionary."

"What happened?" Cora cried.

"Heaven help us. Helen!" Prince Friedrich called.

"Is he all right?" called the baron. "I can move these vehicles!"

"He's fine," Merritt called over his shoulder as he settled a hand on Owein's neck.

Owein rose to his feet and shook confetti from his white-speckled fur. *I'm fine,* he echoed, and the footsteps of a dozen guards thundered in the carriage hall, rifles drawn and bayonets gleaming.

Lady Helen rose to her feet. "I want to know the cause of this travesty *this instant*! I've had *enough*!"

One of the guards approached and shouldered his weapon. "My apologies. We . . . I don't know."

"Then retrieve someone who *does*." Lady Helen's voice took on a dark tone. "There are men stationed everywhere! Surely someone saw something!"

The guard bowed. "I was stationed just outside the first door. I didn't see anything. Only felt the gusts, as you did." He shook his head, as though confused.

Owein shook again, trying to rid his body of the residual jitters in his chest and legs. Had . . . Had someone meant to hurt *him*? Merritt hadn't been nearby . . .

Puffing out his chest, Prince Friedrich asked, "And who among you has wind spells? This was a wind spell!"

"None of us are wizards, Lord Leiningen." The guard offered another bow. It made sense—they all wore red, not blue.

"Lady Helen and Lady Cora have wind spells," Hulda said quietly to Merritt, but her voice carried.

Cora paled. "I . . . I could never! I'd kill myself!"

Lady Helen put a hand on Cora's shoulder. "Her constitution wouldn't allow it. And she was just outside there!" She swept her hand to the open door. "Right in your view." She jutted an accusing finger at the first guard. "And I was standing right beside you, Miss Larkin."

Hulda nodded. "It did not emanate from you, I know that."

"It wasn't me!" Cora cried. "Look, I'll prove it!"

"Cora, don't!" Lady Helen snapped just as Cora threw her hands out and blew a forceful but harmless gust toward the gold gilt carriage. It didn't budge. Lady Helen seized her wrists and wrenched them back.

Cora doubled over, wheezing instantly.

"Fool girl." Owein didn't miss the tightness in Lady Helen's voice as she embraced her youngest daughter. "Out of the way, she needs fresh air. Move!"

The guard stepped aside, and Lady Helen, putting a supportive arm under Cora's shoulders, escorted her toward the door. Cora couldn't stand up straight, and the wheezing continued. Her free hand clutched her chest.

What can I do? Owein asked, the jitters intensifying.

"Nothing for now," Merritt said aloud. "Let's get out of here."

They followed the others back outside, into the cool morning air. Cora sat on the cobblestone just outside the carriage house, following her mother's instructions to "Breathe in, deep, out slow. In, out."

Merritt said, "That was directed toward Owein."

Baron von Gayl turned about. "It fell on him?"

"I'd moved away, so he was the only one near it." Merritt's eyes narrowed as he took in the carriage house. His hands formed fists at his sides. "Like someone was waiting for the opportunity."

You think they want to hurt me, and not you. His stomach sank, like when he let his dog side eat something it wasn't supposed to.

Merritt's mouth pressed into a hard line. *I do.*

"But why?" Hulda wrung her hands together. Paled. "I guess it's obvious, isn't it?"

They don't want me in the family, Owein said, and Merritt translated it for the others.

Prince Friedrich, within hearing distance, rushed over. "We would not go through all this trouble if we didn't. The queen herself said—"

"Lady Briar has made it very clear she's unsatisfied with the arrangement," Hulda murmured.

Baron von Gayl reeled back. "You're blaming my wife? She's not even here!"

"She distinctly insisted on not coming," Merritt snapped. "The first attack was the night before your arrival."

"Precisely! We were at the hotel."

"You were with her that night?" Hulda asked. "The entire time?"

The baron's face flushed. "I . . . That is . . ." He glanced sheepishly at Prince Friedrich. "We stayed in separate rooms. She insisted. And . . . she retired early. But she often does."

Prince Friedrich's jaw set.

But I wasn't in the breakfast room, Owein tried.

"But Owein wasn't in the breakfast room," Merritt repeated, clearing a rasp in his voice. "That was only me and Ernst."

"But that other dog was." Hulda sounded truly shaken. "And the hounds are very similar in size and color to Owein. It's been him this whole time, and we didn't see it." She curled in on herself. "I didn't see it."

"I believe this tour ends here." Prince Friedrich pulled down on his coat. "We will return to Cyprus Hall at once."

⌒⍟⌒

The scene was familiar by now. Cyprus Hall filled with watchmen. A constable interviewing members of the staff and family, others taking notes. Why was it wherever Owein went, trouble followed?

It's really more their fault, he told himself as he moved about the house freely; people tended not to suspect dogs of much unless a turkey leg had gone missing. *Everything was calm and normal until Merritt and Hulda showed up. Trouble follows* them, *not me.*

Though it did start to feel like trouble had a bone to pick with Owein, personally, this time around.

He checked in on Cora in her room. Didn't enter, but stuck his nose in the crack left by the door. Blightree had returned straightaway to help her—his necromancy included a healing spell, and the Leiningens had luck spells on their maternal side, so her breathing had improved. Good. Lady Helen was with her now, having already given her testimony and complaints to the constable.

Owein noted that while Briar seemed a very likely suspect, Blightree had also been absent from the tour. But he also didn't have wind spells, and from what Owein understood, a person couldn't merely purchase hurricane-level gusts. Though the royal necromancer was hardly a regular person. Still.

He went downstairs, where he heard Briar loudly protesting from the drawing room, "—absolutely absurd! You're wasting your time with me. Have you spoken with Belinda?"

Belinda was Lady Helen's maid, whom Briar had been with this morning, giving her an alibi for the carriage house. Then again, as Merritt had covertly pointed out, the suspect was most likely a member of the Leiningen family or their staff. How else could they so precisely track Owein's movements? (Or Merritt's. Owein thought maybe this could still be about him, since a lot of people had tried to kill or imprison Merritt recently.) So Belinda might provide a good alibi, but what if she was keeping secrets to protect Lady Briar from retribution?

Why did people have to make things so complicated? It was giving Owein a headache.

He did think, maybe, it was someone outside of Cyprus Hall. Someone like Beth—or, rather, someone *like* Beth but *stronger*—could discern where Owein was without entering the house. Clairvoyancy was tricky like that.

When everything was said and done, the constable met with Prince Friedrich, and of course Owein lingered nearby, as good as invisible in his canine form.

"We'll reach out to Palmerston and Colin," Prince Friedrich said, referring to Cora's older brothers, "and see if they've been in town."

The constable nodded. "We'll also follow up with other registered elementists with wind spells in the area."

"And the carriage house." Prince Friedrich, who usually had a kind and paternal tone, sounded stern. He glowered.

"The queen's men are already on it. I will certainly report to them, yes," the constable agreed. "I appreciate your patience, my lord."

And as easily as he'd come, the constable and his men departed.

It will be okay, Owein offered, but the prince didn't hear him.

Merritt's voice rang behind him. "Friedrich," he said, and Owein turned in time to see Hulda elbow him. "*Prince* Friedrich," he amended.

"I am terribly sorry about all of this," Prince Friedrich said, noticing Owein for the first time. "I don't have a lead to follow or a direction to take. Briar was here the whole time. She has a witness. I believe her."

"Of course," Hulda offered, keeping her voice low. "She's your daughter. Believe her you must."

Owein heard what Hulda didn't say: *But that doesn't mean I have to.*

"I think," Merritt said, "this time, it would be better for us to take Owein somewhere else."

A flash of remorse crossed Prince Friedrich's features. A deep breath raised his shoulders, and his lips quivered with ready words. Then, all at once, he deflated. "Of course. I understand. Do you have somewhere to stay?"

Hulda nodded. "I've made arrangements."

Where? Owein asked, but Merritt kept his focus on Prince Friedrich.

He nodded and kneaded his hands together. "I'm terribly sorry for all of this. God let it be sorted quickly." He sighed. "It might be best for you to leave while Helen is preoccupied. She will try to talk you out of it. Throw a fuss, at the very least."

"Thank you," Hulda said, just as Merritt called Owein to him.

And like a good dog, Owein followed.

Chapter 28

Hulda, Merritt, and Owein arrived at LIKER headquarters in the evening. She'd been careful not to tell anyone where they were staying, just in case the culprit was still out for Owein. If this nonsense *was* tied to the impending betrothal contract, hopefully their disappearance would calm things down.

Hulda didn't want to believe that Lady Briar, or any of the Leiningens, were responsible for now *three* attempts on Owein's life, if that's what the first two were. The Leiningens were a hospitable and well-bred family. Even Lady Briar, while deeply opposed to the betrothal, contested it in a dignified manner. Then again, Hulda had learned the hard way not to take others at face value. She needed to follow her gut. Perhaps run through some augury exercises tonight and see if the future would give her a peek at the solution for this ever-growing problem.

After meeting with Miss Richards and obtaining keys, Hulda, Merritt, and Owein went around to the back of the building and entered it through a clandestine door, not unlike what she did at the Bright Bay Hotel in Boston. She found one of the spare rooms on the second floor and opened the door. The air had a brisk chill to it, so she quickly swept over to start the fire.

"Owein wants to know how long we'll be here," Merritt said, plopping down on the edge of the bed and dropping his suitcase at his feet.

"I'm not sure. At least the night. I'll send word to Lady Helen in the morning. I'm sure by then there will be news from the palace. No one can use such spells on the queen's property and get away with it."

She coaxed the fire to life and took a moment to warm her hands by it. Stood and stretched her back, then crossed to the window to draw the diminutive draperies, letting in some light. It was only then she realized how still the room had become. Glancing over, she saw Merritt and Owein locking eyes, having another of their tacit conversations she would never be privy to.

She sighed. "Well?"

Merritt cleared his throat. "He wants to stay with the Druids."

She reeled back a little, surprised. "The Druids?" The image of the nude woman—Morgance, apparently—throwing herself at Merritt rose in her mind. She dismissed it sharply. "LIKER is perfectly fortified. The Druids don't even have a room in the city."

Merritt paused, frowning, before speaking again, his voice growing hoarse. "I told him as much. He's insistent." Another pause, then, to Owein, "I'm *getting* to it. He says he wants to see them again before he leaves, and if someone really is after him, they wouldn't look for him in the middle of a late-winter forest." He hesitated before repeating Owein verbatim, "'They're my friends, and I won't see them again after we return to the States.'"

"I'd rather you be where we can keep an eye on you." Hulda folded her arms, as if doing so would quash the uneasiness building in her. "We don't know enough to make any safe bets."

Merritt paused, then gave Owein what Hulda could best describe as a "warning" look.

She rolled her lips together. "Go ahead. You needn't censor him on my behalf."

Giving her an apologetic look, Merritt said, "He says he's not a child anymore. And while I may legally be responsible for him in America, he can do as he wants in England."

Hulda frowned. Waited for a wave of trepidation to pass before speaking. "He is, technically, correct." A new ache pulsed behind her forehead. She closed her eyes and rubbed it. "How well do you know these Druids?"

"I don't think it's a terrible idea." Merritt spoke softly, as if doing so would ease the situation. "Outside of what happened with Morgance"—Owein perked up at that; Merritt hadn't shared the information with him—"they seem responsible. Owein has gotten very close, very quickly, with Kegan and Fallon. They said they'd still be in the area, and they *did* give us that communion stone." He turned sharply to Owein. "*That* is not necessary. If you want to be treated like an adult, act like one."

Hulda deemed it better not to know what that last exchange was about. "If we use the communion stone and they're willing, will you return here by noon tomorrow? The last thing I want is to organize a search party scouring the countryside for you." She strode closer and crouched before the terrier. "We care about you, Owein. You're our family."

A soft whine emitted from Owein's throat. He dipped his head in acknowledgment.

"There's no guarantee they will answer." Merritt's voice wheezed, and he cleared it again. Pulled the selenite rod from his suitcase and activated the rune on it. "Sean? It's Merritt. Are you still nearby?"

About twenty seconds passed before a rich Irish voice responded, "Aye, Merritt. Have you changed your mind?"

"We've a situation at hand I'm sure Owein will be happy to fill you in on. We've departed from Cyprus Hall for the moment. Owein was hoping you might have room under your tent for him tonight."

Another hesitation; Hulda assumed Sean was talking it over with his comrades. "How far out are you?"

Merritt glanced to Hulda, silently asking if they should divulge their location, or perhaps arrange to meet elsewhere. Deeming it safe, she nodded.

Merritt related the address.

"We'll come to you," Sean replied. "Make it easy on you. Need a few things in town, besides."

"That's very kind of you. Thank you." Merritt waited for further response, but the communion rune dimmed, ending the conversation.

"Well, there you go," he said to Owein. "Back by *noon*."

Owein replied with an airy bark. A span of silence followed.

Standing, Merritt slid the stone into his pocket. "He wants your help writing a letter to Cora." He took a moment to listen to further instruction. "'I don't want to run away from this,'" he added, speaking verbatim again.

A small smile pulled on her lips. "I would be happy to help, Owein. Let's aim to be precise, for Merritt's sake."

~⍥~

As Hulda had the neater handwriting, she penned the letter for Owein, trying to keep it as much in his voice as she could, making suggestions where she found them prudent. It was a single short page, but it would do the job nicely enough.

Lady Cora,

I'm sorry about the trouble this has caused. I hope you're feeling better after the incident at the carriage house. I want everyone to stay safe, so we'll proceed with caution. I appreciate your patience, kindness, and friendship. I hope one day I'll have a voice to express that myself.

Sincerely,

Owein Mansel

Hulda sealed and addressed it. She'd post it on the morrow, if they didn't head straight back to Cyprus Hall. They could only take the situation one day at a time . . . though time was a commodity she was quickly running low on. BIKER could not go on without its director forever.

Owein took to pacing the hall, listening for Sean's arrival. Merritt sipped water slowly, staring off into space, thinking about, oh, his book or some such. He had a tendency to daydream, but such was the mind of a creative.

"Did we ever decide on flowers?" he asked later, voice returned.

"Hmm?" Hulda glanced up from the receipt book she'd opened only a minute before. "For the wedding?"

He nodded.

"I believe lilies are in season. I'll have to check with Miss Taylor." Beth had been helping with the arrangements while Hulda was busy stitching BIKER back together. The thought made her oddly melancholy. "I wish I hadn't postponed everything."

Merritt lifted his head. "What do you mean?"

"The wedding. We could have been married before Christmas." She smoothed a wrinkle in her skirt.

"Hard to find seasonal flowers at Christmas."

She rolled her eyes. "Flowers hardly matter, in the end. Flowers, the dress, the venue . . . it's all furbelow, in the end."

Merritt smiled. "Pardon?"

She rechecked her words. "Embellishment. Superfluity. Hardly matters." She tossed the receipt book onto a nearby empty shelf. "We'd already be married if I wasn't so deep in work."

"Your work is your life," Merritt objected.

"My work is *part* of my life, and my life is in dire need of balance." She adjusted her glasses. "You are a very critical component, as are Owein and Whimbrel House and the lot of it."

"Careful, Miss Larkin." He grinned. "I might think you like me." He sat up straighter. "December was a hard month."

"It was," she conceded. "But still."

Merritt shrugged. "We could just get married."

She eyed him. "We are getting married."

"I mean now."

She waited for the conclusion of the joke, a witticism of some sort, but when none came, eager nerves began popping in her chest. "Now?"

He smirked.

"And how, pray tell, would we manage such a thing?" It was a nice sentiment, but unrealistic.

"Just head to the closest church, I suppose."

Hulda clucked her tongue. "This isn't the States, Merritt. We're not English citizens. We've no congregation, and banns have to be posted three weeks prior to matrimony."

He stood, shoved his hands in his pockets, and walked over to her, finding a spot to lean against the wall. "Surely pastors can be bribed."

"Surely those who try can be arrested, and I've been arrested enough times not to wish for another," she countered. Considered. "I mean . . . that is, I suppose there's Gretna Green."

"Isn't that in Scotland?"

"Yes, just over the northwestern border. I believe there's a kinetic tram that runs . . ." She shook her head, and the eager bubbles burst one by one. "What am I thinking? We couldn't possibly. We've a potential murderer somewhere about, and it's too far from Owein. Whether or not he's an 'adult,' it wouldn't be responsible in the slightest! And what would we do about the wedding back home? The invitations have already been sent."

Merritt pushed his hair back. "I mean, they wouldn't have to know."

She smiled at the sentiment. "It would be a wonderful secret, but it's simply not feasible."

A familiar Irish voice, louder this time, said, "Well, it may be."

Hulda leapt straight out of her chair, nearly smashing her head into Merritt's. A tall stranger lingered in the doorway, a hawk on his shoulder and Owein already at his knee. He lifted a hand in apology. "I couldn't help but overhear."

Steeling herself with a deep breath, Hulda quickly smoothed her skirts and approached. "You must be Sean. Forgive me, I'm not familiar with your surname."

"Don't really have one." He smirked. To Merritt, he said, "Your fiancée?"

"None other," Merritt answered.

He glanced between the two of them, making Hulda feel oddly self-conscious. "That is," he went on, "if you're not hell-bent on a Christian ceremony, I'm a Druidic priest."

Blood rushed into Hulda's cheeks.

"Really?" Merritt sounded delighted by the idea. "You've license to marry?"

"I do."

Hulda opened her mouth. Closed it. Glanced from Sean to the hawk, to Sean, to Owein, to Merritt, and back to Sean. "I . . . That is . . . This is very unexpected . . ."

Merritt placed a hand on the small of her back. "It's all right, Hulda. It's just a jest."

Another bubble popped.

"No." She stood straighter. "No, it wasn't."

Merritt met her gaze, questioning.

She turned to him. "I want to marry you, Merritt. I regret not doing it sooner. Like you said . . . why not now?" She laughed at the ridiculousness of it. A younger Hulda would have fainted at the prospect! "It doesn't change the wedding details back home. Why not simply . . . elope?"

She could hardly believe the words coming out of her mouth. Judging by Merritt's expression in the evening light, neither could he. Was it too forward of her?

Then she realized something else, and disappointment cooled her fervor. "Though I suppose it's not the best choice, having a wedding anniversary on the eve of your birthday."

Merritt startled. "My birthday?" He paused. "My goodness, it *is* my birthday tomorrow, isn't it?" He laughed, glancing at Sean. "I'm not used to celebrating it."

The sentiment, given in jest, saddened her. "Well, it is. And it wouldn't be wise to congest holidays."

"Honestly, Hulda"—his blue eyes twinkled—"there's nothing I'd want more."

She searched his face. "Truly?"

He grasped both her hands in his; a slip of light from the window glinted off the pearl in the ring, almost like an omen. "Truly and absolutely," he murmured, pressing his forehead to hers.

She grinned; she couldn't help it. "And you won't hold it over my head in years to come?"

"You know what?" He pulled back. "Now that I think about it, I was mistaken when I told you my birthday. I'm certain it's in February. So there's no issue."

She laughed. A tear formed in the corner of her eye. The bubble in her chest grew overlarge, making her feel like she might float away.

Sean asked, "Is that a yes, then?"

Pulling a hand free, Hulda wiped the tear. "I mean . . . if it's no trouble—"

"Absolutely yes." Merritt squeezed her hand.

Sean rubbed his hands together and looked around the barren room. "Let's see here . . . normally we'd do this under an arch—"

Hulda jumped as the room around them warped, a chunk of the ceiling coming down and turning a brilliant shade of green, taking on the shape of an arch over their heads.

Owein started shaking a moment later. His doing, then.

Her cheeks were hurting, she smiled so widely. Everyone was smiling. Merritt was smiling at *her*. Even the hawk seemed jubilant.

From his pack, Sean pulled out an ordinary roll of twine—or perhaps candlewick, Hulda couldn't be sure. He used a knife to cut a long length, then had Merritt and Hulda hold right hands. He looped the twine around them, starting at Merritt's elbow and ending at Hulda's. He then put a hand on either of their shoulders.

"As I bind your hands, so are your lives bound in a union of love, trust, and devotion. Like the stars, your love should be a constant source of light, and like the earth, a foundation from which to grow."

Another tear formed as Hulda stared into Merritt's beautiful eyes, crinkled as he smiled at her. This was not how she'd imagined this happening, not even when she was young and still full of hope for her future. Yet oddly, in this empty back room in LIKER's headquarters, under the watch of strangers and a dog who used to be a house, she couldn't think of anything more perfect.

"May this knot remain forever tied, and may your hands always hold one another. Hold tightly during the storms of life, and be gentle as they nurture one another. I summon the spirits of the four quarters of our world, that this binding may be blessed by the powers of all creation. So let it be, amen."

Bowing his head, Sean moved his hands down Hulda and Merritt's joined arms, bringing them together over their hands. He squeezed once, then released them. "It is done."

Hulda's heart swelled to bursting. "Done? We're . . . married?"

"Under Druidic law and any state recognizing it, yes." Sean winked.

With the hand still bound to hers, Merritt tugged her forward and sealed the ceremony with a kiss on her lips. Hulda thought she'd melt into a puddle right there. Surely this was a dream! Things like this didn't just *happen*, and certainly not to her.

But when Merritt pulled back and Hulda opened her eyes, her world was just as jubilant as before she'd closed them.

Turning to Sean, Merritt said, "So we can never take this thing off, right?" He held up their bound hands.

Sean chuckled. "I would save the string, for sentimentality. And for now"—he scratched behind Owein's ears—"I will take this one off your hands."

Remembering herself, Hulda said, "Noon, Owein. Please. And contact us if anything goes awry."

"He knows," Sean and Merritt said in unison, then exchanged a knowing look.

"Right." Hulda hesitated, then quickly unwound the string binding her hand to Merritt's as Owein restored order to the makeshift arch. She might have stepped halfway into a fairy tale, but she was still mistress of this place while Mr. Walker was in Constantinople, so she escorted Sean, the hawk Fallon, and Owein into the hallway and down the stairs, thanking Sean repeatedly for coming to them and caring for Owein, and for the ceremony, and again for Owein. She saw them out the door, then watched them go down the street, ensuring they were well. The three of them easily blended with the crowd. And Sean was such a large man—he would be able to fend for himself, magic aside. And Owein! He could certainly take care of himself. He'd disintegrated an entire carriage earlier that day. Hulda really shouldn't worry.

She did worry, a little. Caught herself wringing her hands on the way back upstairs to the room where Merritt was looking out the window in the same direction Owein had gone, keeping a watchful eye just as she had.

Hulda closed the door gently behind her. "So."

He turned back from the window, a rueful smile on his face that instantly put her at ease. "So, Mrs. Fernsby. This has been a delightful turn of events."

She held his eye and crossed the room. "Indeed."

She only needed to lift her face to invite his lips to hers, to truly memorize them—their shape, their warmth, the way they flitted across hers. Feeling courageous, Hulda nipped at him, earning a soft growl and both his hands at the small of her back, pulling her in closer, then *closer*, to him.

Abruptly, she broke the kiss, grabbed his collar, and pushed him onto the bed.

He snorted. "Well then."

"I," she stated, pulling hairpins from her hair, "have waited a *very* long time for this, Mr. Fernsby. I do not see the point in dallying."

A familiar mischievousness smoldered in his expression. "I'm sorry, was that dallying? I don't think I received the schedule for tonight's events."

"You don't need one." She placed her hairpins on the side table and shook out her hair, delighted by the way Merritt's gaze darkened when she did. She proceeded to undo the buttons on her dress, Merritt's eyes glued to her every movement. It sent warm shivers up her spine.

This was really happening, wasn't it?

She was utterly exultant at the fact.

Pulling down her sleeves, she asked, "Now, are you going to remove your trousers, or should I?"

Chapter 29

There was nothing better than waking up in the morning next to the man you loved, especially when he was in the nude.

Hulda rolled toward him and buried her face into the side of his neck, blotting out the sunrise pouring through the windows. She was usually up and about this time of day, but given that she hadn't slept particularly well last night, she determined it would be all right to repose for another hour or so. Truthfully, the time she *had* spent sleeping had been quite peaceful, merely fleeting, as Merritt had ensured thrice the loss of her maidenhood. As she adjusted beside him, she noted she would be somewhat sore today, but found she didn't mind in the slightest.

And to her delight, two of her more sultry earlier visions had come to pass last night. She greatly anticipated experiencing the others firsthand.

Merritt groaned beside her and stretched, arching his back, before looping an arm around her, his hand instantly going for her posterior. "Morning," he mumbled, eyes still closed.

Warmth bloomed in her chest and filled her to her toes. She brushed unruly hair from his face, then traced the line of his brow, down the length of his nose. It was all so surreal. She was a married woman. This man was her husband. The sequence of events . . . it was all so unexpected, but she'd learned to be surprised with Merritt.

"Morning," she whispered, occupying herself with his face and his hair. He dozed off a bit longer, though Hulda found herself suddenly wide awake. She didn't mind. She was simply . . . happy.

When Merritt began to rouse again, she took the opportunity to slide from the sheets, which earned her a surly growl from Merritt. She located her glasses, cleaned up at the washbasin in the corner, and got dressed, leaving her hair down for now. By the time she got the Druids' communion stone, Merritt was sitting up, blankets around his hips, rubbing sleep from his eyes. Hulda watched him a long moment, memorizing his every facet, feeling warmer and fuller with every passing second.

He caught her eye. "Is something funny?"

"Just admiring the view," she offered, earning herself a grin. Refocusing, she activated the rune on the communion stone. "Sean? Owein? Is everything all right?"

The reply came quickly. "Hi!" bellowed a child's voice, a boy, on the other end. "Yeah, we got mallow candies! And we're roasting them over the fire!"

"Mallow candies?" Merritt asked.

"Pâte de guimauve," Hulda provided. "Kegan?"

Merritt nodded.

"I'm very happy to hear that," she said. "Is Owein—"

She heard him barking in the background, which answered that question. Everything was fine. She sighed in relief.

"He says he'll be back on time. We're leaving after the mallow candies," Kegan said. "Bye!"

The rune flashed, and the magic cut off.

"Ah, the concision of children." Hulda set the stone on a shelf where it would be easily heard if it activated again.

"Should we send word to Cyprus Hall?" Merritt asked.

"Perhaps. We did make it difficult for them to send word to us." She dug into her bag, setting her hairbrush aside, and pulled out a small box wrapped with ribbon. Tied into the ribbon was a pen with a dragon carved along the top. She handed the bundle to Merritt. "Happy birthday."

He lit up. "What's this?" He pulled the pen free from the knot and turned it over. "This is extraordinary. It's got a little jewel for an eye."

"It seemed whimsical." She tried to hide a smile and failed miserably.

"Thank you." He put it in his hand, holding it as if to test it. He had a funny way of writing where he laid his thumb straight, perpendicular to his index finger, as opposed to down with the other fingers to better grip the utensil, as Hulda had been instructed to do in school. She had never commented on it. He moved to put the pen in his pocket, realized he still wasn't wearing any pants, and set it aside. Pulled the ribbon free from the box while Hulda held her breath. "You didn't have to get me anything."

"Nonsense." She sat on the edge of the bed. "If you don't care for these, we can return them for a different design."

He opened the box. Inside were two gold-plated cuff links. They were simply made, in the style Hulda preferred—she'd never seen Merritt wear cuff links, so she could only conjecture his opinion on the matter. Simple, slightly oval, with a matte finish.

"I thought," she added as he slipped one out of the box, "you might wear them to the . . . *other* wedding."

He grinned. "I think they'll make me look quite dashing." He carefully set the cuff link back, stuck a knuckle under Hulda's chin, and guided her over to kiss her. "Thank you."

She grinned. Rose and returned to that hairbrush, noting Owein's letter beside it. She should deliver it. Tidy up in case Miss Richards or the like decided to check in.

Merritt dressed while she brushed her hair. Remembering her intentions for last night, she dug out a particular receipt book from her black bag, the one that held all her notes on the strange goings-on at Cyprus Hall. She turned the page and jotted down new information regarding the carriage house over a diagram for folding petticoats, along with what she'd learned from the constable, courtesy of Owein. Merritt kissed the side of her neck as she was finishing. "I'm going to find something for breakfast."

"I believe there's a small kitchen downstairs," she offered, and he sauntered off to locate it.

Alone, Hulda retrieved her dice and set the book out on her lap, letting her vision go out of focus, blurring her writing. She rolled her dice carefully, trying to keep them on the book while not moving her eyes from her writing. Tried unsuccessfully for about five minutes, then turned the page back and began again, thinking over the events in her mind the way Professor Griffiths had instructed her to. The rolling of the dice became a rhythm, like the tapping of impatient fingers. She lost one off the side of the book but didn't stop to retrieve it. Just rolled the dice, seeing beyond their blurred markings, keeping a somewhat steady tempo with the scoop and drop, scoop and drop.

Her neck was beginning to ache when her augury seized upon a pattern of threes. She saw the Leiningens and Mr. Blightree around a pedestal with an unfurled scroll upon it covered in neat, tight penmanship. Mr. Blightree held a quill, and Owein approached.

The vision faltered. Hulda desperately tried to hold on to it—

A pen scraping the bottom of an ink vial.

A shod foot as it came down, as though running.

A bead, or perhaps a marble, rolling across the floor.

William Blightree, with tears in his eyes.

Hulda blinked, and the vision dissipated. It was that same premonition she'd had twice before. Flipping back a page, she found where she'd written down the details. Only the first time had included Mr. Blightree weeping. Why had her augury left that off?

Her breath caught. Had that clue already come to pass? Was it no longer the future?

Distantly, she heard a thumping noise. Tilted her head to better hear it, then set the receipt book aside and rose, heading into the hallway. The thumping was coming from the back door of the building. It was about nine in the morning; perhaps a LIKER employee had lost his or her key. As Hulda approached, she heard footsteps on the floor above her, signaling the presence of other employees, though they were likely too far from the door to hear the emphatic knocking.

Why not use the front door, if the back was locked?

Hesitant, wishing she'd brought her black bag with her, she reached the door. Carefully turned the knob and opened it—

Morning sunlight temporarily blinded her. Raising a hand to shield herself, she saw a boy of perhaps seventeen years of age wearing a page uniform. He seemed relieved to see her. "I'm sorry, is there a Mr. Fernsby or Miss Larkin staying here? I was told to try this location."

"I . . . yes. What do you need them for?"

He fetched a crisp letter from his bag. "I'm to deliver this to one of them. Straightaway. He said there isn't much time."

"Much time?" Hulda reached for the letter.

The page pulled it back. "I must give it directly—"

"I'm Hulda Larkin," she said, and snatched the letter, breaking the seal with her thumbnail. Inside was a hasty scrawl without a signature. As she read, a chill swept over her as winter rain.

Please come to Cyprus Hall at once. We have a body.

⌒⊙

Hulda spoke through the communion stone as she rushed down the hall to find Merritt. She passed a few employees on the way but didn't bother masking her speech; they could make of it whatever they wanted.

"We need Owein back as soon as possible. They found someone. Tell him they found someone, and time is of the essence!"

She turned a corner and nearly knocked a tray of bread and tea out of Merritt's hands. "Whoa there." His smile dropped at her expression. "What happened? Owein?"

"They found a body for him," she said.

They both left the tray forgotten in the hallway and rushed upstairs. By the time they'd finished packing and exited the building, Sean, the hawk, and Owein came bounding up the road, the first flushed, all three out of breath. Owein panted hard, his tongue lolling out the side of his mouth.

"I don't know," Merritt said in response to an unheard question. "But we'll find out."

"Thank you," Hulda said to both Sean and Fallon. "Thank you for everything."

They hailed a coach, Merritt doling out a larger-than-necessary sum to the driver with the instruction to "drive like an American."

The man whipped his team, and they rushed down the London streets en route to Cyprus Hall.

⁀੭

A footman was waiting in the drive when the carriage pulled in, and he bolted into the house, leaving the front door ajar. When Merritt stepped out, he heard him call, "—here! They're here!"

Was this really happening? Nerves ran marathons around his limbs and somersaulted his heart. He had assumed there would be so much more time—years, even—before someone was found. What were the chances that a workable vessel had been collected already, before the determined fortnight was even up? It seemed too easy, too planned. Licks of nausea curled up the sides of his stomach. All the calm, blissful feelings from the morning were gone.

Lady Helen rushed through the vestibule to meet them. "I'm so glad they found you! We sent at least a dozen missives. Come quickly."

She ushered them to the blue drawing room, where a pedestal with a scroll was set up. The family was gathered there, minus Briar and Cora. The morning light hit the windows in such a way as to give the space a blue cast in addition to the blue furnishings, making it feel like it was much earlier—or much later—than it was. Baron von Gayl and Prince Friedrich stood as they entered.

But there was no body.

"I don't understand," Merritt said.

"The contract."

Merritt whirled around to see Blightree behind him, looking as though he'd aged twenty years. He had heavy bags under his eyes, and his expression had the sort of gauntness one saw only in the very frail or very hungry. His clothing was a mite disheveled as well.

The man clasped his hands before him. "You must sign the contract before I can do anything with the transfer. I've finished redrafting it, and the queen has approved Miss Larkin's changes."

Merritt glanced back at the pedestal. On the ride over, Hulda had mentioned seeing a vision of one—was this it? "But . . . who? Is it really sound to do this now?"

"I can only preserve the body for so long," Blightree murmured. "I assure you, the family has been rewarded handsomely. It will be a strong body, and a good age, too—only fourteen, just a little older than Cora."

Hulda grasped Merritt's elbow. "But . . . is there not a way to salvage the boy?"

Blightree's head hung like an anvil had been set upon it. "I would spare the lad if I could. I've tried."

"But surely—" Merritt began.

"The boy is my nephew," whispered the necromancer.

The man might as well have stabbed Merritt through the heart with a rusty bayonet. Hulda gasped, and her hold on his elbow tightened.

Oh no. A soft whimper escaped Owein.

Blightree nodded with effort. "He drowned." Tears brimmed in the corners of his eyes. "I was called away last night. I tried to revive him; my magic can keep his heart beating, but his soul is already gone. He won't open his eyes or respond. I never thought . . ." He sniffed. Pulled out a handkerchief and dabbed his eyes. "But at least some good can come of it."

"You should be mourning," Hulda said.

But Blightree shook his head. "There is time for that later. As I said, time is of the essence."

Briar and Cora appeared then behind him, Briar with her lips pressed into a resolute line, Cora with her head down. Their hands were clasped together, but Cora seemed to be dragging behind like a doll. Blightree was close to the royal family. Had they known, perhaps even befriended, his nephew?

Owein shifted closer to Merritt's side. The tension felt thick as cold butter. Merritt didn't sit, but hugged the wall, Owein at his heels. Hulda grabbed his elbow.

"I never noticed," she whispered, taut as the high string of a violin, "that the carpeting doesn't reach the walls."

Merritt blinked. "Pardon?"

"And the cream shades in the carpet," she continued. "That cluster vision I had when meeting with Professor Griffiths . . . it happens in this room. The lighting . . . The lighting made me notice it."

Merritt recalled the vision; she'd let him read it out of that receipt book she'd been marking up. Nothing in it was harsh or violent, but she'd said it felt important. "I guess we'll find out soon enough," he offered by way of encouragement.

She nodded vacantly, then perched on the edge of the closest chair, back erect. Blightree pushed past all of them and stood on the far side of the pedestal. He dipped a large quill into an ink vial. It was nearly empty, and the tip of the pen scraped along the glass bottom.

Hulda jolted. Merritt touched her shoulder, but she wouldn't break the silence. She couldn't commune with him as Owein did, so she simply overlapped their fingers.

"The time has come. Prince Friedrich?"

The prince stepped forward. The room was not overly large, but it still felt like minutes passed before he reached the pedestal. He dipped the pen and began scrawling his name at the bottom of the scroll.

"*Stop.*"

Prince Friedrich's hand stopped midletter. Merritt held his breath and looked around the room, trying to determine who had spoken. At first he thought it Briar, but when he found her, she was focused on her sister, who sat beside her, hands clenched into tight, white fists.

"Cora, what is the meaning of this?" Lady Helen asked.

Cora stood and lifted her head. Red rimmed her eyes, and her jaw protruded with clenched teeth. "I said *stop*! Stop this!"

Her father set down the quill. "What outburst is this? You know—"

"I *know* what you've said!" she shouted, sounding like a completely different person with her voice raised. Gooseflesh prickled Merritt's arms. "I know what I've been *told*, but you would never listen to me. Neither of you ever listen to me!"

Lady Helen's hand swept to her breast.

Tears rimmed Cora's eyes. "I don't want to be forced into a marriage like Briar!"

"Cora," Briar warned.

"Especially not with a barely literate dog!" she screamed.

Owein reeled back.

"He's not a *dog*," Merritt countered. "Not in tru—"

"It's demeaning!" she shouted over him. She whirled on Blightree, taking her plea to him. "Please, I'll do anything else. Just don't make me sign this contract. Don't sign away my future!"

Lady Helen bolted to her feet. "Stop this at once, Cora! This is unseemly!"

"No!" she screeched, and pallor overtook her mother's face. "All I ever do is what I'm told. Sit quietly and take it all with a smile. I'm not a decoration to be painted however you choose. I'm a person!"

So am I, Owein protested, but Merritt didn't voice it.

"That is *enough.*" Prince Friedrich fumed.

But Cora spun toward Merritt and Owein. "Why couldn't you have just left? When the roof fell, you should have just left! It was obvious you weren't welcome!"

"Cora!" Briar grasped Cora's forearm.

Cora ripped away, tears streaming down her cheeks. "If you had just left, no one would have been hurt!"

"What are you saying?" Lady Helen cried.

"You," Hulda whispered, squeezing Merritt's fingers. "You're the one who did it."

"You may go to your room if you insist on acting like such a wretch," Prince Friedrich spat. "Your signature is not required." He picked up the pen.

Pure panic resonated within the young woman. Merritt stepped forward, ready to take control and calm down the situation, but Cora acted first.

"I said *no!*"

She flung out her hands, and gusts as strong as those in the carriage house swallowed the room, sending furniture, vases, pictures, busts, and the contract flying.

Merritt dropped to the floor, pulling Hulda with him. Baron von Gayl shouted, "Get down!" and threw himself over Briar just as a fireplace poker flew over their heads. He raised his hand as an urn sailed toward them and, with a kinetic spell, directed it into the wall, where it shattered into dozens of pieces, swept into the gusts like a torrent of knives.

Owein inched out, and the urn resolidified, only to run into the far corner and shatter again. Cora stood in the center of the room, the center of the storm itself. She stumbled back as the baron tried to seize her with a kinetic spell, but it dissipated as quickly as it had formed. In the back of Merritt's brain, somewhere, he recalled the Leiningen family possessed spell-turning, a wardship spell that nullified other magic.

"Stop!" Lady Helen could barely be heard over the rushing air. She put out her hands and tried to use her own wind magic in the opposite direction of the building tornado, but she quickly dropped to the floor, wildly out of breath, as was the cost of elemental air spells.

But that was the thing. *How is she doing this without faltering?*

I don't know. Owein barked. Several flying items returned to their original places, order to chaos, but the gusts only ripped them away again. When Prince Friedrich grabbed Cora's ankle, a head-sized stone appeared above him and dropped, crushing his hand into the floor. Cora danced away, putting her hands over her ears. The wind, somehow, increased.

Hulda shouted something to him, but the gusts carried it away.

Merritt threw up a wardship spell, and the sound of the gusts pummeling it was more deafening than the storm itself. The force quickly knocked it down. "What?" he yelled, then winced as a chair swept into him. He tried ducking back to where the wall jutted out a little, pulling Hulda and Owein with him.

A hole opened in the floor beneath Cora—Owein's doing—but she spell-turned it before she fell. A lump formed on Owein's back, universal punishment for using alteration magic.

"The *bead!*" Hulda yelled. "I saw a bead in the vision. She must have it. There's nothing else!"

"What bead?!" Merritt gripped her close as a large portrait whipped by them.

"The conjurer's bead, from the Tower of London!" She had to scream at him to be heard, especially as sconces ripped from the wall. The chandelier tore from the ceiling, and Merritt threw up one, two, three invisible walls to hold it in place, which made the bruises from the chair ache all the deeper.

He remembered that bead. Lore said it could negate the effects of magic. He recalled how simple it had looked. Was that because it'd been a fake?

Cora was a member of the royal family. Surely she had *some* access to the Tower of London. Had she seized it for herself? It seemed the only explanation. She must not have used it in the carriage house to "prove" her innocence.

The carriage house. The breakfast room. The bedroom. Good God, she was going to kill them all.

Shielding himself with another wardship spell, Merritt crawled forward to see Cora. He couldn't hear her over the noise, but she was sobbing, tears swept into the wind. She was only thirteen. Surely she couldn't want *this*.

Maybe she'd known Merritt and Owein had moved rooms. Maybe she'd only meant to scare them.

Her fists were still pressed to her ears, like she was trying to drown out the terror she was creating. *Fists.* Could she be holding the bead?

Another hole opened beneath her; this time she fell a ways before spell-turning it, again without consequence. The floor entrapped her leg just above the knee.

And suddenly stones appeared everywhere, stones as small as a shoe and as large as a donkey. Too heavy to be swayed by the wind, the heavy stones dropped with loud *thud*s. One barely missed Briar. Another crushed the chair Hulda had been sitting on.

"You have to stop this!" Merritt bellowed, but his voice, too, drowned in the storm. *"CORA! LISTEN TO ME!"*

A great *thump* sounded behind him, and he caught the tip of a whine before the gale whisked it away.

For a moment, despite the torrent, time seemed to stop.

Hulda screamed. Merritt turned around. Owein's paws reached toward him over the carpet, slowly staining it red as blood seeped into the fibers. Owein's back half Merritt couldn't see. It was trapped under a boulder.

Merritt stared at his uncle, and his entire body flashed cold.

No.

He slammed himself into the boulder. It didn't move. Debris whipped by, cutting into his clothes, his skin, leaving hot, angry marks behind.

No.

He slammed into it again, but the blasted stone was too heavy. Hulda pushed as well, but it wouldn't so much as budge. The sharp edge of a picture frame sliced into Merritt's shoulder, sending a spurt of blood into the breeze.

NO.

Screaming, Merritt shoved the boulder bodily, and it collapsed into sand. A stone consumed by chaos.

Merritt dropped on Owein. The wind swept the sand and blood—so much blood—away. A scream echoed in the room, and distantly he knew it was Cora. Maybe she wanted to stop. Maybe she *couldn't* stop.

But Owein. Owein was dying.

Merritt picked up the half-crushed dog in his arms. Threw up a wardship spell and walked toward the front of the room. The wind knocked his wall down. He threw up another one, and another, until his body grew so weak from use of magic he collapsed to his knees, not far from where Blightree was barricaded into the wall by a broken sofa.

"Help him!" Merritt cried. "Blightree! *HELP. HIM.*"

The old man crawled out, staying low to the ground. A shard of glass whipped by and cut a long line on his balding head, but the necromancer didn't seem to feel it. He put a hand on Owein, whose chest rose and fell in uneven rhythms. He panted, his tongue a lifeless worm. The skin under his fur was slick with sweat and blood.

"I can't!" Blightree called back. "My magic works only on humans!"

"He *is* human!" Tears whipped from Merritt's eyes.

But Blightree shook his head.

"Then *move him*!" Merritt screamed. "Put him in the new body!"

"It's not here! And we can't leave!" Another boulder fell from the ceiling, shaking the room.

Merritt grasped Owein's head in his hands. *Hold on, Owein. Hold on.*

Owein didn't answer. His breaths were growing short.

No. It couldn't end like this. Not like this. Not when they were so close—

Merritt lifted his head. Grabbed Blightree's wrist. "Put him in me!"

"What?"

"Put him in me!"

The necromancer blanched. "I . . . I can't! I don't know what will happen! Two spirits in one body—"

"I don't care!" he bellowed. "We're losing him, damn it! Put him in me *now*!"

The ceiling around the chandelier gave way, and the crystals slammed into the wall behind them.

Blightree placed both his hands on Owein, one on his neck, one on his ribs. He closed his eyes, and the pressure around them seemed to grow heavy, like they were sinking into a lake, deeper and deeper, the pressure increasing with every foot.

Then Blightree stiffly grabbed Merritt's hand, and a sense of supernatural wrongness overtook him, like his spine was being tapped, or his body stretched from the inside out. For a moment, Merritt felt very, very old, like he'd turn into sand just as the boulder did. All of Owein's years, added to his own.

And then . . . power.

That flare of chaocracy he'd felt when the boulder dissolved increased tenfold. It buzzed through his fingers and to the tips of his hair. And something new, something *big*—alteration spells, like everything around him was nothing more than putty, waiting to be shaped by a master's hand. The power pushed and pushed, unsure of its new vessel, unsure of where to go.

Hello, Owein, Merritt thought.

And released it.

He pushed it all out of him at once, uncaring for the consequences. It burst out like it had on the island, when Merritt had pulled trees up by their roots and turned the sky to violet snow. It swept through the room, reorienting the toppled, fixing the broken, breaking the fixed. The walls caved in and warped as alteration spells shrunk and reshaped them. The drawing room crumbled and reoriented itself over and over. The outer wall tore away entirely, sending Cora's building wind with it.

But still the storm raged. Cora was on her knees, screaming, sobbing, and the hurricane spun around her, merciless and unending.

Remember when I had my nightmare? whispered a voice in the back of his mind. A voice with a peculiar lilt to it. *Remember when you tried to stop it?*

Merritt didn't understand. What was he doing? Where was he? Why were his legs twisting backward?

It's okay, the voice assured him. I *remember.*

Merritt's arms moved of their own accord, coming before him, hands pointed not at Cora, but just behind her. The chaos pulled from the walls and centered at that spot, tearing up carpeting and making debris dance like little puppets. Peals like struck glass sounded as one, two, three, four, *five* wardship spells boxed around the building chaos. The magic inside spun and twisted, growing angry. Growing bigger and bigger and—

The box exploded outward, a magical bomb, slamming into Cora's back and knocking her prone. A spherical bead rolled from her hand.

The wind slowed; people covered their heads as debris fell. Coals from the fireplace pattered black against the carpet. Shards of glass from windows, mirrors, and picture frames glittered in a great cascade. Fluff from torn cushions snow-flaked drowsily.

Cora lifted her head, then her hands. Her right hand looked as though the ancient talisman she'd gripped had burned it. She cried as she looked at her palm, then smiled in relief.

A loud *crack*, almost like thunder, ripped through the room. The ceiling split overhead, sending a large chunk of house down onto Cora.

"Look out!" Merritt/Owein shouted. Lady Helen rushed forward. Cora covered her head.

The chunk of wood and mortar froze a few feet above the ground. Baron von Gayl shielded Cora with his body, his left hand up and shaking with the effort of a kinetic spell to stall the chunk from crushing them both.

A new gust, this time from Briar, shoved the great hunk off to the side. The young woman, covered in dust, ran to the both of them. "Oh, Ernst, thank you. Thank you."

The fullness was too much. Merritt/Owein dropped to his knees and vomited, then promptly passed out.

Chapter 30

Hulda paced the length of the library, wringing her hands together, heels clacking where they met the tile between Indian rugs. The blue drawing room was completely destroyed, as was the bedroom above it. The conservatory shared a wall with the blue drawing room and had been badly damaged as well. Other adjoining spaces, including the gallery and grand hall, sported some cracks, as if an earthquake had rolled through. A very nauseous Mr. Blightree had taken over the yellow drawing room, where his nephew's body had been placed under a slew of spells to keep its blood running and lungs breathing . . . spells that had hopefully held up during this whole debacle. Cora was bunkering with her mother in the ladies' morning room, and the local doctor administered to the others in the gentlemen's morning room. Hulda had already been seen, requiring only a few bandages for cuts she'd gotten from flying debris. Now all she suffered from was immense nerves, anxiety, nausea, trepidation, uncertainty, jitters, and suppressed panic.

She still hadn't heard about Merritt.

Servants had flocked in the moment Lady Cora's storm subsided. To think the culprit of all this destruction had been under their noses the entire time, and such a seemingly demure girl! But while thirteen was old enough for an educated child to know better, education did not equal maturity, as Hulda had reminded herself dozens of times to abate her fury. Surely it was only the child's possession of a luck spell that had let her get away with it so long. She'd certainly blown out every ward and stone placed in and near the blue drawing room! Cora had been in hysterics as soon as that cursed bead left her fingers, sobbing and apologizing, her hand burned as if she'd grabbed a hot poker by its sharp end. Hulda didn't understand the working of such magicked artifacts. She wished to learn more, but other things were, presently, more imperative.

Once the magic had ceased, Lady Helen had switched on like a fire rune and taken complete control of the catastrophe. It *had* been her shoe in Hulda's earlier vision. Her shoe, Blightree's pen, and Cora's stolen bead, for what little good the soothsaying had done. Now Merritt's dual-possessed body was in the yellow drawing room with Mr. Blightree, footmen had been sent to retrieve doctors, maids to deliver missives, and Lady Helen had dismissed all other staff for holiday before her house collapsed further. It would cost a fortune to repair Cyprus Hall, between this incident, the breakfast room, and the guest bedroom.

Hulda could not bring herself to care.

So she paced, as quickly as a person could pace without running. *Merritt will be fine,* she chanted to herself. She'd had multiple visions of the future in which he was alive and hale. Still, her hands chafed and her teeth threatened to break from gritting. Somewhere in the household sounded a symphony of footsteps and greetings, likely another person replying to those emergency missives, but Hulda did not crack the door to check. She wished she'd taken the time to eat before coming here, just so her stomach would have something to throw up.

"Hulda."

She nearly tripped over herself, hearing the sound of his voice. Spinning toward the door, she couldn't help but cry out at the sight of Merritt, whole and standing, though bandages stuck up from his collar and sleeves, and his left arm was in a sling. She ran to him and hugged him, earning a gentle *oomph* from the collision. His good arm wrapped tightly around her back and held her close.

Neither of them spoke. He smelled like iodine and frankincense and dust, but he was warm and breathing. Hulda's tears soaked into his shirt. If he felt them, he didn't comment.

After an eternity, she pulled back. Touched his face just below a cut on his cheekbone, which he'd gotten shielding *her*. "Does it hurt?"

"Oh, everything hurts *immensely*."

Pulling on his arm, she led him to the closest sofa and made him sit. Knelt on the carpet beside him. "Owein?"

"Not in here anymore." He rubbed his chest as though it were sore. "Blightree moved him to the body, but he hasn't woken yet."

Fear tightened her middle. "And if it doesn't take?"

Merritt worried his lip, then shook his head. "I suppose a spirit in the walls of Cyprus Hall would fix the place up quickly."

Hulda chewed on the inside of her cheek. *If Owein stays. If he's able to.* What if the shock of nearly dying was too much, and the boy finally passed on to the other side?

Her resolve started to crumble.

Merritt's hand came under her chin. "Blightree seemed hopeful. As hopeful as he can be. How are the others?"

She swallowed. Let out a breath. "I haven't checked on them in a while."

Merritt glanced toward the door. "Certainly noisy out there."

"As should be expected." She smoothed her skirt. "No one is dead, outside of . . ." She couldn't bring herself to say it. The memory of that boulder crushing Owein, the mewling sounds, the blood, she'd rather forget her own name than remember that. Swallowing, she steeled herself. "Cora's all right. She's apologized to everyone over and over and has made herself sick from sobbing."

"I don't think . . ." Merritt paused, as though carefully choosing his words. "I don't think it was entirely her."

"This time, perhaps not. She seemed wildly out of control. But the other times, it was. The carriage house, the breakfast room . . . I'm not sure what will become of her."

He rolled his lips together. "I wonder if it will nullify the contract."

Hulda drew her brows together. "What of it?"

"I signed it, Hulda."

Her mouth formed a silent O.

"Blightree insisted I sign it before he'd pull Owein out of me. So I did. I didn't want Owein's soul to be lost on a technicality. It's done."

"I see." She mulled over this. Would she have done any differently? Probably not.

He leaned forward, planting the elbow not in a sling on his thigh, and rubbed his face with his hand. "I just . . . don't know."

"How can we?" She set her hand on his knee. "And to think . . . Poor Mr. Blightree. To have the loss be in his own family. He must be devastated."

"He is."

She ran her thumb over his kneecap. "And Owein . . . That line is a necromantic line."

Straightening, Merritt ran his hand down his face. "It is. I asked Blightree about that, before I left. But . . . his nephew . . . hadn't shown any skill, despite the bloodline. Not something we need to worry about at the moment, anyway." He rested his chin on his knuckles, a faraway look settling into his blue eyes. "We just have to hope both body and spirit survive. The delay . . ."

He trailed off, unfinished. If only to distract him, Hulda said, "In good news, the baron's act of bravery seems to have done very well for his marriage. Briar was fussing over him when I left, ensuring he was comfortable."

A half smile pulled at his mouth. "That's good."

Hulda nodded, unsure what else to say. They both seemed at a loss for words. So they simply sat there in each other's company, worrying in joined silence, waiting for any sort of word on their future.

Chapter 31

He opened his eyes to blurs. Blinked, and the blurs changed shape. Blinked again, and saw *color.*

The ceiling was yellow, with white wainscoting crossing it and delicate blue flowers painted along the panels. He stared at it for a long time, trying to understand it. Trying to remember the color of the flowers' leaves. Oh, right. Green.

The room didn't smell like much. Rooms always smelled like something, so the lack of scent was jarring. Woke him up a little bit. Something was . . . different. Not wrong, just different. He was too big, too long. His skeleton wasn't shaped as it should be. Had he used an alteration spell and forgotten about it?

Memory assailed, and he winced. His body had been crushed. He recalled . . . pressure more than pain. Panic. Wind and weakness. He wiggled his toes. They were still there, but with no fur between them.

Though he was very tired, very heavy, he found the strength to lift his paws, then stared at them longer than he had at the color green, trying to comprehend them.

Hands. He had hands. Ten digits covered in pale skin. He wiggled his thumbs first, then forefingers, middle and ring fingers, pinkies.

Turned them over and studied his nails. They were very clean. Turned back and traced the paths on his palms.

He was on a narrow bed of some sort, maybe a table. He noted absently that it was digging into his shoulder blades. So, carefully, bit by bit, he sat up. The room spun despite his slowness, sending a wave of dizziness through his skull. He cradled his head, finding hair there. Pulled his hand away.

He was . . . human.

He looked down at himself, at the simple nightgown he wore, which was almost the same off-white as the tablecloth beneath him. He had a flat chest and a stomach, hips and legs and bare feet. He stared at the feet. Wiggled his toes.

Smiled.

"I'm glad to see you awake," said a prim British voice to his right. Owein turned to find two people seated in chairs against the wall. Blightree and . . . oh yes. Queen Victoria.

"We've had quite the episode, haven't we?" She tapped her hands on a small chest in her lap. The wood was painted . . . red. He could see red! "But your guardian has signed the documents, and I intend to keep you both to your word."

"Cora?" Owein asked. He didn't have a voice—it was a rasp, the way Merritt sounded when he used too much communion. "Merritt?"

"They're both hale enough." Reaching over, the queen took Blightree's hand. "And will be no worse for the wear once my dear man has recovered from his services to you. It's a big and rare spell combination, moving spirits about."

Blightree patted her hand. He looked a little queasy, a little sad, but well enough.

To Owein, Victoria asked, "How are you feeling?"

He blinked. Touched his chest. "Different." There was a little more voice this time.

Victoria handed the chest to Blightree, then crossed the room, her long skirts swishing, to a pitcher of water. She poured just a little into a cup and handed it to him.

It felt strange, holding a cup. Having thumbs. Owein brought the water to his lips. The first bit drizzled down his chin, but instinct took over, and he drank. He remembered, distantly, drinking like this. Not from a cup this fine, but he'd been human before.

"I'm afraid that, while you do fascinate me," the queen went on, "I'm not able to stay." She retrieved the chest from Blightree and held it tightly. "This item is very powerful and is not meant to be used by young girls who have not fully harnessed their magic." She clucked her tongue.

"What will . . ." Owein coughed. "What will happen to her?"

"To Cora? She'll be on strict probation for the next year at *least*." She sniffed with displeasure. "You should be more concerned for the guards at the tower. I've the mind to behead the lot of them, but then what can one do when the culprit has a luck spell that turned their heads?"

Owein jolted. Victoria offered a close-lipped smile. "Regardless, their consequences will be severe. Cora . . ." She considered a moment. "Cora is young and stupid. I've spoken to her directly, and I do believe it is sheer *stupidity* that caused all this." She waved a hand, not caring to clarify. "It is fortunate for her that she is so high in society. Were she not, I would not be so lenient. But she is family. Of course, I will still make sure she rues this day. I've not yet determined the extent of my wrath." She tapped a finger on the box. Quieter, she said, "Even I wouldn't dare to use this artifact, or any of them, unless the situation were dire. I am a strong wizard, Mr. Mansel. But these were created for the first of us, those imbued with the fullness of magic and the abilities to control it. I think they will be taken out of the public eye indefinitely."

He considered this. "Will you give her a chance?"

"Hm? You'll need to clarify. More water?"

Owein shook his head. "Cora. She was so miserable. About the . . . marriage."

Victoria exhaled slowly through her nose. Tilted her head slightly to the side as she regarded him. "I am impressed that the central victim to her crimes has such mercy."

"She didn't mean to hurt me, I don't think." *Crushing bones, panic, the room spinning and growing dark.* Owein shook himself like he would have as a dog, and it came out as a half shudder, half convulsion in his new body. "Just . . . scare me away," he finished.

"Can you be so sure?"

Owein shrugged. The gesture felt both queer and familiar to him. "I've lived a long time, Your Majesty."

She smirked at that. Took a moment to collect her thoughts. "I am not without heart. In truth, Briar had almost swayed me." She glanced back at Blightree. "I was fortunate enough to marry someone I love. I certainly understand the appeal, though I would have entered matrimony regardless. Such is the duty of the ruling class." She raised an eyebrow. "But I will make an amendment, for your sake. If Cora finds another suitor who *will add to the noble bloodline* by the time she is eighteen, I will disregard her obligation to you. You will, of course, keep the body."

Owein looked down. Flexed and unflexed his fists, tightened his stomach. He was hungry. "Thank you. She'll be happy to hear it."

"I intend for her not to be happy for a good while. Perhaps I shall take her on as a ward." She turned, directing the idea to Blightree. "Let her follow me around and do *my* bidding for a year or so. Give her a true taste of responsibility. I think she'll not complain about her duties after that."

Blightree nodded. "It is a sound idea."

"I am, again, terribly sorry for your loss." Walking over, she clasped his hand.

Owein wiggled his toes again. "What was his name?"

"Pardon?" asked the queen.

"His name." Owein pointed to himself. "The one who sacrificed so that I could live."

Blightree's eyes watered. "Oliver. Oliver Whittock. Thank you for asking."

Owein nodded. "Thank you, for helping me. For giving me a voice again. And hands."

A few tears spilled over the necromancer's face as he smiled. "My dear boy, you are very welcome."

෨

It was fascinating how efficient a household could be, despite the collapse of a good chunk of the house itself. Merritt supposed that was a benefit to living in a mansion. Even when entire rooms collapsed, there was still space left over.

The kitchens had been unharmed, and so Merritt and Hulda were able to get a simple lunch. Prince Friedrich, also with bandages poking out of his sleeves, dropped in for a bit to speak with them, to apologize, and to see how everyone fared. But duty called, and he soon departed again. There was a lot of hustle and bustle about the arrival of Queen Victoria and an alarming number of people from the Queen's League of Magicians—in part to reacquire the bead and clean up the social mess, as nobility cared far more for the social ramifications of their deeds than the physical ones. As neither Merritt nor Hulda had a drop of royal blood in them, they weren't privy to exactly *how* the issue was being handled, but Merritt was sure that, once everything calmed down, Lady Helen would tell them all about it, whether they wanted to know or not.

And so, needing to take their minds off the suppositions and unknowns, Merritt located a chess board and set it up, which was how he learned Hulda was a far more adept chess player than he was.

"Check," she said. Merritt moved his king over one square. She did the same with a rook. "Check."

Merritt moved the piece back.

"Really, Merritt, just surrender." Exasperation weighted her words.

"In true war, this is how an army stalls so reinforcements can come in," he countered.

She looked at him over the rim of her glasses. "You've no reinforcements. Check."

He moved the piece over one square.

"For heaven's sake. *I* forfeit." She knocked down her king with a flick of her finger.

Merritt grinned. "And *that* is how I never lose at chess."

Folding her arms, she rolled her eyes. "You're intolerable."

"You're stuck with me, my dear."

"Unless I travel somewhere that doesn't uphold Druidic law. Russia, perhaps."

He set up his pieces again. He'd chosen the black, despite knowing that meant Hulda would go first. He had always liked the black pieces, for one reason or another. But he paused, a polished pawn in his hand. Black like Owein's undercoat. He sighed.

"Don't suppose we can scatter these and have you take a peek, hm?" He placed the pawn on the board.

Her hand stilled as she set down a bishop. "I'm afraid to."

The door opened just then. A maid slipped in, nodding quietly to them before fetching their tray. She slipped out just as quietly.

Merritt returned his king to his square in the back. "Your turn."

Hulda moved a knight out front. Merritt copied the move. She pushed out a pawn, and he mirrored it.

"You'll lose, that way," she said, pushing out another pawn.

"We'll see."

The door creaked again, perhaps the maid returning for the pitcher.

"I guarantee it." She moved another pawn. He copied her. She captured his pawn with her first knight.

"Ah," he said, and inched out his rook.

"Hello."

They both startled. Merritt's knee hit the corner of the chess board, knocking down several of his soldiers. A footman had entered the room, albeit without the jacket that went with his uniform. A foot*boy*, rather. The lad was an adolescent, with the slightest bit of baby fat still in his cheeks. Dirty blond hair swept just over his eyebrows, trimmed short in the back. His eyes were gray, chin on the sharper side. He'd have a well-defined jaw when he was older.

He smiled hesitantly. "I suppose I do look a little different."

It was the accent, more than the words, that made Merritt's heart break apart and reorient itself. It wasn't quite British, not quite American, but something other, something learned a long time ago, warped only slightly by environment, because until now he hadn't had a voice to warp.

Hulda stood. "Is . . . Is that you, Owein?"

The boy lifted his hands, studied them, turned them over. "It feels odd, being this tall. But yes, it's me."

Merritt stood as well. "Tell me something only Owein would know."

They both glanced at him.

Merritt shook his head. "I'm sorry . . . I just want to be sure."

The boy considered for a moment. "Sometimes you hum 'Turkey in the Straw' when you get dressed. And you tried to feed me an onion at Christmas, but Beth smacked it out of your hand and jammed your middle finger."

Merritt laughed. Tears filled his eyes with each chuckle. He crossed the distance between them in four strides and threw his arm around the boy. The top of Owein's head came to Merritt's clavicle.

"Owein . . . it's really you." Hulda came around, and when Merritt released him, Hulda turned him to her. Pushed his hair off his head. Looked him over for . . . signs of injury? Likely just to assure herself that he was real, hale, and whole. "Did it . . . hurt?"

"I don't remember," he said. "But it fits a lot better than Merritt did."

Merritt grinned and wiped his eyes. "I did get one thing out of it." He looked around. Grabbed a cup off the table with the pitcher and brought it over. "Let's see . . ."

He concentrated on the cup, feeling a rumble, almost like a growl of hunger, zip up his torso. The cup shuddered in his hand and melted just enough to bend out of shape.

Hulda gasped. "Chaocracy! Why didn't you tell me?"

He blinked a few times to dismiss the confusion curling through his thoughts and reorient himself. "I was trying to *melt* it," he said with a frown. "Not enough magic, I suppose. But I *felt* the way you did it, Owein. It sort of contextualized things for me. I, um . . ." He set the cup aside. "I can see why they want you."

Owein folded and unfolded his hands together. "I'm not ready to do any magic yet. I'm still getting used to . . . this." He gestured to his whole self. "Maybe we can take the cup home and mail it back?" His voice jumped midsentence.

Merritt grinned and wiped his eyes. "Ah, the joys of puberty. You haven't gotten to experience that yet. What a way to greet humanity."

Owein cleared his throat. "You're welcome, for not stealing your voice anymore."

New tears brimmed, but Merritt ignored them, instead hugging his uncle once more. "I think I'm going to miss our private conversations," he said, kissing the top of his head. "But I'm so, so happy to have you back."

Owein, despite having only been technically human for a couple of hours, was exhausted. Blightree said that was to be expected; his new body and old spirit had both undergone a lot of stress. His reintroduction to everyone was also tiring. Half the Leiningens treated him like a newcomer, and not like he'd been living at their house for the last week and a half. But it felt wrong to sleep when there was a very important issue to discuss, and an important person to discuss it with.

Her door was unlocked. Owein rapped softly with a knuckle—he could do that now—and cracked the door open. "Cora?"

Her room was dark, only one drape drawn. She sat on the far edge of her bed, facing away from him, hunched over. He'd never seen her hunched before. She always sat up so pristinely, with a spine Hulda would envy. Turning her head just enough to glance over her shoulder, she asked, "Who's there?"

Owein stepped into the room. "I wanted to talk to you before I leave."

She turned more, looking at him, her brows knit tightly together.

Owein glanced down at himself. "You didn't know him, did you?"

"Who?"

"Oliver Whittock."

It took her a moment. Then her eyes widened and her lungs took in a sharp breath. "He's the one . . . You're . . ."

He reached her and held out a hand. He'd decided that might be the best way to do it. "Owein Mansel. It's nice to meet you again."

She stared at his face for several seconds, then weakly took his hand. "You talk funny," she managed.

He shrugged.

Pulling her hand away, she dropped her head. "I'm surprised you want to talk to me."

He wasn't sure what to say to that, so they lingered there in painful silence for a minute. "The queen . . . she said she'd make an amendment—"

"I know." She whispered now. "My mother told me."

More stiff silence.

"Thank you," she finally added. "I'm sorry . . . I'm so sorry. I was so scared. I still am." She opened her hand to the circular scar on her palm. "I won't let him heal it." Blightree, she meant. "I need to remember this."

"We're okay," he offered. "All of us."

She shook her head. Her lip quivered. Once she'd steeled herself, she said, "I never meant to *hurt* you. Not really. I wanted to shake up that room to scare you off, but I did *so much* . . ." Her gaze lingered on the scar on her palm. "I didn't think I'd be able to do so much damage. It scared me. That's why I bought the next spell. And Maksim"—the hound who'd been injured, she meant—"I thought he was you. The room was mostly empty. I thought I'd scare you, and it would be so obvious you were the target that you and the others would run right back home . . ." Her voice creaked into nothing. She sniffed. Owein waited while her throat cleared, but when she spoke again, it was barely a whisper. "But he moved, and I hurt him *and* the baron. I didn't mean to. I didn't trust myself anymore."

"Cora—"

"But Briar gave me courage," she continued, barely audible. She didn't lift her head, wouldn't look at him. "I thought I'd try one more time. That carriage was so big, I thought for sure it would hit the one next to it and stop, but it didn't. I'm glad . . ." She swallowed. "I'm glad you were so fast, Owein. I'm glad I didn't kill you."

You almost did, he thought, thinking of the storm in the drawing room, but he didn't voice it. He didn't think she needed to hear it.

"Thank you," he offered, taking a step back, giving her space. "For giving me a body."

She still didn't look at him. "It wasn't me. None of this was me."

"I know. But you're part of it."

She brushed the back of her hand across her eyes. "I suppose so."

She said nothing more, even after a few more difficult minutes. So Owein turned and started for the door. He'd just reached it when Cora said, "Owein?"

He glanced back.

"Can I . . . write to you?" She still didn't look at him. "Not . . . now. Not for a while. But I think . . . once things are more normal, once I've fixed them . . . maybe I would like to."

"Yes," he answered simply. He didn't think the response needed embellishment.

She said nothing more, and neither did he. Owein slipped into the hallway, closing the door behind him, and carried his weary body toward the guest bedrooms. Paused and dug deep to find the energy to do a little more.

Taking the stairs down to the sitting room, he found Hulda and Merritt speaking quietly to a red-eyed Lady Helen. Their words cut off when he got close; he no longer had the invisibility of a household pet. Still, Lady Helen gave him a close-lipped smile. "I really am so glad for you, Owein. I can't wait to see what you grow into."

He looked from her to Merritt, then back again, unsure whom to ask. "I wanted to talk about the contract."

Merritt rolled his lips together. It felt like he wanted to say something the others couldn't hear, but his communion spells only worked on plants and animals, and Owein was neither of those anymore.

"Merritt signed it." Hulda spoke hesitantly—they had told him this earlier, before he'd reintroduced himself to the Leiningens. Owein understood her confusion.

"I know. But . . ." He chose to focus on Lady Helen. "I would like to sign it myself."

She stood a little straighter. "You would?"

He nodded. "You made a promise to me, and you kept your end." He ran his hands down his footman's shirt—it was all they'd had on hand that would fit him, though it was a bit large. "I want to keep my promises, too. I want to sign it."

He had just over four years to get used to the idea of marrying someone. Strange, thinking about the time. Four years would have gone by very quickly if he still lived within the walls of Whimbrel House, yet it seemed like an eternity now.

The Leiningens had some rough edges, but Owein was learning everyone had rough edges. Granted, some were rougher than others, but even those might smooth out, with enough time and care. They were a nice family. Yet even if they hadn't been, Owein would have kept his promise. He didn't need Merritt's help to do that.

And so, under witness of Lady Helen, Hulda Larkin, Merritt Fernsby, and Mr. Blightree, Owein approached the contract once more. Holding a freshly dipped quill, he wrote his name in shaky, unpracticed letters right under Merritt's.

In the morning, they sailed back for Rhode Island.

Chapter 32

The door to Merritt's bedroom opened as Merritt struggled to put on cuff links by himself. "Heaven help you," said his friend Fletcher, jogging across the room. "You can't look good even for your own wedding?" He grabbed Merritt's stiff shirt collar and straightened it, then tugged on the shoulders of his blue vest.

"What?" Merritt glanced at the small mirror on the wall. "I think I look rather dashing." In truth, he always thought he looked strange with his hair pulled back, like it somehow made his face bigger, though Beth had combed his waves into a rather nice-looking tail.

Fletcher took the cuff links from him and attached them himself. "Usually it's the bride who takes too long, not the groom."

Turning away from the mirror, heart doing a little flip, Merritt murmured, "Fletcher . . . are they here? Did they come?"

Fletcher clicked the last cuff link into place and looked up, his face a stoic mask. It lasted for about two seconds before his white-toothed grin broke. "Yes, even your mother."

Merritt sighed, laughed, and cried all at once. Stood back and wiped his eyes on his knuckles, then thanked his friend when he offered a handkerchief. "Praise the Lord," he murmured.

"Don't get distracted." Fletcher took a step back and looked him over. "You can have the family reunion *after* your vows."

"Of course." He dabbed his eyes again and folded up the handker-chief. "I'm keeping this."

Fletcher merely shrugged and held out his arm. "Shall I walk you to the altar?"

Merritt shoved the man and escorted himself to the door, unable to quell the smile on his face. He hurried down the hall and the stairs and through the reception hall. Out the door, where he could see the small wedding party seated before a large green arch with white April flowers on it. An outdoor wedding was a little eccentric, but the licensing had all been done through the church, and what was his relationship with Hulda if not a little unconventional?

He saw them almost immediately. His mother, Scarlet, and Beatrice took up the front row of chairs, his mother on the aisle, her body turned as she spoke to Hulda's mother across the way. Her parents were stern folk who didn't laugh enough, in Merritt's opinion, but they were kind and seemed happy about the situation, and that was all Merritt could ask for.

Despite Fletcher's admonition, Merritt went straight to his mother, who cried out and stood at the sight of him. He embraced her tightly, taking in her familiar smell.

"Oh, my boy," she said into his hair, "you look so dashing!" She pulled back and dabbed at her eyes with her own handkerchief. "I think you've grown again."

"I believe I will be two inches short of six feet the rest of my life." His voice croaked, though not from the use of communion. He'd barely used the spell over the last month since returning from England. Few might be aware, but the average shrub and dormouse didn't make great conversation.

His sisters stood as well; Scarlet leaned over and kissed his cheek. "We have many introductions to make, after," she said, tilting her head toward the second row, where a man and three boys sat. That would be Merritt's brother-in-law and his nephews, whom he'd never met. His heart pulsed to bursting, almost like he'd felt when sharing his body with Owein. He nodded to the family. In the row behind them looked to be Beatrice's brood. Her girls waved at him, making him chuckle. The next row held the Portendorfers.

"She's coming!" cried out Danielle, Hulda's younger sister. She, her husband, and her children sat behind Hulda's mother, and behind them was Beth and, surprisingly, Myra, though the latter wore a short veil on her hat to hide her face. Owein sat beside Beth, his hair neatly combed back. His new jacket fit him well, but Merritt had a feeling it wouldn't fit him much longer; that boy still had some growing to do. Their eyes met, and Owein smiled. Merritt could almost hear his words inside his head, like he was the dog again, saying something like, *Will this take much longer?* Or *When can we eat?* The thought stirred nostalgia, and Merritt found himself pulling out Fletcher's handkerchief again. Baptiste took up the end of the row, beefy arms folded over his chest, looking very satisfied with himself. If nothing else, the luncheon would be splendid.

Shaking out his nerves, as he really *shouldn't* be nervous, having technically already been married for a month, Merritt went over to the very patient pastor. "Thank you," he said.

The pastor nodded, and the small congregation rose as Hulda and her father stepped off the porch of Whimbrel House.

Heaven help him, she was beautiful. She wore a colbalt dress with *lace*, far more lace than Merritt had ever thought he'd see on her, though it adorned only her collar and sleeves. The dress had a wider collar than she normally preferred, elongating her neck and presenting that lovely collarbone of hers. Matching lace hung from her veil. Her arm looped with her father's, and she held a very simple bouquet of white daffodils to match the archway. A light blush crossed her nose as she met his eyes. Merritt grinned, then reached out his hand as she neared.

As Hulda slipped her hand into his, her father said, "Do take care of her."

"I shall do nothing but," Merritt replied, and pulled her toward the pastor. He held both her hands in his and smiled; she mirrored it.

The pastor began saying . . . something. It sort of went in one ear and out the other. Merritt couldn't look away from Hulda's eyes, which glimmered nearly green in the late-morning light. It had rained all last week, and they'd worried they'd have to move the wedding inside, but God had gifted them with sunshine today.

I love you, Hulda mouthed, and Merritt silently repeated it back, squeezing her hands. Her hair, what he could see of it under the veil covering it, was elaborately braided and pinned, and Merritt found himself very eager to ruin it.

Hulda tipped her head to the pastor, signaling that Merritt should probably pay attention now.

"Repeat after me," he instructed, and Merritt did.

"I, Merritt Fernsby, take you, Hulda Larkin, to be my wife, to have and to hold from this day forward, for better or for worse, for richer, for poorer, in sickness and in health, to love and to cherish, till death us do part, according to God's holy law, and this is my solemn vow." Then, before the pastor could instruct Hulda to do the same, Merritt added, not really loud enough for the audience to hear, "Hulda, I am a better man because of you. I am a *found* man. You have changed everything in my life for the better. I honestly don't know how I lived before you. I want your face to be the first thing I see in the morning, and your voice to be the last I hear at night, forever and always. I will gladly haunt this house with you for eternity."

Hulda laughed, and tears brimmed on her eyelashes. Merritt broke their handhold long enough to lend her Fletcher's handkerchief. "I told you I hate crying at weddings," she said, and a few in the congregation chuckled. When the handkerchief was again stowed away, she repeated after the pastor, "I, Hulda Larkin, take you, Merritt Fernsby, to be my husband." Her voice choked; she took a moment to swallow. "To have and to hold from this day forward, for better, for worse, for richer, for poorer, in sickness and in health, to love and to cherish, till death do us part, according to God's holy law, and this is my solemn vow." She glanced to the pastor—she was a rule follower, after all, and when he nodded, she murmured, "I never realized how boring I was before I came here."

Merritt laughed.

She fought a smile. Lowered her eyes to their hands. "You are a light, Merritt. You are *my* light. You are everything that is good in this world. So genuine, so chivalrous, so imaginative. I'm so happy I get to partake in that imagination with you. In this *life* with you." She blinked a few times, clearing tears. "You have written me a happy ending, and I cannot fathom a better story than ours."

Warmth wound from his shoulders, down his torso, and into his toes.

The pastor waited a beat, then, over his Bible, said, "I now pronounce you man and wife. You may, Mr. Fernsby, kiss your bride."

Merritt tugged Hulda forward and crushed his lips to hers, grabbing her around the waist and dipping her. Applause rose up from the small crowd, and he was fairly certain that was Beth letting out a loud *whoop!* in the back.

Righting Hulda, he broke from her, pleased to see the grin on her face. It was *really* official now, though, in truth, they would always celebrate their anniversary on his birthday. And Merritt really, truly, didn't mind.

The families mingled as Beth and Baptiste set out the luncheon. Merritt formally met Richard Moore, Scarlet's husband, and his three nephews, Matthew, Albert, and Andrew. George Blakewell, Beatrice's husband, clapped him on the shoulder. "I've heard only good things, my man. I think we ought to smoke cigars sometime." And his nieces, Bethany and Maggie, seemed charmed by him regardless of what he said, though that might have been the power of his very nice vest.

When Merritt introduced Owein as his "nephew," Scarlet and Beatrice assumed he came from Hulda's side, while the Larkins presumed he was a Fernsby. Merritt didn't bother to clarify.

They ate together, they laughed together, they celebrated together. It was probably the best day of Merritt's life, but he was all about progress and intended to have even better ones to come. It wasn't until the sun threatened to set and guests began taking to their boats for the journey back that Merritt spied Baptiste putting away dinner and slipped over to speak to him.

"You know," he said offhandedly, "I think I *can* handle it."

Baptiste glanced up. "Handle what?"

"The story. About your previous incarceration." He shrugged. "Surely we've known one another long enough for you to let me in on the secret. I won't judge you for it." He was fairly certain Baptiste hadn't murdered anyone, or they wouldn't have let him out.

Baptiste continued his cleanup, and for a moment Merritt thought the conversation over before it had begun. But without looking up, Baptiste said, "Cheese."

"Pardon?"

"Cheese," he repeated, meaning Merritt had heard him correctly the first time. "I worked with three men to steal wagon full of cheese. Sold it over border, in Belgium."

Speech fled Merritt for a good few seconds. "You . . . You stole *cheese?*"

A small smile ticked up the corners of Baptiste's mouth. "Was very expensive cheese."

Merritt snorted and clapped the man on the shoulder. "Somehow, I think that makes me like you more." He checked his pocket watch. "I'm going to see my mother off. Hold down the fort, hm?"

Nodding, Baptiste picked up a stack of dishes from the table, then glanced out a north-facing window. Frowned. "I thought you said the dog died?"

"Hm?" Merritt followed his line of sight. Owein walked the shallow wilds a way out, and sure enough, a dog was trouncing beside him. From this vantage point, it *did* look remarkably like the brown terrier Owein had spent the last few months in.

"It . . . did." Uncertainty dropped Merritt's voice. "I'm sure it did. Huh." He scratched the back of his head, ready for the tie holding his hair back to come out. "I'll ask about it." But first he'd tend to his mother. With luck, he'd be seeing her again soon. He already had an invitation to spend the weekend in Concord with Beatrice and her family, and Peter Fernsby certainly wouldn't prevent Merritt's mother from visiting her daughters, now would he?

"I'll help clean up after the guests leave. Thank you, Baptiste." He clapped his shoulder once more and wound his way into the cool air, where his family, both new and old, awaited him.

༄

It wasn't hard, really, to adapt to being human again. Owein's soul remembered it, even if his memory didn't quite. Memory was finnicky that way; the older it got, the more slippery it became, and there was very little magic—at least, *his* magic—could do about that. But Owein Mansel had been human again for an entire month, almost to the point where he didn't think about himself as *human*, just merely Owein.

The dog had started following him about a quarter hour ago. He'd thought it was a fawn at first. Then he thought it was *his* dog, the mutt Silas Hogwood had snagged off the streets to stuff him into for easy transport. But the pattern in the fur wasn't quite right, the ears were too high, and it was missing the white patches. That, and this dog was a girl.

When he stopped, surveying the pinks and violets of a breathtaking spring sunset, the dog caught up to him and licked his hand.

"I know you're not the same," he said offhandedly, enjoying the layers of red in the sky. He didn't think he'd ever tire of seeing the color red. "Are you going to tell me who you are? I have a hunch."

The dog barked and loped ahead, tail wagging, ready to play. Owein didn't have communion—Merritt had gotten that somewhere else in the family line. But he'd lived as a dog long enough that canine instincts had embedded themselves in his subconscious. In a strange way, he almost *felt* the animal's response.

"When you're ready, then." He picked up a stick about the length of his forearm. "I don't mind if you stay."

The dog barked an agreement, and when Owein threw the stick, she bolted across the island to chase after it, startling a nesting whimbrel as she went. Owein watched her go, pausing where the stick landed. Instead of bringing it back, however, the dog simply waited there and barked at him again, inviting him to play.

A smile on his lips, Owein ran after her, glancing over his shoulder once to the house that used to be only his and the people tarrying outside it, enjoying the last of the celebrations. He was happy to be there. Happy to see Hulda and Merritt together. He'd known they were meant for each other before anyone else did. Really, this wedding was his doing. For the moment, everything seemed just as it should be.

And yet, something within him, something deeper than his terrier instincts and his magic, whispered that his adventures were only just beginning.

Epilogue

August 11, 1847

To Mrs. Hulda L. Fernsby,

I'm writing to you in response to your letters. They've been reviewed by my committee and voted upon; we are very interested in meeting with you, and in seeing the extended formal proposal you'd mentioned previously. There is a medical certificate we may be able to grant your organization in regard to the access of cadavers, but we will require extensive documentation as to how they're used to keep that certificate registered.

The committee is reconvening on September 14 in Washington, DC. I have set aside three hours' time to meet with you specifically, as well as any colleagues you feel best represent your case and your proposition. I hope you will be able to attend.

I think it best to keep this under seal until everything is set in stone. For that very purpose, I hope you will forgive the brevity of my letter.

Sincerely,
Loren Loughty
Chairperson
Congressional Committee for the Continuation of Wizarding

ACKNOWLEDGMENTS

Thank you so much for reading another book in this ongoing story. The Whimbrel House series is very dear to my heart, and I'm so grateful to everyone who gives it a chance.

I want to give thanks, again, for my wonderful husband, Jordan, who is such a great support to me and who was so kind and generous during a very hard year when writing became particularly difficult for me. *Boy of Chaotic Making* is our victory.

Thank you so much to my editor, Adrienne Procaccini, who sees the merit (pun intended) and potential in my feeble creations and guides them to the light. Another thank-you to Angela Polidoro, who cleans up my messes and whips these manuscripts into shape!

Thank you to Leah O'Neill, who is a very dedicated friend and beta reader for me, and to Rachel Maltby and Julie Daines, who know a lot more about history and the *ton* than I could ever hope to know.

My utmost appreciation for all the staff behind the scenes that copyedited, proofread, kerned, styled, and bound this book so that I could share it with the world. Y'all do a great job.

Yet again, thank you to the Head Honcho, the Big Guy Upstairs, for all He has blessed me with. I owe You one (million).

ABOUT THE AUTHOR

Charlie N. Holmberg is a *Wall Street Journal* and Amazon Charts best-selling author of fantasy and romance fiction, including *The Hanging City*, *Star Mother*, the Paper Magician series, the Spellbreaker series, and the Whimbrel House series, and writes contemporary romance under C. N. Holmberg. She is published in more than twenty languages, has been a finalist for a RITA Award and multiple Whitney Awards, and won the 2020 Whitney Award for Novel of the Year: Adult Fiction. Born in Salt Lake City, Charlie was raised a Trekkie alongside three sisters who also have boy names. She is a BYU alumna, plays the ukulele, and owns too many pairs of glasses. She currently lives with her family in Utah. Visit her at www.charlienholmberg.com.